NO OTHER CHOICE . . .

"I ain't goin' in no tipi like no savage woman," Josie said, pulling away from Caleb.

"I didn't know you were afraid of anything, Jocelyn Hardwick," Caleb taunted, gently nudging her toward the tipi. His green eyes seemed to see right down into her soul. He caught her by the shoulders, forcing her to look up at him.

"This is the way it is, Josie," he said. "Tomorrow it will snow, a huge, deep snow that will bury this village. We can't leave here till spring."

Josie blinked rapidly, fighting tears.

"We're safe here," Caleb went on. "When spring comes, we'll leave, and I'll take you to a fort and see to it you get back home." He paused. "If that's what you still want."

The plea in his voice made her glance up. Again his gaze locked with hers.

"There's no choice," he added. "I'll take good care of you, Josie."

Josie's shoulders sagged with resignation. Long-held tears tumbled down her cheeks.

Strong arms went around her and pulled her close. She turned in Caleb's embrace and rubbed her cheek on his shirt. His breathing quickened. Before she could pull away, his lips captured hers. Worse, she felt herself responding.

Caleb bent over her, pressing her tightly to his chest, while his lips drove all thoughts of fears from her mind. . . .

BOOK YOUR PLACE ON OUR WEBSITE
AND MAKE THE
READING CONNECTION!

We've created a customized website just for our very special readers, where you can get the inside scoop on everything that's going on with Zebra, Pinnacle and Kensington books.

When you come online, you'll have the exciting opportunity to:

- View covers of upcoming books
- Read sample chapters
- Learn about our future publishing schedule (listed by publication month *and author*)
- Find out when your favorite authors will be visiting a city near you
- Search for and order backlist books from our online catalog
- Check out author bios and background information
- Send e-mail to your favorite authors
- Meet the Kensington staff online
- Join us in weekly chats with authors, readers and other guests
- Get writing guidelines
- AND MUCH MORE!

Visit our website at
http://www.zebrabooks.com

BRIGHT
MORNING STAR

Kathryn Fox

Zebra Books
Kensington Publishing Corp.

http://www.zebrabooks.com

ZEBRA BOOKS are published by

Kensington Publishing Corp.
850 Third Avenue
New York, NY 10022

Zebra and the Z logo Reg. U.S. Pat. & TM Off.

First Printing: October, 1998
10 9 8 7 6 5 4 3 2 1

Printed in the United States of America

To my first love,
Gene Autry

Thank you for all those wonderful Saturday mornings.

To my greatest loves,
Donnie, Brad, Matthew, and Daniel

Thanks for enduring, guys.

Chapter One

"If you're up there whorin', you better git down here right this minute, or I'm a-comin' up after you." Josie Hardwick shoved away an errant strand of dark hair and jammed the old felt hat firmly onto her head. Placing a booted foot on the bottom step, she craned her neck to see the rooms lining the balcony of the saloon's second floor. *He's up there all right. Rolling around with some slut.*

She turned, and her gaze swept the empty saloon behind her. Her nose wrinkled against the stale odor of whiskey mingled with the pungent scent of a sawdust-littered floor. Red-checkered cloths covered empty tables. The only patron was a lone man hunched over his drink, one foot propped against the brass rail running the length of the oaken bar. Behind it, the bartender slowly dried glasses with a towel and watched her.

"Petey? Petey!" her voice echoed with a cavernous ring. Scowling and moving up a step, she sighed. She'd told her addled brother not to go near the saloon when she left him alone in the wagon. Now she'd have to haul him out like a sack of 'taters. *Hell to spit!* She spent most of her time rescuing either Petey or Pa from their own mischief.

"Do you hear me? I know damn well you're up there! I saw you jawin' with that whore from all the way 'cross the street!" She shifted the too-heavy Hawken rifle from her left arm to her right and jerked another glance over to the bar. She hated tight places with strange people to her back. "I'm comin' up!" She started up the stairs, her oversized boots clumping on the bare boards.

As she reached the first landing, her brother stumbled out of an upstairs room, his shirt half buttoned, his breeches clasped together by one hand. "For God's sake, Josie. Stop that hollerin'. I'm a-comin'," he grumbled, stopping to hitch up his pants.

"You got no business up there with that floozy," Josie hissed, tossing her head toward the fleshy woman standing at the top of the stairs, stuffed into a black corset and hose.

Petey cast a wishful gaze up at the woman and frowned. "Don't you go callin' Lulu no floozy. She's a real nice—"

"Whore," Josie finished with a withering look. "Now, git your backside 'cross the street and into that wagon." She flung out an arm encased in a coat sleeve three inches longer than her fingers.

Petey hesitated as if to defy her, but another scathing look shriveled his rebellion. "All right, Josie. Just stop that hollerin'. You got everybody a-watchin' us." He glowered and nodded toward the swinging doors, where the crowd stood three deep peeping over the edge.

She felt a hot flush reach her cheeks before she grabbed her brother by the ear and hurried down the steps. Suddenly, the barrel of the cumbersome rifle tripped her. Petey pitched into her back, and together they fell, head over heels. With each revolution, the gun gouged her side, threatening to discharge at any time.

The floor rushed up to meet her, and she shut her eyes in anticipation of the impact. They struck something and stopped tumbling. Josie's nose rubbed against the soft muskiness of leather. Slowly, she pushed her hat up from over her eyes. Rows of fringe adorned the buckskin mere inches from her nose. Colorful beading led to a tanned neck and face. She lay sprawled, facedown, lengthwise a stranger. A crooked smile narrowed gold-flecked green eyes, and a handful of silky brown curls fell across his forehead. He was the purdiest thing she'd ever seen.

Caleb stared back at the dirty-faced urchin who had barreled down the stairs at him. She blinked and long lashes swept her clear sapphire-blue eyes. Rivulets of grime streaked her face, and stringy strands stuck out from under the battered hat.

"Let me go, you big oaf," she said, pushing against him. Her hat tumbled off, loosening a cascade of long black hair. "Now look what you done." She snatched up the hat, stuffed up the unruly mane, and jerked the headpiece down over her ears, making them stick out like wings. Beneath the smudges, a pretty pink blush suffused her face.

A giggle from outside brought Caleb's attention back to his predicament, reminding him how foolish he must look sprawled on the floor, his hat at a ridiculous tilt, staring openmouthed at this ragamuffin. A crowd had gathered outside, guffawing while the girl berated him in a voice that surely carried all the way down the street.

"What are you grinnin' at?" she demanded as she rolled off him.

"At you," Caleb said, pushing himself up on his elbows. "Who let you out with a gun this size?" He nudged the fifty-caliber rifle with his boot.

A blast skittered the gun across the floor. Wood shavings rained on him as a hole appeared in the oak paneling on the side of the saloon. Caleb glanced over at Shorty, the barkeeper. He sucked in his breath as his gaze jumped from the pile of people on his floor to the crowd now bent double with laughter. Caleb stood, then reached down and offered Josie his hand.

"I can git up myself," she snapped, jerking her arm out of

his grasp and scrambling to her feet. A cloud of dust rose from her clothes as she brushed at the sawdust. Caleb sneezed.

Primly, she smoothed back loose curls of hair. "You made me git dirty," she scolded as she flicked away one last wood shaving.

I wonder how she can tell? Caleb guessed the clothes carried more than a day's worth of dirt.

"You made me waste a good ball too." She picked up the rifle and eyed the still-smoking end.

"You're likely to kill somebody with that thing." Caleb jerked down his shirt and swept his hat off the floor. From his height, he could barely see her face beneath her hat's broad brim.

She raised her head and narrowed her eyes. "Who I kill's my business. If you hadn'ta got in the way, none of this woulda happened."

"Me!" Caleb felt a pinch of annoyance. "You charged up the stairs, bellowing like a bull." He waved an arm toward the balcony.

"I was not bellowin'." She slammed the rifle butt on the floor to accentuate her words. "I was tryin' to git my brother's attention. You hunkered yourself over here and stuck your nose in it," she shouted.

"I thought you were going to shoot Lulu, the way you were waving that gun around," Caleb shouted back.

"Maybe I should've." She threw a warning glance back to the top of the stairs, where Lulu cowered behind the railing. "That way there'd be one less whore."

"You sure have got a big mouth for somebody so little." Caleb stifled an unwanted smile. Her face was screwed into an expression of pure defiance.

"And you sure got big feet for somebody so skinny." She stuck her chin out and crossed her arms.

Her expression challenged him to better that one. A renewed surge of laughter burst from the crowd outside. Caleb McCall wasn't a vain man, but his large feet had always been a sore point. Somewhere to his left, a woman's high voice chimed into the laughter. He glanced at the girl. She was thoroughly enjoying his humiliation. "Somebody ought to teach you some manners," he growled.

"Somebody like you? Humph."

Her smug expression begged him to try. He was sorely tempted to call her bluff, to yank her breeches down and tan her bottom. She'd thrown down the gauntlet, and he couldn't pick it up. All he could do was back down, and the gleam in her eye said she knew it.

Minutes ticked by, punctuated only by an occasional twitter from the crowd. Caleb began to feel foolish. They were locked in a staring contest. Hands on hips, she met his gaze unblinkingly.

From the corner of his eye, Caleb saw Petey stuff his hands in his pockets and heave a huge sigh. He shuffled away out of sight. Shorty hurried toward the door, encouraging onlookers to leave before the sheriff showed up and demanded explanations. Transfixed, Caleb wondered how he could get out of this with his pride intact.

"Petey!" Josie shouted suddenly, breaking the glaring match. The boy jumped and spun around, red-faced. Directly above him hung an elaborate portrait of a buxom, nude woman.

"You ain't got no business ogling such filth," she scolded, snatching up her gun and striding over to the boy. She grabbed the top of his ear again and marched toward the door. They slammed into the swinging doors, sending one panel dead center of Shorty's midsection.

"Ooph!" He clutched his stomach and doubled over.

Caleb removed his hat, scratched his head, and laughed as the pair disappeared into the crowd. Bachelorhood didn't seem so bad after all.

"Why'd you go and embarrass me like that?" Petey stumbled forward as Josie let go of his ear. Clutching at the worn side of a ramshackle wagon with one hand, his other hand fumbled for a better hold on his pants.

" 'Cause you ain't got the sense God gave a goose." She turned and planted both fists on her hips. "You know better than to go in a place like that."

Petey stuck out his lower lip in little-boy fashion. "Just because we're twins don't give you the right to push me around all the time."

"If I didn't boss you, you'd just git yourself kilt someplace. Now, git on the wagon." After patting the gaunt mules affectionately, Josie swung up into the seat and gathered the reins. Petey stood below her, staring at the ground, scuffing at the dirt with the toe of his boot.

"Aw, c'mon, Petey," she cajoled. "We gotta git goin'."

"I ain't never gonna learn nothin' 'bout women," he mumbled, and kicked at a pile of horse dung.

"You ain't gonna learn nothin' in a place like that 'ceptin how to lose what money you got."

He scowled darkly and looked up. "You and Pa won't let me do nothin'."

Her heart lurched. Petey was the only person in the world she gave two hoots about. She hated to hurt him, but she had to treat him that way. He didn't seem to understand anything else. Besides, it was for his own good.

"Now, you know that ain't true. I let you go huntin' with me yesterday."

"Hunting bird eggs ain't huntin'." His lip drooped lower. "Leastways at home I could go squirrel huntin'."

"C'mon, Petey. I don't wanna argue today." She sighed and realigned the leather reins through her fingers. "How about we buy ourselves a piece of sticky peppermint from the store? Would you like that?"

Instantly his eyes lit up, and he scrambled into the wagon seat. "I love you, sis," he said, throwing an arm around her shoulders and giving her a squeeze.

Josie smiled, flicked the reins across the mules' backs, and glanced at her brother. He stared straight ahead with the store already in his sight, his anger forgotten. At twenty-one, he was a man by all measures except his mind. Don't seem fair, she thought. As a child, he was distracted, a little slower in his thinking. Instinctively, she had shielded him against their five brothers.

She sighed and stared at the mules' bony rumps. Pa'd whup them both when he learned Davie wasn't waiting on the docks like he wrote. Her oldest brother had changed his mind and decided to stay in the Tennessee hills. The thought of one of Pa's switches whining through the air made a chill run over her. Nope, Pa wouldn't like one of his brood defying him. Pa didn't like spirit in any of his young'uns.

"Want another?" Shorty asked as he leaned over, lifted the shot glass, and wiped at the wet circle beneath it on the varnished wood of the bar.

"Nope. Two's my limit when I'm working." Caleb pushed his old felt hat back with one finger. "Even after all that."

"When you pullin' out?" Shorty worked his way down the bar with his damp cloth.

"Tomorrow morning, first light." Caleb tossed down the last of the Old Gideon and turned his back to the bar. He looked out the wide saloon window onto Liberty Street. Wagons still rolled into Independence. Wagons loaded with furniture, farm implements, children, and household clutter—wagons headed for Oregon.

"You sure this is the last one?" Shorty murmured behind him.

Caleb continued to stare out the elaborately painted window. Gold and green scrolls decorated the glass, spelling out SHORTY'S DRINKING ESTABLISHMENT. In his memory, he saw great lines of wagons stretching across the prairies, families he'd led westward, families for whose lives he'd been responsible.

"Yep." He turned back and picked up his glass. "I'm getting too old for this."

"What'cha gonna do afterward?" Shorty asked.

"Thought I might buy a little spread in California. Raise a few horses."

"You oughta get married." Shorty tossed his cloth to the back bar and propped his chin on his hands. "Man like you's had chances. More'n most, I'd bet."

Caleb toyed with the empty glass. "Never seemed to be any time for a full-time woman, what with the wagon trains and trapping."

"You oughta think about it. A man needs a steady woman and some kids." Caleb stiffened. He looked up and saw the question in his friend's eyes. In all the years they had known each other, Shorty had never asked him about his reaction to children, and he'd never offered an explanation. Shorty knew better than to ask. "You want me to get like you? Still calf-eyed over the same woman after all these years," Caleb teased, lightening the mood. Shorty colored from his white, starched collar to the roots of his red hair. Married close to thirty years, he and Mary were still as much in love as when they were kids.

"You need one like what just left here." Shorty grinned triumphantly. "She'd keep you in line."

Caleb shook his head. "Makes me glad I never found the time. A woman like that would put a man off marriage for good."

"She shore do rule the roost, don't she?"

"I expect she gave Lulu a good scare too." He swung his long legs around and stood as another customer stepped up and slapped the counter for service. "Give Mary my best."

"Will we see you before you leave?" Shorty asked as he moved away to wait on the newcomer.

"Sure. I'll see you for supper tonight."

The wagon train waited on the outskirts of town. Soon, he'd have to join them. Caleb turned again to the window. Then, another wagon rumbled past the saloon, a lightweight, home-made vehicle with a canvas top stretched tightly over iron rungs. A young man handled the reins, and beside him a young woman held an infant tightly in her arms.

Caleb watched the family pass and felt a sharp regret. He turned away and reached over the counter for the bourbon bottle. Briefly, he caught his own reflection in the huge mirror dominating the back bar. Maybe Shorty was right. Maybe he should have married years ago and raised a family instead of leading wagon trains down the Oregon Trail for the last ten years. Now, thirty-five was too old to start.

Caleb held up a silver coin and flipped it into the air when Shorty glanced at him from beneath a cocked brow. The bartender caught it easily, but frowned as he pocketed it. Pouring another drink, Caleb reminded himself he'd never broken his two-drink rule, especially on the night before a train left.

"You sure you don't want another?" Shorty asked sarcastically, eyeing the generous portion Caleb had sloshed into the glass.

Caleb laughed. "Well, hell. It's my birthday."

"Your birthday? Why didn't you say something?"

"I've never been here on my birthday before. We should've pulled out weeks ago."

Shorty looked up as another wagon rumbled past. "Think you'll have any trouble starting this late?"

"I don't know. The fellow heading up this group says they'll travel light and do what I say." Caleb shrugged. "I've heard that before."

From the wagon seat in front of McCuller's Store, Josie watched the tall, buckskin-clad man saunter down the street. Mr. McCuller'd said he was wagon master Caleb McCall, who had a train waiting on the edge of town. Caleb McCall. She whispered the name to herself. It had a nice ring to it. The train would be pulling out in the morning, the storekeeper had said.

Josie chewed the side of her mouth and glanced toward the door. Thunderation, it took Petey forever to pick out a piece of candy.

Wagon master. That meant he had plenty of experience with Injuns. Josie shivered at the thought, remembering her mother and husband's death. Nothing would make her drive this team of mules back to the Rockies with only Petey for company. Nothing would terrify her again like the trip here, *I ain't spendin' another night jumpin' and listenin'.*

Caleb moved farther down the street, towering over the ladies he tipped his hat to. *Yep. A body'd be safe with him. Now, how can I go about gittin' on the train?* Slipping her hand into her pocket, she jingled the few coins left. Wagon trains cost money, precious money Pa'd miss for sure. Josie gnawed the other side of her mouth. There had to be some way. Some way to get on that train.

Petey interrupted her thoughts by wandering up, cracking a mouthful of peppermint. "Petey, go in there and git me a plug of that tobacco McCuller's got behind the counter," she ordered, tossing him a coin.

Her brother stared at her with open mouth. "Chawin' tobaccy? You don't chaw, Josie."

"Just go git it and don't ask so many questions."

Business was thriving from outfitting wagon trains, Caleb thought as he strode down the dusty street, dodging emigrants scurrying past him. They bustled in and out of the stores, packing their wagons with last-minute supplies. The wide dirt street accommodated a large number of vehicles parked haphazardly, spilling over onto the tree-studded lawn of the steepled brick courthouse.

Suddenly the blue-eyed hellion from the saloon blocked his path. She stood with legs spraddled, rifle resting easily in her arms, her jaw stuck out like a bad toothache.

"You the wagon master of that train on the edge of town?" She spat a long amber stream of tobacco juice at his feet.

Caleb glanced down at the damp spot in the dirt, then back to her face. "Yeah. That's my train."

"Heard you was lookin' for some scouts."

Petey tugged on her arm. "But, sis. You ain't no—"

She silenced him with a well-aimed stomp to his foot.

"Yeah," Caleb said slowly. "I'm looking for a few men."

She stood straighter and shouldered the heavy rifle. In hilarious contradiction, long lashes swept her eyes while she shifted the wad of tobacco. "I'm askin' for the job."

The corners of Caleb's mouth twitched, but he didn't dare laugh. Pushing his hat back, he leaned against the wall of the building, then crossed his arms. "You got any experience scouting?"

"Sure. Wouldn't be here if I didn't." She whacked on the plug with renewed vigor.

"Ever kill anybody?" As he watched the color drain from her face, Caleb wondered if she knew how fragile she looked in the too-big clothes and shoes, despite the wad that would choke any good tobacco chewer.

"Kilt me many a man." The chomping slowed, and her shoulders drooped a little.

"Where'd you shoot 'em?"

"Where?"

"Yeah. Between the eyes? In the leg? Where?"

"Ah . . . between the eyes."

"Josie, you ain't never—Ouch!" Petey yelped when another well-placed kick connected with his shin.

"Bleed much?" Caleb asked calmly, watching her grow paler.

"Bleed? Yeah, buckets."

"Bury 'em yourself?"

She dropped the rifle butt to the sidewalk. "No. Petey here did it for me." She swayed a little and clutched the business end of the gun for support.

"Sis, you know I ain't never—Owie! By God, quit kickin' me. You done flattened my foot. Just look at my ear.

You done made it longer a-pullin' on it all the time and—
Dadlim!'' Petey grabbed his shin. ''You know good and well
you is scared silly of Injuns, Josie. Why you want to scout for
'em?''

She deftly ignored him and peered at Caleb. ''You gonna
hire me?''

For a split second, Caleb wondered what she felt like beneath
those baggy clothes, wondered if any beauty lurked beneath
the streaks on her face. Mentally, he shook himself. *Caleb,
you've been on the prairie too long.* Luckily, the ball in her
jaw erased all serious thoughts from his mind.

''I think I've got enough scouts, Miss . . .''

''Ain't no Miss. Just Josie.'' She nodded her head while
shooting Petey a withering look for the triumph evident on his
face. ''You sayin' you can't use me?''

''Not this time.'' Somehow, he knew she'd put a mark by
his name in her book, and the thought of having her for an
enemy bothered him. ''Now, Miss . . . Josie. I've gotta be
getting to my train.'' He nodded and moved past them. As she
walked away, their voices drifted back to him.

''Why'd you spit out that tobaccy, Josie? You ain't been
chawin' it long. How come you're drinkin' out of the horse
trough? The whole bottom's full of slimy green stuff. You sure
don't look good, sis.''

Caleb picked his way between the wagons until he reached
a white two-story house on the outskirts of town. Bright red
geraniums grew in wooden crates by the walkway. He smiled
as he took the steps in one stride, remembering the delight on
Emmy's face the day he'd nailed together the planters.

The cool interior of the house hit him as soon as he opened
the door. A little silver-haired woman in a cherry wood rocker
by the window looked up from her tatting as the door swept
open.

''Caleb. Good morning.'' Her eyes twinkled in the immensely wrinkled face, and her timeless smile didn't betray her nearly eighty years. "Have you had something to eat yet?" She put down the needlework and rose from her chair in a whisper of skirts.

"I ate at Shorty's."

She frowned and shook a bony finger. "A young man like you needs nutrition, Caleb, instead of fare from a saloon."

As she moved toward him, he admired the care she took in her dress for a woman of her age. Two pearl combs held hair nearly the same color swept up into a fashionable style. Self-consciously she smoothed a striped calico bibbed apron that covered the gray taffeta day dress perfectly fitted to her still-slim figure. Townsfolk said she was once a great beauty and turned the head of every man in town, but Philip Osgood had captured her heart.

She and Philip had lived happily for forty years in this house, although Philip was gone much of the time, taking wagon trains west. Caleb had met the man, who had become a legend along the Oregon Trail, soon after he drifted into town, and had liked him instantly. Philip had taught him all he knew about wagon trains and the Oregon Trail. Caleb had grieved with Emmy when Philip was killed in the street outside Shorty's saloon by a pack of outlaws. It seemed fitting a man like Philip should have died somewhere along the trail he'd loved.

Ever since Philip's death, Caleb had lived with Emmy. He faithfully paid her rent for the entire year even though he, too, was gone much of the time, and she mothered him as if he were one of her own precious children she'd shared with Philip.

"Caleb, you've been drinking, and in the morning too. For shame."

His jaw worked as he fought the urge to laugh at the expression on her face and the picture they must make while she scolded him with her finger—he well over six feet tall, and she barely reached the middle of his chest.

"You'll ruin your health drinking the brew Shorty serves over there. Now, come, dinner's about ready and there's hot biscuits.'' She patted his arm affectionately, her lecture satisfactorily delivered for the day, and moved off toward the delicious smell of baking bread.

Caleb slowly climbed the stairs to his room. He didn't plan to return to Independence after delivering this train safely to Oregon. He'd miss Emmy and her neat, clean house. It was home. At least the only one he was ever likely to have.

He stuffed his few belongings into saddlebags hanging over the end of the bed, took his fifty-caliber Henry rifle down from the pegs by the door, and laid it across the chair. After pouring some water out of the pitcher, he splashed his face and dried it on a clean towel hanging above the bowl. He walked over to the window, where sheer curtains fluttered in the gentle breeze. Far below, a lone wagon rumbled toward the group circled at the edge of town. Down the street a team of skinny mules hung their heads at the hitching post. Caleb smiled, thinking of the tobacco-chewing waif.

Downstairs smelled like fresh bread, a warm, yeasty scent permeating every cranny of the house. In the dining room, Emmy busily placed steaming plates of food onto the table set for six, the total number of her boarders.

''Take your hat off, Caleb,'' she reminded him without looking up.

Caleb smiled as he removed the offending Stetson and tossed it down onto the floor by his chair. She moved around the table with the energy of a young woman. Leaving her would be the hardest thing.

Caleb started to speak, then stopped to take a sip of cool water to clear the lump from his throat. ''I'm leaving tomorrow.''

''I knew that. You're getting a late start, aren't you? Philip used to say when spring is this warm, there'll be an early fall on the plains and early snow on the passes.''

''Yes, ma'am, but we plan to move quickly.''

''When will you be back?''

Damn, this is going to be hard. ''I'm not coming back this time.''

Her hand stopped midway between the plate and the bowl of vegetables. A clock ticked on the carved mantel of the fireplace, filling the silence that fell like a leaden curtain. "Not coming back? Why, child?"

"I think it's time I moved on. After ten years, I think I'm too old."

"Nonsense," she chided, setting down the bowl of butter beans. "My Philip was older than you when he still led trains."

Caleb didn't remind her that if Philip had quit when he should have and not stepped into an argument between a settler and a known outlaw, he might be alive today. "It's time I moved on to something else."

"What will you do?" she asked weakly.

"I thought I might try ranching."

"Look for a good woman, maybe?"

"Now you sound like Shorty." Emmy kept her eyes turned away, but Caleb thought he saw tears glisten for a moment.

"He's right. A good man like you, Caleb, needs a woman."

Caleb smiled and laid his hand over her small one. "There aren't many like you."

The little woman blushed bright red, and dismissed his comment with a wave of her hand and a smile. "You ought to get yourself a woman, Caleb. Have some children." Emmy sat down in the chair opposite him and stared directly at him.

Caleb pushed his food around, feeling the heat of her gaze. Then she moved to the chair beside him, and her small, thin hand rested on his large brown one. She squeezed it firmly, her strength surprising. Caleb looked up. "You can't let the past ruin the years you have left, child." She stroked his stubbly cheek, using her favorite name for him. Straightening one of the wayward curls that hung over his forehead, she said, "I'll vow if you set your mind to it, you could land a pretty wife." She tucked a strand behind his ear and smiled brilliantly.

Caleb watched her face, seeing the lingering beauty of her youth, the beauty that had bound the heart of an adventurer to the little prairie town of Independence and kept him returning there each year. "I'm going to miss you, Emmy. Philip was a lucky man."

"He always wanted a boy like you."

Caleb knew she referred to the three sons she and Philip had buried out behind the house in the little cemetery. "Philip was like a father to me. I owe him my life many times over. Not just for him being there when I needed him, but for the things he taught me."

"You remember all those lessons by lamplight?" she asked.

Caleb nodded.

"You put them to good use and write me, you hear?" Emmy rose and busied herself around the table.

Caleb felt a twinge as he saw a tear slip down her cheek. "I'll write you and let you know about that woman."

Emmy smiled with misty eyes. "I'll look for those letters every day."

"What you gonna do, Josie?" Petey shouted, looking up to where his sister balanced precariously on the porch roof.

"Shh! You want everybody in this blessed town to hear you?"

"What're you gonna do up there?"

"I'm gonna git us on this wagon train. I ain't makin' that trip scared to pieces again." She slipped on a loose shingle and crouched as it rattled to the ground.

"What good's trompin' around up there gonna do?"

"Shh! You wait with the team and leave the rest to me."

Josie inched her way to the window she'd seen Caleb standing in earlier. She'd get on that train if it killed her. Even if she had to use her feminine wiles—as the preacher back home used to call them—to do it. Better to die of embarrassment than to get scalped. She leaned over the windowsill and tumbled into the room. One of her unlaced boots slid off and clumped her on the head.

"You in, sis?" Petey yelled loud enough to be heard clear out to the train.

Josie stuck her head out the window. "Shut up, Petey. Git on back to them mules and wait for me."

He shrugged and ambled down the street out of sight.

God, please don't let him get into any more trouble, she prayed as she turned back toward the room. She was inside a real, honest-to-goodness room, she realized with a rush. One with rugs on the floors, mattresses on the beds, and clean water. The faint scent of lavender clung to the bed. A set of worn saddlebags lay in a corner. She paused, listened, then crept over to them.

She untied the leather thong and drew out a brown linen shirt. *Looks big enough for me and Petey.* She held it up to her chest, and it swept her knees. Pressing it to her nose, she inhaled leather and homemade soap. *It smells just like Mr. McCall.* She rubbed the coarse material against her cheek, and her imagination took wing, putting her in the arms that filled those sleeves.

"Where's your mind, girl?" she asked herself, mimicking her father. "There ain't no time for foolin' around," she whispered softly.

Carefully, she unbuttoned her shirt and tossed it to the floor, undid her pants, and kicked them aside. The wooden floor was cool to her feet as she padded across the room. A mirror with a diagonal crack hung over the washstand. She squinted into its face and tilted her head. "You ain't so bad," she told herself, rubbing at the ring of dirt that encircled her neck and made ridges on her skin. "Not bad for an old woman of twenty-one." With a careful swipe to her disarrayed hair, she strolled over and crawled into the bed. Now, all she had to do was wait, wait until he came back, then scream. She reckoned a fine, upstanding man like him would have to take her along. His sense of honor'd see to that, she thought smugly, remembering a like situation Betty Jean had gotten into back home.

Seconds passed. Then minutes. Josie picked at the covers,

wiping at the dirty smudges her arms made on the sheets. No one came. She strained her ears to hear footsteps on the stairs. Nothing. She ran her hand over the smooth sheets. Ma'd never had anything this fine, not even at home in Tennessee. Josie flopped over onto her side and stared out the window. *Wonder what he's like when he ain't bein' stuck up?* She plunged her nose into the pillow and breathed the same scent that filled the clothes.

By the time an hour had gone by, Josie's eyes drooped. The soft breeze stirred her hair, and the coolness of the linens invited her to lay her head back in their fragrant depths. Only when she jerked awake did Josie realize she had slept.

Heavy footsteps clumped up the stairs. Her courage fled. With one motion she leaped out of the bed, scooped up her clothes, and dove for the window. Behind her, the door scraped open. Clutching her garments against her chest, she cowered outside the window on the porch roof, in full view of the entire town. To her left, Petey strolled down the street, hands shoved into his pockets. *Dear Jesus, don't let him see me and start shoutin' stupid questions up at me.*

"What in the devil—" said someone inside the room. "All right, whoever you are, come out."

The unmistakable click of a gun's hammer drifted out the window. Josie pressed closer to the side of the house. She heard boots thud across the floor. A tanned hand brushed back the curtains. A curly head poked out. He looked in the opposite direction first. Josie squeezed her eyes shut. "Please, Lord," she whispered. "I didn't mean all them things I did. But if you're gonna strike me dead, please do it now."

Chapter Two

"Caleb!" A feminine voice drifted up from downstairs.
"Caleb?"

"Be right down, Emmy," he called, drawing his head inside
without looking to where Josie cowered against the house.

The hammer clicked back in place. Footsteps receded toward
the door, it brushed open, then closed. The room grew quiet.
She exhaled and sagged to her knees on the roof.

"Josie. You is naked as a scraped hog!" Petey stood in the
front yard of the house, staring straight at her, his fists jammed
on his hips. "Why ain't you got no clothes on, sis?"

Josie threw on her pants and shirt, crawled to the edge of
the porch, and jumped. She winced as she hit the ground, but
the blow didn't stop her. Rolling to her feet, she scooped up
her hat, grabbed Petey's arm, and dragged him down the street
behind her at a dead run.

The afternoon sun shone brightly when Caleb stepped down
from the steps of Emmy's house. He turned and looked back

toward the second floor. The curtains in her room stirred slightly. She'd slipped away while the other boarders ate, and he knew she was crying.

A tall buckskin mare waited at the hitching post. Caleb patted her nose, and Cindy nickered into his hand, finding the slice of apple he'd smuggled out of the house. After slinging his saddlebags over her back, he swung up into the saddle. Prancing with anticipation, the mare trotted off down the street, her ears pricked forward toward the distant cluster of wagons. As they passed the livery stable, Cindy strained to see the fine black colt she'd just weaned. Mr. Todd, the liveryman, had agreed to sell the horse and give the money to Emmy.

As they reached the edge of town, a small detachment of cavalry rode in, jostling one another and trading jibes. A young farm boy passed them on a lumbering draft horse. He turned, openmouthed at the impressive picture the division made in their fresh uniforms.

"Where ya'll headed?" he shouted at them.

"For the Bozeman Trail." One young soldier stopped his horse. "You know, where that Injun Red Cloud's been harassing the wagon trains. We're here to put an end to that." He laughed and glanced at his comrades.

Caleb ground his teeth together as he passed them, a cold anger building in him at the naïveté of the farm boy. The blue and gold of the calvary uniforms was burned on his memory, and flashes of pain twisted his heart. Their laughter followed him, and he could almost feel the heat from the fire, hear the screams, see Fawn's face. He didn't unclench his teeth until the town fell far behind him.

The westward-bound families looked up from their individual chores as Caleb rode into their midst. Used to their stares, he smiled grimly to himself as he heard whispering behind him. He'd gained a reputation over the years—some of it deserved and some not. His choice of dress added to the gossip; he wore a full set of buckskins, from the intricately beaded shirt and pants to the knee-length boots made especially to fit his large feet.

Cindy delicately jumped over a stack of crates between two wagons. Parked in a circle, the forty wagons provided a corral for the horses. Caleb dismounted and let her go graze, then turned and searched the crowd for the train's organizer. A small, slim man walked out from behind one of the wagons with hand extended.

"I'm Jim Statton." He grinned. "You must be Mr. McCall?"

"That's right." Caleb took in the man in one glance. Short and balding, his hair receded from the top of his head, leaving only a few wisps along the sides. Poor pickings for scalping was the first thing to run through Caleb's mind, then he scolded himself for thinking it.

"I'm pleased to meet you, Mr. McCall. All of my people are here. Some arrived just this afternoon."

An educated greenhorn. "I'd like to meet and speak to the others as soon as possible," Caleb said shortly. Educated easterners were the worst kind. No common sense. But Statton's grin was infectious, and Caleb clasped the man's outstretched hand firmly.

Caleb pulled a crate into the center of the crowd and hopped up onto it. "You folks gather 'round." As he waited for any late arrivals to come forward, he looked down onto the faces that would come to rely on him for their very life, some faces that wouldn't live to see Oregon.

Near the back of the group a young woman stood apart from the crowd. A dark, scowling man stood close by her side, his hand gripping her elbow. She clutched an infant against her chest. Caleb frowned. Years on the trail had taught him to spot trouble. The pair in front of him fit the mold—a young wife terrified of her husband, judging from the furtive glances she gave him and the way she tried to sidle out of his grasp; a possessive, domineering husband. More than one jealous husband had caused a fight on a wagon train.

"My name's Caleb McCall," he shouted over the crowd's buzz. "I'm your wagon master. I've made this trip ten times, so I know this country well." Heads nodded in approval.

"I've a few simple rules," he continued. "What I say goes, no questions or arguments, not when it involves the safety of the train. Those of you who have horses to pull your wagons will need to trade for oxen as soon as we reach Alcove Springs. Horses won't last once we get to the mountains." Murmurs rippled through the throng.

Caleb drew a breath. The next announcement always brought an argument. "If any of you are carrying heavy furniture, leave it here. Your animals and wagons are more valuable, and there'll be too much of a load with stuff like that." He looked over the crowd and waited for the inevitable.

A short, red-haired man stepped forward. Carrying a Bible stuffed firmly beneath his arm, the little man wore a self-satisfied smile that stretched his ruddy face and further disfigured his misshapen nose. Throwing out his chest, he tugged up his trousers with his free hand.

"Mr. McCall, my name is Isaiah Crockett. My family and I find your attitude objectionable." He nodded to a pale woman tending to a group of squirming children. "What we choose or don't choose to take in our wagons is our concern. We have things my wife cherishes deeply."

Caleb saw a blush creep over the woman's cheeks and doubted she'd ever had a thing she cherished deeply. Looking down on the man standing below him, Caleb sighed. Every train had one, he reminded himself with a slight shake of his head.

"If you don't like my rules, Mr. Crockett, you're free to wait right here until next spring for another wagon train with a different wagon master." The little man swallowed, blinked, and shifted his feet.

"We're getting a late start as it is," Caleb said in a threatening voice. "I can't afford for one wagon to slow down the rest. If we aren't over the mountains before winter, we'll die. Is that understood?'' Caleb's eyes drilled into Crockett's as a rumble went through the crowd. The man opened his mouth to comment, then snapped it shut. ''Are there any more questions?''

At the back, the young blond woman wrenched away from her husband and stepped forward. Holding the baby pressed against her shoulder, her fingers worried her dress skirt. Several times she glanced back at her husband and his frown deepened. ''Are . . . we likely to encounter any Indians, Mr. McCall?'' she asked.

Caleb glanced at her husband. He stood with arms crossed, his expression unchanged.

''Yes, ma'am,'' Caleb said with a nod. ''I've dealt with all the tribes from time to time. The Lakota, the Cheyenne, Crow, Blackfoot, Pawnee.''

The woman shifted the baby to her other arm and licked her lips. Glancing again at her husband, she started to speak. But before she could form the first word, her husband stepped forward and jerked her arm. She cringed away from him. His eyes locked on hers, and he dragged her away toward the wagons. The unmistakable sound of a slap drifted back over the still twilight.

Caleb trembled with fury as the people in the crowd looked at one another. Violence toward a woman had always angered him, as well as overbearing, insecure husbands who resorted to striking their wives to obtain the obedience they could not get through respect. They disrupted the train, made trouble where there was trouble enough. He glanced down. The faces of the crowd looked up to him, and he knew that sooner or later that couple's trouble would be his. Men like that ought to spend a few months out on the prairie with nothing but grass and snakes for company, then they'd appreciate females a little more, he thought wryly.

''No more questions?'' he asked, trying to hold his voice even. ''Good, we'll pull out at daylight.'' He hopped down off the crate, whistled, and caught Cindy's bridle as the crowd dispersed.

"Crockett will be trouble," Statton said, moving up beside Caleb and nodding toward the man hurrying his family away.

"So will the couple in the back. I've had troublemakers before." Caleb threw a stirrup over the saddle and checked his cinch. "The prairie has a way of breaking them of their bad habits."

"The Tolberts," Statton said with a shake of his head. "Anna and Eric. A strange pair."

With a final jerk of the strap, Caleb turned to face Statton. "Make sure folks dump off their excess baggage. I know some of the things mean a lot to the womenfolk. They won't like leaving them, but their stock will mean more when we get to the mountains."

"I'll speak to them," Statton promised.

"Good night." Caleb swung into the saddle. The setting sun gilded the layer of dust that lay in a blanket around Independence as he set off for Shorty's house and Mary's famous chicken dinner.

Josie took a bite of the dry biscuit and chewed slowly. The rough boards of the wagon bed pricked through her worn pants. The sultry night that swirled around them was filled with pinpoints of light and an orchestra of insects. Petey shifted his weight and the mules fidgeted.

"How come you want to git on that wagon train so bad, sis?" he asked, sliding closer to her side.

Josie shrugged. "I just ain't particular to making that trip back by ourselves."

Petey mulled over what she'd said. She hoped it satisfied his curiosity, and she wouldn't have to explain further.

"How come . . ." he began slowly, stretching his feet out as far as the narrow wagon bed would allow. "How come you don't just pay?"

" 'Cause Pa don't hold with spending good money for such. He figures we oughta be able to make it on our own."

"Is that why Ma and Johnny and the others got kilt? 'Cause Pa didn't join no train?"

A chill ran up her spine. Sometimes Petey's insight gave her the willies. "Yeah, I reckon that's why."

"That why you got in Mr. McCall's room naked? To make him take us along? I ain't scared of the Injuns, Josie."

She could think of no words to describe the fear she felt at the mention of Indians. How could she admit her fear to her brother when he looked to her as mother, father, and sister?

"How long we gonna sit here in this wagon?" He fidgeted, then rose up on one hip to pull a splinter from his breeches' seat.

"Till morning, then we'll tail that train out of town." She wished she'd brought along an extra blanket to sit on.

"Seems to me somethin' ain't right 'bout followin' and not payin'."

Josie didn't answer him. What could she say? As if sensing her confusion, he edged closer, flung an arm around her shoulders, and snuggled her closer to him. "I'll look out for you, sis. Ain't nothin' gonna happen you and me can't handle. Ain't that the way it's always been?"

"Yeah, I reckon." She ran a hand down Petey's cheek. Rough stubble pricked her hand, reminding her for all his innocence, he had grown into a man. For a moment she dropped her role of protector and laid her head on his shoulder. "I love you too, Petey."

Caleb stretched out on the bedroll, clasping his hands behind his head. Mary's chicken dinner lulled him into a wonderful drifting between sleep and wakefulness. Sunset was a pink sliver near the horizon, darkening until overhead stars glittered, dwarfing the immense prairie for a few hours. As the darkness closed in around him, so did his memories, like clear nights when he lay and watched a multitude of stars through the open smoke hole of a Lakota tipi. He had wondered then, as now, what was really up there. The Indians said their gods lived beyond the points of light. The whites taught their one God lived there, in a place called heaven. Which one was right?

Caleb sighed and turned over onto his side and gave way to the sleep tugging at his eyelids. The dirt-streaked face of an urchin drifted into his mind. Deep blue eyes wavered before him. Long, dark wisps of hair fell across his bare chest, tickling his thick mat of hair. She smiled, her lips thin and pink. Then they lowered onto his, soft and supple. Caleb reached out to entangle his hands in the dark cloud. He jerked awake, his heart pounding.

He sat up and stared into the fire, seeing her image instead of the flames. Was it Shorty's words about a woman that had made his dreams and thoughts take this turn? Was it his self-imposed celibacy playing with his thoughts? Caleb shook the battered coffeepot. It sloshed, and he poured another cup, rose, and walked toward the train.

Most of the campfires had flickered into embers and the wagons were still and dark. Caleb strode softly, not even the parched grass crackling beneath his stride. He passed among the wagons, checking wheels and harnesses, looking for trouble or problems that might arise. Finding himself by the Tolberts' wagon, he paused and studied the conveyance. It was made from a farm wagon. Iron reinforced the chassis and bars stretched across the bed from side to side, supporting the canvas top. As he pondered whether the construction would be trail-worthy, the unmistakable moans of a man's passion came from inside the wagon. Caleb turned, intending to hurry away. Then the crack of a slap joined a woman's sobs mingled with a man's climax.

"Be still, you Indian whore," a labored voice said from inside.

Decency told Caleb to leave, that it was none of his business. But as he turned, the wagon began to creak and shake. A woman sobbed at more muffled curses.

Caleb stared into his cup, clenching his teeth against the

anger welling up in him. Eager to get back to his own fire, he walked away. With his head down, absorbed in thought, he ran straight into Statton.

"McCall! Golly, you scared me." Statton pulled up his suspenders. He held a pistol in one hand. "I was going to . . . I wasn't looking for anyone to be about."

"I couldn't sleep. Thought I'd take a turn through camp, see what needs doing tomorrow."

Statton glanced in the direction from which Caleb had come. "I see you were entertained by the nightly show." He nodded toward the wagon. "Everyone here has heard it. They go on every night. My wife says it's disgraceful. I tell her she'll hear worse than that before this train is over."

"Living this close, I expect so," Caleb said, edging away from the embarrassing conversation.

"Tolbert." Statton shrugged. "He's a strange bird."

Caleb glanced back toward the wagon where a lantern now burned low.

"They come from Minnesota. Said they were going to Oregon to join his brother on a farm there. A strange marriage, if you ask me. She's scared to death of the man."

As they both watched, Anna Tolbert climbed from the wagon. She pulled the thin cotton wrapper closer, glanced around briefly, then fled into the darkness. Caleb frowned. He'd have to say something to the women about venturing so far from the train for some privacy.

A buzzing fly landed on Josie's face. She wriggled her nose, then slapped at the offending insect. "Wake up, Petey." She elbowed him, asleep on the other side of the wagon bed. "Git up. We gotta git moving if we wanna tail that wagon train."

"Aw, Josie." Petey propped up on his elbows and frowned. "Why don't you join the train instead of sneakin' around about it."

"You know good and well why." Josie stood in the wagon

bed and shook the jacket she had used as a pillow. "I told you last night Pa didn't give me enough money to pay to join no wagon trains. We just gotta drag along behind."

Petey struggled to his feet and cast a longing glance toward the saloon. "Josie, do you think I could—"

"No. You ain't goin' in there after no whore. We gotta git goin'."

"You don't understand a man's needs. He's gotta have a little—"

"I understand all I want to know 'bout men," she snapped.

With a heartfelt sigh, Petey scrambled to the wagon seat. "I ain't never gonna git a chance at no woman. She's the only one I even seen near 'bout since we left Tennessee. And there sure ain't none out in them woods where Pa's got us."

"You'll live." Josie clamored to the seat and picked up the reins. She'd purposely left the mules hitched all night so they could pull out right behind the train. Pa'd be mad enough when she came back without Davie. He'd skin her for sure if she spent good money for protection from the Injuns.

She flicked the lines, and the mules stumbled forward. No one moved along the deserted streets. Petey propped one foot against the wagon's side and pulled his hat across his face. He snored softly and she smiled. Her twin always could sleep— anywhere, anytime.

They rumbled out of town, and the rolling prairie stretched in front of them. Without Petey to talk to, her thoughts turned to her encounter yesterday with the wagon master. She remembered how his arms had encircled her, how his scent had enveloped them both. She shook her head. *There ain't gonna be no man. Not even if he's so purdy you'd walk him down to the front row in a revival meetin'.* She sighed and leaned back against the wagon seat, letting the memory of his gold-flecked jade eyes flit through her mind.

Chapter Three

Caleb cantered toward the wagons as the sun peeped over the flat horizon. The wagons were milling crazily, nearly running into one another, tangling traces and harnesses. A deafening din from barking dogs, screaming children, and shouting drivers accompanied the confusion. Sharp cracks of whips over the oxen's heads punctuated the noise. This kind of fray in the mornings would slow them down, and the train couldn't afford that.

With practiced ease, Caleb trotted in among the wagons, shouting orders and suggestions. In short time they all creaked down the trail in a line. Most of the women and children walked alongside to save the stock. Men drove the oxen on foot, holding a long bullwhip, yelling "gee" or "haw" for left or right turns. Dogs trotted beneath almost every wagon, their pink tongues hanging out in the midmorning heat.

A big crowd of people huddled at the edge of town to watch the train pull out. Today Caleb barely had time to glance their way, yet he plainly saw Emmy waving to him from Shorty's buggy. He'd traded the heavy buckskin shirt for a white linen one, and the collar flopped against his neck in the warm wind. Stopping and raising his hat, he saluted her, then galloped away after the others.

The line of wagons rolled slowly, and Caleb rode up and down the column, watching for breakdowns and lagging teams. A sweating Jim Statton pulled up beside him, hatless, his shirt open at the neck.

"Early to be this hot, isn't it?" He mopped at his forehead with a drenched handkerchief.

"Yep." Caleb glanced toward the western horizon. "We're in for a storm tonight."

"Think so?"

"Always does when it's this hot this early." Caleb drew his lips into a tight line. "We'll circle the wagons before dark." He wasn't in the mood for conversation this morning. Statton stayed by his side for a time before riding off into the unmerciful dust and heat.

The faces of the travelers on the passing wagons were a blur to Caleb. Recognition would come as they progressed, but he made it a point not to get too close to his charges. Too many dangers and hazards waited to take a life.

Before noon, those walking wearily dragged their feet. Caleb unbuttoned several buttons on his shirt to let the hot breeze cool the puddles of sweat beneath the fabric. He galloped back a distance, then dropped the reins so Cindy could graze while he watched his charges roll past.

As the dust cleared from the last wagon, he noticed another cloud of dust far to the rear of the train. A lone wagon pulled by two shuffling mules dogged the train. "What in the devil—" He gathered Cindy's reins and galloped toward the straggler.

Josie stood up in the seat and shaded her eyes. Someone from the wagon train rode back toward them, kicking up a cloud of dust. "Thunderation," she muttered, and flopped back into the seat.

"What's the matter?" Petey asked, yawning and cracking open an eye.

"They've seen us. There'll be hell to pay for sure." Josie hunched her shoulders and pulled her hat low over her eyes. "You keep quiet and let me do the talking. You hear?"

Petey nodded as the cloud of dust drew nearer.

Josie didn't glance up when the rider drew alongside the wagon and then fell in with their pace.

"Where you folks headed?" he asked.

Josie risked a peek at the man from beneath the brim of her hat. One look at his face and her heart leaped into her throat.

"We're going back home." She flicked the reins, and the mules picked up their speed.

"Where's that?" His voice quivered as his horse changed to a trot to keep pace.

"Up in the edge of the mountains." Josie glanced at him.

"You're a long way from home, aren't you?" He leaned down, trying to peer at her face beneath the hat. "What's the matter? No other scouting jobs open?"

She gave the reins another flick and ducked her head lower. "Had to meet somebody in Independence, if it's any of your damn business."

The nearest mule plunged and brayed as Caleb grabbed the reins and jerked the team to a halt, nearly throwing Petey from the seat. "You got a good reason for hanging way back here instead of with the train?" he growled.

Josie stared at the floorboards of the wagon, hesitant to meet those eyes again. "That's my business."

"I'm making it mine." He reached over and snatched off her hat. "Don't you know it is dangerous to travel out here by yourself?"

" 'Course I know that." Josie grabbed her hat away from him and jammed it back on her head. "Some folks ain't got all the money in the world." Raising her eyes to meet his, she tingled from a slight shock. Straight white teeth gleamed in a tanned face. Despite the anger in his voice, his eyes twinkled as if he knew all her secrets. She scowled deeply, hoping he'd take the hint and leave.

"Is it the fee? Is that why you're dragging back here, bait for every cutthroat we come across?" He paused, but Josie didn't respond. "Bring your wagon on up. Forget the money."

"Don't you reckon you better ask them folks about that first, Mr. Smarty?" Josie pointed at the train with the end of her bullwhip.

Caleb looped a long leg across his saddle horn and pushed his hat back with one finger. A light brown ringlet fell forward over his eyes. "I'm the wagon master. What I say goes."

Josie jerked her hat lower. "Proud of yourself, ain't you? We don't take charity."

"Yes we do, sis," Petey interrupted eagerly. "I mean, I'd like to ride with the other folks. There'd be singing around the campfire and dancing and—"

"Shut up, Petey." She gritted her teeth. "I swear, sometimes . . ."

Caleb laughed, a big, warm masculine sound, and Josie was glad he couldn't see the gooseflesh the sound brought to her skin.

"Now, that's what I like," he said. "Somebody who speaks his mind."

"I like him," Petey whispered, and nudged Josie with his elbow.

"What do you say, muleskinner? Want to join us?" Caleb taunted.

Josie flung a murderous glance at her grinning twin. If Pa was waiting for them by the trail like they'd planned, he'd whup her for sure if he saw her come sauntering in with a whole wagon train of people. He wouldn't give her the chance to explain before he'd cut a branch. He'd say his money was too hard to come by, too hard to grub from the ground to waste it on conveniences and comforts. After all, her and Petey'd made the trip to Independence alone, hadn't they? But then, they hadn't seen any Injuns either.

Mustering all the dignity she could, Josie straightened, stuffed her hair back underneath her hat, and picked up the reins. "I reckon my brother's made the decision for us. But we ain't takin' charity. I'll work out the fee till we drop off."

"Have it your way." Caleb tipped his hat, and had turned to ride away, when Josie stopped him.

"Mister!"

He looked back over his shoulder.

She hesitated, willing her voice not to tremble, willing her hands not to shake. "Thanks."

He placed one finger against an eyebrow, dipped his head at her, then galloped away.

Josie flicked the reins and urged the mules into a trot. Even at their best, they wouldn't catch up with the train before dark, and she hoped he wouldn't come back to check on them. His presence unnerved her as no man ever had. And she didn't like being unnerved. It made her vulnerable, made her start thinking about things—things like husbands and babies and—

"I think he likes you." Petey cut into her thoughts.

"Oh, shut up." She frowned and shoved her hat forward over her eyes.

True to Caleb's prediction, a ground-jarring storm blew in at sunset. The clouds had started gathering after the noon stop and increased as the afternoon went on. Before dark he ordered the wagons circled. They had barely completed camp, when lightning began to arc along the horizon. Loud cracks of thunder roared overhead, spooking the exhausted animals into flight. The driving rain poured off his shoulders and Cindy's haunches as they dashed across the prairie in pursuit of the stock. Together, along with Statton and his party, they rounded up all the stragglers, while the squall diminished as quickly as it had appeared.

The remaining clouds scuttled across the sky and bright stars peeped between the dark wisps. Campfires blinked to life, lit from the sparse wood available, and soon the combined smells of supper drifted on the damp evening air. Caleb rode through the camp, Cindy's hooves making a soft squishing noise on the rain-soaked ground. He planned to sleep tonight within the circle of wagons, a long-honored sense of foreboding pricking at his scalp. Nothing had happened to make him wary, yet something had put him on guard.

Josie shivered in her wet clothes and wished the mules would hurry. In the distance, campfires flickered. Somehow, the spots of light made the night less lonely—that and the thought that where those lights were, so was Caleb. They had hurried all afternoon to catch up, but the strong oxen had outdistanced the stubborn mules. Anyway, she was glad for one more night alone, one more night away from Caleb's disquieting closeness. Caleb. She liked thinking of him that way.

"Wake up, Petey." She elbowed her brother again.

"Wha—" Irritably, he shifted, pushed his hat back, and sat up straight. "I wish you'd quit punching me. You're gonna make me fall plumb off this wagon. When'd it git dark?" he asked, looking around them.

"Right after the sun went down."

He shot his sister a withering glance. "Don't turn yore sharp tongue on me. You know''—he turned toward her and shook a bony finger—''if you'd talk a little nicer, some fellow might come along and take you off our hands."

"Oh, yeah. And where's this fellow gonna come from? Out of Pa's mine? They gonna dig him up?" Josie spat back.

"There's been fellows by asking about you." Petey flopped against the wagon's side.

"Oh, you mean them trappers with no teeth, and wolf guts flung around their necks? Or was it the old crazy man with one eye who thought he was a moose and wanted to drink out of the creek? Which one you want for a brother-in-law?"

Her challenge didn't change Petey's expression. He intently

studied her face. "Don't you git lonely, Josie?" he asked, losing the taunting tone in his voice.

Josie hauled on the reins to halt the team and shoved the brake forward with a booted foot. "I reckon I do." She jumped to the ground and pulled out a sack of biscuits from beneath the wagon seat. "We better not make a fire. No telling who else might take a notion to ride up."

"Aw, Josie. We got to eat biscuits for the next three weeks?"

"I'll shoot us something in a few days when I go hunting for the train." She took a bite of the dry, crumbling bread and grimaced against its staleness. "Eat your supper."

After their brief supper and a swig of water from the same canteen, she and her brother crawled beneath the wagon and covered up with damp, ragged, dirty blankets.

"You sure we ain't safer in the wagon?" Petey murmured.

"I got the mules hobbled. What you gonna do if it rains again? The way you snore, you'll drown sure, sucking all that water in."

As their voices died, she became aware of hoofbeats, soft steps made by unshod ponies. A bunch of them, Josie figured as she cracked open an eye and watched them pass. Their movements were almost soundless except for the whisper of the grass as they passed. *Barefooted horses. Injuns!* Josie cringed in her blanket, sure she'd feel a knife at her throat at any moment. Old memories assailed her as she remembered her mother's death. She pulled her hat down over her eyes. The mere mention of Indians was enough to make her heart jump clean out of her chest. As swiftly as they had appeared, the band of Indians disappeared, paying the lone wagon no attention. Josie climbed out and stood. The remnants of the storm clouds obscured the moon, casting the prairie into darkness. She looked toward the wagon train. Was this an attack? Would she stand here and watch a slaughter—again. Her heart flew to her throat as the Indians passed as slim silhouettes between her and the distant lights.

"C'mon, Petey. Git up!" She kicked at Petey's backside beneath the blanket.

"Thunderation, Josie. Cain't you let a body sleep? What's the matter." Petey shoved down the blanket and rubbed his eyes.

"Injuns."

"Injuns!" Petey sat up and cracked his head against the wagon's axle. "Ow!" he muttered as he scrambled from under the wagon.

"Let's go." Josie climbed into the seat and slapped the reins against the mules' backs. The wagon lurched forward, leaving Petey clinging to the side.

"Wait, Josie. By God—" He grabbed for the wagon seat and hauled himself aboard. "Where we goin'?"

"We're gonna join that wagon train."

"Thought you didn't want no charity?"

"Injuns change things," she said, and slapped the reins again, sending the team into a fast, shuffling walk.

Caleb strolled through the camp as if he were simply visiting. He took special note of the children, their faces expectant and filled with excitement, oblivious of the dangers lying in wait for them. A shiver passed over him. He had made the right decision letting this be his last wagon train.

Halfway around the circle of wagons, he saw Josie coming. She had the mules in a fast trot and she was cracking a long bullwhip over their heads.

"What's the matter?" he asked, catching the nearest mule's bridle as she jammed on the brake and hauled back on the reins.

"Injuns," she panted.

"Where?"

She turned and pointed back in the direction she had come. "There. Between us and you."

Caleb's glance swept her from head to foot. She was scared

to death, but was she exaggerating? Had she heard an owl and let it spook her? No, he told himself, his gaze falling to the Hawken rifle propped against the wagon seat. *Whatever else she is, she's no scatterbrained female.*

"How many of 'em were there?"

"I dunno. Twenty, maybe thirty."

A curious crowd had gathered behind them. "Don't say anything about this," Caleb whispered, moving closer to her. "Pull on in here," he said in a normal tone. "Crockett, move your wagon up some."

Several men helped move the unhitched wagon up so Josie and Petey could slide into place. She jumped down, and her wet clothes slapped against her legs as she landed. Caleb silently helped her unhitch the mules and turn them loose inside the circle of wagons. He waited until the last of the curious had dispersed before he spoke.

"I'm gonna ride out and see what I can see," he said, laying a mule collar in the back of the wagon. "These people will panic if they think Indians are on our trail. Don't mention what you saw until I come back. Understand?"

She looked up at him and nodded. Her hands were steady, but her eyes were full of fear. "Can you keep him quiet?" he nodded toward Petey.

"Petey, you keep yore yap shut, you hear?" she hissed at him.

The boy frowned, then nodded.

"You want me to go with you?" She lifted the Hawken from the wagon seat.

Caleb started to chuckle, then caught the frown on her face. "No. I need you to stay here so people won't suspect trouble."

She nodded solemnly and he turned to go.

"Mr. McCall?"

He stopped and turned.

"Thanks for lettin' us join up."

Caleb touched his hat and strode away. Back at his own fire, he whistled low for Cindy. When she trotted up, he threw his blanket and saddle across her back. She turned her head to look at him as if to ask if he'd taken leave of his senses.

"This won't take long, girl," he said as he jerked the cinch tight and dropped the stirrup. Picking up his Henry rifle, he swung into the saddle and rode in a wide circle around the train. Back toward the east, he picked up Josie's wagon tracks and followed them west until the tracks were marred by hoof-prints. He swung down from the saddle and knelt. Unshod prints. He looked toward the train. "How'd she know that?" he asked himself. Remounting, he followed the tracks as they led away from the train without wavering. After he'd followed them for more than a mile and was convinced the Indians hadn't doubled back, he swung Cindy around and headed back for the train.

Stopping by his camp first, he unsaddled her and turned her loose. Then he returned to the wagon train. By then all campfires were out and the wagons were still and dark. He strode the length of the train until he found Josie's wagon. One body was rolled in a blanket underneath and another slept in the wagon body. Glancing around, he saw no one else watching, so he leaned over the wagon bed and lifted the hat that covered the body's face. Cold steel slid up his cheek.

"Whoever you are, you better git yore damn hands off my hat," Josie said low and even.

"It's me. Caleb McCall." Caleb dropped the hat, his heart pounding.

Josie jerked the hat off her head and sat up. "What'd you find?"

Caleb studied her anxious face. What kind of woman was she to pull a gun on a man and never blink an eye? "You were right, but they've headed north. Must have been a hunting party."

"They was huntin' all right, but it won't no buffalo." She wriggled out of the blanket and jammed her hat on her head. "Dad-blamed Injuns cain't be trusted."

Caleb felt a ripple of anger at the remark, but then, he'd

heard the same before. "You'll be safe here. Stay with the train tomorrow."

She nodded and he headed back to his own fire, contemplating Josie. Just the sight of her made him laugh. Wonder what made her the way she is? he thought as he flipped out his bedroll and lay down. Where was she from and what had she seen? Obviously, she'd been looking out for herself for some time, and Petey too. An uneven warble broke the quiet, and Caleb shifted uneasily.

Caleb sat on a rise beyond the train, one leg hooked over the saddle horn, and watched as the wagons rumbled past. Everything was going smoothly, at least for then, but he couldn't lose the eerie feeling that something was about to go terribly wrong.

His gaze shifted to the end of the train. Josie had stubbornly insisted on positioning her wagon at the end of the line, where she and her brother suffered everybody else's dust. Caleb rotated the wagons regularly, the lead wagon today becoming the drag wagon tomorrow, but she still insisted.

Caleb took off his hat and wiped the sweat off his forehead with his shirtsleeve. God, that woman, if that's what she was, could be exasperating. In addition to riding drag, she collected firewood for the entire train every night. To earn her way, she said. Every evening after they circled the wagons, she and her brother would disappear with their one rifle, then reappear later, each one's arms loaded down with scraggly brush and a few sizable branches from a nearby coulee.

He peered through the dust cloud, and there she was, struggling with the mules, urging them on as they slowed and threatened to balk. She stood up in the wagon and efficiently popped the braided leather whip inches above their ears. In all the days he'd watched her, she hadn't once touched them with the stinging end.

Their wagon rolled past, only a few feet away. She glanced

toward him. Her teeth tightly clenched together, she thinned her lips into a line. That had to pass as a smile. It was the closest anyone got out of her. Except Petey. He got the real thing. When she smiled at him, her face lit up with a puzzling mix of devil and angel, a smile that curved her lips, showing surprisingly even white teeth.

Where had she come from? Why did she live as she did? No prying would release the answer from her. She didn't talk to anyone on the train except Petey, and he trailed her footsteps like a pet dog. It was evident he adored her. It was also evident Petey wasn't all there. Maybe that was why she scolded him one second and fiercely protected him the next.

Realizing the train had passed him by while he daydreamed, Caleb shook his head. He wiped his face again and punched Cindy in the sides. As he cantered past Josie's wagon, almost hidden in the cloud of dust, he pulled back on the reins and fell in beside her.

Josie sneezed, blew her nose into a man's handkerchief, then cracked the whip over the mules' heads again. "Haw, Briny, haw," she shouted to the outside mule and hauled back on the reins to turn him to the left. The cloud of dust choked her, and filled her mouth with grit. She leaned over the side of the wagon to spit. When she raised her eyes, she looked straight at Caleb's beaded moccasins.

"You folks all right back here?" he asked, pulling back on his horse's reins.

"We're comin' along." Josie straightened and sat up on the seat, her eyes to the front.

"You don't have to ride back here, you know. You can pull up nearer the front. Let somebody else eat dust for a while."

The grit was filtering back into her mouth again, but something in the way his eyes twinkled kept her from spitting over the side again. She swallowed the scratchiness. "We ain't got that much farther to go anyhow." Holding the reins between her knees, Josie shook out the damp handkerchief and tied it across her mouth.

"Suit yourself." The little buckskin mare reared and plunged against the reins. Caleb's legs tightened on the worn western saddle.

Glancing away from his powerful thighs, Josie tugged the handkerchief higher over her nose.

In a spray of sand, Caleb galloped ahead toward the rest of the train. Josie sighed and stared at his receding back, admiring the effortless way he maneuvered the horse in and out of the wagons. She sighed again. He sure was a fine figure of a man. Scolding herself in muted mutters beneath the cloth, she ordered those kinds of thoughts out of her mind.

Petey awoke with a loud snore and a fit of coughing. "Hell to spit, sis. This dust's thicker'n pea soup. How can you breathe?"

"Tie your handkerchief 'cross your mouth."

Petey pulled the soiled fabric from his pocket and shook it out. Josie reached over and grabbed it away. "Better not. You might catch more than dust from this."

"How come you don't go on ahead like Mr. McCall said? It'd be fair. Everybody'd have to ride back here sooner or later."

"I said I ain't takin' no handouts. We ain't far from home, nohow."

Petey rolled out his bottom lip. "It ain't charity. I'd just like to breathe once before we get home."

"I ain't movin', and that's that." The space between them and the next wagon had grown wider, so Josie stood and urged the mules ahead with a snap of the whip. Ahead, Caleb charged in and out of the line, waving his hat at a lagging team of oxen.

When the wagons stopped at noon, a hot wind whipped up dust devils in its path. The train circled, the families struggling with thirsty and tired oxen, irritable drivers and children. Men unhitched the horses and took them to a coulee for a drink from a waterhole. Women scurried around, shoeing children back to the train and getting a meal together.

"Look at that," Petey said, elbowing Josie in the side as she pulled the sack of biscuits from beneath the seat.

Josie pulled her hat lower to shut out the glare and followed his finger. A lone woman with a baby in her arms walked away from the train with a determined stride, oblivious of the hot wind that whipped her skirts around her legs, her eyes focused on the low hills to the north.

"Maybe she's goin' to the bushes," he suggested with a shrug.

"There ain't no bushes out there, stupid," Josie said, an uneasy feeling settling over her.

"You don't reckon she's gonna do it out in the open," he whispered, his eyes round.

"Petey, you ain't got the sense you could slap in a gnat's ass with a butter paddle," she muttered as she grabbed her gun and jumped down from the wagon. "Stay here. I'll be right back."

Josie trotted across the ground toward the woman. "Ma'am," she called. The woman didn't turn or indicate she'd even heard her.

"Ma'am. Mr. McCall says it ain't safe fer womenfolk out here alone."

Still no response. Josie caught up with her and grabbed her arm. The woman stopped, whirled, and leveled a gaze on Josie that jarred her to her soul. The woman's eyes were wild and unfocused. "Lord amighty," Josie breathed.

The woman caught her arm and squeezed it until Josie swore the blood had stopped running into her fingers. "Are you the one who saw the Indians last night?"

"How'd you know that," Josie whispered. "Ain't nobody supposed to know 'ceptin me and Mr. McCall."

"Tell me. What did you see?"

"All I seed was a small bunch of 'em. Mr. McCall said it was a huntin' party."

The woman squeezed tighter. "I have to know if it was him."

"Who?"

"My husband."

Josie whistled low. "Yore husband is an Injun? You ain't married to that feller with you?"

"He will come for me and the child." She bobbed her head. "He's following us just beyond those hills." She pointed at the low humps in the north.

Josie pushed her hat back and scratched her head. What if the woman wasn't crazy? What if she was telling the truth? "You just come on back with me, ma'am." Josie broke the woman's grasp with her other hand, took her elbow, and turned her back toward the train. "Show me where yore wagon is and I'll take you to it."

Meekly, the woman turned and began to shuffle back. Just as they neared the train, a dark man stepped out from behind a wagon.

"Anna." His voice snapped her to attention.

She glanced around to look at him, and her eyes widened.

"Come along, Anna, and stop bothering this gentleman. He has work to do." His words were level and measured, belying the anger in his eyes.

"I ain't no gentleman," Josie snorted, "but that's all right. Folks make that mistake sometimes. She weren't a-botherin' me none. I just—"

"Come along, Anna," he said firmly.

"I'll be right along." Anna smiled brightly, but it didn't stir the glower from his face.

"I said come along *now.*" His voice took on an ominous tone.

She bowed her head in submission. "Yes, Eric." Together they walked away, the man's hand firmly on Anna's elbow, urging her on a little too quickly, Josie decided.

"Quair folks," Josie murmured, scratching her head.

Chapter Four

The hot wind whipped at Caleb's shirt, flapping the linen material against his damp skin. The sun baked down on the back of his neck as he squatted beside a fresh set of hoofprints. Rising, he looked to the west, where the wagon train toiled along in its own dust cloud. They were being followed, and whoever it was was content to sit back and watch. What were they waiting for? If it was a party of renegades, they would have swooped down on them before then.

He mounted Cindy and galloped toward the train. Pulling her into a trot, he paralleled Jim Statton's wagon. The little man was sweating and swearing as he walked alongside his wagon.

"Everything all right?" Caleb shouted above the squeak and groan of the wagon.

"Damned hard-headed oxen!" he shouted back.

Caleb laughed. "Let's circle for the night by that coulee over there." Statton looked in the direction Caleb pointed, and nodded.

Galloping to the lead wagon, Caleb cut in front of the team

and rotated his finger in the air. "Circle 'em up," he yelled. The man on the wagon nodded and pulled his team into a circle. Others followed and soon the train was a tight coil.

Caleb rode back to Josie's wagon and saw that she and Petey had slid into place. When Josie pulled the grimy bag from under the seat, he saw Petey grimace.

"What's the matter, Petey? Can't stomach biscuits again?" Caleb drew Cindy to a dancing halt by the wagon.

Petey glanced over at his sister, covered his eyes with his hand, and shook his head. Josie elbowed her brother and shot him a venomous glance.

"Ain't no use in wastin' good shot when there's food here to eat." She held up the cloth bag.

"Sis, there's more grit in them biscuits than there is flour."

Josie took a rebellious bite, and Caleb heard the grit crack between her teeth.

"Come over to my camp later, Petey." Caleb raised a rabbit slung over his saddle horn. "I'll cook supper for you." The idea had just hit him, but now seemed the perfect way to get to know the pair better. Something about Josie stayed in his thoughts, intrigued him. Rough around the edges, she appeared to be one of the most capable women he'd ever known. She took what life dished out, handled it the best she could, then went on. He liked that. "Sure will, Mr. McCall," he answered, his eyes bright.

"Traitor," Josie mumbled, spitting dry crumbs everywhere.

"Josie, you can come too. Just don't bring the bread." Caleb laughed at her murderous expression and rode away.

As he neared the Tolbert wagon, he noticed Anna standing by the side of the wagon, looking toward the north. Puzzled, he reined in by her side. "Can I help you, Mrs. Tolbert?"

"No," she answered shortly, still staring off in the distance.

Caleb followed her gaze to the line of hills. "Where is your husband?"

"Out there."

Alarm went through him. What was Tolbert doing off alone?

He picked up his reins, preparing to gallop out and give Tolbert a good tongue-lashing, when Eric emerged from the wagon.

"What do you want, McCall?" he growled.

Caleb glanced at Anna. She didn't acknowledge Tolbert's presence.

"I saw your wife staring off in the distance, and she said you were out there."

Eric's face darkened murderously. "Anna, have you been bothering Mr. McCall with more of your silly stories?"

She turned, glanced at them both, then sat down on a crate and began to rock the baby clasped to her chest. As she rocked and hummed, Caleb recognized the strains of a Lakota lullaby.

He raised his eyes to meet Tolbert's.

"Anna," Tolbert shouted.

She stopped singing and sat, frozen in fear, her eyes on Tolbert's face. "Go inside the wagon."

Meekly, she obeyed.

"My wife is not well, Mr. McCall." He smiled a cold smile that never reached his eyes. "A difficult birth."

Caleb nodded, a stone of fear growing in his heart. The Tolberts were going to be trouble, all right. At that moment, Josie sauntered up, hands stuffed in her pockets.

"Mrs. Tolbert not feelin' well again?" she asked them both.

"No," Eric said in a calm voice. "She's not."

"Well, it ain't safe fer her to go a-traipsing off into them bushes like she done. Mr. McCall here'll tell you that. If she cain't find no bushes, I can teach her to pee sorta standin'." Josie hooked her thumbs into her belt. "Do it all the time myself."

"Yes," Tolbert said, flushing profusely, "I'll keep that in mind."

Josie moved away, throwing Caleb a victorious glance, as if she'd just imparted some nugget of wisdom.

Caleb watched her shuffle away. Now, what connection could there possibly be between Mrs. Tolbert and that hellion? He didn't like this. No, indeed.

* * *

The sweet smell of rabbit stew was just beginning to bubble out of the iron pot, when Caleb heard a shuffle behind him. Petey pranced into the firelight, followed by a disgruntled Josie.

"Here we are, Mr. McCall," Petey announced.

"Have a seat." Caleb pointed to the opposite side of the fire. As he ladled the fragrant stew out of the pot, Petey's eyes followed his every move, and when he handed the boy the bowl, he began to dip the stew with his fingers, shaking off hot gravy.

"Petey, for God's sake, don't gobble like a hog," Josie scolded.

Abashed, Petey wiped his fingers on his pants and looked into the bowl, willing the stew to cool itself.

When Caleb handed Josie a bowl, she took it with long, slender fingers. Gracefully, she balanced the bowl on her knee and stirred it with the spoon Caleb gave her.

"Josie, I didn't know you and Mrs. Tolbert were friends," he said, dipping himself out a portion.

"We ain't. Not friends exactly. I just talked to her the other day and she seemed mighty sad 'bout somethin'." Josie spooned out a bit and neatly ate it.

Caleb took a bite of his supper. "What did she say to you?"

"Well, when I seen her, she was walking out away from the train, headed for them hills to the north."

Caleb paused. "Walking away from the train?"

"Yep. At first I thought she was goin' to pee, but she had the baby grabbed up against her and she looked like she didn't know what she was doin'." Josie took another bite and daintily licked her lips clean.

"What did she say?"

"Well." Josie paused and seemed to ponder her answer. "She asked me iffen I was the one what seen the Injuns."

"She knew?" Caleb sat up straighter, the hair on the back of his neck rising.

"Yep. Then she said her husband was an Injun and he was a-comin' fer her and the baby."

Caleb put down his bowl and stood. He walked to the edge of the firelight and stared out across the starlit prairie.

"What's the matter?" Josie's voice asked behind him.

"She told me the same thing."

"I heared some of the womenfolk a-talkin' when they was goin' to the bushes yesterday, and some of 'em said she was teched in the head and that she and Mr. Statton's wife was sisters."

Caleb whirled. "What else did you hear?"

"I don't keep with repeatin' gossip." Josie took another bite of stew as calm as a spring breeze.

Caleb squatted down beside her. "I want you to talk to her and see what you can find out."

"You sure is nosy fer a man." She looked directly into his face, and the blue of her eyes startled him.

Caleb rose. "Those Indians you saw are following us. Have been for days. Something is going on here, and it involves Anna Tolbert. I know it, but her husband won't let anyone near her except maybe you."

"And you want me to find out what's goin' on?"

"Can you do that for me?"

Honey, I'd do anythin' fer you. "I'll see what I can do." Josie set the bowl by the fire. "You stay put, Petey. Here, use my spoon." She licked her utensil clean and handed it to him.

Gratefully, the boy dug into the meal.

"I'll be back directly." She shoved her hands in her pockets and strolled off toward the train. Once she was away from Caleb's firelight, she took off her hat and wiped her forehead. When he squatted down beside her, she thought she'd plumb pass out. Them eyes. Ma'd once had a ring as green as them eyes.

She found Anna seated on a crate, rocking the baby, Eric nowhere in sight.

"Hi," Josie said, flopping down on the ground at Anna's side.

When Anna didn't answer, Josie plunged on. "How's the baby?" She pulled back the baby's blanket. A copper face crowned with a head of black hair poked out.

"Jesus Lord," Josie muttered under her breath. "He's mighty purdy," she said to Anna.

"He is Red Cloud's son," Anna said without shifting her gaze from the night beyond the lantern light.

"He ain't yore husband's young'un?"

"He is Red Cloud's son. He is coming for us."

"Well, if this Red Cloud's comin' fer you, how do you know?"

"The owls tell me."

"Owls?"

"I hear them call at night. He is speaking to me."

"Anna!" Eric Tolbert shouted her name and Anna jumped. "What lies have you been telling this time?" He yanked her head back with a handful of hair.

"Oh, we was just chawin' the fat, Mr. Tolbert," Josie drawled as evenly as she could muster. "You know, woman things."

He let his hand slip away from Anna's hair and flushed. "I'm sorry, Josie. It's been a long trip from Minnesota and, as you can see, my wife is not well."

"Well, I think she looks just fine. Maybe a bit tired. I'd be glad to help her with her chores iffen you want me to?"

"No. Thank you, Josie."

Seeing a chance to leave, Josie smiled, nodded, and shoved her hands deeper into her pockets. Then she turned and walked away, taking all her strength to shuffle and not break out in a dead run. Feeling Tolbert's eyes on the back of her neck, Josie felt rather than heard his threats. "What kind of danged trouble have you got me into this time, Caleb McCall," she murmured as she wove in and out of the wagons, nodding and answering others' nods as she tried to make her path look random and not headed straight for Caleb's fire.

Suddenly, an arm caught hers and brought her up short. Someone yanked her into the shadows. "What did you find out?" he whispered into her ear.

"You like to have scared me to death," she scolded, turning in Caleb's arms to face him.

"Tolbert's following you," Caleb whispered. They stood in the shadow of a darkened wagon.

Josie peeped around the wagon and saw Tolbert wandering from fire to fire, his eyes searching everywhere. "You don't reckon he'd hurt me, do you?"

"He'd kill you if he had the chance," he whispered again.

"Quit a-blowin' in my ear," she said, pushing his cheek away from over her shoulder. With his lips so close, she couldn't concentrate on anything.

Tolbert swung in their direction, headed right for them. Had he seen them? Josie's heart pounded against her ribs. There was nowhere to go. Abruptly, Caleb jerked her around, pressed her back against the wagon, and proceeded to kiss her . . . soundly.

"Oh, pardon me," she heard someone say. Caleb's body completely covered hers. His lips were pressed against hers, soft, caressing. Then, as the footsteps receded, he relaxed against her and his lips gently left hers. Dormant desires sprang forth as if it had been only yesterday when she was a young woman in love. How long had it been since a man had put his arms around her? How many years since someone gathered her close, as Caleb was now doing? How long since someone made her feel loved?

Caleb's heart leaped into a pounding beat as he felt Josie relax beneath him, felt the curves of her body meld into his. Her arms snaked up around his neck. Her touch was gentle, womanly. This is crazy, he told himself as want uncoiled within his body. *This is the muleskinner, for God's sakes!* But there, in the dark, she was a warm, gentle woman, a woman soft and pliant in his arms.

"Tolbert's gone," he whispered.

"Uh-huh," Josie answered.

Surprised at his reluctance to step away, Caleb let his hands glide down her arms and stepped back.

A wedge of light caught her face. She stared up at him, the blue of her eyes intense.

"Tarnation," she breathed. "Where'd you learn to kiss like that?"

"I'm sorry. It's all I could think of."

"I ain't arguing with yore choice."

Caleb peeped around the wagon. The campground was quiet, no one in sight. "What did you find out from Anna?" he asked again.

Josie studied the toes of his moccasins. "She said her husband was Red Cloud and that he was coming fer her."

Silence greeted her answer. She raised her eyes. Caleb's face was pale even in the dark.

"What'd I say? You know this Red Cloud?"

He nodded. "I know him."

"She said the baby was his too. I seen the baby and he's dark and his hair's as black as a stack of black cats. Uh, you can let me go now."

"Sorry." He released her and stepped back. "I better go talk to Jim Statton."

"Mr. McCall."

He turned toward her.

Her face was split with an ear-to-ear grin. "You sure do kiss good."

"Why didn't you tell me about Tolbert," Caleb demanded. Jim Statton straightened from where he was mending a wagon wheel. His shoulders sagged as if under a great burden. Wiping his hands on a rag, he shook his head. "I don't know," he said softly. " I . . . just couldn't think." He raised his face to look Caleb square in the eye. "I swear I didn't know about the Indians until yesterday though. Anna kept muttering something about Red Cloud following us, and we thought she was talking nonsense again. Last night I rode out of camp and checked around. There they were, right off to our northeast."

"What puzzles me is why you lied about knowing the Tolberts?"

Jim shook his head and looked out across the dark prairie. "You don't know what kind of hell we've lived since we left Minnesota. Tolbert's temper, Anna's distraction, the beatings, the nightly abuse. I don't know." He shrugged and turned to look at Caleb. "Do you really think Red Cloud will come? Surely he has found another squaw by now to warm his bed and make him forget all this."

Caleb silently shook his head and looked down at the ground. How little the white man understood the Lakota. Their children were sacred to them, and they would move heaven and earth to get them back if taken. If Red Cloud believed Eric Tolbert had taken his child, nothing would stop him.

"He'll come. You can count on that. *When* is the question." Caleb turned to look toward the northeast. "Help me find some men to ride ahead as scouts and some to ride as guards. As soon as we reach Fort Laramie, we'll stop and tell the army what's going on." The words fell bitter from his tongue. Any dealings with the army soured his stomach.

Jim nodded. "I'm sorry."

"We'll have to be extra careful from now on. No one leaves the train alone. Is that understood?"

"Understood. I'll post some sentries tonight."

Caleb looked off toward the north. Red Cloud was there. He could feel it in his soul.

Caleb rarely slept soundly now, and when he did he kept Cindy hobbled close by. No one left the train alone, and the women walked out onto the prairie to relieve themselves only in groups. He'd seen no sign of the Lakota. None at all. But he wasn't lulled into a sense of security. He knew they were there, barely behind them and out of sight, waiting for the appropriate moment to approach the train. The only hope was that they would reach Fort Laramie first or that he could talk to Red Cloud.

As the wagons rumbled along day after day across the dusty desolation of the plains, bumping along in the knee-deep ruts left by their predecessors, Caleb's thoughts turned more and more to the chief that shadowed them. Red Cloud. *Mahpíya Lúta.* The name brought forth vivid and sometimes painful memories. Many years had passed since he'd seen the warrior who had made such a name for himself among his people. An ardent supporter of the Lakota Nation, he was among the most feared Indian leaders. He objected to the whites taking the hunting grounds of the Lakota, forcing his people to range farther and farther from home for the buffalo they depended on for their livelihood. He must have loved Anna Tolbert to have led his people this far afield during the hunting and gathering season.

Late one afternoon, as they were circling the wagons, Isaiah Crockett stepped into Caleb's path. "Myself and some of the others would like more information on what we can expect from the savages in these parts." The little man rocked back on his heels and adjusted the Bible he carried under his arm. Behind him gathered a group of sheepish observers, obviously the victims of one of Crockett's rousing sermons.

Caleb stopped Cindy and pushed back his hat. "Mr. Crockett, you can't expect anything from the Indians. Expecting them to act this way or that gets people killed."

Crockett shifted his feet and glanced back over his shoulder at his followers. "Just the same, we'd feel better knowing that you're well versed in their behavior." The little man's tiny black eyes glinted as though he were privy to a secret.

"If you're dissatisfied with my services, you're welcome to look for another guide once we reach Fort Laramie."

Crockett's face reddened. "I understand you used to live with the savages?"

The question stunned Caleb. Few people knew about that part of his private life. "At one time, a long time ago."

Grinning triumphantly, Crockett dug deeper. "I also understand that you had an Indian wife?"

Caleb's anger grew. "My personal life is none of your business, but yes, I did."

"How can we be sure you won't sell us out to the savages, if we meet any?"

The ignorance of these people never ceased to amaze him. "I have never sold anyone out, Mr. Crockett, but I might make an exception in your case." Caleb leaned out of the saddle toward Crockett, and was about to put the man in his place good, when a voice chimed in.

"You lived with the Injuns?"

Caleb swung his gaze from Crockett's broad face to where Josie stood behind him, her eyes huge and her arms full of wood. "Yes, I did."

She frowned and chewed on her bottom lip. "Weren't . . . weren't you scared?"

For a moment she looked vulnerable, almost frightened. Caleb quickly dismissed such a ridiculous thought. "Nope."

She swallowed, turned, and disappeared behind a wagon, Petey scurrying after her.

Before Caleb could ponder her curious actions, Statton rode up. "Crockett, I thought I saw the wheel of your wagon wobbling. I'll go back and take a look with you. Can't have anybody lagging behind now." Statton shot Caleb a glance that warned him to keep his temper.

"Sure, glad for the help." Crockett turned, then stopped and pivoted back toward Caleb. "I'm watching you. You just remember that." He sniffed and stalked back toward the train.

"You oughta know by now that there's always ones like that," Statton said. "Don't let him get to you."

"Guess you came at a good time."

Statton shrugged. "I heard his talk last night around the campfire."

Caleb let out the breath he was holding and eased himself back down in the saddle. "I know, but that man . . ." He let his words drift off as he looked over Statton's head. Poised on the rise of land directly to the north, motionless except for the wind that ruffled their feathers, sat three Indians. Caleb squinted. Lakota.

The Indians inclined their heads toward each other and slowly begin to ride toward the train. Spurring Cindy, Caleb galloped toward the front of the train and turned them into a tight circle.

"Get some crates in between those wagons," he shouted over the din. "Pull in closer."

Josie's wagon slid into place last. Caleb drew Cindy to a halt as Josie turned a dirt-streaked face toward him. Her blue eyes were pools of fear.

"Injuns?" she asked quietly.

"Red Cloud. Pull your wagon on in tighter."

Obediently, she flicked the reins and urged the mules forward.

"You got plenty of ammunition?" Caleb asked her, wishing he could do something, anything, to take that stricken look off her face.

"Yep, got plenty." She patted at the pocket of her tattered coat. "Reckon we're gonna need it?"

"I don't know. Hope not. Get down under your wagon."

"Mr. McCall?"

"Yeah?"

"Be careful?" Her eyes huge, she still smiled. "Cain't have you kilt, you know."

"Don't worry. I know what I'm doing."

"I know." She held his gaze for a moment, long enough for him to get another glimpse at the woman beneath the dirt and rags. Then she frowned and glanced away. "Just don't want to have to bury you. Take too much time to bury your feet." She didn't smile or even look at him, and he rode away grinning, silently admiring her sharp wit.

He leaped the pile of crates between the wagons and galloped along the outside circle of wagons. Guns poked out from beneath canvas covers, behind barrels, and under wagons.

"Nobody shoots until I say. You people got that?" he shouted above the chorus of crying children. Then he wheeled and rode slowly out toward the braves who had come to a halt about a hundred yards from the train. Statton joined him.

"You don't have to do this. Go back to your wife," Caleb said firmly.

"Ellen's fine. If this is Red Cloud, then he's kind of a relative, wouldn't you say?"

Caleb glanced over at Statton's sideways grin and chuckled.

The three braves, painted for war, sat quietly on the broad backs of their ponies as Caleb closed the gap between them. Their long headdresses of eagle feathers denoted their rank in the tribe. Naked except for a leather loincloth, the men were tanned and muscular, especially the calves of their legs, which ended in brilliantly beaded moccasins. Caleb looked down briefly at his knee-high boots. The pattern and workmanship were the same.

The braves' eyes admired Cindy as he stopped, signed friendship, and waited for them to make the next move. The man in front, apparently the leader, nudged his horse closer.

"Wanblí Ska, iskahuhanska tawa sunkmurryta ska yuhá yeló."

Caleb was momentarily taken aback by the use of his Lakota name and the lilting Lakota dialect. He hadn't heard either for many years. He peered closer at the man in front of him, disguised beneath paint and feathers.

"Two Bears? Is that you under there?"

The Indian's face split into a smile. *"Wókiksuye nitakola. Waste yeló."* Two Bears set his headdress dancing with the enthusiastic bobbing of his head.

"How could I forget you? I beat your butt good the last time I saw you."

"No, White Eagle. I beat yours," he replied in halting English.

"I see your memory is as fleeting as your looks." The Indian's smile faded, and, from the corner of his eye Caleb saw Statton brace for a fight.

"You are in great danger, my friend," the brave replied. "You must turn and go back to the white man's town, where you will be safe. Bad people are with you. Red Cloud is very angry."

"Where is he?" Caleb glanced to the rise over which the Indians had ridden.

The Indian turned toward the west and waved the six-foot lance adorned with eagle feathers in that direction. "He is there."

"Yeah, I thought so. What does he want?" he asked, knowing full well what Red Cloud wanted.

Two Bears hesitated, presenting the stony face practiced by warriors. Caleb's memories rushed back. He and Two Bears had spent many hours together after Spotted Bear had brought him to his village when he was only ten. From that day on, he'd lived as a Lakota. Spotted Bear's wife, Morning Star, had sewn his clothes, fed, and loved him as though he were one of hers.

"He wants the child, his son, born of his wife," Two Bears said.

"The woman has returned to her own people. She wishes to live with them and her white husband."

"Her husband is Red Cloud." Two Bears slammed the lance into the ground.

"You needn't try any tantrums on me. I'm wise to your tricks."

Seconds ticked past. The Indian's scowl slowly dissolved into a smile. "You have learned much, White Eagle, since you earned your name."

"I can't give the woman over to Red Cloud. You know that. If she has chosen to return to her white husband, Red Cloud'll have to accept that."

"Tol . . . bert is no husband. He is cruel. The Lakota do not beat their women."

"Some white men do, but it's up to the women to decide if they want to stay. What if she were to talk to Red Cloud, explain that she wants to live with her own people? Think he'd let her?"

Two Bears shook his head.

"Perhaps the white husband would give Red Cloud his wagon to keep the peace," Caleb answered.

Statton shot Caleb an incredulous glance.

"I will send a message. Red Cloud does not know I come to you. He will be very angry."

"We don't want a war. We want only to pass peacefully through your country. These people will not settle here. They will go farther west to Oregon to farm."

"I will bring you Red Cloud's answer."

Without another word, the warriors wheeled their horses in unison and galloped over the rise, their feathers streaming out behind them.

"Think Red Cloud'll talk?" Statton asked.

"Probably not." Caleb lifted his reins and turned Cindy toward the train. "It's time I had a talk with Mr. Tolbert."

Chapter Five

Caleb strode into the Tolberts' camp right after dark. Anna knelt by the fire pit, stirring a pot suspended over the flames on an iron tripod. The baby lay close by her side, wrapped in a blanket.

"Oh, Mr. McCall. Do come in." She snatched up the infant and scurried away to find her husband.

He emerged from behind the wagon carrying a piece of harness in his hands, frowning. "What do you want? I'm busy. I have to patch this harness before tomorrow."

Anger heated Caleb's cheeks, but he swallowed his growing loathing of the man before he spoke. "Can I see you privately?" Caleb nodded slightly to where Anna sat on a wooden crate, rocking back and forth and singing to the child in her arms— singing a soft Lakota lullaby. As the tune drifted toward them, Tolbert silenced her with an angry glance.

"I'll be right back, Anna. Supper better be ready. And for God's sake, put that brat down long enough to fix my meal."

Anna nodded and laid the infant close by her side.

"What do you want?" Tolbert demanded angrily as they moved away.

Caleb paused, trying to remember the words he'd rehearsed all day. He wanted Tolbert to cooperate, but didn't want to make him angry, not at first. "I'll level with you. Your presence and that of your wife's on this train has endangered all of us."

Tolbert frowned. "I don't know what you mean."

"I mean the baby. Why didn't you tell me about Red Cloud?"

Surprise glinted in Tolbert's eyes for an instant, then he covered his reaction with a scowl. "It's none of your damn business."

"Anything that happens on this train is my business." Caleb struggled to get a grip on his temper.

"My personal business is none of your affair. Besides, I've seen the way you look at her." A slow, self-satisfied smile spread across Tolbert's face. "You're just like the rest. You think because an Indian had her, you can get a little. She's mine, McCall, to do with what I wish." Tolbert leaned forward and stabbed Caleb's shirt with one finger.

Caleb ignored the barb and backed away, irritated by the twitch in his cheek muscle. "Red Cloud's men are behind us, getting closer every day."

"He won't attack us, not with her along." Tolbert pointed toward his wife. "Why do you think I brought her?" He smiled smugly.

Caleb swallowed his anger again, letting Tolbert's filthy remark go unchallenged, although his very soul urged him to smash the man's face. "He'll wipe out this entire train to take back what he considers rightly his."

Tolbert stared at Caleb, and an evil light crept into his eyes. "I want to see him beg for her," he whispered hoarsely. "I want to see his eyes when I uncover the baby and show him that head of black hair. Then, when he really wants her, I'll make him watch while I take her right there, show him who the husband is."

The man's insane. "He'll kill you if you touch her like that."

"Better to die at his hand than to live the rest of my life chained to an Indian whore and a bastard."

Caleb regretted it the moment his fist connected with Tolbert's jaw. The little man fell with a great thud into the dirt and looked up with surprise, rubbing the growing lump on his face.

"I'll get you for that," he growled. "I'll get you when you're least expecting it. Go ahead and have the bitch. I know you want her, have wanted her from the beginning. I can tell you what it's like." Tolbert rolled onto his hands and knees and crawled forward. "Would you like that? I can tell you how soft she is and how easy—"

Caleb raised his hand to strike the man again, this time intending to put all his force behind it. Suddenly, a fist shot out from behind him, knocking Tolbert back down.

"Josie!" Caleb turned to find Josie glaring down at the man. She shook her hand and put her knuckles in her mouth.

"The bastard had that coming," she said. "Ain't no way for a man to talk 'bout his wife." Then she shrugged and nodded at Tolbert, sitting up rubbing his chin. "Caught him off balance. Most of the time I don't knock 'em down, just stun 'em a mite."

Laughter bubbled up in Caleb's throat, killing what was left of his anger. What kind of woman was this? Kiss like an angel and fight like a man. Caleb pivoted on his heel and strode away, eager to put distance between himself and Tolbert, but Josie soon caught up with him.

"You want his wife, like he said?" she asked, trotting up beside him.

Caleb glanced down at her floppy hat barely reaching his shoulder. "You get right to the point, don't you?"

"Just wondering." Josie shrugged. "Heard some folks talkin' last night."

They raised their eyes at the same time, and her gaze drew his like a magnet. But he found her stare too intense, too probing. Her innocent, unwavering eyes seemed to see through

him and into his darkest secrets, those he didn't care to bring
to light or share. Turning his face away, he swiped at another
streak of dust on his pants. " 'Course not.''

"She sure is purdy though." Josie nodded over her shoulder,
and Caleb followed her gaze back to where Anna bent over
her prone husband.

"Yeah, she sure is." He turned to go, uneasy with Josie's
painfully direct questions. She stuck right by his side as he
walked.

"You like women like that? I mean, them that's soft and
such.''

Caleb stopped and looked down on her. She tipped her face
up and waited expectantly for his answer. Unbidden, his eyes
darted to her lips, remembering how soft, how warm, they had
been. "Yeah, I guess I do," he admitted slowly.

"Ain't got much use fer women like that." She shook her
head. "Too weak, no disrespect meant fer Mrs. Tolbert. She
can't help she's teched.''

Caleb cupped her shoulder in his hand, letting his palm linger
on her warm flesh. "A woman can be soft and still not be
weak. A man needs a strong woman out here.''

Josie shook off his touch. "Well, men ain't nothin' but
trouble. Ain't good fer nothin' but drinkin' and swearin' and
gettin' babies.'' Her expression changed. Gone was the defiant
look, and vulnerability took its place. She ducked her head and
walked away, leaving Caleb wondering.

"Come on in, Two Bears," Caleb said without lifting his
eyes from the rabbit that sizzled grease onto the fire. As boys
they'd played the game, each reading the other's thoughts,
anticipating the other's moves.

"*Iyúha nehouéya, Wanblí Ska,*" a voice replied from the
darkness behind him.

"You know I didn't hear you come up. Have you forgotten
our game?''

Two Bears' copper face widened into a grin as he stepped into the light. "I remember the game, and I am pleased that you remember. Living with *wasíchu* has not ruined your ears."

Caleb poured himself a cup of coffee and another for Two Bears. The brave squatted by the fire and took the tin cup while Caleb leaned back against his saddle. "Yeah, I guess I'm probably still more Lakota than white."

The warrior made a face at the coffee, then stared into Caleb's eyes. "Then why do you live as a white man?"

"Oh, I don't know, after . . . what happened, I couldn't stay." Caleb looked away from Two Bears' intense gaze.

"If you change your mind, there is always room in my tipi."

Caleb glanced up. "I can never return to the Lakota. Too many bad memories." He tossed out the coffee. "Did you talk to Red Cloud?"

Two Bears rose from the fire, walked a short distance away, and folded his fringe-clad arms across his chest. Again his face became the mask of a warrior. "He wants his son and Running Elk."

Caleb frowned. "You know I can't hand the man over to him. I think I can make Tolbert pay, but he'll never give up the child if for no other reason than Red Cloud wants him."

"Red Cloud does not want white man's things." Two Bears whirled around in a flurry of dark hair and fringe. "He wants Tolbert's scalp for his lodge pole, and he wants the woman and child."

"I can't give him that. These people are my responsibility."

Two Bears' face softened. "I know this. I fear for you, my brother."

Caleb looked into the ebony eyes that mirrored the brave's compassion and remembered in flashes their childhood together, remembered Spotted Bear's insistence that the orphaned white child retain his native tongue and teach English to the other boys. The wise man often told them that one day their lives might depend on their speaking the white man's language. "Is Red Cloud still following us?"

"Yes." Two Bears nodded. "He comes."

"I guess we'll have to be ready, then."

Two Bears nodded solemnly, then, as quietly as he'd come, he slipped away without another word. Caleb picked up the blackened coffeepot and poured another cup. He sighed and stared into the orange flames of the fire. He knew Red Cloud, and he was as good as his word. If he wanted Tolbert's scalp, then he'd walk through hell to get it. Caleb threw the rest of his coffee into the fire and strode off toward camp.

"Where you goin', sis?" Petey rose up on his elbows as Josie crept over the side of the wagon.

"I'm goin' to the bushes," she hissed. "Go back to sleep."

"You reckon them Injuns is really out there?" he whispered urgently.

"If Mr. McCall says they are, I reckon they are. Now, hush up."

Petey lay back down and Josie crept away. Although going to the bushes by herself was a welcome idea, since she couldn't lose Petey from underfoot lately, what she really wanted was a turn through camp. The families intrigued her. Their faith in each other, their love for one another, drew her like a herd of cows to fresh water. There'd never been any love in her family. Her father dominated the whole bunch of them, even Ma. Poor Ma. At least she was rid of the old bastard. Josie stuffed her hands into her pockets and kicked at a pile of manure.

Voices made her look up. Ahead, Caleb lounged against a wagon, hat pushed back, talking to a group of men, a length of rope in his hand. A covey of young girls giggled around him, and he smiled at their twittering. Josie ducked behind a water barrel and watched. Soft leather pants fit long legs perfectly from bulging thigh to large, moccasined feet. As her gaze swept over him, her heart thudded. The chattering girls moved away, hands over their mouths, whispering among themselves.

Josie crouched farther behind the barrel when Caleb pushed away from the wagon and moved in her direction. Her cheeks flamed. What if he caught her squatting there? What kind of excuse could she give? She shrank farther back into the shadows. As he grew closer, his footsteps crunched in the dirt, then stopped. Curiosity overcame her. She decided to risk a peek. Cautiously, she slid one eye past the barrel. He was looking directly at her.

"Josie?"

"Thunderation," she muttered, stood, and stepped into the light.

"What are you doing back there?" He smiled at her, his green eyes flashing with gold bits.

Josie ducked her head so he wouldn't see her red face. "Nothin'. Just lookin' around."

"Looks to me like you were hiding from somebody." Laughter tinged his voice.

Tilting the brim of her hat, Josie peeped up at him. "Weren't hidin'. Just watchin' the folks hereabouts."

His long fingers moved nimbly as he threw another knot into the length of rope. "You know," he said with a crooked grin, "I bet you're pretty under all that dirt." He wiped at her face with one finger.

"Leave me be." Josie jerked her head away and swatted at his hand. "And quit makin' fun of me."

"I'm not making fun of you."

His hand caught her elbow. She looked up into kind eyes that wrinkled at the corners.

"I meant what I said."

Josie looked at her feet.

"There's a little lake over that rise." He pointed to the north. "Some of the ladies went over after dark to have a bath. Why don't you join them?"

"With Injuns all around?" she asked incredulously. "Nope. Don't want to run up on no Injuns." The thought of a band of savages catching her swimming nude made her blood run cold.

"Some of the men went to stand guard. I think it's safe enough."

She opened her mouth to protest, then snapped it shut. A bath. How long had it been since she'd had a bath—a real all-over bath, not just a quick wipe to the necessary places? "Maybe I will." She scuffed at the dirt with her boot. Sure sounded tempting. "You don't reckon them men'll peek, do you?"

He laughed, a rich, deep sound that sent her senses reeling. "I don't reckon they'll peek. In fact, I told them they'd be struck blind if they did."

"Well, you'll have a bunch of blind folks tomorrow. Never knowed a man who wouldn't."

His laughter rippled down her spine like a cool mountain stream.

"You say what you think, don't you?" He cocked his head to the side.

When he smiled, her palms began to sweat. "I cain't leave Petey. No tellin' what kind of trouble he'll go and git himself into."

"I'll keep an eye on Petey. Go on and have fun. Just be careful." With a playful pinch to her cheek, he winked at her and turned to saunter off.

Long after he disappeared from her sight, she stood in the same spot with one hand against the cheek he'd tweaked.

She heard the squeals and giggles before she ever reached the lake. A soft sound to her right brought her Hawken up to bear.

"Whoa, missy. It's Jim Statton," a voice said from the darkness.

Josie lowered the gun without comment and headed for the lake. The waters glistened in the moonless, starlit night. The women from the train were clustered at the other end. When Josie walked out onto the damp sand, they ceased their laughing and playing and fell silent, clinging to one another. Ignoring them, Josie moved down the shore to where a group of young willows hung over the water. Leaning her rifle against a stump, she glanced around, then shucked out of her ragged coat and trousers. She slid down the suit of underwear and discarded knitted socks. The sultry dampness of the air caressed her skin. With one toe she tested the water, then waded in over her head. Flipping over onto her back, she floated, remembering humid summer days in Tennessee and a favorite secret swimming hole. Water filled her ears, muffling the splashes and giggles from the other side of the lake to a muted buzz. Overhead the stars winked in and out of existence in a black canopy. Josie kicked away from shore and paddled out to the lake's middle. The water was as warm as bathwater, heated beneath the day's relentless sun. She closed her eyes and let the gentle thud of sounds lull her.

Drifting and daydreaming, she lost track of time and place. Suddenly, she realized the lake was silent. She shot straight up in the water. The other swimmers were gone. Insects buzzed their nighttime music accompanied by the sound of gentle waves lapping at the shore. She shivered, wrapped her arms around herself, and waded toward the shore. A loud crack broke in the quiet. Josie ducked down in the water.

A figure moved in the shadows beneath some low willows on the other side of the lake. Even squinting her eyes, she couldn't make out who it was except that it was a man. The shadow moved again, and she dove beneath the water, surfacing under another clump of trees, several feet away. "Hell to spit," she muttered softly. Her gun was propped out in full sight along with her clothes.

The man stepped out of the shelter of the trees, walked down the shore toward her, and stopped. Josie seethed and longed for her gun loaded with rock salt. Probably some bastard who thought he'd catch the women naked. As he drew closer, Josie saw that he was dark and slim. He glanced several times at the hill hiding the train, fidgeted with his suspenders, then resumed his pacing. Josie ducked under again and crawled through the squish on the bottom to the edge. As she slid out of the water, her fingers inches from her gun, another shadow appeared from nowhere. Josie eased back into the water. They were too far for her to identify, but the second man was an Indian. She was sure of it. Long hair swung around his shoulders and the fringe of a loincloth swayed around his legs. The pair stood in the water's edge for several minutes, then the man pressed a sack into the Indian's hand. They parted and the first man headed over the hill toward the train.

Josie clenched her teeth together to keep them from chattering despite the warmth of the air. Minutes passed as she juggled the pieces of what she had seen, then another movement onshore sent her diving back beneath the overhanging willow branches. A tall, lanky man stepped from the shadows. He took off his hat and ran his fingers through a mass of curly hair.

"Mr. McCall?" she whispered urgently.

"Josie?" he answered. "Where are you?"

She let out a silent sigh of relief so great, she trembled. "I'm here. In the water."

"Didn't you hear the rest of the women leave?" he asked, a hint of distress in his voice.

"No," she said, shaking with cold. "If I'd a heard 'em, I'd a come too. You think I like it out here alone?"

"Come on out, and I'll walk you back." He stepped out into the faint light, a smile on his face.

Josie paused and crossed her arms over her chest beneath the water. "I cain't. My clothes is over there."

"I'll turn my back." He chuckled as he turned around and crossed his arms.

"You just better not look," she threatened as she scrambled up the bank, scampered over to her clothes, and shrugged them on. "I've shot folks for less." The wet clothes clung to her shape, but she didn't care. All she wanted was to get back to the train as fast as she could. She buttoned the last button and reached for the Hawken. "You see anybody when you come down here?"

"No," Caleb answered, turning around. "Why?"

"They was two men here before. One of 'em was an Injun."

He frowned and stepped closer. "Are you sure?"

"Looked like one to me. 'Course, I couldn't make out who they was."

He studied her face, then smiled. "You're not pulling my leg, are you?"

"No, I ain't," she answered, indignant.

"Seems strange I didn't see anybody on the way here."

"They was here. Yonder's their tracks." She pointed to where the man had stood.

Caleb squatted down by the place she indicated. Bare feet, booted feet, moccasins, even horse prints dented the wet sand. A large set led off toward the train, but disappeared in the stubbly grass. Two Bears should be long gone, riding for Red Cloud. If guards had been left behind, he'd have seen them long before then.

Caleb glanced up at her. Long black hair hung in a wet curtain from beneath the hat. The cotton shirt molded to a full bosom. "You see Indians behind every bush," he said, and stood. "Come on. Folks will wonder about us and come looking."

Slinging back her hair, she started in front of him down the slope toward the train. The sassy sway of her hips in the overlarge pants brought to mind the vision of her in the lake. When she didn't arrive with the other women, he'd gone looking for her. Then he saw her from the tip of the riser—milky white skin against dark water, long limbs gracefully treading the water. She intrigued him—fire-breathing hellion by day, innocent seductress by starlight.

They walked in silence until they reached the edge of camp, then stopped and faced each other.

"You look better washed." Caleb grinned and touched the end of her nose.

"Ain't much on washin'," she said with a shrug. "Give a body phewmony, it will. You watch out for Petey like you said?"

"He's all right. I put him to oiling harnesses," Caleb answered.

She pulled off her hat and jammed it between her knees. Long strands of hair snapped as she ran her fingers through it, twisted it into a knot, and jammed the hat down on the coil. He followed her hands, wishing deep within him that his fingers were combing her hair, touching her skin. She looked up at him. Without the coating of dust and dirt, her skin was smooth and creamy. Full lips turned up into a smile. Caleb closed his eyes and lowered his head toward her.

"Mr. McCall?" The sound of his name brought him up short. He opened his eyes. Bright-blue doe eyes stared at him, droplets of water glistening on her lashes. He was so close to her, he could have licked the moisture off with a flick of his tongue. She had no idea he had been about to kiss her. Neither had he.

"I ain't foolin' 'bout them men."

Confused for a moment, Caleb frowned.

"You know, by the lake."

Caleb shook himself mentally. "I know you think you saw somebody, Josie, but I was right there on the hill. I'd have had to see them, and I didn't see anybody except you in the water."

Her eyes narrowed, and she cocked her head to the side. "How long was you standing in them shadows?"

Caleb knew his flush gave him away. "Not long."

A slow, seductive grin spread across her face. "You want me to make yore explanations in the mornin' when yore blind as a bat?"

Chapter Six

Several days later the wagon train entered the hilly country at the foot of the Rockies. The hardest part of their journey lay ahead of them—the deep chasms and steep slopes of the mountains. A large group of men rode guard around the wagon train. Three more rode drag, and Caleb and Statton rode out front. The night after Josie saw the men at the lake, Caleb had chosen to tell the whole train of the danger following them, conveniently leaving out his reasons for knowing. And while he'd explained their predicament, Tolbert had glowered at him from the edge of the group and occasionally rubbed his jaw, a reminder of his threat for revenge.

Caleb hoped Red Cloud had changed his mind, since there'd been no answer to his message, but he doubted it. Only days away from Fort Laramie and the safety of the army patrols, they'd seen no sign of the Lakota, or any other tribe, a disquieting coincidence, Caleb thought. He encouraged his guards not to fall into carelessness. Red Cloud was sure to make some sort of move, and soon.

Midafternoon in the second week after Caleb's nocturnal

visit from Two Bears, about fifty Lakota warriors appeared on a rise directly in front of the train. Caleb hauled on Cindy's reins, sending the usually docile mare dancing along the ground. The braves wore their finest, their faces covered with colorful war paint, and they sat motionless with the feathers on their lances waving in the slight breeze. Caleb looked up at the ridge, hoping to pick out Red Cloud.

He squinted and pulled down the brim of his hat to cut out the glare of the sun on the yellow sand. A band as large as this had more in mind than talking. "Circle 'em up!" he shouted to the lead drivers, and the wagons slowly turned inward. The guards kicked their horses into a gallop and rode up beside Caleb. "Get everybody inside the circle and load all the rifles. The rest of you concentrate on protecting the women and children. Don't worry about your wagons. Maybe I can bargain with them."

Caleb rode slowly toward the group of Indians, making sure his hands were nowhere near his revolvers. A tall Indian sat at the front of the wedge of warriors. Plaited into his long, black hair, two eagle feathers hung over his left ear. One of the feather's edges was serrated, designating that he'd counted coup four times in battle by touching the enemy with a coup stick. Numerous quills banded the other feather, signifying that the owner received many wounds but had killed his enemy. Red paint streaked the brave's face and formed handprints on his body and that of his horse. He wore only a simple loincloth and beaded moccasins. Caleb rode straight up to the band, face-to-face with the feared Red Cloud.

A thousand memories assailed Caleb as he signed friendship and waited for a response from the man he hadn't seen for almost ten years.

"Lila téhan, Méhpíya Lúta. It's been a long time, Red Cloud." Caleb shifted his position in the saddle so he could keep all the braves in his line of vision.

"Wí oyta yeló, Wanblí Ska," Red Cloud replied. "Many moons, White Eagle." His English was flawless, although spo-

ken hesitantly with the slightly guttural accent of Lakota. He looked over Caleb's head and nodded toward the train circled for attack. *"Ota obni niobtu yeló?"*

"Many innocent people are with me." Caleb's gaze locked with the chief's. "Don't make them pay for Tolbert's mistake."

Red Cloud nodded toward the wagons. "When I returned to our home, Running Elk was gone from our tipi, taken by Tolbert, dragged away, my people said." His face was unreadable, but Caleb knew the man, knew the pain was still fresh.

"I don't argue that you've got a score to settle with him, but punishing all these people, that's worse than what he did."

Red Cloud turned toward Caleb and scowled. "What right have you to tell a chief what is right and wrong?"

Caleb pushed his hat back and hunched his shoulders as he shifted in the saddle. "Of all the white men you know, I guess I've got more right than most."

Red Cloud bunched his eyebrows into a deeper frown, then his face relaxed into a small, stiff smile, the smile of a man carrying great responsibilities, carrying the burden of others' lives. Caleb well understood the pressure.

"What is your offer, White Eagle?" Red Cloud asked.

"Let me talk to Tolbert, make him pay you in supplies and food."

Red Cloud looked surprised, and Caleb hurried to finish. "Oh, I know bolt goods and beads won't ease the pain, but your village is hungry. Make him hurt a little without starting a war."

"What of my woman?"

"She has returned to her own people. She wishes to live as one of them now."

Red Cloud glanced toward the train again. "Running Elk did not leave my tipi willingly."

"How do you know that for sure?" Caleb saw the chief's jaw tighten. "How do you know her thoughts when she saw Tolbert again?"

The only outward indication of Red Cloud's emotion was

his Adam's apple bobbing as he swallowed. But beneath the fierce war paint, Caleb knew emotion and memories washed over him. He had truly loved Anna Tolbert.

"When I returned to the village and found Tolbert had taken her—" Red Cloud's voice trembled with the still-remembered sorrow. "Our horses were tired from the hunt. I took a fresh one from the village and rode very fast, far in front of my braves. I caught up to him, but before I could attack, one of his men shot me in the shoulder. Still I followed them. I came upon them again before the dark. They had her on the ground. They pulled her dress up, and they came into her." Red Cloud moved his hand indicating intercourse. "Many times they did this, many men."

Caleb's face blanched as the image of what Red Cloud was suggesting came to mind.

"I can see that you did not know," the chief said softly.

"No, I didn't." The same cold anger Eric Tolbert seemed to generate everywhere he went rose in Caleb.

The proud chief shifted uncomfortably, and his voice broke as he spoke. "I could not attack. My warriors were far behind me, and I was wounded. I followed them until they came to the white man's village." He swallowed again, and Caleb saw raw emotion in his eyes. "There were many of them, too many for us to take them there. We have waited until now."

Caleb's throat tightened at seeing the emotion displayed by a man who could take a life in the blinking of an eye but could also show great compassion to those of his tribe. "Neither of us wants a war, Red Cloud. Many good men will be killed. Many of mine and many of yours. Think over my offer."

The Indian gazed off into the distance. "Perhaps there would be some honor in taking Tolbert's goods. The women clamor for new beads, glass ones brought by the white man, and new material for dresses." He turned back toward Caleb. "My people will be hungry and cold when winter comes. The buffalo have moved far away. We ride many days to hunt them, leaving our women and children alone. The Crow are raiding our villages, stealing our women and our food." He gazed off into the distance again. "I will consider your offer. Meet me here tonight when the moon rises over that ridge." Red Cloud pointed his lance toward the far hill. "I will give you my answer then."

The chief turned his horse and trotted back over the rise, the rest of the party falling in behind him. Caleb let out a sigh of relief. At least, Red Cloud hadn't attacked the train. But why? *Why didn't he kill us all and take Mrs. Tolbert and the child?*

True to his word, Red Cloud sat atop the appointed rise, silhouetted by the full moon as it rose above the brush and rocks. Caleb rode slowly up the incline toward him. Behind him, the campfires of the wagon train flickered like fireflies in the night.

Red Cloud didn't speak, and continued to stare at the wagons below as Caleb reined in his horse. *"Lipanpi tuke wanje el onhun honwó?"* he asked, lapsing back into Lakota.

Caleb turned and pointed. "Your son is there, in that wagon, the one that's a little shorter than the others."

"Is he like his mother?" he asked, his voice thick.

Caleb hesitated in his answer, unsure of the Indian's mind. When they had lived as young braves together, nearly twenty years before, Red Cloud was honest and reliable, a natural leader. What had the loss of his greatest love done to him? What kind of man had he become in the past years?

"No," Caleb said slowly, "he is dark like his father."

Red Cloud smiled a small, brief smile.

"He's all she has, Red Cloud," Caleb interjected. "She is . . . not well. She is . . . touched."

Red Cloud grimaced as though a knife had pierced him. Then he nodded slowly. "The child should stay with her."

"What of the rest?"

"I will accept your offer."

Caleb knew the offer was an insult to the proud man, that no amount of plunder could replace the life of one of his people, of his Running Elk. His acceptance was the only way he could save face for not attacking the train.

"You've made a smart choice, wise for you and for the Lakota."

Red Cloud didn't acknowledge the compliment, and his gaze drifted once more to the train. "She was happy with me. She ran and played with the children and kept me warm at night. We would have made many beautiful babies together, Running Elk and I." His look grew wistful. "My warriors will ride into the camp for the goods," he said abruptly, shaking himself out of his reverie.

"I'll go tell them." Caleb started to rein Cindy around, then he paused and looked back. "It is good to see you again. Remember how we used to give Morning Star a fit?"

Red Cloud grinned. "My mother laughed at your tricks and scolded me for mine." The smile faded, replaced by a look of concern. "Have you never taken another woman?"

Caleb paused, painful memories blocking other thoughts. "No, I haven't."

"You should find yourself a woman."

"Don't know of any that'd have me."

Red Cloud paused a moment longer, then he was gone in a flurry of feathers without another word.

"We're not gonna give them savages the things we spent hard-earned money for," chimed up Crockett from the crowd that surrounded Caleb. "We'll fight 'em, by God, and kill every last one of 'em." He tenderly caressed his long rifle as if it were a woman.

"Talk like that'll get us all killed," Caleb shouted from the top of a crate. "You're buying your freedom is what it amounts to." The crowd had grumbled and groaned as he explained the chief's demands. Now they were downright nasty.

"What'll happen the next time some bloodthirsty savage

decides he takes a liking to our plunder? We supposed to hand over more to the varmints?'' Crockett bellowed.

''If you want to stay alive, Mr. Crockett.'' Caleb glared until Crockett stepped back.

Reluctantly but obediently, the travelers gathered up flour, sugar, mirrors, cloth, and other supplies. The pile grew larger and larger at the center of camp as family after family added to it.

''McCall will pay for this, that I can guarantee. Just as soon as we reach civilization, I'm contacting the authorities.'' Crockett tossed an armload of things on top of the pile.

Several of the other families griped, each discussing what they would have done different and the threats they would have carried out against the ''bloodthirsty savages.'' Suddenly, warriors appeared from nowhere. Women stifled their screams with the backs of their hands. Men tightened their grips on their rifles. Caleb walked forward, keeping an eye on the situation for signs of trouble.

''Here it is, Red Cloud,'' he said to the chief. The other two warriors rode over to the pile, jumped off the bare backs of their mounts, and sorted through the goods, tossing them haphazardly here and there in their haste to see it all. But Red Cloud's eyes swept the crowd, and Caleb knew he was looking for one face.

From the corner of his eye Caleb saw Eric Tolbert lounging in the shadow of his wagon. He crossed his arms over his thin chest and watched the tanned, virile men as the firelight rippled off their flexing muscles.

Tolbert's face twisted with subdued anger while Red Cloud's eyes swept the camp. Pushing away from the wagon, Tolbert started across the circle toward the leaping fire. More warriors had joined the first two, and together they were making a fine mess. Caleb's grip tightened on his gun as Tolbert neared, jealousy and rage warring across his face.

The movement wasn't wasted on Red Cloud, and he stiffened when he spotted the object of his most intense hatred. Caleb gently laid his hand on Red Cloud's leg in an effort to remind him of the bargain.

"I will keep my word, White Eagle," he muttered softly, never taking his eyes from Tolbert's, although a crowd of people stood between them.

Once they had satisfied their curiosity as to the nature of the gifts they were about to receive, the Indians quickly brought in pack animals and loaded up the goods on three ponies and travois. Several braves approached some of the settlers for more, but Red Cloud quickly intervened. The ponies plodded out of camp into the night with the warriors following behind. Red Cloud waited until the last of the men disappeared before he moved, and then he made straight for Tolbert's wagon.

Tolbert stepped into his path, his rifle cradled in his arms. "What do you want, you filthy savage?"

Red Cloud paid the insult no mind and pushed the man out of the way with the shoulder of his horse.

Tolbert spun around to regain his footing and raised the rifle. Caleb grabbed the barrel. "What's the matter with you, Tolbert? You want to get us all killed?"

"He ain't going in my wagon," he muttered.

Before either of them could react, Red Cloud reached out and parted the canvas. Inside, Anna clutched the baby to her bosom and rocked, singing a tuneless lullaby. The swarthy face at the rear of the wagon sparked no recognition. She smiled absently and snuggled the child closer to her bosom. Red Cloud remained motionless in disbelief, disbelief that this shell of a person was the same warm, loving woman who had come to him so eagerly.

"Running Elk?" He crooned her name, and for a moment Anna stopped rocking and looked puzzled, fastening her eyes on the strange face at the door. But to Red Cloud's disappointment, no recognition shone in the smile, merely the fleeting shadow of a memory, hardly enough for her troubled mind to latch on to. She watched a moment longer, then resumed rocking and humming. Sadly, he dropped the canvas.

"I'll look after her." Caleb's voice was a whisper. "Perhaps someday she'll recover."

Red Cloud turned to face him, his usually immovable expression filled with sorrow. "You have chosen the white man's ways?"

"Guess so. Doesn't seem to be any place for me with the Lakota. I'm going to Oregon."

Red Cloud laid a hand on Caleb's shoulder. "Your soul is Lakota. Someday you will find I am right. Until then, you are welcome in my village." Effortlessly, the chief vaulted onto the horse's back. He cast one last look at the wagon, and a scathing one at Tolbert before he kicked the horse and galloped into the night.

"What're they doin', Josie?" Petey whispered as he inched closer to his sister lying prone beneath the wagon.

"Don't know. I cain't see no more." From their vantage point at the end of the train, they had seen the Lakota ride into camp. Josie ran a shaking hand across her face.

"It's all right, sis." Petey's arms went around her shoulders.

She patted his hand. Sometimes he could be downright affectionate. Then sometimes, his addledness could be aggravating.

"Think they'll kill 'em all?" he asked.

"Now, I don't know that either. You think I read minds?" While she answered, she frantically searched the distant crowd for Caleb.

"You don't have to be so ornery." He pouted. "I was just wondering."

Outlined against the bonfire, the savages formed eerie figures, their hair long and wild, their naked bodies golden in the light. Josie spotted Caleb standing a ways from the crowd. She shook her head as the memories of war cries echoed in her brain.

Then the braves began to stream out of camp, loaded down with cooking utensils, blankets, and other trinkets. Josie covered her head with her hands when she realized the braves were

headed right for them. The thud of galloping horses made the
ground tremble, and Josie flattened herself against it. Then the
hoofbeats passed her and moved into the distance. She peeked
over her arms. The settlers, apparently none the worse for wear,
milled around camp.

She crawled out from beneath the wagon, stood, and brushed
off her pants. Petey wriggled out behind her. Leaning against
the wagon seat, well away from her grasp, was her rifle. Foolishness like that would get her killed, she mused, remembering
diving beneath the wagon without the weapon. A horse's loud
snort made her jerk her head around. The beast was so close, she
could see the pink inside his flared nostrils. Her eyes traveled up
the lean, muscular neck of the animal and straight into the
painted face of a fierce warrior. Ice water filled her veins, and
her fingers tingled. Starlight made him look all the more eerie,
casting blue sparks in his loose, dark hair. He was a vision out
of a nightmare.

The stallion danced for a moment, then the brave leaned
down and touched her shoulder. "Tell your enemies that Red
Cloud counted coup on you. It will give you strong medicine,"
he said softly in perfect English. Then the stallion reared and
lunged into a ground-eating gallop.

Chapter Seven

Grumbling spotted the train after Red Cloud's Lakota left, dissatisfaction with Caleb's handling of the situation. After a customary turn through camp, he rode to the top of a hill and surveyed the prairie, glistening beneath starlight. Did the settlers know how lucky they were to still be alive? Did they realize how rare such a transaction was completed successfully without bloodshed? No, he decided. They'd probably never believe that an Indian would keep his word, that he would honor the promise he made.

After another scan of the area, Caleb slowly rode back to his own campsite far outside the confines of the circled wagons. He unsaddled Cindy and stretched out on his rough wool blanket. Overhead, tiny pinpoints of light punctuated the dark sky against the Milky Way.

A deep breath brought to him the mingled scents of earth and herbs, dust and faraway rain—a heady fragrance he had learned to love in his years of solitude on the prairie. A slight breeze stirred his hair, and his eyes drooped heavily toward sleep.

Suddenly, his eyes flew open. He sorted through the hum of insects, the rattle of Cindy's chains, and the chirp of crickets, wondering what had awakened him. The hair on his neck prickled. He inched his hand toward his revolver. An owl's faint hoot drifted from a small thicket of willows. He flipped over onto his stomach. That was no owl.

An answering hoot, slightly different in tone, came from another direction. Caleb slid his revolver from its leather holster and checked the chamber. Cindy snorted, lifted her head, and sniffed at the air. She pricked her ears forward, flared her nostrils, and stared intently toward the wagon train. After a few seconds she shied and trotted closer. Her ears flicked back and forth to catch any sound.

Knowing Cindy had never been wrong before, Caleb crawled over to his Henry repeating rifle leaning against his saddle horn. He felt around in his saddlebags, brought out a box of shells, flipped open the lid, and spilled them into his hand. The magazine of the rifle full, he dragged it back to his bedroll, then lay down to wait.

From his prone position, he could see the camp. The evening fires were faint ember glows. No one moved, and the wagons were dark. As he watched, a shadow passed a wagon. Caleb squinted and cursed himself for not following Emmy's advice to buy a pair of spectacles from McCuller's Store. Another shadow flitted by. His heart pounded. Dammit! He pounded his fist on the ground. Red Cloud had promised to let them go. Now he'd face as an enemy the man he'd known for years as a brother. With a revolver in his right hand, Caleb crept to Cindy's side and loosened her hobbles, then scurried across the open ground to the edge of the train.

No one moved among the wagons. He knew he was already too late when the first scream rent the air. Falling to his knees, he rolled beneath the Statton wagon. Moccasined feet moved stealthily through the camp. His thoughts flew to Josie. She and Petey were on the end of the train, their wagon parked on the other side of the circle. He stood, jerked open the canvas, and shook Statton awake.

"What is it?" Statton asked sleepily. Another shriek jarred him awake. "Sweet Jesus!" Grabbing his gun, he leaped out of the wagon, and together they roused several more families. Yips and war cries filled the air along with shrill screams and moans of the dying. They were under full attack. Caleb slipped from wagon to wagon until he came upon a large group of Indians stripping the Crocketts of their possessions. He raised his rifle and pumped out round after round. The attackers whirled toward the barrage of shots before they fell.

Clouds scuttled across the moon. Caleb squinted. What tribe were they? In the orange glow of burning wagons, they appeared to be Lakota. But even his alliance with Red Cloud wouldn't hinder him from protecting his train.

From wagon to wagon, he and Statton slipped, firing into the midst of the Indians. Flames leaped high into the air when fires reached the volatile canvas tops, throwing an eerie light on the carnage taking place around them. Women tried to flee, their long white nightgowns streaming out behind them, some with children in tow. Indians pursued them, often catching them by their hair and hauling them backward until they lost their footing and fell.

"Come on, Josie. You gotta get up." Petey tugged at her back, trying to turn her over.

"Leave me alone," she muttered, her face pressed against the dirt. She couldn't bear to lift her head and face what she knew was going on around them. The shots had started as she drifted off to sleep under the wagon. When she'd opened her eyes, the first thing she saw was a pair of moccasined feet creeping past, inches away from her nose. Memories of her family's brutal death came rushing back. Cold fear flooded her veins.

"Come on, Josie. I can't go without you." Her brother shook her again. "We gotta go help them folks."

"Didn't nobody come help us, did they?" She pulled her coat over her head.

"Sis, you know that was 'cause Pa was stubborn, and we was travelin' alone. This is different. You're the only one knows how to shoot that rifle a-yours."

"I cain't. I just cain't." She buried her head deeper in the wool. She heard Petey scrambling around and felt when he left her side. "Where do you think you're goin'?" she asked, risking a peek.

Petey stood beside the wagon, examining his slim knife. "I'm goin' to help these folks. Just 'cause you're scared don't mean I cain't go." He ran a finger down the narrow edge of the blade. "Mr. McCall's been good to us, better than our own kin back home." He rammed the knife down into its leather pouch. "I ain't a-gonna sit by and watch 'em all git kilt." Leaning down, he peered into her face. "You comin'?"

"Thunderation." Josie wiggled out from under the wagon. "Hand me my shot bag and powder."

Petey obliged, a triumphant twinkle in his eye. Josie snatched up her gun and jerked the leather pouch and horn from his hand. "And you can stop that danged grinnin'."

A loud report jarred the air. Caleb whirled. In the center of the melee stood Josie, her fifty-caliber Hawken snugged against her shoulder. Fire spurted from the end of the barrel and the pan's flash illuminated her face. Behind her, Petey crouched with one hand on her shoulder, a small skinning knife in the other.

"Get down!" Caleb shouted at the pair, but the din around him drowned his words. Shouldn't have given Statton my Henry, Caleb thought as he crouched and sprinted toward them. Striking Josie broadside, he gathered her beneath him and stuffed her under a nearby wagon.

"You make a damn fine target while you stand there reload-

ing that relic,'' Caleb scolded while disentangling himself from
her arms and legs.

"I can do for myself, thank you." She shoved at him indig-
nantly and hurriedly rammed a ball down the gun's barrel.
"This here Hawken can do more damage than that little pea-
shooter of yorn."

"Take this anyway." He pressed one of his revolvers into
her hand. "What about him?" he asked, nodding toward Petey,
crawling beneath the wagon with them.

"Long as Petey's got his knife, you don't worry about him,"
she said, jamming the cork into the end of her powder horn.

Surveying the frailty of the small blade and the broadness
of Petey's grin, Caleb decided to worry. "We're going to head
over toward those wagons on the edge of camp. Keep low and
keep your back to mine. Petey, you follow close." Half dragging her behind him, Caleb scrambled out, and stood. Josie's
gun roared next to his temple, momentarily deafening him.
Putting one finger in his ear, he whirled to his right in time to
see a brave stop, grab his chest, and fall on his own ax.

"That one woulda split your skull," she said calmly as she
rammed home another ball, licked her finger, and put a bead
of moisture on her sights.

Back to back they crept toward the only untorched wagon—
the Tolberts'. Petey, knife drawn, crouched and followed behind
them. Josie jolted against Caleb as her gun barked again, picking
off an Indian climbing into a wagon. His revolvers answered,
taking down two more raiders. Scattered shots popped across
the encampment as the last few survivors tried to defend themselves. Dead littered the ground, settler and Indian alike. Indians
swarmed over the wagons, rummaging through the contents,
tossing out things into small piles. All around, wagons blazed,
tongues of flame licking through the canvas tops. Caleb's heart
sank. His train was lost.

"Something's wrong," he muttered, flattening himself
against the untouched Tolbert wagon.

"Whatcha mean?" Josie sidled up beside him, Petey hot on her heels.

"This wagon isn't touched." Before the words were out, the wagon shuddered, and Caleb stiffened, training his guns on the rear. Eric Tolbert parted the canvas, looked around, and slipped to the ground. He paused, glanced around again, then hurried out into the darkness away from the train.

"Where's the woman and baby?" Josie whispered.

Caleb waited, but they didn't follow. Sliding to the back, he jerked open the canvas. Anna Tolbert huddled in a pile of quilts, holding the baby. Her tangled mass of hair framed a face dominated by wild, vacant eyes. Knees drawn up against her chin, she inched backward until she pressed against a trunk.

"Mrs. Tolbert, it's me, Caleb McCall," he soothed as he climbed into the wagon. "I'm not going to hurt you. You have to come with me." He reached out and she shrank away. "We have to get out of here before the Indians find you."

Her eyes cleared and reason returned. "Indians?" Her hand flew to her mouth. "My God, Red Cloud."

Moving faster than he could have anticipated, she crawled past him, leaped out of the wagon, and ran across the clearing, clad in only her nightdress.

"No!" Caleb scrambled after her. Her golden hair fanned out behind her as she dashed toward the main fight.

"She's slap-assed crazy," he heard Josie observe with a low whistle.

As he sprinted after Anna, he stumbled over bodies in his haste. Each dead warrior wore Red Cloud's colors, yet there was something eerie about the morbid scene, some nagging detail that didn't fit.

Caleb dodged braves calmly scalping their victims, others setting fire to remaining wagons. A group yipped victory, holding bloody scalps aloft. Behind him thudded two sets of feet as Josie and Petey ran along with him.

Anna waded into the worst of the fight, blood staining the hem of her nightdress and a thick ooze covering her feet. She approached a tall, bronze Indian rifling a wagon and caught him by the arm. He spun around with murderous rage on his face and raised a stone ax. She calmly stared up at him, a slight smile parting her lips. Caleb slid to a stop and reached for his gun, but before he could aim and fire, a slender blade glinted in the air. Petey's knife found its mark dead center the Indian's chest.

Caleb grabbed Anna and pulled her away. She slumped heavily against him in a dead faint. Dragging her backward by the collar of her gown, he pulled her into the protection of a half-burned wagon.

"Stay here with her." He shoved her at Josie. "I'm going to see if there's any others alive."

"You want me to go with you, Mr. McCall?" Petey asked.

Caleb smiled briefly at the anticipation on the boy's face. "No, Petey. You better stay here and protect the women."

He grinned broadly and nodded. "Yes, sir."

The stench of death was nauseating, and morning mists shrouded the infant sun. The thin canopy of dawn saw an end to the carnage as the warriors collected their scalps and loot and searched for their ponies.

Creeping along beside the charred skeleton of a wagon, Caleb spotted Statton's body stretched out on the ground. Caleb bent low and ran across the open area toward him. A shrill whistling split the air. He turned his head in time to see the stone knife coming before it sank deep into his knee, sending shards of pain through him. Loose dirt crowded into his mouth and nose when he struck the hard ground. A whirring sound filled his ears as blackness swirled up to envelop him.

The scorching heat of the sun warmed Caleb's face, and a loud buzzing worked its way into his mind. He tried to put his hands over his ears. A fierce pain stabbed through him. Breathing heavily, he lay still, trying to focus on where he was, what had happened. The buzzing wavered in tone and intensity. He thought he'd go mad if he couldn't shut it out of his mind. Clapping one hand over his right ear, he shifted his weight to the left and tugged at the arm bent beneath him. Pain filled him again. *At least one ear is better than none.* Dirt and gravel was in his mouth, and his nose itched as his head began to clear. He turned in the direction of the annoying buzzing.

Clouds of flies rose from a nearby body when a turkey buzzard landed softly in their midst and extended his wings in a gesture of dominance. He slowly turned his great ugly head. Caleb hated buzzards, but at least he'd temporarily stopped the flies.

The scavenger took an awkward step forward, extending his wings for balance. He continued in his awkward gait until he stood right by Caleb's left foot. Cocking his head to the side, the bird took a tentative peck at a blue bead on Caleb's knee-high boots.

"Go on, you bastard." Caleb kicked his right leg. The buzzard squawked and hopped a short distance away. A dead body caught the bird's eye, and he moved in its direction, startling another cloud of flies. Caleb's stomach tightened as the scavenger pulled at the corpse. Rising up on his elbows, he saw the horror of the night before spread out on the prairie.

Caleb rolled to his side, gritting his teeth against the pain. He grabbed the knife with both hands and pulled. The blade slid out, bringing with it a fresh flow of blood. His head fell back, and sweat dribbled down his nose and dropped into the dirt.

"I'll die of thirst if I stay here," he murmured to himself, struggling into a sitting position. Grasping his brown linen shirt with both hands, he tore off a wide strip of the fabric and wound it around his knee to stanch the bleeding.

A shadow glided along the ground, announcing the arrival of more scavengers. Five more joined the first, and still others circled overhead. Caleb looked around him and found the rifle he'd dropped the previous night. Briefly wondering why the

Indians hadn't taken it, he used it as a crutch to pull himself to his feet.

Putting his weight on the gun, he took a hopping step. Bodies lay everywhere, some scalped and others horribly disfigured. Hoping for some sign of life, Caleb made his way through the mutilated camp. Most of the wagons were emptied and charred, the horses stolen or chased away. Approaching Statton's wagon, he found Statton cleanly scalped, lying on the ground. He wore a surprised expression at the stone ax sticking out of the center of his forehead.

"Oh, God." Caleb fell heavily to the ground. The heat smothered him, wrapped around him, suffocated him. With two fingers he closed Statton's eyes, then everything went black.

Gentle hands soothed his brow, and the sun no longer parched his face. Something poked at him, sending fire through his body. Caleb lashed out, thinking the buzzards had found him. His flailing arm struck a leg.

"Ouch!" the voice said.

Someone caught his free arm.

"Mr. McCall?"

The voice was familiar.

"Mr. McCall, wake up."

He opened his eyes. Petey stood over him, blocking the sun.

"You're hurt real bad," said Josie's gentle voice. "We gotta get out of here."

"Mrs. Tolbert and the baby?" His voice croaked, and he wished he had a drink.

"I don't know. Me and Petey left to chase away a bunch of Injuns, and when we come back, she was gone."

Struggling to his elbows, Caleb tried to get up. "I have to find the baby. He'll die out here."

Josie took one arm and Petey the other. Together they stood him up, shoving his gun stock beneath his arm for support. Nearby, their wagon was hitched to the two mules. Before he could ask why the Indians hadn't taken the stock, a bright splash of color caught his eye. An arrow stuck out of the wooden body of a nearby wagon.

"That's odd," Caleb muttered.

"What?" Josie asked.

"I didn't see any braves using bows." Shaking off their restraining hands, he hobbled over, jerked the arrow out of the wood, turned, and looked around him. Most of the victims had been killed at close range with axes, tomahawks, and knives like the one that had gone into his leg. Why would the raiders leave a single arrow? Was it meant as a sign, a clue intentionally left?

As Caleb turned the arrow over in his hands, he pieced together scattered events of the night. The faces of the attackers weren't the faces of Lakota. The war paint was applied in the same pattern as the Lakota but without the care each man took to draw the symbols that gave him strength in battle.

Caleb looked closer at the arrow, finely turned, smoothed to silkiness for straighter flight. Feathers, meticulously trimmed and dyed, adorned the end. About halfway down, three slashes cut into the shaft carried a different color—blue, red, and yellow. "Crow," Caleb murmured out loud.

"What are you talkin' about?" Josie watched him with fists planted on her hips.

"A band of Crow attacked the train."

"Injuns is Injuns," she said with a shrug.

"But why? Why would they disguise themselves as Lakota, their own enemies? Scalps taken without honor won't mean anything." He turned the arrow again. The answer lay in his hand, but just then his mind was too scattered to figure it. He broke the arrow in two pieces and let them fall.

"Where do you think you're goin'?" Josie scolded as he started down the length of the decimated train.

"I have to find the baby."

With dread he approached the Tolbert wagon, miraculously untouched except for the wheel spokes broken with an ax.

Maybe Anna had fled back here. He jerked open the canvas cover. The interior was empty.

Letting the cover fall closed, he backed away and looked beneath it. He hadn't seen Eric's body among the dead, although some were disfigured beyond recognition. Josie had said she left Anna beneath the Crockett wagon. Caleb turned and started up the other side of the camp. He heard a groan. Everything had looked the same the night before. How could he remember which wagon they were under? He quickened his pace. Another groan. He stumbled and felt Josie slip her hand under his arm. A moan came from beneath the scorched and broken body of the Crockett wagon. Only a pile of rubble remained of the heavy Conestoga the man had insisted on bringing. Caleb tried to lean down, but a stab of pain made him grab his knee.

"You stay there," Josie ordered. "Petey, steady him while I take a look." She dropped to her knees and scratched away the boards. Anna's face appeared beneath a heavy beam. Crushed by the weight of the lumber, she cradled the baby in her arms, protecting him by the mass of her own body. Her face was blackened and burned, but she grasped Josie's shirt-sleeve and hung on.

"We've got to get her out of there." Caleb stumbled forward.

"She ain't goin' nowhere," Josie said, looking back over her shoulder. "She's jammed under there. Ain't enough of us to lift the boards clear."

A tear ran down Anna's cheek and her lips moved silently.

"What is it, Mrs. Tolbert? You want a drink of water?" Josie asked, rocking back on her heels.

Anna shook her head. Then, in tiny movements, she tugged the baby's blanket free from beneath her body, dragged the infant toward her face, and snugged it to her once more. Josie pulled back the baby's cover. Completely unharmed, the baby sucked his fist hungrily. Anna thrust the bundle toward her, an unspoken plea in her eyes.

"You want me to take the baby?" Josie asked.

Unable to move her head, Anna blinked rapidly in answer.

"But, but ... I don't know nothin' 'bout babies," Josie sputtered and glanced over her shoulder.

Caleb felt as helpless as Josie looked. The very thought of caring for an infant terrified him. No, never again. "We'll get you out," he promised.

Gently, Josie took the baby, and Anna smiled weakly and blinked away tears. Her smile slowly faded and the life went out of her eyes.

Josie stood and held out the bundled infant to him. He stared into the baby's tiny button eyes, black as charred wood like his father's and so like his own infant daughter's lost to him long ago. A sharp pain stabbed at his heart. "The first order of business is to feed you." Once the words were out, their meaning sunk in. He pushed back his hat and scratched his head. Where, in this vacant, empty land would he find nourishment for an infant? He glanced toward Anna, the front of her blackened gown dampened by milk leaking from her breasts. The idea that formed in his mind repulsed even him, but if the child was to live, he had no other choice.

"Pull the boards away from her," he commanded, taking the baby from Josie.

"Why?" she asked. "Ain't no need to get her out now."

"The baby's got to nurse."

The look Josie gave him was one of pure astonishment. "You ain't gonna ... a dead woman?"

"That baby needs food. You got a better idea?"

"No." She darted a pleading glance at Petey. "Well?"

"Sounds like a good idea to me," he said with a shrug. "Remember them pigs Pa suckled on their dead ma that time Lenny Webster shot the sow when he was high as a Georgia pine? Them little piggies done just fine till Ma could milk the cow."

Scolding him with a look, Josie jerked away as many boards as she could. She ripped apart Anna's gown and placed the infant at her breast. Hungrily, the baby drank the milk with little gasping noises. After one breast grew slack, Josie shifted him to the other. He eagerly drained that side as well, then began to fret and squirm.

"Oh, Lord. You reckon that milk's gonna make him sick?" Josie frowned and picked up the baby. He rewarded her with a loud burp and a grin.

Despite the unlikely surroundings, Caleb couldn't help but smile at the child. He'd be hungry again, long after his mother's body grew stiff. Then where would they get milk?

Chapter Eight

Josie's eyes widened. "You mean I gotta jab a hot knife right to your leg?"

"If we don't cauterize it, it'll fester." Caleb grunted and straightened his leg.

A thin bead of sweat broke out on Josie's upper lip. She and Petey had dragged Caleb back to his campsite. Now he lay on the ground, propped against his saddle, his face pale and clammy. His leather britches were split to the knee, exposing the ugly, jagged knife wound. "I cain't," she whispered, shaking her head.

"Yes, you can." He raised his head. "Build a fire over there." He shifted to his left side and yanked a broad-bladed knife from a leather pouch sewn into his boot. "Put this in the flames."

Her hand closed around the carved bone handle and she glanced at Petey.

"You reckon he's already ravin'?" he whispered, his eyes wide.

"Get some wood like he says," she ordered.

When Petey returned with scraggly twigs and brush, Josie laid a fire, struck a spark with her flint, then sat back and waited. Caleb's head rested against the saddle seat, his eyes closed. Absently, she poked at the fire. Was he conscious? His face was growing paler as the puddle of blood beneath his knee grew larger. The bandanna tied around his leg hadn't hindered the seepage. She batted at a fat buzzing fly that lit on the blood-soaked cloth.

When flames leaped from the bed of orange coals, she placed the knife-blade tip in the fire. Caleb hadn't moved. He looked so alone, so defeated. She reached up, hesitated, then raked her fingers through the thick brown curls tousled over his forehead.

Glancing up through thick lashes, he smiled, then grimaced. "I think it's ready," he said, his voice strained. Josie's hand froze. Could she give him this pain even if it was for his own good? Compassion tore through her and her insides ached. He caught her wrist with one hand and squeezed gently. "Go ahead," he whispered.

She pulled her hand free, rose, and retrieved the knife from the fire. The blade's end glowed bright cherry red. "Petey, come hold his arms."

"You don't have to hold me down. I can't cause any trouble," Caleb said.

"Just the same, I don't want you a-floppin' all over the place." She knelt by his side and glanced up at her brother. "Hold him good now, Petey."

"Wait." Caleb caught her wrist. "Hand me that saddlebag first." He pointed behind him.

When Petey obliged, Caleb pulled a bottle of whiskey out of the leather case, uncorked it, and took a deep draft. He wiped his mouth on his sleeve and set the bottle down firmly. "When I say, press the blade against the wound." He lay back on the blanket and gathered a bunch of wool fabric in each hand. "Now."

Josie stared down at the gaping flesh, then glanced to his pale face. Her vision wavered, and she swayed slightly. A warm hand closed over her wrist. She cracked open an eye. Caleb winked and squeezed her hand. "What's the matter, mule-skinner? I'm at your mercy. Don't you like that?"

She shook her head. "I ain't never done nothin' like this. Only hogs when Pa'd cut off their nuts."

Caleb laughed, then took another drink with trembling hands. "Don't go that far. Just the leg, please." Tipping the bottle toward her, he asked, "You want some?" Although he was pale and sweating heavily, his eyes sparkled with mischief.

She slanted a glance at him. "If I get liquored up, I might forget you ain't a boar hog."

His face sobered and he squeezed her hand again. "Go ahead. It won't get any better the longer we wait." Pain filled his soft voice.

Josie took a deep breath and grasped the knife in both hands.

"Wait." Petey caught her arm. "Here, Mr. McCall." He handed Caleb a short length of wood.

Caleb took the wood and clamped it between his teeth. He nodded, then closed his eyes.

Josie shut her eyes and plunged the heated blade into the center of the wound. The scent of burning flesh filled the air around them. She jerked the knife away, leaving a patch of blackened flesh. Caleb stiffened, then fell back limply. The stick fell to the blanket. Dropping the knife, she scrambled to his shoulders. "Caleb?"

Petey pulled her aside and put an ear against Caleb's chest. "He's all right, sis."

Josie sighed and rocked back on her heels. Her hands shook, her insides quivered. What was this strange feeling rushing over her at the sight of this virile man lying unconscious before her?

Caleb peeked open an eye. The bright sun obscured every-thing else from sight except its own glare. Wondering if he was alive, he shifted his weight, and the searing pain that ran down his leg assured him he was. Turning his face away from the light, he saw someone kneeling beside him. Josie's face filled his vision. She stroked back his hair with tenderness her rough exterior hid.

"How you feelin'?" she asked.

As he shook his head, another figure moved between him and the sun. Petey grinned at him, holding the baby in his arms.

"We was beginning to think you was a goner. You gotta git up. Can't lay here in this sun no longer." She tugged at his arm, struggling to get him to his feet.

Clamping his teeth shut, Caleb grabbed his gun, braced it under his arm, and staggered to his feet. With Josie on one side and the gun on the other, he hobbled to the waiting wagon, fighting dizziness. Her grip on his arm was strong and sure, and he allowed her to help support him.

He grabbed for the tailgate of the wagon. The hot world spun, and he fell through a black void.

"Pa'll kill us fer bringin' somebody home, Josie," Petey said as they bumped along in the wagon.

"He won't notice 'cause he'll be mad as a rattlesnake in an outhouse when he finds out Davie didn't come." Josie shifted her position in the wagon bed, stretching out her aching legs. A hot breeze ruffled her hair as she lifted her hat and wiped at her forehead. Thunderation, could it get any hotter? She sloshed the canteen and sighed at the hollow sound it made. Not much left, and she'd need all she could get to keep Caleb's fever down.

The wagon lurched forward. Caleb groaned and clawed for his leg.

"Easy now, Mr. McCall." She caught his hands between hers. "You'll pull off the bandage, and I'll have to do it up again."

He opened his eyes and croaked, "Cindy?"

"Who's he callin' for?" Petey asked over his shoulder. As

he looked away from the dim path they followed, the wagon hit another tooth-jarring bump.

"You watch what you're doin'. Dumpin' him out won't help matters none," she snapped.

"Reckon he means the mare?" Petey asked.

"You askin' about the horse?" Josie bent over him again, throwing shade across his face.

Caleb nodded.

"We tied her on the back. Had to. She kept followin' us around, stickin' her nose in your face."

"The baby?"

"The baby's fine." She patted a bundle of rags beside her. "He's asleep right here."

"Water?"

Gently, Josie raised his head and poured a small amount into his mouth. "Not too much, now." She lowered him back onto the bed of blankets. The wagon jolted, nearly throwing her out. "Thunderation, Petey. Be careful and for once don't turn this dad-blasted wagon over like you usually do."

She pulled off her bulky jacket and stuffed it beneath Caleb's head. "There. Bet that's better, ain't it?"

Caleb moaned and licked his dry, cracked lips.

"What we gonna do about that baby?" Petey asked.

"I don't know." Josie sighed and smoothed Caleb's cheek. "I ain't never handled no babies before."

Petey turned on the board seat. " 'Course you have. Don't you remember little John?"

A hand clutched at her heart. Little John. Her own precious baby. Dead when he was only a few hours old. Sudden tears burned the backs of her eyes, and she silently cursed her brother for making her remember what she had tried so hard not to think about since finding the Tolbert child.

"Milk," Caleb whispered.

"Think he wants us to give the baby milk?" Petey turned around again.

" 'Course I know he needs milk, but we ain't got any right

here,'' she snapped, and wiped away a tear that squeezed from her eye.

The setting sun was casting a deep lavender over everything, creating an eerie appearance when they made camp for the night. Together Josie and Petey struggled to lift Caleb from the wagon and lay him by the fire. He mumbled and tossed his head. ''The mare . . . a foal . . . milk.''

''I bet he's tryin' to say the horse's got milk,'' Petey said, dusting off his hands and rubbing the small of his back.

''Ain't you bright? 'Course that's what he's sayin','' Josie snapped as she pulled the blanket up under Caleb's chin and puffed to catch her breath. He sure was heavier than he looked.

''How come you're mad with me, sis?'' Petey asked innocently, rolling out his lower lip and watching her with big, sad eyes. His expression suddenly shifted. ''You ever milked a horse before?''

''Sure. I milk one every day.'' She snatched his hat off his head. ''Tarnation, but you're stupid sometimes.''

''I ain't near as stupid as you are ornery.'' He yanked the hat away and crammed it on his head. ''Always a-scoldin' and a-fussin','' he muttered, jamming his hands deep in his pockets.

''Quit poutin' and go git me some firewood.''

He answered with a grunt and ambled away. Suddenly, he stopped and turned. ''Josie, what you gonna do about his . . . ? I mean, he ain't been all day, and it's night. What you gonna do?''

''I'm gonna put a diaper on him, that's what. Just like the baby.'' She tried to ignore the horrified look that came over Petey's face,

''You ain't gonna . . . ? It ain't proper.''

''I ain't worried about proper, Petey.'' She climbed into the wagon bed and knelt by Caleb's side. ''He's done soaked these clothes, and me and you cain't wrestle him in and out of this wagon all the way home. He don't know what's goin' on anyhow.'' A quick yank untied the leather strip serving as his belt. She pulled it loose, then grabbed the top of his leather pants. Her mother's voice rang in her ears as she tugged, scolding her about the sins of the flesh and including bits from Reverend Brown's latest sermon. As the trousers began to slide off, Caleb began to struggle.

"Petey, come over here and help me."

Petey shot her a fearful glance, then grabbed Caleb's arms while she tugged at his trouser legs.

"Dad-burned tight pants," she muttered.

With strength she didn't guess he could have, Caleb thrashed around, shoving at her, grabbing at his pants. Petey gave her a terrified glance.

"Ain't you gonna help me?" she scolded, prying Caleb's hand off her arm.

"I ain't helpin' you strip no strange man." Petey crossed his arms over his chest and stuck out his jaw.

Josie sighed. Reverend Brown's sermons played louder in his head than hers. While Petey's expression went from disapproving to horrified, she climbed atop Caleb, straddled his waist, and pinned his arms to his sides with her knees. "Mr. McCall?" She patted his cheek.

He stopped tossing his head and looked at her.

"You want to pee all down your leg again and have to wear them skin pants wet tomorrow?"

He blinked, but she couldn't be sure he understood her.

"We cain't stop this wagon every whipstitch. 'Sides, there might be Injuns on our tails."

He ceased struggling, blinked, and blushed. A tug of conscience went through her as he turned his head away. A man like him wasn't used to depending on anybody, let alone being as helpless as that little baby.

"Under the circumstances, don't you think you could call me Caleb?" he murmured.

"Least you got enough blood left to blush. Now, be still . . . Caleb." Josie slid to his side and grabbed the pants again.

"Thirty-odd years of looking after myself, I'm not about to let a shirttail girl diaper me." He lunged toward her, his hands poised to push her away. But before his head cleared the make-shift pillow, he grimaced and fell back. His arms lay still at his sides.

Josie tugged the buckskins away, then stopped. They'd have to roll him around to get those longjohns off. She cut a look at Petey, and he moved another step away. She shrugged, drew her knife, and slashed through the fabric. "Petey, come here and pull off his drawers."

"Uh-uh," he answered. "I ain't havin' no part of this."

"Petey, get over here right now."

With chin thrust out, he shook his head. "Nope. You started this."

Mumbling oaths about Petey's stubbornness, Josie closed her eyes, grabbed a handful of fabric, and pulled. The mutilated longjohns slid off easily.

"Oh, Lordy." Her eyes ranged upward over his naked lower half, but stopped when she met his emerald stare.

He closed his eyes against her wide-eyed expression, and she couldn't be sure he understood. Or did he choose to pretend to hide his shame? Gently, she rolled him to the side and slid a square of material up under him. Then she rolled him to the other side, pulled the material up between his legs, and tied it in a knot.

"Now," she said with a familiar pat. "You go ahead when you have to. I've nursed men before. Don't bother me none."

He cracked open an eye at the false bravado in her voice. She stood at his feet, hands planted on her hips. He let his head fall back into the pillow. What had he gotten himself into? These two were barely able to take care of themselves, much less an injured man and a baby. The nursing might kill him before the fever had a chance . . . or he could die of humiliation.

"Yeah, Pa. He's alive, he's hurt real bad."

Caleb lolled his head to the side. They had traveled all day, and his fever had climbed by the hour. Pain and chills racked his body. Snatches of memories stayed in his mind—Josie wiping his forehead, Josie changing the diaper.

"You drug home a stranger when you didn't even bring my Davie? Another danged mouth to feed." This was a different voice, a man's voice.

"T'weren't nothin' I could do about Davie, Pa. He changed his mind. We couldn't just leave the feller there."

"All right, bring him along, but you'll do the tendin'."

Caleb opened his eyes and raised his head. In front of him was a tumbledown cabin and an old man wagging an angry finger in Josie's face.

"Yes, Pa," Josie answered, lowering her head.

Threads of the conversation wove their way into his mind. Hands grabbed his coat and his legs and lifted him clear of the wagon. The scent of pines and the moldy smell of a thick mat of pine needles filled the cool air.

"Whar ya want him?" a grimy man said, holding Caleb's legs. Another held his shoulders. They all stood on the porch of the cabin.

"Bring him inside," Josie said, and pushed open the door. "Put him over here in my bed."

A rough mattress protested loudly as they dropped him into its softness. Their footsteps faded. Someone lifted his bandage. A sharp, stabbing pain ran down through his leg, and the world spun.

"You see to it that my supper's ready on time, you hear? Bull Hardwick don't wait on his victuals, you hear?" Pa stuck his head in the door and leveled a threatening look at Josie.

"Yes, Pa," she replied. The door slammed shut, and she let out a sigh of relief. At least he wasn't too angry. Thankful to be alone, she shuffled back to her bed. Caleb's eyes were closed, and his face turned away. He sure is handsome, she thought, brushing a curl away from his face.

A kettle of water steamed over the last of the supper fire.

Josie quickly poured a pan full and carried it over by the bed. She pulled back the bandage, revealing the angry, festering wound. Gently, she cleansed the area, rubbed on some of Ma's herbal liniment, and rebandaged it. Then she paused for a good look at the man, and her heart sank. Nobody could live long with a nasty wound like that.

She pulled up the rocking chair, sat down, and wiped his face with cool water. His jaw was strong and prominent, his skin an even brown from hours under the sun. Tentatively, she ran her fingers through his snarled hair. The fevered heat of his scalp warmed her fingertips. He moaned and mumbled, and she jerked her hand away. If she didn't get that fever down, he'd surely die.

She filled another pan with cool water from the bucket outside. Pulling away the top of his longjohns bared wide, firm shoulders. Thick hair scattered across his chest drew her hand to its softness. How would that mat feel pressed against her bare skin? Her fingers walked across his chest, then stopped at a peculiar puckered scar on his breast. On the other side was an identical indentation. She ran her finger across its knobby surface and wondered what could have caused such an evil scar.

A warmth stole through his body. Soft hands moved across his chest, sending tremors through him. He opened an eye. Josie stood over him, at least he thought it was Josie. Her hair hung long, tied at the base of her neck. She turned startled eyes toward him and tried to jerk away.

"Warm water feels good." He squeezed her arm slightly before letting her go.

"You needed a bath," she said, moving a step away. "You scared me."

"Where am I?" The faint scent of food drifted by his nose. Rough, hand-hewn beams hovered over him, and above that the underside of a shake roof.

"You're in my cabin." Josie moved toward the fireplace. She lifted the lid of the pot and stirred the food bubbling inside. Then she scooped a spoonful and gracefully lifted it to her lips.

He lowered his eyes to walls of great logs, mud chinking in between. A blue enamel pot, steam rattling the lid, simmered over a low fire in a huge fireplace. Glancing toward the tiny front window, he reckoned dawn had barely broken. Another day lost.

The baby whimpered, and he raised his head to search the room for him. Another mew, and Caleb spotted a tiny foot poked above the edge of a large basket.

He tried to sit up and swing his feet over the side of the bed, but his head swam and a hot flash of pain went through him. Trembling, he lay back down, grateful for the cool sheets. A quilt covered the bed on which he lay, not the ordinary utility quilt but the fancy kind women fussed over for months.

Reaching down under the covers, Caleb laid a hand over his knee, still warm to the touch. How long had he been out? His fingers brushed the diaper. Scattered memories flooded back. He glanced toward Josie and found her watching him.

"Don't worry about that, Mr. McCall." She nodded toward his lower half. "I got seven brothers. Ain't nothin' I ain't never seen before."

"All the same, I think I can handle that for myself now." Caleb pushed himself into a sitting position against the pillows in the bed. "And please stop calling me Mr. McCall. Call me Caleb."

She avoided his glance, went to the wobbly table, and plunged her hands into a bowl of flour.

"What about the baby?"

"The young'un's all right." She poked her foot at the basket on the floor.

"How long have I been here?"

" 'Bout a week now. Weak as a kitten you was. I been a-feedin' the baby mare's milk. That's all I could think of. Got a cow from the Andersons yesterday for him."

Caleb shook his head to dispel cobwebs threatening to overcome him again. He pulled back the covers and examined his leg. Bandaged neatly, the garlicky aroma of an herbal poultice surrounded it.

Josie moved closer and offered him a bowl of thin soup. "Here, eat this. It'll put back some of the strength you lost while you was sick."

Caleb took the bowl and noticed that her fingers were long and slim, yet cracked and rough. Her faithful hat was gone. He raised his eyes to her face. Little wisps of dark bangs clouded her brow.

"What are you and Petey doing up here alone?" he asked, taking a tentative sip of the soup.

"I ain't alone. Pa's here and Petey and my other brothers and kin." She glanced away quickly, rose from the side of the bed, and walked over to the fireplace to add a log. "You better finish that soup 'fore it gets cold," she muttered over her shoulder.

Caleb wanted to ask her more, intrigued by the disappearance of her rough exterior, replaced by this gentle woman. Josie looked down at the infant as he began to fret.

"Let me have him," Caleb said, quickly setting down the bowl.

"I named him Joshua." She picked him up, walked over, and handed him to Caleb. Her fingers brushed his. Their eyes met briefly before she glanced away. The baby quieted instantly when nestled close to Caleb's fuzzy, bare chest. "He likes you," she said.

Caleb looked down into the little face. "Yeah, I guess he does." He tickled the baby's chin with his index finger, then laughed as the baby tried to put the finger into his rosebud mouth. Caleb shifted him to one arm and picked up the bowl of soup.

"I never had much time for young'uns and such. I was always too busy." Josie moved back to the bowl of dough and attacked it viciously.

"I'd make time for this one." Caleb chuckled when the baby made a face at the taste of his skin. "Are you married?"

Josie stopped kneading the dough with her hands in midair. "Used to be. He died."

Her answer was short and without feeling.

"I'm sorry."

"Don't mind. Happened a long time ago." She slapped dough and slammed it onto the table.

Her self-consciousness was evident. Caleb smiled. "Do I make you nervous?"

"Yeah. I mean no. It's just . . . I don't git company much."

"You have any children?"

Josie stopped, wiped her hands on a dirty cloth, then moved to the door. Without a word she yanked the bucket off its peg and went out of the door, slamming it behind her, leaving Caleb to wonder about the woman who had saved his life.

Chapter Nine

Josie stepped onto the cabin's porch and closed the door behind her. Crisp air teased her nose and stung her lungs as she breathed deeply. She pulled her coat tighter and shivered. Wonder what kept Pa and the boys from their dinner, she thought. I oughta get on down to the mine and see.

Instead, she took another deep breath of the fresh air and walked over to a broken-down corral fence. She crossed her arms on the top rail, rested her chin on them, and sighed. In the distance, the snowy peaks of the Rockies poked their heads over the horizon, beckoning her with their steep slopes and majestic heights. Her thoughts drifted to the man in her bed.

She had not had time to reflect on this growing feeling for Caleb until then. Something about him drew her closer, warmed her from the inside, touched something unfulfilled within her. She closed her eyes, seeing again the attack on the wagon train, smelling the smoke and the blood, hearing the screams and wrenching shrieks. The scenes passed in her head and her stomach tightened as she saw Caleb sink to his knees, the knife wedged deep in his leg. Her heart began to pound. The image of his face, pale, surprised, scared, flashed before her and imprinted itself behind her eyelids. Even when she opened her eyes again, his face was still there. Vulnerable. Needing. And she needed him. Lord knows, Ma'd always said she was too plainspoken. She chided herself for such blatant thoughts, but she did want Caleb McCall.

Josie hopped up on the top rail and studied a faraway peak. One time she'd thought the same thing about Johnny. Tall, handsome, and blond, Johnny cut a wide path wherever he went. When he started courting her, she'd thought nobody'd ever been so lucky. But that'd been before she married him. Johnny. Even his name still made her cringe.

She climbed down off the fence and walked slowly toward the woodpile, the bucket forgotten. Caleb's clean good looks were a welcome relief from Pa's grimy, disheveled boys, as he called his miners. She'd fussed over Caleb all the way home, feeling his forehead and checking the filthy wound, drawing questioning looks from Petey. Pa'd throw a fit if he knew how she really felt. Once they had Caleb in the cabin, her father had quickly washed his hands of the whole affair and returned to the depths of his mountain to mourn Davie's absence.

Caleb's care had fallen to her. The severity and condition of his wound had appalled her once she unwrapped it. The cauterizing had been too late, and infection had set in. Long red streaks ran up his leg nearly to his hip, but Ma's garlic poultice had helped draw out the corruption from the putrefied wound.

Living for so many years as she had with a house full of men, she didn't pay any attention to their careless displays. But the sight of Caleb's youthful, muscular body tugged at places within her she'd forgotten existed.

Caring for him the past week had brightened her dull life. Cleaning him, seeing to his needs, hovering over him as fever tortured his body, had helped fill her days, but nighttime was her favorite. At the end of the day and her duties, she could take down her hair, brush it out, and put on the one feminine garment she owned—the nightgown her mother had given her on her wedding day. Drawing a light shawl around her shoulders, she'd sit in the rocking chair by Caleb's bed and watch his face in the silvery moonbeams streaming in through the high window. She'd almost forgotten what a man looked like with a groomed beard and hair, his face washed clean. Especially one with all his teeth.

"Josie! What you doing out there mooning? Where's my dinner?" Pa trudged up the hill toward the cabin, his dull-witted helpers following blindly behind.

Josie didn't bother to answer right off and watched her father as he grunted and puffed, his legs and lungs beginning to fail him after years deep in the mine. Neither he nor his miners ever bothered to wash, and on cold winter nights the smell in the cabin made her eyes water.

"I better not have to wait for my dinner, girlie, or you'll be sorry." He stopped in front of her, puffing to catch his breath.

"Dinner's ready," she answered, shrugging off his anger.

He pushed rudely past her without answering, followed by the other men who didn't give her a glance. Except Petey. He grinned at her from a blackened face as he passed. She turned and watched as they filed inside without so much as wiping a boot, and sighed. Once they were finished eating, she'd have to sweep up all over again.

Bull stopped in his tracks when he saw Caleb sitting propped against the pillows, his eyes open and alert. "Well, the dead do rise. How do you feel?"

"Much better. I'm sorry for the trouble."

Bull waved a grimy paw as he flopped down in his appointed chair. "Didn't put me out none. Josie there took care of you."

She stepped inside the door and lowered her eyes.

"You mean all the time?" Caleb asked, raising an eyebrow.

"Where's the food, girlie?" Bull banged on the table with his fist, rattling the tin plates already set there. One by one the other sullen men sat down at the rickety table. Oddly, they didn't look up the whole time. Caleb folded his arms across his chest and watched Josie ladle a fragrant stew onto the plates and then draw brown biscuits from a Dutch oven built into the chimney of the fireplace. The men ate silently and hurriedly, their eyes flicking to Bull's plate, measuring so they'd finish when he did.

Bull signaled the end of the meal by sopping up the last of the stew gravy with a bite of his biscuit and popping the piece into his mouth. He slowly chewed the last piece, savoring the taste before swallowing and laying down his fork on the plate. At once the rest of the men followed suit, leaned back, and folded their arms.

"Fine victuals, Josie." He belched loudly. "Did you bring in a bucket of water?"

Josie shook her head, grabbed her coat, and went outside.

"Rest yourselves a few minutes, boys." Bull pushed back his chair, and the miners shot glances between themselves. Caleb guessed they weren't accustomed to being given a moment's rest.

"Well now, I'm right pleased to see you better." Bull came to stand by the side of the bed, his massive hands on his hips. He was obviously not one for personal grooming. Dark-haired like Josie, his beard hung ragged and dirty well past the open neck of his shirt. Soil covered the mine-blackened hair that hadn't known a comb for years.

He ran his eyes up and down Caleb's length. "You ever do any minin'?"

"No, can't say I have."

"That your baby?" Bull pointed to the infant, now fast asleep in Caleb's arms.

"No, he's not mine. I was wagon master on a train bound for Oregon, when we were attacked by Indians. Me, the baby, and your daughter and son were the only survivors."

Bull whirled on Petey. "You mean to tell me you and Josie wasted good money travelin' with a train?"

"We didn't pay nothin', Pa," Petey answered, cringing into the corner. "We brought everybody wood for our part."

"You better not have squandered my money like that." Bull raised a beefy arm in threat, then turned back toward Caleb, rubbing his stubbly chin. "Seems mighty funny to me that the leader would git away and nobody else."

Caleb narrowed his eyes at the clumsy accusation. "I was wounded, and I guess they took me for dead."

"That'd explain it all right," he said sarcastically. "What you gonna do with the baby?"

"I don't know. I hadn't given it much thought," Caleb replied, some inner voice warning him not to tell the miner all the truth.

"You pretty good with that gun?" Bull nodded toward Caleb's revolver and holster hanging over a straight-backed chair.

"I can hold my own." Caleb rose to the challenge in the other man's voice, and their eyes locked in a steely gaze.

"You rest, and we'll see you at supper." Bull abruptly ended his interrogation. "Josie? Josie!"

"I think she went for some water," Caleb said.

"I'll catch her outside. Come on, boys."

The boys rose in unison from the table and followed. The door slammed behind them, leaving Caleb alone with his thoughts.

Bull cut across Josie's path as she struggled up the hill behind the house with the buckets of water. He made no attempt to help, but stopped beside her with his hands jammed in his pockets.

"You make sure you got supper ready on time."

"Yes, Pa."

"What do you know about that fellow?" He jerked his head in the cabin's direction.

"Not much. He ain't been awake too long."

"Seems like somethin' is fishy to me, seein' as how all the people on the wagon train was kilt except him and you two.

Wonder if he robbed 'em?'' Bull's eyes took on a dangerous light that made a shiver run down Josie's back.

"No, he didn't. I mean, he'd a had it with him, wouldn't he?'' She didn't want to think what Bull would do if he thought Caleb carried valuables. Maybe she could sway him from his line of thinking.

"Just you let me know if you find out anythin'."

"Yes, Pa."

Bull and his men continued down the hill and disappeared into the stand of aspen at the bottom of the gully. Josie let out a long breath and picked up the heavy buckets of water.

She sloshed some out as she pushed open the door with her foot.

"Here, let me help you.'' Caleb tried to sit up, but he grabbed the edge of the bed and fell back against the pillows.

"Don't need no help. Been doin' this for years.'' She set the buckets down by the hearth.

"You shouldn't lift things so heavy."

Josie shrugged. "Don't matter none. Long as I can manage, I ought to do it. Least that's what Pa says."

Caleb shifted the baby's position and leaned back against the pillows. The sheet had slipped down around his waist, and Josie's mind flew to the times she'd changed his diaper. Caring for him when he was little better than a corpse was one thing, but seeing him now, half naked, propped up in her bed very much alive, was entirely another.

She lifted the bucket and filled the black cast-iron kettle with water, then swung it over the fire. Picking up a stick, she stirred the flames to life. Then she stooped and dragged a large dishpan from beneath the ragged cloth covering the cabinet and filled it half full of cool water from the spring.

"Want a drink?'' she asked him.

He nodded, and she poured some of the water into a cup and walked over to the edge of the bed. Their hands touched briefly as he took it.

"That baby's right attached to you, ain't he?'' She leaned

over and moved the blanket aside to reveal a rosebud mouth pursed in sleep.

"Yes, I guess he is." Caleb smiled down at the sleeping infant and traced the pudginess of a cheek with his finger.

"He's purdy."

"His mother was beautiful," Caleb answered simply.

Something akin to jealousy rippled through Josie when her eyes met his. She sprang up and busied herself with the dishes. Moving back over to the fire, she swung the now-steaming kettle out and emptied it into the dishpan. "How come you're so attached to somebody else's young'un?"

Caleb couldn't resist a small smile. He liked seeing her like this, without the tough exterior she'd worn since he met her. He wanted to keep her talking, to hear her melodious voice tinted with the twang of the Tennessee hills. "His father's a good friend of mine."

"You gonna give him back?" She grabbed the pan's edges with a towel and hefted it onto the table.

"If I can find him."

Josie took a bar of soft lye soap and rubbed it between her hands in the water. Then she moved over to the table and tossed the first of the dishes into the pan. "He looks like an Injun to me," she said with her back turned.

Her insight floored him at first, then he realized she must have seen the resemblance or heard the rumors on the train. After all, she'd cared for the infant for days while he lay unconscious. "He is. He's half Lakota."

Josie sloshed water onto her boots as she whirled around. "Don't let·Pa hear you," she whispered urgently. "That baby won't be safe here."

Caleb frowned. "Don't worry. The father doesn't even know where we are. For all he knows, we're halfway to Oregon by now."

"It ain't that. Pa hates all Injuns, little and big. Just don't mention it to him."

She looked so frightened, he quickly agreed. "All right, I won't."

She turned back to the pan, but her hands shook as she lifted a dish into the soapy water.

"How long have you lived here?" Caleb saw another flash of sorrow cross her face.

" 'Bout four years, I reckon. Pa and the men got a mine down the hill." She tossed a dish to the side and swiped at a curl with a soapy hand. "Oh, better not mention you know that neither." She shook her hair back and blew the curl away. "Pa, he's funny about people knowin' he's got that mine."

"What's he digging for? Gold?"

"Yeah, what little of it he's found. But he keeps hopin'. That's what keeps the boys here."

"Your brothers?"

Josie shrugged. "Some of 'em. Some of 'em are my brothers-in-law."

"You said yesterday you got a cow from some neighbors, the Andersons?"

"Yeah, they live over the next ridge, but them women . . ."

She let her words drift off, and he heard her swear softly. He grinned, imagining the scene—Josie, marching over the hill, her Hawken in her arms, bargaining the unsuspecting men out of their favorite cow. He leaned over to lay the baby on the mattress at the foot of the bed and the sheet slipped down around his thigh. As he reached for it, he saw her glance in his direction, then look away.

She finished the rinsing and drying and went to the door to throw out the water. Then she came back inside and filled the kettle again. "I think it's time you washed yourself. I'll git the water all ready for you, and go outside and pull a towel off the line." She hurried out the door.

Caleb leaned back and smiled. He hadn't flustered a woman that way in many years. And he liked flustering Josie. For some reason, she was having a similar effect on him, he thought as he felt his loins tighten.

* * *

Red Cloud rode at the head of his band of men. It would be good to get home. He threw his head back and breathed in the dusty, damp morning air. The air was still cool, but it would warm quickly as the sun climbed. Ahead loomed the mountains, guardians of his sanctuary and his people. He wouldn't rest until they joined his band in the hidden valley where they'd spend the winter.

This winter would be better, he thought, glancing back at the travois and horses loaded with goods from the wagon train. No one had taken a single buffalo this year, even though his warriors rode far to hunt and kill the great beasts that supplied all their essential belongings from food to ceremonial masks. Yes, the white man's goods would make it an easier winter. He'd made a wise choice, he thought sadly, the image of Running Elk's lifeless eyes flashing in his memory. Instead of death and honor, he'd at least given his people life, he thought with a twinge of guilt. From now on that would have to be the way of the Lakota if they were to survive—life itself in place of honor.

His band trailed out behind him as they topped a rise. Suddenly, a rear guard warbled a quivering whistle. He stopped and turned his horse. Black smoke drifted straight up into the clear, still morning air.

Quietly, he spoke to his second in command. Two Bears would take the majority of the band home while he and another brave, Wounded Elk, galloped back toward the train.

The same ground they had covered during the night took into the afternoon to cover again, but soon they were within sight of the wagon train. Red Cloud slid from his horse and flattened himself against the ground at the crest of a hill overlooking the camp. Almost all of the wagons were smoldering, burned down to the axles. Bodies lay strewn about, and huge flocks of buzzards busily picked the carcasses clean. Red Cloud inched closer. Mixed in among the white bodies were those of

Indians. But the corpses were so bloated, it was impossible to identify them.

Commanding Wounded Elk to stand guard, Red Cloud crept toward the train. He reached the first wagon, and the stench made his stomach heave. He hid behind the wagon, peering out to make sure this wasn't a trap. Satisfied as to his safety, he moved to another wagon and another. All around were the scalped and brutalized bodies of the settlers. As he approached one of the bodies, a large turkey buzzard challenged him. Its beady black eyes defied him for the carrion at his feet, but Red Cloud didn't give ground, and the bird hopped off toward another victim.

With his toe, Red Cloud shoved the body over onto its back. The pattern of his own war paint, his own carefully chosen colors, glared back at him. He squatted down and examined the bloated face closer. There was something about this warrior, something . . . He rocked back on his heels. Crow! They were Crow! But why his war paint? Why had they wanted the settlers to believe his people responsible? Red Cloud glanced around. Perhaps this was a ruse, an attempt on his life. He'd defeated the Crow soundly in a battle not many moons before.

A woman's body, arms and legs snarled, stretched out on the ground in front of him. Her white gown was stained red with blood. Where were Anna and the baby? Frantically, he began to turn over all the bodies, but without success. At the end of camp he spotted a pile of charred lumber. Wolves had dislodged some of the boards by digging. Red Cloud dropped to his knees and yanked aside the boards. The hem of a woman's gown appeared. Throwing dirt in a fan behind him, he tore at the ground until Anna's bloated face poked out. He scratched around the body, but the baby wasn't there. Slumping to the ground, Red Cloud covered his face with his hands and wailed his own death song.

The stench from the body overcame him, and he vomited the little he'd eaten that day. Weak and drained, he lay in the dirt beside his wife. Suddenly, his eyes focused on a bit of leather clinging to one of the boards. He reached out and pulled it loose. The single piece of fringe from a buckskin shirt held a brilliant blue bead. He ran the bit of leather between his fingers. The baby was missing, and now this. White Eagle. He had the child.

Red Cloud scrambled to his feet and circled the site. Buzzards' three-toed tracks and the coyotes digging had almost obliterated the trail, but he eventually found the trail he sought—White Eagle's slightly off balance moccasin tread, placing his right foot heavier than his left. Alongside he found two more sets of tracks, one narrow set of boot prints, and another wider set.

Red Cloud followed the tracks up the hill. An empty whiskey bottle lay atop cold ashes. Dried blood spots soaked into the sand in several places. He touched the red stains. White Eagle was injured. Following the trail, he found a wagon tread and the hoofprints of a shod horse. A low whistle brought Wounded Elk with the horses. Red Cloud mounted his pony and turned toward the distant mountains. He'd have his son back.

Eric Tolbert huddled in a thicket of brush and watched Red Cloud and Wounded Elk. He was feverish from lack of water and sleep, but his mind had sharpened. His thoughts were now crystal clear, not clouded as they were when he had to look at that bitch and that little Indian bastard every day. No, sir, now he could think perfectly clearly, and he knew Red Cloud would go after McCall and the baby.

He'd seen the wagon master leave with the baby, but then his mind was fuzzy, and he could figure no way to follow. Now Red Cloud would lead him straight to them. He'd kill the baby and McCall and put his past behind him forever, put behind him the betrayal and the embarrassment. He could return home and begin life again. A new crop of pretty, young girls would be of age now, and he could relate his tales of the West again, make them gasp and cover their mouths with horror. In fact, he could already feel his body responding in anticipation of their soft, sweet flesh.

He shook his head free of daydreams and led his captured horse out of the brush. He'd give the Lakota a head start, and then he'd follow. In their stupidity, they'd never know he was there.

Chapter Ten

When Josie returned, Caleb had taken the pan of water into the alcove, drawn the curtain, and begun to bathe. She blushed at the sound of sloshing water, remembering the many times she'd done the same when he was unconscious.

Heating another pan of water, she prepared to bathe the baby to keep her mind off the naked male beyond the curtain. Many years had passed since she'd cared for a baby. Her sister's brood had kept her busy at home while girlhood fantasies filled her head. On the threshold of womanhood, she had longed for a man and babies of her own to hold and love. Then . . . She shook her head. No, she wouldn't think about that anymore.

Josie unwrapped the baby from his blanket and soiled diaper, then lifted him into her arms. His tiny copper face split into a smile as the cool air hit his warm skin, and he wiggled in her grasp.

"You like that, don't you?" She lowered him into the pan of water, where he smiled and kicked as she squeezed the cloth over his chest.

"You look like you were born to that," Caleb said softly, pulling back the curtain.

His brown curls held tiny beads of water even though he rubbed it with the ragged towel. He stood on his own, leaning against the bed for support, naked from the waist up. The two curls lying on his forehead made him look boyish and yet handsome—something Josie found uncomfortable in such a small cabin.

"Like I said before, I ain't never had much use for babies," she said gruffly.

"You and your husband never had a child?" he asked, pursuing her unanswered question from before.

"He died when he was born." She turned her attention back to the baby, and silence fell between them.

"I'm sorry." A wave of weakness overcame Caleb. He sat down on the bed and leaned back against the pillows. The stubborn set of her jaw said she wouldn't answer any more questions on the subject, although his curiosity burned. Crossing his arms over his chest, he watched as she finished the baby's bath. He hadn't taken a really good look at a woman in many years—even longer, since he'd vowed never to marry again. These days his imagination drifted to a life in a cabin much like this one. An isolated cabin far up in the mountains, far away from the infractions of the coming settlers, alone with only the mountains and a woman that was totally his.

She is attractive, he decided, turning his head to watch Josie smile at the baby—even wearing the ragged breeches and cast-off shirt. Curly hair made tiny wisps around her face. Underneath the men's clothes, her slim curves were those of a mature woman. She certainly affected him like a mature woman, and Emmy's words rang once again in his ears. "A good man like you, Caleb, needs a good woman."

Finished with the baby's bath, Josie laid him on the table while she fastened on a clean diaper and wrapped him in a clean blanket. She put him up on her shoulder. His tiny brown face peeked out, and Caleb laughed. "He likes you. I think you ought to give him a name."

Abruptly, she handed him the child. Not much chance of a husband for her with Pa around. She'd faced that fact soon after Johnny's death. Pa'd made it clear no man would tie himself to the likes of her. The best she'd ever do would be to live with and look after him and his boys. No one would burden themselves with a widow with no property and no prospects, he'd told her often enough.

"Come over here and talk to me." Caleb patted the cushioned bottom of the rocking chair beside the bed.

"I cain't. I got to git supper started." She reached beneath the sink and started rattling pots and pans around. "Pa'll be powerful mad if it ain't ready on time."

"Have you always lived here with him? Since your husband's death, I mean."

Josie turned toward him. He was looking down at the baby, smiling. She sighed and dragged out a pot for supper. He could stir up a mess of questions, and she'd talked more to him than she had to anybody in the last four years. The only way to shut him up was to give him some kind of answer. "I was born in Tennessee. During the War Between the States, everything was so tore apart, Pa wanted to leave and come west. Most of the men at home left to fight." She snorted in disgust. "But not Pa."

"We all set out, five wagons of us—me and Ma and Pa, and some neighbors. That's where I met Johnny, on the wagon train. He was my husband." She glanced over at Caleb, but his head rested against the pillows, his eyes closed. His strength was slow in coming back, and that suited her just fine. The only thing that made the days and nights bearable now was him. She wanted to beg him to stay, but she didn't dare. With a heavy sigh, she sat down and began to peel a pile of potatoes—and daydream.

* * *

The sound of scuffing chairs and heavy boots awoke Caleb. He struggled up in the bed and found the cabin filled with Bull and his miners as they trooped in to eat the evening meal Josie had prepared. Caleb noticed she didn't eat with them, content to stand back and serve, offering refills of coffee and food from the stove. Her face was flushed from the heat, and a few tendrils of hair had drifted down her cheeks and hung in damp ringlets in front of her ears. Her eyes darted quickly from her father to the other men, anticipating their needs before they voiced them. Caleb felt a sudden revulsion at the subservient way her own kin treated her.

Across the table, Petey ate in silence, but he cast sympathetic glances toward his sister. She intercepted each one, communicating with him in a secret way. Out of the entire family, only Petey seemed to acknowledge Josie's presence at all. Petey took a fresh biscuit from the plate and slipped it into his lap. He glanced over at Josie again, and as Bull took the last one, Caleb knew Petey's biscuit was for Josie.

After their meal, the men filed outside to sit and swap lies, as was their habit each night. Petey hung back, then slipped Josie the biscuit as she passed. She squeezed his arm gently.

Once the cabin was clear, she fixed her own plate and Caleb's. She sat down at the cluttered table and ate, casting furtive glances toward the door as though she were afraid of being caught.

Darkness had closed in around them when they finished. Josie quickly set the cabin to rights, fed the baby, and handed him to Caleb. She drew the curtain closed on the alcove with him inside, and he could hear her rustling clothing outside. Then she blew out all the lamps except the one that made a rosy circle on the inside of the curtain. Caleb closed his eyes. The curtain swished as she closed it, and the rocker groaned as she sat down. He didn't open his eyes, preferring to prolong the mystery. The scent of roses intertwined with the smells of supper. Obviously, the only feminine necessity she had was a bar of rose-scented soap stashed somewhere. Her breathing was soft and even and arousing. He shifted uneasily in the bed, and the baby protested for a moment with a sleepy whine. Her fragrance swirled around him, accompanied by the gentle swish of the rocking chair.

When Caleb awoke, he felt stronger. He was restless, eager for the outdoors, eager to find Red Cloud and return his son, eager to leave this woman who tantalized him to near distraction. Josie's moving about in the early dawn had awakened him. She had stirred around in the kitchen, filling the coffeepot and poking the fire to life. Her white gown barely discernible in the darkness, she had knelt and peered into the firebox of the cookstove, pulling the light cotton fabric tightly across her body.

His eyes darted to the chair at his side. A blanket hung over the arm, and he guiltily realized she still slept sitting straight up in the chair, giving him the comfort of her bed. He reached over, laid his hand on the blanket, and her heat warmed his palm. His heartbeat quickened at the thought of her so near all through the night, and the memory of his dreams troubled him deeply.

The combined snoring of Bull and his men would cover an Indian attack, Caleb thought as he sought to cover his ears with the pillow to block out the noise. He'd turned over and was about to close his eyes, when he noticed Josie had stepped closer to the bunk beds, peering down into the men's faces. Moving toward the nail that held her clothes, she cast one more glance backward, then pulled her gown over her head. In the dim light, her body was a ghostly softness, her curves full and smooth, her hair a long, dark shadow around her shoulders. Caleb knew he should look away, but his eyes had a will of their own, and he stared at her nakedness unashamedly. She took her shirt from the nail, pulled it over firm breasts, and buttoned the front. Then she took down the soiled denim pants and pulled them up fine, long legs. She stuffed her shirttail hurriedly into the pants when she heard a set of feet hit the floor.

Bull sat on the edge of his bunk, holding his head in his hands. He coughed once and spat a plug of mucus onto the floor. Then he rose, scratched, and ambled outside to relieve himself. Without a word of complaint, she took a handful of leaves caught up in the firewood, wiped up the spit, and threw them into the fire.

Caleb softly turned over, putting his back to her. His anger flared as he thought of the conditions and treatment she received from her own father. The Lakota treat their women with honor, he thought ironically. His thoughts drifted to Emmy's neat, comfortable house back in Independence. That's where she belongs, he thought, the scene playing out in his mind. In a white house with sheer curtains ruffling in the breeze, wearing a fine white gown waiting for—Suddenly, the image of the man coming home to her appeared in his mind and the meaning of his thoughts hit him. No! He was too old to think about such. He was too old to . . . marry. Wasn't he?

"You ought to get yourself a woman, Caleb, and get some children." Again, Emmy's words rang in his ears.

From that moment, he began to see Josie in a different way. Instead of the streak of dirt on her face, he noticed the soft curve of her lips and how she pursed them when faced with a problem. Instead of the cracked nails, he noticed long, slender hands. Instead of grimy, slick clothes, he noticed delicate curves underneath, neatly outlined by her lack of undergarments. She deserved some time off. And, by God, as soon as he could, he'd see to it she got just that.

After Josie had finished breakfast for her father's army, Caleb sat up on the edge of the bed, testing the steadiness of his feet on the floor.

"You sure you're ready for that?" she questioned, watching him from the stove where she warmed milk for the baby.

"I want to get outside and sit in the sun. Come with me."

"Oh, no. I gotta git dinner started or Pa'll—"

"I don't care what Pa says. Come outside with me." Caleb held out his hand.

She smiled a slow smile that crinkled the corners of her blue eyes. Caleb guessed she did that all too rarely.

"All right, for a little while. But you gotta take half the beatin' if Pa catches us," she teased, an irresistible twinkle in her eye.

"Gladly, now, help me up."

She quickly fed the baby, then laid the sleeping infant in the center of the bed with pillows piled around. Slipping her hands under Caleb's arms, she helped him steady himself on his feet. Pressed close to his bare chest, the stiff, curly hair tickled her cheek. Blushing at the intimacy of the touch, she hurried to get his shirt. He slipped his arms into the sleeves of the buckskin, pulled it over his head, and hobbled across the floor. Josie ran ahead and peeped out the door.

"This way. Got somethin' I wanna show you," she whispered conspiratorially.

Obediently, he followed her out onto the porch. He paused and inhaled deeply of the air scented with the sharp smell of pine. The view from the front porch of the cabin was magnificent, a broad green valley beneath them, spreading to the foot of another high range of mountains. The peaks of the Rockies poked above the branches of huge blue spruce and pines.

"Follow me down here. Careful now," she urged, and started off down the hill beside the house. His limping steps became surer as the slope leveled out.

She led him through a thicket of blue spruce fifty feet tall, their roots buried in a carpet of needles. Carefully holding his elbow lest he slip, she guided him over roots and fallen branches until they reached a small, open meadow. Thousands of columbine lifted their exquisite flowers toward the morning sun. Red, blue, yellow, and white, the blooms filled every inch of the meadow in a riot of color.

"Ain't it purdy? I come here when Pa don't know. Makes me feel calm in here." She laid her hand over her heart, and Caleb felt his own heart lurch at the happiness in her voice. Her eyes sparkled with anticipation until she met his, then her glance slid away.

Caleb limped out to where the columbine grew as high as his waist on the glacial-rich soil of the alpine meadow. Josie followed and pointed toward a large rock sticking out of the cloud of flowers. More tired than he cared to admit after the short walk, Caleb sat down. Josie sat beside him. She reached out and picked a handful of the fragrant flowers, then held them to her nose.

The stillness filled their ears, broken only occasionally by the distant, haunting call of an eagle. Caleb plucked a brilliant blue blossom and tucked it behind Josie's ear. She turned toward him. There wasn't a trace of the foul-mouthed urchin who had confounded his life for the past weeks in the face that smiled up at him. In her place was a very young, very vulnerable woman who had already experienced too much pain.

"Tell me about your husband," Caleb asked, letting his fingers linger in her hair.

Josie sighed and looked away toward the distant peaks. "I met up with him on the wagon train. His family had joined the bunch of us going west. He was some older than me, and I fell in love with him the minute I saw him."

Something about the wistful way she said that made a chill run over Caleb.

"He was tall and blond, and he could outshoot any man on the train. Pa, he didn't like the idea at first when Johnny spoke for me. Said he needed me on the farm we was goin' to buy out west. But Johnny, he had a way about him, and he charmed Pa till he said yes."

Her expression changed, and she turned. "Then we run into a bunch of men who talked about finding gold out here, and Pa got the fever. He forgot all about the farm. All he thought 'bout was findin' gold and gittin' rich. He stopped in Fort

Laramie and wired my brothers in Tennessee for 'em to come out and hit it big along with him. I found out I was pregnant about two months after we got married.'' She smiled sadly. ''Musta happened on our wedding night.''

Tears sprang to her eyes, and Caleb knew he should stop her from dredging up painful memories, but he wanted to know more, to know everything about her.

''It was rough crossing the prairie and we was just about in the mountains when my time come. Ma and me delivered the baby in the back of the wagon while Pa and Johnny fretted outside. It was a little boy, like Johnny wanted.''

The threatened tears coursed down her face as she talked, and Caleb wondered if she'd ever told anybody else these things. ''What happened to him?'' he asked softly.

With both hands Josie wiped at her cheeks. ''We was down there at the foot of the mountains when the Injuns found us. They'd been a-following us for a long time, and Pa knew it. We'd made it that far on our own without a scout, and Pa thought we'd be safe once we was in the mountains.''

''You mean you weren't with a train?''

''No. Oh, no. Pa wouldn't wait for a wagon train.'' She shook her head. ''He was so het up about the gold, he grumped all the time somebody was gittin' his. Anyway, the Injuns found us late one night.'' Wrapping her arms around herself, she rose and stepped away. ''We was asleep in the wagon, me and Ma, and Johnny and Pa was sleeping outside, under it. They come outta nowhere. We didn't hear a sound till they started shootin' arrows into the wagon. Pa, he jumped up and . . . and run into the trees . . . and left Johnny to fight 'em on his own.''

Her voice wavered and her shoulders shook. ''He stood 'em off as long as he could. Ma and me were shooting from inside the wagon, but one crept up and jerked open the cover. He saw Ma first and dragged her out. The last time I saw her—''

Her voice broke, and Caleb longed to wrap her in his arms and tell her nothing else bad was ever going to happen to her. But he stayed seated, watching the heaving of her shoulders.

"The last time I saw her they was dragging her away into the dark. The same Injun reached for me, but Johnny stuck his skinning knife in that one's back and kilt him. Then a whole bunch of 'em come up. They grabbed Johnny . . . and ripped off his clothes. Then they started cutting away little—little pieces of him, little slivers of his skin."

Josie bowed her head and sat down. "It was a long time 'fore he died." She covered her face with her hands and cried.

Caleb knew about torture. His blood ran cold at the thought of dying that way. Hesitantly, he put his arm around her shaking shoulders and drew her to his chest. The water from her tears ran between her fingers and made small circles on the leather of his buckskin pants.

He put his hand behind her head and pressed her face to his shoulder. Her sobs shook his body, and he gently caressed her back. Slowly, she let her arms slip up around his neck, and a fire burst forth in Caleb. He let his arms drop lower and pulled her tightly against him, his chin resting on her hair. She looked up, an expression of surprise beneath her tears. He dipped his head and captured her lips, hungry for the softness of a woman. Her gasp of surprise was a soft intake of breath, then she responded, moving her lips seductively beneath his. He shifted his position and clasped her closer to him. Through the fog of passion filling his mind, he tried to remember when was the last time he'd kissed a woman.

Her soft surrender to his caresses further fired his wants. With difficulty, he pulled free of the kiss. "We'd better get back," he said softly.

Josie pushed away, her cheeks flaming. He saw the humiliation in her face, saw the wall that shielded her against the world go back up, and he cursed himself for his impetuousness.

"You're right. We better git home. Pa'll come looking for us, and I sure don't want him to find this place." She reached to help him stand.

He caught her hand and held it a second, looking up into the depths of her cobalt eyes. "Josie . . . I . . ."

"Don't say nothing," she pleaded sadly. "Leave well enough alone. Don't spoil it." She helped him to his feet, drawing his arm about her shoulders.

He hopped stiffly back across the meadow toward the trees. If she noticed the reaction she had on him, she didn't let on, and he silently willed his body to behave itself.

Far above the meadow, a rocky outcropping gave Bull a clear view, and he ground his teeth as he watched the embrace below. If not for the girl, his wife might be there today to feed him and warm his bed. He swore and clutched his rifle tightly. By God, Josie was a better shot than to let the savages take his Emily. After all, he himself had taught her to shoot when she was a child. But over the years he'd made her pay for her mistake.

The strange man she'd dragged home was falling in love with her. He'd known from the start it would happen when he put her in charge of his care. Ordinarily, he didn't hold with allowing unmarried women to nurse injured or ill men, but he made an exception in this case. After all, she'd been married once and had had a child.

He was desperate for help in the mine, and Josie was his best chance to acquire that help. Things were beginning to fall into place. Once she bedded the stranger, she'd have him hooked and he wouldn't want to leave her. She'd make it plain she had no intention of going away and leaving her poor old father to fend for himself. Then he'd have another strong back for the mine.

He was close to a strike. He could feel it in each bucketful of worthless rock he carried out of the ground. Very soon he'd be a rich man, and he'd no longer have any use for his sorry offspring. Bull licked his lips as he watched Josie melt in Caleb's arms. Yes, the man'd fall all right, and fall hard if Johnny was any indication of her abilities. Yes, sir, very soon now he could quit this rocky and desolate piece of ground and move west, west to green, bountiful Oregon. Once there, he'd buy land and raise horses, and maybe farm a little, enough to keep his hand in it, he dreamed.

He shook his head and realized the two had left the meadow and were headed for the cabin. He had to hurry, he thought as he turned away and scurried down the hill. He had to beat Josie to the cabin and scold her for being late with supper. Maybe he'd knock her around some this time just to make the stranger more sympathetic toward her. Bull grinned foolishly as he hurried, half walking and half sliding down the rubble-strewn hillside.

Chapter Eleven

Bull rounded the corner of the cabin when Josie and Caleb emerged from the spruce wood. His face flushed red with anger, he fell into step beside her, inches from her ear, shouting at her with every step.

"I expect my dinner to be ready when I git here, girlie," he roared, shoving a blackened face into hers. "What do you think I'm gonna eat, eh? You want me to have to fix it myself after I've worked all day in the mine?" His yellowed teeth clicked together as he talked.

Josie stopped abruptly and spun to face her father. They glared at each other for several seconds.

"After all I've done for you, is the way you repay me?" Bull glanced over at Caleb, moved around in front of Josie, and stood in her path, forcing her to stop in front of him. Lightning-quick, he smacked her full in the face.

Josie reeled backward a step or two. Caleb slapped his thigh for his revolver, then remembered he hadn't worn one since Josie brought him there. He lunged at Bull and grabbed his arms with more strength than he thought he'd regained. The surprised look on Bull's face said he, too, had underestimated Caleb's condition.

"Let go, McCall. This is none of your affair," Bull ground out, narrowing his eyes.

"It's all right." Josie gently laid her hand on Caleb's arm while holding the side of her flaming cheek. "It's my fault. I shoulda been here."

Caleb met and held the old miner's eyes, silently promising swift retribution if it ever happened again. Then he reluctantly let his hands drop.

Bull quirked the corner of his mouth, a small, evil smile that said he'd gained an advantage. "Now, git along in there and fix me and my boys something to eat." He shoved Josie, hitched up his filthy pants, and stalked after his daughter, leaving Caleb standing in the yard, feeling helpless.

Later, after having eaten their fill, the men filed outside and wandered back down toward the mine. Hoping for another small grasp of authority, Bull stayed a few more minutes to hound Josie with threats if supper was late again. Then, with a triumphant look, he stalked out of the cabin and followed his men down into the gully.

Caleb intentionally stayed out of the cabin while the miners ate, afraid of what he would do if he came too close to Bull. The baby would need a cradle board and he'd seen some vines just in the edge of the forest.

Josie didn't look up from cleaning off the table when he hobbled in, his arms laden with aspen branches and vines. Her cheek bore a red handprint. She glanced up as he let the wood fall to the floor, then looked away. "What's that for?" she asked.

"To make a cradle board for the baby." When she didn't answer, Caleb stepped closer. "Does this happen often?" he asked, touching her cheek.

Josie flinched and stepped away. "Don't matter. It's a sorry mess I've gone and got myself in, but ain't no cure for it." She made a last swipe at the table with the dishcloth.

"You ever thought about leaving, going back to Tennessee?" With a groan, Caleb eased himself down into a wobbly chair.

Josie shrugged. "They're all I got. What am I going to do? Go back to Tennessee alone?"

"What about your brother Davie? Can't you stay with him?"

Josie's laugh was bitter and dry. "Davie, he turned out the bunch of us years ago. Said he wanted better in life. Said he didn't have no use for no-counts."

It was on the tip of Caleb's tongue to say, "Come and go with me," but he bit back the words. What was the matter with him? In a few short days he'd managed to make a complete fool of himself. He was far past the age of acting like an idiot over a woman, he thought. But then, he'd also thought he was past the age of wanting a woman as badly as he wanted Josie.

Josie met his eyes over the table, dishcloth poised in midair. He realized several seconds had passed.

"I thought ... maybe ... maybe ..."

Josie frowned, and Caleb let his words drift off. Shrugging her shoulders, she continued to scrub at the table. "Pa ain't so bad. Least he took me in when Johnny died. I was another mouth to feed."

"Out of the goodness of his heart?"

"Somethin' like that." Josie avoided his eyes and rinsed out the dishcloth.

Bull and his boys reappeared at dusk, and Josie had supper on the table for them. Without a word of thanks to either her or the Lord, they dug into the food. Morsels dropped onto the floor, and Josie stood to the side, ready with broom and cloth to clean up their messes.

Caleb couldn't eat. He'd eaten some things he wasn't proud of in some places he didn't like to think about, but the sight of these grown men slobbering over their food like hogs was more than he could take. His developing hatred for Bull Hardwick deepened.

When the men filed outside, Josie fixed Caleb and herself a plate and wiped clean a small place on the table. Darkness crept in around them, exchanging the day's sounds for the night's. The cabin was quiet except for the occasional clink of a fork against a tin plate.

The gathering twilight softened Josie's face. As she ate daintily, careful not to drop a crumb, Caleb's gaze was drawn to her lips again and again.

Josie glanced up when Caleb's chair protested as he shifted and dropped his eyes to his plate. He had been watching her again. She could feel his eyes on her. His long, tapered fingers played with his fork, pushing food around on his plate. The ridges of her spine tingled, remembering where those fingers had caressed.

All too soon Bull and the boys tromped back inside. Josie turned her head as they stripped down to their filthy underwear and flopped into their bunks.

"Petey, you git out in the morning and check them rabbit boxes we set. I'm mighty hungry for some fresh meat."

"Yes, Pa," Petey answered from the dark.

"Yore worthless for everything else, boy. Maybe you can find us somethin' to eat besides these damned beans." Bull accentuated his words with a loud passage of gas.

Snores soon filled the air, and Josie blew out the last of the lamps. Faint moonlight lit the baby, peacefully asleep in the crook of Caleb's arm, his little fists straight over his head.

"Here, you take the bed tonight." Caleb stood, walked into the other room, and yanked back the covers. "I'll sleep outside in my bedroll."

"Are you sure? How's your leg?" Josie rose and followed him.

"It's fine." He handed her the baby. "I've taken your bed long enough." He couldn't tell her the scent of her in the bed covers was driving him mad with want. "I'll leave the baby here with you. He'll have to spend enough nights outside once we're on the trail.'' A strained silence fell between them. Until that moment, there'd been no mention of his leaving.

''You'll leave soon, then?'' she said after a pause.

''I thought maybe in a few days.''

Without a word, she turned away and began to gather up dishes.

Caleb fetched his bedroll from his saddle and spread it out on the front porch. He lay down and pulled his hat over his eyes. The night was cool and damp, and he reached down and pulled up the blanket. The sharp scent of pine sap filled the damp night air. From far away came the hauntingly lonely cry of a wolf. Caleb could sympathize with his plight. Josie made him think about things he thought he'd left behind years before in a Lakota camp when he buried Fawn and his daughter. Those years, although long past, held precious memories for him, memories of home and hearth, of Fawn waiting for him in their tipi at nightfall, of the softness of a woman's body joined with his in the dark, of knowing she was totally his.

A soft rustle at his side alerted him. He slid his hand beneath his blanket for his gun. Josie softly closed the door behind her. Her hair tumbled loosely down her back over an old worn wrapper. Caleb raised his hand to touch her, then jerked it back.

''Couldn't sleep.'' She sat down on the edge of the porch by his side. ''Thought I'd come out and git a breath of fresh air.'' She avoided his eyes and swung her bare feet back and forth.

She'd lied. She'd hardly had time to try and sleep. Caleb shifted and turned onto his side.

''Tell me about your wife,'' she asked in that mellow drawl of hers, keeping her face carefully turned away. ''Did you love her, or did you marry her for . . . your comfort.''

Her neck was smooth and creamy in the low light. The ragged gown hung seductively off one shoulder.

''I loved her. Very much.'' Her frank question didn't anger him as it once had when others asked about his past. Some men did marry Indian women—squaws, they called them—in order to have someone to cook and clean and for sex.

"How 'bout yore young'un?"

"How'd you know I had a child?"

Josie shrugged. "You talked when you was feverish."

"That must have been some conversation I had with myself."

"You did ramble on some." She turned toward him, waiting expectantly.

"My daughter was killed when she was a baby." The words rushed out.

A flash of sorrow passed over Josie's face. "What happened?"

Caleb sighed and put his arms behind his head. Absently studying the boards above him, he let the memories come flowing back. "The Lakota raised me. Fawn and I were children together. When we were old enough, I took her as my wife."

"Was she purdy?" Josie stared out across the moonlit yard, her face turned so he couldn't read her thoughts.

"She was the most beautiful woman I had ever seen."

Josie shivered and drew her wrapper tighter.

"We married in the autumn on a day that the aspens rained yellow leaves." His wistful smile was like a knife in her heart, and she ached with the jealousy that suddenly rose in her.

"Our village sat in a grove of trees," he continued. "The children ran through them, rolled in them. Those first days were . . . wonderful. By late spring she was pregnant."

Caleb pushed up on his elbows and kicked aside the blanket. "The baby was born in the dead of a terrible winter. Food was scarce and the weather was brutal." He looked out toward the mountains, their snow-covered tops shining in the moonlight. "Late one night—" His voice broke, and he ran a hand through his hair. "Late one night, a band of Crow attacked the camp. They killed women, tiny children, the old, and as many of the warriors as they could, including the war chief. Our village was too small to fend off such a large attack." He turned to face her. "Fawn and the baby died instantly."

Josie tucked her hand beneath her armpit to keep from reaching out to him, afraid of his rejection.

"I was stunned, in shock," Caleb continued. "We covered ourselves with ashes and tore our hair in grief. Some of the Lakota talked of war with the Crow, but others urged caution. The dead of winter on the plains was no time to wage war, the elders warned. So we waited until the spring. By then the Crow were gone."

Josie stared at her feet. Her memories of Johnny were brief, fading more over the last few years. Now she had trouble remembering what he'd looked like. Beside her in the dark, Caleb sighed softly, and she found herself envious of the Indian maid who had known Caleb McCall intimately, envious of the nights they slept together, envious of the child she'd borne him.

"You still reckon Crow burned the wagon train?"

Caleb nodded and sat up on the porch's edge. "The Crow fear Red Cloud because he has powerful medicine. They must know about the baby. He's Red Cloud's weakness, and they know that. If I get him back to his father and he decides to live among the Lakota, he will one day be chief. The Crow think he carries the same medicine as his father."

She glanced at Caleb. The want in his eyes mirrored burning within her. She didn't resist when he slid an arm across her shoulders and pulled her closer. He slipped his hand into her hair and pulled her face toward his. The now-familiar scent of aged leather rose to meet her as he gathered her to him. His lips came down on hers, and he drew in a shaking breath as he pulled her to him and fell back onto the blanket. Josie sprawled across his chest, entangling her hands in his hair. His hands, gentle and warm, stroked the length of her back and brushed across her hips.

Startlingly aware of his arousal and sensitive to his building wants, she couldn't bring herself to pull away. Something in her longed to be touched, to be loved, to be held. She blindly followed as his hands swept lower, sending tingles up her spine.

His heart thudded against her chest, its thumping increasing with each caress. The trembling in his arms told her he struggled to control his long-neglected needs.

The fabric of her threadbare gown slid up her thigh, and the cool night air against heated skin made gooseflesh pop out on her.

"We oughtn't be doing this," she murmured into his neck.

"Uh-huh," he murmured as his hands roved up her rib cage and brushed across her breasts in slow, mesmerizing strokes. She threw one leg across him, and his hand followed its creamy length down her thigh, almost to her knee, then moved up. She groaned against his lips as he brushed over the warmth of her inner thighs.

He wrapped his arms around her and rolled as though to pull her beneath him. Then he stopped abruptly. His eyes flew open. He broke the kiss and pushed her away.

"What's wrong?" she asked, her face flushed with excitement and sudden embarrassment.

"I can't." He sat up and swung his legs over the edge of the porch. "I can't do this to you." He arched his back and put his head in his hands. "And I would have too." He raised his eyes to meet hers. "Right here on your father's porch."

Josie jerked the front of her wrapper together and flung back her hair. Humiliation and sorrow burned across her face. She felt like a whore. Hell, she had acted like a whore.

Caleb cursed himself. What had this woman done to him, to his well-ordered life. Making love to a man's daughter on his front porch? What was he thinking of? *You weren't thinking, McCall.*

"Josie." His fingers brushed her cheek. "I'm sorry. It has nothing to do with you. I promised myself when Fawn died . . ." Her look withered his words. He felt the ache of her pain deep in his chest. Her needs were as strong as his, yet she, too, held back.

Without a word she quietly rose, went inside, and pushed the door shut with a gentle shove. Caleb lay back on his blanket.

Overhead, the stars winked knowingly. God, how he wished he had a bucket of cold water, but his knee ached and the river was too far away to limp to in the dark.

A sudden stirring in the bushes outside the clearing of the yard brought Caleb back to awareness. He reached for his revolver. The rustling came again, then a strange warbling call. The hair on the back of his neck rose, and every nerve in his body screamed. Crow! Caleb eased back the hammer of the revolver and wished for his knife in the boots inside.

The woods were silent, but he knew they were there. If he made a move, they'd be on him. He searched the dark depths of the woods. Not a leaf moved. Not a bird chirped. The forest was eerily quiet, as though poised, waiting.

Minutes passed. His hand ached from holding the gun cocked. He shifted his position. Nothing happened. He moved to get a better look at the edge of the clearing, and still nothing happened. He settled into a position feigning sleep, his revolver drawn and ready. Not until the pink of dawn filled the sky did Caleb realize he hadn't slept all night.

As soon as the sun came up, Caleb made a show of rising from his blankets. He stretched his arms far above his head, then moved off the porch toward the woods to relieve himself. He holstered the gun but left the slip of leather that held it in place hanging loose. Stepping into the edge of the forest, his eyes immediately searched the needle-littered floor for signs. Several moccasin tracks confirmed his suspicions. He squatted to examine the faint depressions in the forest floor. The tracks were too plainly in sight. The Crow wanted him to know they had brazenly stood only feet from him in the darkness. Caleb rocked back on his heels. The baby was no longer safe with him.

Josie was cleaning up the cabin after breakfast when Caleb ducked to enter the room. He paused in the doorway, watching her before she noticed his presence. He would leave here and never see her again—and for some reason that saddened him greatly.

"It's time for me to go," he said bluntly.

She jumped and turned at the sound of his voice. "You mean now? This morning?"

"We had visitors last night." Caleb strode across the room and picked up his boots. "A bunch of Crow warriors spent the night on the edge of the woods." He sat down at the table and pulled them on. "They want the baby. Red Cloud can protect him better than me."

"What you gonna do?" she asked in a shaky voice.

Caleb picked up his rifle from the corner and checked the magazine. Finding it loaded, he clicked it shut, picked up his saddlebags, and slung them over his shoulder. He stopped in front of her, hating the way her eyes implored his for an answer when he had none to give. "I'll try to find Red Cloud and return his son," Caleb said softly.

The baby cooed from his basket on the floor. Josie picked him up and pressed him to her shoulder. "Let me change him." She turned away and laid him on the bed, where she changed his diaper and clothes. Then she wrapped him tightly in his blanket.

Caleb stepped outside and picked up the cradle board he'd made from smooth aspen wood and vines. He gently fitted the baby into the board and hefted it onto his back. Josie's hands trembled as she tied it securely with rawhide straps. Tears glimmered in her eyes when he turned around.

"Josie . . ."

"Jocelyn," she whispered. "My name is Jocelyn."

"I like Josie better." Caleb put a finger beneath her chin. "It fits you."

The corners of her mouth quivered, and she looked away.

"I can't thank you enough for what you've done for us." He guided her face back toward his, making her meet his eyes.

"Woulda done the same for anybody." Playfully, she pushed at his arm. "Now, go on. Git."

Caleb started toward the door, then paused with the latch in his hand. He could feel her standing behind him, so close, in fact, that he could hear her breath making a ragged sound as she forced down her tears. In one motion he set down his rifle and swept her into his arms. He caught her tightly against the front of his leather shirt, wrapping his arms around her. Damn this predicament. He laid his face against the silkiness of her hair and rubbed it against his cheek. Damn the Crow. His lips crushed hers in a desperate kiss, trying to burn her into his memory. Damn the promise he'd lived with too long. Her gentle hands caught the back of his neck and pulled him closer. Caleb moved his lips, seducing her with their firmness, and Josie responded freely, passionately.

"Good-bye, Josie," he murmured, setting her firmly away from him. His body ached, his need for her was so great.

"Good-bye, Caleb McCall." She stepped back and laced her fingers together in front of her. Holding her head at a stubborn tilt, she fought not to give in to the storm of tears threatening to break.

Caleb moved swiftly out the door before he changed his mind. He'd saddled Cindy earlier and now he swung into the saddle and gathered the reins. Cindy pranced forward, and Caleb stopped her as Josie came out of the cabin.

"Remember me?" She stepped to his side and lifted her face.

"Now, how would I forget a dirty muleskinner like you?"

She smiled even though her eyes swam with tears. No knife would ever cut him as deeply as the pain in her eyes. He turned toward the wood, and soon the branches and needles of the spruce forest swallowed her up.

Chapter Twelve

When Caleb lost sight of the cabin, he turned north toward Powder River country. That's where Red Cloud would have taken his band of people for the winter, Caleb reasoned.

Golden leaves peppered him as he wound his way down the mountain. Cindy daintily stepped over roots jutting up into her path. A shallow stream gushed over rocks, cutting through a steep ravine. He pulled Cindy to a stop and allowed her to drink. After kicking his feet loose from the stirrups, he threw one leg over the saddle horn and stared into the water. Vague images of the time he was sick drifted through his mind.

He remembered very little, only disjointed and jumbled images of Josie's face above him and of the bumpy ride in the wagon. He remembered pain, scorching pain, as if his leg were on fire. But above the pain he remembered her hands—firm, gentle hands tending him, comforting him, reassuring him.

He dismounted and sat down on a convenient rock. Josie's face floated before him, teasing the uncertainty in his mind about leaving. The last image he summoned was the way she'd looked last night when he pushed her away—her cheeks flushed and her raven hair tumbling about her shoulders. Scuffing at a pebble on the ground, he cursed himself again as he'd done often that morning for the rules he'd imposed on himself. Why did he still feel he'd betray Fawn if he took another woman to wife?

Caleb looked up at the sun that shone down through a canopy of yellowing aspen leaves. It was nearly noon. Soon he'd have to stop and eat, but for now he wanted as much distance as possible between himself and Josie. That way he couldn't change his mind. He swung back into the saddle and punched Cindy gently in the sides.

She had begun to pick her way down the mountain again, when something red among the cascade of yellow leaves caught his eye. Caleb started to pass it, disregarding it as another leaf or his imagination, when Cindy pricked her ears forward and flared her nostrils. She nickered softly and backed away from the dense wood facing them. Caleb urged her on. She refused to move and backed up another step.

Squinting into the wood, Caleb drew his gun and stepped down off her back. He dropped the reins on the ground, and with a gentle pat and soft word he moved toward the splash of red. A rotting log a few feet from the edge of the obscure trail held an arrow identical to the one left in the Crockett wagon. Red, yellow, and blue slashes angled across the shaft. Caleb jerked it loose. The paint was fresh . . . and recent. From the feathered end dangled an amulet. Caleb jerked the necklace free and held it up. A tiny, finely beaded pouch of soft leather in the shape of a turtle hung from a rawhide string decorated with colorful quills. A chill rippled down his spine as he ran his finger over the beading. He pulled open the bag hardly bigger than his thumb and poured out a pile of soft, gray ashes into his open hand.

Fawn's mother had made and beaded the pouch to hold the ashes of his daughter's umbilical cord. Caleb ground his teeth at the irony. Carefully kept ashes warded off evil and brought good luck.

Hot tears stung the backs of his eyes as he turned the necklace over and over in his hands. On the day she was born, he'd crept around the tipi and peeked inside through a slit in the back. A man's presence, any man, was forbidden at a birth, but he'd been frantic about Fawn. Through the slit he'd seen her calmly squatted in the center of the lodge, grasping a pole firmly embedded in the ground. Her buckskin dress piled up around her waist and an old woman of the tribe, a midwife, sat near her feet, holding a soft piece of young buffalo hide.

Perspiration dampened the long, dark hair that clung to Fawn's flushed forehead and cheeks. As he watched, she threw back her head. He knew she wanted to scream. She wouldn't. All Lakota births were accomplished in silence.

Suddenly, the old woman scrambled to her knees and placed her hands between Fawn's legs. Fawn ducked her head between her elbows and strained mightily. A small red form emerged part of the way from her body. She bore down again and a wet, slick baby slid out. The old woman caught the baby in the buffalo hide. She held the child by its heels as thin mucus streamed from its mouth. Then the infant began to cry softly. The old woman had smiled and laid the baby on a bed of furs. Then she took hold of the cord still attached to Fawn's body. She held it for an instant, then gave it a yank. A large, slippery mass slid out, and Fawn collapsed onto the fur bed. Carefully, the old woman had wrapped the afterbirth in a soft skin and disappeared from the tent to hang it in a tree to dry.

A few days later she would return, cut a length from the now-dry membrane, and carefully deposit it into the tiny bag. The child would now, according to custom, enjoy good fortune. Caleb smiled and rubbed the soft leather between his fingers. All that was left of his beautiful daughter were these few ashes.

They're close, he thought as he glanced over his shoulder. In fact, he felt as if they were all around him, taunting him, playing with him like a cat with a mouse. Tucking the beaded pouch safely into his jacket, he ran back to Cindy and sprang

into the saddle. Kicking her into flight, he headed back up the
mountain toward Josie.

Josie stood on the porch and looked after Caleb for a long
time after he disappeared into the spruce forest. She'd hoped
at first he might change his mind and come back. He hadn't
returned. She shrugged and went back inside to begin the end-
less cleaning. Why'd she even bother? she thought as she kicked
at a biscuit lying on the floor. The place would look and smell
the same once the men finished their supper.

She took down the water bucket from its rusty nail, jerked
on her old ragged coat and the felt hat. As she opened the door,
something zinged by her head and struck the log wall with a
thud. She whirled. An arrow, its shaft still quivering, had
embedded itself in the door facing. She froze where she stood,
unable to move her feet or her arms. The woods seemed alive
as she slowly turned her head and scanned the edge of the
clearing.

Another arrow sailed past her head and stuck waist level in
the logs. Josie dropped the bucket and fled inside. She slammed
the massive door behind her, bolted it shut, and secured the
shutters over the windows. *Petey,* she thought with an eerie
feeling. *I wonder where Petey is. And Pa and the boys.*

She lit a lantern and turned the wick low to give off only a
dull glow in the semidarkness of the barricaded cabin. She
carefully took down the old Hawken rifle that hung over the
fireplace. A bag of black powder and a small pouch of lead
balls hung on the end of the gun.

Her hands shook badly as she stood the old gun on its stock
and poured a small amount of the powder into the end of the
barrel. The soft black powder spilled across her hands and onto
the floor. She withdrew the tamping rod from under the barrel
and rammed down the powder. Then she put in a patch of cloth
and tamped it down also. She dropped the lead ball down the

barrel and rammed it home. After replacing the rod, she was ready.

The front window had a small hole cut into it, barely large enough to poke the end of a gun through. Josie peeped out between the shutters. The yard beyond was still, bathed in the glorious morning sun of early autumn. She moved to get a better view of the clearing around the cabin and saw nothing. The only sounds were those of birds warbling in the forest and the gentle sigh of the wind in the tops of the pines.

Minutes ticked by, and Josie's heart pounded. It must be past dinnertime, she thought, listening for the raucous sounds the men made coming up the hill toward the cabin. But the forest was still. Her palms perspired and the gun barrel grew unbearably heavy. The exertion of keeping the ancient weapon aimed out the window made her arms quiver.

Overhead, something scraped on the roof. She held her breath and listened. There, it came again! She turned her eyes toward the ceiling. They're on the roof! The scraping sound increased. They're tearing off the shingles to get in! She crossed the room, listening. A sound came from the other side of the fireplace. She shifted the gun to her left hand. For once she was glad she'd won all those shooting matches at home, even if it didn't get her any beaus.

Padding softly across the room, she paused directly beneath the sounds. She could see daylight now between the shingles. They had pried off the first layer and were struggling with the next one. Its edges were securely nailed. Josie raised the old gun and took aim dead center the moving shingle. She seated the stock of the gun firmly against her shoulder, closed her eyes, and slowly squeezed the trigger.

The roar of the gun filled the tiny space in the cabin, and Josie's ears rang. Eighteen inches of fire spewed out of the end of the barrel as a neat round hole appeared in the shingle. A heavy thud followed by scurrying feet echoed in the quietness left by the roar. The recoil from the blast sent Josie sprawling onto the floor and wedged her beneath the table. Her head swam from the impact and she wasn't sure, but she thought her shoulder was broken.

Gingerly, she crawled out from under the table. She moved her shoulder and found it was whole. The sounds from the roof had stopped. Josie tried to peer through the hole the ball made, but the light was blocked. She stepped closer and squinted. Something warm and sticky dropped into her eye. She wiped a dirty sleeve across her face. It came away a brilliant red.

Suddenly, stomping, impatient hooves pawed the yard. Josie ran to the window to peep out even as she reloaded the gun. Twenty or thirty painted warriors rode their ponies into the clearing. They stayed close to the edge of the wood, as if they knew they were out of range. A tall man sat at the center of the group, and Josie knew immediately he was the leader. His long, dark hair was tied back with a handful of eagle feathers, each one carefully cut into patterned edges. His horse's sides were covered with painted handprints. The warrior's legs were long and tanned, and he wore only a breechcloth and moccasins, even though fall nipped the air. But even the paint didn't disguise the long, ragged scar running across his bare chest and stomach.

He waved his hand, and his companions melted back into the forest. Some rode around toward the back of the cabin, and some disappeared into the wood beyond. Damn, Josie thought, and wished her father hadn't insisted on windows on the back of the house. She glanced briefly over her shoulder toward the shuttered rear windows and, seeing nothing, turned her attention back to the tall Indian.

As she watched, he moved toward her. When he reached the porch, a gentle nudge sent the horse clattering up onto the rough boards. He carried a lance decorated with quilled and trimmed eagle feathers that dangled from a stone blade. With one powerful move he stuck the lance into the wooden floor of the porch, then trotted away, back to the edge of the clearing. He turned his horse and simply sat there, watching her watch him.

Behind the cabin, she could hear the horses milling about. Memories of the night Johnny died came anew to her mind, vivid memories of faces, wild and painted into grotesque expressions. She stifled a terrified scream with the back of her hand.

"White woman!" the Indian called to her in perfect English. "We will not harm you."

"Yeah? I've heard that before, Injun." Josie heard her own voice answer with more courage than she felt.

"We want McCall and the baby. You will go free."

Her mind flew as she felt her chest tighten with fear for Caleb. Was he far enough away by now? Or was this another Indian trick? Had they already killed him and the child? Her head ached with too many thoughts.

"Do you hear the words of Crazy Elk?" the Indian shouted.

"I hear you." Josie hoped her voice sounded spunkier than she felt. "McCall ain't here. He left days ago."

"You lie. McCall was here last night. We watched you from the shadows while you lay with him." His voice held a note of sarcastic contempt.

"You're wrong, Injun. You saw me with one of the men who works with my father." He didn't answer right off, and Josie peered closely through the hole in the shutters. He sat silently on his horse, pondering what she'd said—she hoped.

"McCall is your man," he said after a lengthy pause.

"He ain't my man." Josie raised the gun up to the peephole. "I don't want no filthy man."

A smile slowly spread across the brave's face. "The white woman has not yet had a good man to teach her obedience. Maybe Crazy Elk will show her."

His sneer was evident even across the thirty or so yards between them. An idea formed in her mind. Her bravado entertained them. Maybe it would hold them long enough for Pa and the boys to come up. "I don't want no kind of man, Injun or no. They're all the same," she shouted out the window.

"Give us McCall and you will live. My patience grows short."

Josie cursed silently as the brave adeptly sidestepped her challenge. "He ain't here, I tell you. He's gone, and good riddance."

Suddenly, the crack of pistol shots reverberated through the trees. Leaves rained down on the heads of the assembled braves. They were caught unaware and struggled to control their plunging mounts. The rain of shot fell from the sky, and confusion muddled the well-organized band. From around the side of the house Caleb charged on foot, a blazing revolver in each hand. The cradle board bounced crazily and the baby wailed. Caleb fired the revolvers consecutively, aiming directly among the horses' hooves.

"Open the door, Josie!" he bellowed as he sprang up on the porch.

Josie hesitated only a second before she drew aside the bolt and swung the door open a crack. Caleb charged inside, and she slammed it shut and drew the board across it as a hail of arrows beat on the outside.

"Is there any way out of here?" he asked quickly.

Josie's eyes widened. "Under my bed's a tunnel to the mine. I found it runnin' away from a beatin' one time."

"That's my girl." Caleb smiled at her, the little wrinkles piling up around his eyes. "Now, what are we going to do about this noise?" The baby's cries intensified as Caleb slipped off the cradle board.

"Wait, I got an idea." Josie ran to the cabinet, jerked aside the curtain, and scratched through tins and bags of supplies. "Here it is." She drew out a small cloth bag tied in a knot. She ripped a piece of cloth away from a rag in the cabinet and untied the bag. White granules of sugar poured out in her hand. After putting a good pinch of sugar in the square of material, she tied all four corners together. "Sugar tit," she said, and held the cloth to the baby's mouth. He grabbed the cloth eagerly and began to suck, quieting his squalls.

"Thought you didn't know anything about babies," Caleb teased, hefting the board back onto his back.

"Don't." Josie quickly tied the thongs. "But I know plenty 'bout how to keep the peace." She gave the straps a final tug.

Caleb grabbed her hand and pulled her over to the bed. He reached down and lifted up the mattress and the lid to the box on which the bed sat. The scent of damp, musty earth poured up out of the hole. Caleb got a lamp from the table and poked it down into the shaft. A breath of air came up to them.

"Good, the entrance isn't blocked. Once we're in, there's no coming back. Understand?"

Josie nodded silently and took one more look around the cabin before she followed Caleb down the earthen stairs carved into the sides of the tunnel. He held the lid up long enough for her to slip through, then he lowered it, careful not to disturb the bedclothes and give away their exit.

The walls of the shaft quickly became rock, and Josie wondered who had dug this shaft. What was it for? Maybe the others had used it for the same reason they did.

They were slanting constantly downhill now, going deeper and deeper into the bowels of the earth. Twice Josie slipped and fell on the slick floor before a faint light appeared. Caleb shrugged off the cradle board and handed it to her. Crouching low to the ground, he moved forward slowly, a revolver in each hand.

The mouth of the shaft they were following emptied out into the main corridor of the mine her father had worked from sunup to sunset the last four years. The light they had seen came from a ventilation hole dug in the roof of the mine shaft. With a cautioning wave, Caleb eased out into the tunnel.

A small sound made the hair on the back of Josie's neck rise. Caleb reached around and pushed her flat against the wall behind them. They slid toward the mouth of the shaft, and the light became brighter. Caleb abruptly stopped inside the opening, and Josie moved up beside him. A small gasp escaped her lips. She rushed past him. His hand plucked at her shirt as she passed. Her Pa, brothers, and brothers-in-law were thrown about like rag dolls, their bloody bodies bludgeoned and scalped.

The sound of feet crashing through underbrush frightened them both. Caleb snatched her to her feet and jerked her back inside the mouth of the cave. He wedged his shoulder against the wall, holding Josie tightly against his chest. She couldn't have heard a whole tribe of Indians for the pounding of her heart and his as they stood motionless against each other. He wrapped his left arm around her and cocked his pistol with his right hand.

"Stay here." Pushing her against the cool, smooth rock wall, he stepped back outside.

The opening of the shaft sat on a rocky expanse of the mountain in plain sight from all directions, affording little protection. Despite his orders, Josie followed him, crouched low to the ground. A sound in the edge of the woods caught her attention. The rustle came again, and the high tinkle of metal against metal. Caleb clucked softly, and Cindy answered with a soft nicker. She trotted over and he caught her bridle.

"We have to get out of here." Caleb grabbed at Josie's sleeve.

She stood over the bloody, almost unrecognizable body of her father. She should feel grief, she thought, but all she felt was relief and shock. "Petey?" she asked suddenly, realizing he wasn't among the dead. "Where's Petey? I've gotta find him."

"If he was out here, he's dead, Josie. Now, come on before we are too." He put one foot in the stirrup and reached back for her arm.

"No." She jerked away. "I have to find Petey." She spun around and ran toward the mine. A branch cracked in the dense pine thicket to their right. Caleb crouched behind Cindy and waved Josie to the ground. Another cracking branch gave away the stalker's location. With gun drawn, Caleb crept toward the thicket. Cautiously, he parted the thick undergrowth.

Josie poked her head over the rock and saw Caleb stumble

backward. He lost his footing and sat down hard. Then one of the mules ambled out into the open. Astride her with two rabbits flung over his knees was Petey.

"Petey." The word rushed out. She could have faced anything except the death of her twin. "Where've you been?"

"I ... I went to check them rabbit boxes like Pa said." Petey's eyes flew wide at the sight stretched before him. "What happened?"

"Injuns."

"They dead?" Petey pointed at the bodies.

"They're all dead."

"I ... I heard the racket." Petey paled and swung his gaze toward Josie. "Come back to check on you."

Josie stepped forward and rubbed his leg. "I'm all right. Caleb come back just in time."

"They don't hardly look real, do they, sis?" He nodded toward the blood-soaked ground.

"I don't know how you missed getting killed, Petey." Caleb swung into the saddle. "But come on before they kill all of us." He leaned down and caught Josie by the arm, tossing her up behind him.

"Wait." Josie laid her hand on his shoulder. "Petey can't ride that mule. He'll fall off and break his neck. He ain't never rode nothin' without fallin' off."

Caleb turned in the saddle and looked into her face. "He's going to have to. Cindy can't carry three of us, and if we don't get gone, the Crow'll find us any minute."

With a nudge to Cindy's sides, they clattered across the exposed rock and down a little-used trail, opening into the same meadow where Josie had taken Caleb that peaceful day not so long ago. Right on their heels, Petey clung precariously to the bouncing mule. Behind them they could hear the whoops and shouts of the Indians as they found the trapdoor. Caleb urged Cindy into a full gallop as they cleared the steep incline. Skirting the meadow, they lost themselves in the deep forest. Caleb leaned low over the mare's neck. Josie shut her eyes and buried her face in the back of his coat. Behind her she could feel the cradle board bouncing against the rawhide thongs that bound it to her back and hear the thud of Petey's mule. She prayed that when their flight stopped, Petey and the mule would still be together.

On they flew until Cindy's sides heaved with the exertion. Not until they were well away from the summit of the mountain did Caleb slow their pace. They came out of the forest into a cool, green glade nestled at the feet of the high hills around them.

Caleb looked back over his shoulder and laughed. The mule trotted out of the trees, Petey clinging to the short mane. The animal's sides heaved as she stopped beside Cindy, and Petey grinned in triumph.

"That sure was fun. Can we do it again sometime?"

Caleb shook his head as he dismounted. He led the mounts right up to the rock wall and tossed aside limbs and brush. The blackness of a cave entrance yawned before them.

The damp, musky smell of the interior enveloped them as they entered. A breath of cool air wrapped around them, then moved into the darkness deeper inside the cave.

"We'll stay here tonight," Caleb said, leading Cindy over pebbles in the entrance. "We can even have a fire. The smoke'll be drawn away, down into the cave, and come out someplace up there. They'll never know we're here even if they've followed us."

Josie didn't answer while she fumbled with the straps of the cradle board, loosened it, and held it in her arms. She commanded her feet to carry her over to the wall, then slid down it into a heap on the damp earth.

Petey left the mule to Caleb and sat close by her side. "I sure am glad you ain't dead, sis." He rubbed her forearm as he spoke.

Josie blinked away tears. "I'm glad you ain't either, Petey." She threw her arms around him and cried softly.

Caleb turned at the sound of Josie's sobs. She had pushed

away from her brother. Tears stained her face, and she stared vacantly at the opposite wall.

After jerking off the saddlebags, Caleb emptied out the few remaining supplies he'd packed that morning. He lit a fire from dried wood piled inside the cave entrance and cooked a pan of beans and a pot of coffee. He poured himself a cup and sat back on his heels, studying Josie over the rim. The life seemed to have gone out of her. Pulling some jerky from his shirt, he rose, walked over to her, and squatted down. "You better eat. There's no telling how long we'll have to run like this. Better keep up your strength."

She shook her head and put it down on arms crossed over her knees. Petey gave her a pat, then rose and filled a tin plate. The baby whimpered from his nest in the cradle board. Josie turned her head, rose, and took him out. When she pulled back the blanket, his flat, copper face worked itself into a deep frown before he thrust a fist into his mouth.

"He's hungry," she stated, looking back over her shoulder at Caleb.

He moved over to the horse and felt Cindy's bag. A little milk dripped out, but not nearly enough to sustain the child for long. Caleb threw out the rest of his coffee, then took his cup and gently squeezed out Cindy's precious milk. When the cup was about half full, the milk gave out.

"This is it, little one. We've got to get you to somewhere there's some milk, and soon." He smiled down at the child and handed Josie the cup.

Without a word, she ripped off a scrap of her shirt, dipped it into the milk, and placed it in the baby's mouth. He sucked hungrily and squirmed when it was dry. Over and over she repeated the process, wearing the same absent look.

Darkness fell outside, and the deep, dark recesses of the cave became more so. The temperature dropped, and a cold wind whistled through the opening. The flames flickered and danced. Caleb poured himself another cup of coffee, sat down, and leaned back against the opposite wall to watch Josie rock the baby. The firelight danced in the blue depths of her eyes, shadowed the lines of fatigue on her face, and put blue highlights into her raven-black hair. It had come loose from the tie at the back of her neck, spilling across her shoulders. He took another sip of coffee. Pleasantly bitter, it warmed his stomach, and his eyelids drooped. The scant serving of milk had satisfied the baby, and he fell asleep with the rag of cloth still firmly in his mouth. Josie gently pulled the rag out and placed the infant in the fur-lined cradle board.

"Sis? Want me to tell you a story?" Petey asked from across the fire. She nodded and patted the ground next to her. He scurried over, threw a comforting arm across her shoulder, and began to recite. "Once upon a time there was these three bears, and they had this shack of a house up high in the hills. Now, Pa bear . . ."

Caleb closed his eyes and let the singsong cadence of the mountain twang lull him into drowsiness. He didn't know how long he'd been asleep, when a sound jerked him awake. His hand automatically flew to his pistol. Across the remains of the fire, Petey lay curled with his knees in his chest, jerking from a nightmare. Josie, propped against the cave wall, laid a comforting hand on his side. He sighed, turned over, and slept peacefully.

She glanced toward Caleb and found him awake, watching her. Holding out her hands to warm, she moved nearer the fire. The dancing yellow flames were mesmerizing. Her head ached, and her thoughts were unconnected, drifting in her skull like bits of ice in a spring thaw.

The picture of her father lying spread-eagle on the ground floated in front of her eyes. His eyes focused unseeing on the sky, and his forehead was split in two with an ax. She felt an emptiness, a sadness at losing the last of something. Pa and her brothers had never shown her love, only misuse and abuse. But they were all she had. The last of the Hardwicks. Now she was totally on her own, in a strange land she knew nothing of save the one small cabin on the hill. She had no husband, no skills, no money. The despair of her situation came crashing down on her and tears slipped down her face. Why couldn't she just pick up and leave, go back to Tennessee, make her own life there? she thought irritably, swiping at the tears with the back of her hand. She was too scared, that's why. Too scared of the unknown, too scared of the Indians between the Rockies and the Smokies, too scared of being alone. A sob escaped her lips, and she pressed her hand over her mouth.

Warm fingers touched the streaks on her face. Caleb's thumb wiped at one side. He had come to sit by her side. Warm green eyes studied her face, then crinkled into a smile. He took her shoulders and pulled her back against his chest. The soft brushed leather caressed her face, and the earthy scent somehow made her feel safe. Wrapped tight in his arms, she let the sorrow come pouring out. Hard, jerking sobs shook her body. It felt good to cry, to let go, to have someone else take charge for a while.

She moved as his beard tickled her cheek, and she felt him chuckle deep in his chest. One arm beneath her breasts, he pulled her down onto his blanket and snuggled her against his length. Then he reached down and pulled one blanket over them both. The strong thud of his heartbeat comfortingly in her ear. When had she felt so . . . so protected? Not ever that she could remember. Pa never made her feel this way. Johnny didn't either. She should get up, she thought, aware of the heat from Caleb's body warming hers. What if Petey woke up and found her like this? What would he say? Caleb's breathing fell into an even rhythm that lulled her. She'd worry about her feelings tomorrow, she decided with a sob.

Caleb watched the dying fire long after its flames had turned to embers. Occasionally, he threw on a piece of precious wood to keep it alive. Josie's sobs had turned into involuntary jerks, and he knew she'd cried herself into an exhausted sleep. The nearness of her body tormented him, but the need for rest overcame his other needs. Josie moved in her sleep, snuggling her back closer to him, and his body cried out with want. Visions of nights with Fawn tormented him, nights filled with velvety passion, making love in front of the dying fire, her dark hair spilling down around her face and softly sweeping his chest, her eyes reflecting the orange of the embers. Dully, he shook his head to dispel the ghosts, and tightened his grip on Josie.

"You can't let the past ruin the years you have left, child." Emmy's words echoed dimly in his thoughts.

"I won't," Caleb heard himself whisper into Josie's hair as his eyes closed. "I won't, Emmy."

Chapter Thirteen

The first shafts of morning sun stabbing in through the mouth of the cave awakened Caleb. His arm rested intimately across Josie's ribs, and her back pressed tightly against him. Rolling her away from him, he left the blanket. A glorious September morning greeted him. The air was cool, but not uncomfortable, and had a nip of fall to it. Caleb leaned one hand against the wall of the cave and looked out at the distant peaks, the misty memories of the previous night's dreams still haunting him. The sun was warm on his chest, and he closed his eyes and let it spread through him until a small sound made him turn. Behind him, Josie stirred beneath the blanket they had shared.

Picking up a few twigs from the pile by the door, he soon had the fire crackling and last night's coffee warming in the pot. He watched her sigh softly and turn over, throwing one arm over the place he'd slept. She ran her hand across the empty blanket, then opened her eyes to stare at the blank rock wall beyond. Color flooded her cheeks as she turned over and met his eyes.

"Good morning," she murmured, hastily straightening her clothes.

"How do you feel this morning?" he asked, frowning at the gray circles beneath her eyes.

She stood and walked over to Petey. He still slept peacefully, his fists curled beneath his cheeks. She patted his arm, then returned to the fire. "Numb, I guess," she said as she rubbed her hands together, then turned her back.

"Where'd Petey get that story he told last night?" Caleb asked.

Her cheeks turned a pretty pink. "Oh, out of some book a traveling preacher man left with us. Petey, he always lived in his head. Always has wanted to see the world, he says. That's why he likes them stories about princesses and princes and all that."

"You two are close."

"Yeah, I guess we are. We're twins, you know."

"You told me."

"Oh, yeah. I guess I did."

Caleb knew his gaze disturbed her. The intensity of it disturbed him. She glanced at him once, then diverted her attention.

"What do them drawings mean?" She pointed to crude etchings on the facing walls, caricatures of horses and men in battle, bringing in game to a waiting village, rings of children playing beneath a brilliant yellow sun.

"Ancient Lakota drawings. They've been coming here for hundreds of years."

Josie whirled to face him. "Here? To this cave?" Her eyes widened with fear.

"This is a sacred place. Young braves come here to seek their first visions. The wood over there and the cut grass for the horses, they're all replaced by each user."

Her eyes searched the dark recesses of the cave, as if she were sure a Lakota warrior lurked there. "We gotta git out of here. What if they followed us?" she said, a note of rising panic in her voice.

Caleb threw the last of his coffee into the fire and calmly stood. "Those weren't Lakota that attacked you. They were Crow."

"Crow? How do you know?"

"Believe me, I know the Crow when I see them."

"What difference does it make, Crow or Lakota? They'll kill us on sight."

Caleb shook his head. "Makes all the difference in the world. That baby is half Lakota. We're taking him home."

"Home?"

"To Red Cloud."

"Oh, no. Not with me, you don't." She shook her head until her hair billowed out around her. "I've done had all the Injuns I want for a long time."

Caleb saw the fear and pain in her eyes, but he was tired and worried. He knew how stubborn she could be. Today his patience wouldn't stretch that far. "You'll go where I go until I can get you to a fort. We have to get that baby somewhere there's milk." He narrowed his eyes, ready for another argument.

"There's milk at a fort. I ain't goin' into no Injun village, no matter how good a-friends you are with 'em." Josie balled her hands into fists at her side.

"You mean we're going to an Injun camp? Live there with 'em?" Petey asked, sitting straight up.

"Yeah. For the winter anyway. That is, if we can convince your sister." Caleb nodded toward Josie.

"Mr. McCall, can I ask you something?" Petey rose to his feet.

"Sure."

Petey bunched his forehead into a frown. "Have they got women in this Injun camp?"

Despite the look Josie shot him, Caleb had to laugh. "Yeah, Petey. They got women, but not the kind you want."

Petey frowned, then brightened. "Oh, I know what you mean.

You think I want one of them loose women. Nope." He shook his head solemnly. "I want me a wife."

"A wife!" Caleb and Josie exclaimed at the same time.

"Yep. I heard them Injun women were purdy and smart. I want to court one."

Caleb shook his head. "Most folks won't agree with you on that."

"See what you've gone and done." Josie stomped her foot and whirled on Caleb, pointing a finger at her brother.

"I didn't have anything to do with this." Caleb held up his hands and shook his head.

"You put them ideas in his head." She crossed her arms and jutted out her chin. "I ain't goin' to no Injun camp."

"You'll either go with me or stay here." Caleb stepped forward until they were head to head. "Name your choice."

Josie's eyes were full of anger and fear. "Injuns have done took everything away I ever had. It don't matter to me what tribe they belonged to. Why should I risk gittin' kilt just to return a half-breed baby? I ain't goin' nowhere with you."

The punch came totally without warning. If not for the untimely dropping of a coffee cup, Caleb wouldn't have seen Josie's fist coming straight for him. He ducked, and she fanned the air, losing her balance and nearly falling into the fire. She flung back her hair and advanced on him again.

Utterly confused as to what had brought on this violence, Caleb obligingly backed around the fire pit staying out of her range, his thoughts flying. To his left, Petey hopped from one foot to the other, mimicking a fight, punching the air with his fists.

"Give it to him good, sis."

"I won't go into Injun territory with nobody, least of all you, Caleb McCall," she spat out as she tried to maneuver closer to him.

If her aim hadn't been so good, Caleb would have loved a good laugh over this, imagining the picture the two of them must have made with Petey dancing accompaniment. But as it was, she was coming too close to connecting with his left cheek. She swung again, and Caleb jerked his head back in time. She had put everything she had behind that punch, and the momentum carried her forward. Catching her toe on the rocks of the fire pit, she lunged across the glowing embers. Caleb caught her underneath her arms and dragged her safely away. Once clear of the fire, he released her and backed away, ready for another onslaught.

Her hair was a dark tangle around her head and her jaw worked in anger. "I ain't gonna follow you like a puppy to any damn place you want until you take a notion to drop me off at some godforsaken fort between here and Missouri." She shoved her hair off her forehead. "I've had enough of this life. All I want to see is them green hills of Tennessee." Her voice quivered. "And if I have to whip yore ass to git there, I'll do it." Anger faded into sorrow as her voice broke and her chin began to tremble. "I want to go home."

Caleb took her gently by the shoulders. "Listen to me, Josie. I'll take care of you. Nobody'll hurt you as long as you're with me. Petey too. Trust me." The words seemed to soothe some of her fear. Slowly, her fists unclenched. The fire of combat left her eyes.

Caleb drew her into his arms. "I meant it. I'll take care of you."

"Are you gonna kiss her now?" Petey's face was a mixture of hope and disappointment as he paused, one foot in the air and both hands still clenched, waiting for the next punch.

Before the dew dried off the grass, they were on their way. The baby drank what little milk the mare had left and obligingly dropped off to sleep. Riding behind Caleb, Josie found herself surrounded by a fairyland of color. The trees were edged in their fall colors. The frost had not yet turned the grass to brown, and its vivid green against the yellow of the aspen trees dotting the far hillsides addled the senses. As they rode, Josie's arms tightly clasped around Caleb's waist, he entertained her with stories about the Lakota. *He's trying to convince me they ain't gonna scalp me on sight,* Josie thought. Even though she didn't believe him, she laid her head against his back, grateful he cared enough to try.

Although he rode loosely, swaying effortlessly with Cindy's gait, Josie knew he watched for signs of the band of Crow. It appeared they had given up the chase and returned home to prepare for the coming winter. But she knew better. In this savage land, she'd learned to expect the worst, because that's usually what she got.

They rode steadily north toward the Powder River. Caleb pointed out landmarks, calling the country the last refuge of the Lakota. He told her how once they had descended on Minnesota Territory in great numbers, eager for the deep forests and swift streams where food was abundant. But now, with the constant advance of the whites, they had been pushed back nearly into the high Rockies. He told her how the plains were once black with buffalo, how brave warriors hunted the great beasts on swift ponies. Sadly, he told of the movement west of the whites and how with that movement came the end of the buffalo and the end of a way of life.

Josie listened with her cheek against his back. She heard the sadness in his voice, felt the tension in his muscles when he talked of the end of the days of the Lakota. Now the children went hungry, he said, if the herds wandered south instead of north. Brave, painted warriors now hunted rabbits and birds to feed their children.

"How do you know where to find Red Cloud?" she asked when he stopped talking.

"When I was a little boy, I used to hear Father talk about a beautiful lush valley where the Lakota could live in plenty, protected from the white man and the cold winter wind."

"You reckon that's where he's holed up?" Josie twisted around when she heard Petey's mule stumble. Petey smiled and waved at her.

"I don't know. I hope so."

Shifting her legs so the saddle's apron wouldn't pinch, Josie asked, "How come he's hiding way up here anyhow?"

"Last summer Red Cloud refused to sign a treaty with the government."

"Why?"

"The army set up a meeting in Fort Laramie last June. Many of the important chiefs were there—Red Cloud, Red Leaf, Man-Afraid-of-His-Horse, Old Spotted Tail."

Josie clung tightly as Cindy slipped, then regained her footing on the narrow ledge they followed.

"The army said this would be a lasting peace, expecting the Lakota to sign away rights to their land so gold miners could pass through on the way to Montana Territory."

"Sounds like a good deal to me." Josie twisted around and watched Petey clinging to the mule as the incline increased.

Caleb snorted. "The army thought so too. Everybody did but Red Cloud. Then Colonel Henry Carrington rode into the fort with his detachment of men."

"They start a fight?"

"He was headed for the Bozeman Trail, the trail that passes right through the best hunting grounds. Red Cloud took it as a show of force. He walked out, saying the army intended to steal the land all along. He said they never intended to allow the Indians a choice." Caleb reached his arm around to catch Josie's belt as Cindy lunged the last few feet up the steep incline, then stopped. "His people followed him, and they went back up into these hills to hide."

Caleb took off his hat and wiped his forehead with his arm. Below them, the earth dropped away to nothing. Out in front stretched range after range of snow-capped mountains.

Petey's mule scrambled up beside them, and he slid to the ground and stepped away, an unnatural bow in his legs. "Damn if that mule ain't got a plank fer a backbone," he said, rubbing his backside with both hands.

Caleb handed Josie to the ground, then swung down himself.

A small clump of pines huddled on the edge of the cliff. She walked over and leaned against one. The view was breathtaking.

"You reckon the army'd come up here after Red Cloud?" she asked, drawing in a deep breath of the biting air.

"If they can find him." Caleb stepped to her side. "He's been harassing wagon trains along the Bozeman for months. Sweeping down out of the mountains, striking, then disappearing like gray ghosts."

Josie turned to face him. He stood so close, her nose brushed his shirt fringe. With his face turned to the side, staring out over the valley, she could well imagine him with feathers in his curls, wearing a loincloth, the wind in his hair as he galloped along bareback. She shivered, remembering the mysterious scars marking his chest.

"What are them marks on your chest?" She stared across the valley, yet sensed that he tensed at her question.

Caleb glanced down at her, one eyebrow cocked quizzically.

"I seed 'em when I was tendin' you." She looked at the ground, and his gaze warmed her cheeks.

"They're Sundance scars," he answered shortly.

"Sundance?" She turned to face him and saw the skin stretch tight across his jaw. "What's that?"

"It's a Lakota ceremony. A celebration of sorts, a test of bravery."

Having heard tales of Indian ceremonies, Josie let the subject drop, but his answer piqued her curiosity about the life he had lived so long ago.

On the morning of the third day, Cindy gave no more than a dribble of milk for the baby, and he cried fitfully in hunger. Caleb frowned as Josie tried again to comfort the infant. They were paralleling the Powder River with no sign of the Lakota, or any other Indian for that matter. He hadn't told her of his doubts, but he was truly afraid he'd led them all to death, that no such valley as he had thought existed.

As the afternoon sun dipped behind the trees to the west, the chill of the air undeniably carried a hint of snow. Caleb stopped on the next rise and looked westward to the Rockies' snowy peaks. "Snow," he said, pointing to the faraway summits. "It'll get here tomorrow, maybe the next day."

"You reckon it'll be a blizzard?" Josie asked, her voice muffled by his shirt.

"Maybe we should stop here, put up a shelter." Even as he spoke, he knew they wouldn't last the winter with no stores. Especially the baby. He wouldn't last another week without milk.

They camped for the night in a secluded rock-rimmed area on the banks of a swift stream. Caleb hobbled Cindy and the mule, setting them to graze in a grassy coulee near the stream. Josie slid the cradle board off and gently rocked the baby to quiet his fussing. A little water from the stream quieted his hunger temporarily, and he slept peacefully.

Caleb drew a string and a fish hook from his saddlebags and waded out into the stream. Petey followed close on his heels. Josie watched for a moment and stifled a smile when Caleb slipped, then caught himself. He glanced back toward her with a crooked grin. Leaving him to his embarrassment, she pulled her coat tightly across her chest and, folding her arms for warmth, wandered down the banks of the river in search of firewood.

The brilliant red sunset faded and the forest took on the soft lavender of dusk. A few brave insects tuned up for a last serenade before the impending snow fell, quieting their songs with its white death. The waters of the stream gurgled and tumbled over smooth stones. Josie paused, watching the mesmerizing motion that swept along swift little minnows, darting about the bases of rocks. How she envied them their freedom.

Suddenly, a strong arm clamped her arms to her sides. A hand covered her mouth. She struggled, half hoping this was one of Petey's jokes and vowed to kill him if it was. But the hands that held her were slimmer, more powerful than her brother's. A strong, musty odor surrounded her, not an unpleasant one, but one that reminded her of the outdoors, of smoky cabins and roasting meat. The captor dragged her backward away from the edge of the water and into the shade of a rock overhang. He hadn't spoken a word, and her imagination ran wild. Suddenly, his grip on her loosened. She tested her strength against him and found she could slip easily from his arms. Free, she whirled and saw Caleb standing in the shadow of the surrounding rocks, a revolver pressed to the temple of a painted Indian warrior. Fear filled the man's eyes as he listened to Caleb's voice whispering in his ear. To the left, Petey stood with his mouth wide open.

They spoke to each other several minutes, then Caleb smiled broadly and holstered the gun. The Indian turned and slapped Caleb on the shoulder.

"You two know each other?" she asked, stepping a safe distance away.

"This is Rotten Stomach," Caleb said. "He and I are old friends."

"Cain't say much for his name." Her gaze was drawn to the black gap in the Indian's front teeth.

Caleb translated and Rotten Stomach threw back his head and laughed loudly.

"He has some . . . interesting personal habits," Caleb said with a wink. "He can't seem to keep a wife."

Caleb translated into Lakota, and Rotten Stomach guffawed again. The two men turned and walked back downstream, leaving Josie to follow on her own.

Caleb threw logs on the small fire until it leaped and crackled. Josie walked over, picked up the baby, and cradled him against her chest. She listened but didn't understand the conversation going on between the two men. Petey sat down cross-legged opposite her and wriggled closer to Caleb every few minutes. Occasionally, Caleb motioned in her direction, and the Indian would turn and stare at her. She kept her eyes cast downward, reluctant to meet the man's frank stare. She'd never felt more naked, more helpless without even her Hawken for protection. She slid a glance at Caleb. He looked relaxed and comfortable, at ease in this man's presence.

The chill of the evening set in, and she moved closer to the fire, taking the fretful baby with her. Caleb had caught four little trout. Now he speared each one with a stick and held them over the fire. As he and Rotten Stomach talked, the fish sizzled and bubbled over the flames, filling the air with its tantalizing scent. Almost absently, Caleb removed the meat from the stick and handed it to Josie. She accepted and scowled when his eyes met hers. He smiled slightly before diverting all his attention back to Rotten Stomach.

The three men ate their meal, totally ignoring her. Petey glanced at Caleb and then the Indian as though he understood every word they said. Josie offered the baby the last of the scant milk from Cindy, adding a little water to it to make it stretch, then rocked him gently until he slept. She felt her own eyes droop as the monotonous tone of their voices blended with the heat of the fire to lull her to sleep. Standing the cradle board securely against a rock, she spread the blanket out near it and crawled beneath the covers.

Sometime in the dawn hours, a cold draft awakened her. She grabbed at the cover. Her fingers touched soft leather. She started to scream, but a large hand clamped over her mouth.

"Shh. Do as I say," he whispered in her ear.

"I won't. You git your own—"

Caleb tightened his grip. "Keep that mouth of yours shut and listen," he hissed. "I told him you were my woman and that's the way it has to look. Else he'll make an offer for you. He was impressed with your . . . assets."

Josie twisted her head around. He was grinning broadly. "It'll only be for appearances. Don't worry." Something about the way he said that angered her more than if he had insisted on more than appearances.

He dropped his face onto her shoulder and began to nuzzle

her neck. "What about Petey?" she asked, tilting her head and pushing him away.

Caleb nodded to where Petey was already asleep by the fire, wrapped in one of Rotten Stomach's extra blankets. "He doesn't share your fear, I see."

"Petey ain't got sense enough to know what to be scared of." She wrenched her blankets around and turned over to face Caleb.

"Do you?" His eyes drilled into hers, his face only an inch or two away. Scathing words sprang to her lips, but her heart remembered the meadow, and, unbidden, her eyes found his lips.

Suddenly, Caleb jerked her around roughly so she faced away from him. He dragged her back against his hips, snuggling her intimately into the curve of his body. Rotten Stomach glanced over at them once more before he spread out a buffalo robe and lay down. Caleb curled his arm possessively around Josie's waist. Casually, he threw a leg across her knees. A silent chuckle rumbled in his chest and Josie seethed. He was enjoying this masquerade too damn much.

When she awoke at dawn, he was gone, and his spot on the blanket was cold. She glanced toward the fire. Petey and the mule were also gone, but thankfully, the baby still slept in the cradle board. "Reckon he's left us?" she asked the sleeping child as she got up and rolled up the blankets. The coffeepot still sat over smoldering embers of last night's fire. Laying her hand gingerly against its side, she found the pot still warm.

As she finished the last of the coffee, a crashing in the bushes to her right brought her to her feet, a surge of fear rushing through her veins. Cindy and the mule stepped gingerly out of the tangle. Caleb swung down, and Petey urged the mule out into the grass. Rotten Stomach had disappeared.

"Where's your friend?" she asked as vinegary as possible.

Caleb swiftly tied the bedding behind the saddle and tore up the fire. "We're not far from Red Cloud's camp. He's gone on ahead."

Again Josie felt a rush of fear. He really was going to take them right into the heart of an Indian camp. Her palms turned damp and cold, and she felt all the color leave her face. Mechanically, she moved around, securing the fretting baby to her back, seeing that nothing was left behind. Suddenly, a hand clasped her arm. She turned and looked into Caleb's face.

"I promised I'd take care of you, Josie, and I will," he whispered as his eyes held hers. "The Lakota mean you no harm."

Josie nodded and looked away. Somehow she knew once she entered this world of his, she'd never be the same.

Chapter Fourteen

The north wind carried a hint of snow, creeping up Josie's sleeves and making her shiver. They rode steadily northeast into ever-increasing altitudes, following Rotten Stomach's careful directions. Ahead of them, Caleb said, lay the mysterious valley he'd heard about from the time he was a small child, the carefully guarded valley where a whole tribe might hide and wait out the season when they were most vulnerable.

About noon they left the forest and entered a long, narrow passage between two towering walls of solid rock. Caleb constantly watched the high edges of the rough gray granite with his rifle drawn. The narrow path wound through the rocky canyon, then abruptly spilled out into a vast, flat valley. Sharp peaks towered over and surrounded the valley on each side. A sparkling stream snaked through the center of a grassy meadow and thousands of tipis perched like mushrooms along the bank. Lodgepoles stuck out of each skin, bony fingers reaching for the sky. At the top of each dwelling a thin column of smoke ascended straight up into the leaden sky.

Dogs, children, and horses milled around in between the

lodges. Women halted their chores by the stream to turn around, their bronze faces flanked by long, fat braids. Beaded buckskin dresses dangled to their calves, and they gathered their children to them as Caleb and Josie rode past.

Her heart hammered, and her ears filled with the imagined screams of her mother and her husband as they passed the outskirts of the village. She peeped one eye around Caleb's back and watched row after row of tipi, each sewn in a similar manner but painted in varying colorful images. More people wandered out of the lodges to watch, and she buried her face in Caleb's back.

She heard Caleb's soft "whoa," and Cindy halted. Josie raised her head. A huge lodge stood directly in their path. Supported by twice as many poles as the others, bright pictures decorated its sides—paintings depicting battles and hunts with brilliant red clouds overseeing each scene.

The flap of the tipi opened and a slim brave stepped out. *"Wanblí Ska! Mison, le hinhina ki nite kecem yeló,"* he said, a smile splitting the tanned, chiseled face. Josie cringed as his dark gaze swept her. She crouched behind Caleb, unable to bring herself to face the warrior.

"Wokisuye ciciuay yeló, Mahpíya Lúta," Caleb answered in the lyrical tongue. Then, in English, "I have a present for you, Red Cloud."

So this was the feared Red Cloud. Josie peeped around Caleb's shoulder. He didn't look so fierce. In fact, he looked a lot like the other men surrounding them.

Caleb swung down off Cindy's back, leaving Josie exposed. When he held up his arms, she eagerly jumped into them. Behind her, she heard Petey plop to the ground.

"Golly," he murmured beneath his breath, taking in all the faces that crowded closer.

Caleb untied the straps holding the cradle board on Josie's back and placed it in Red Cloud's arms. The warrior frowned.

"Le nicinca yeló, Mahpíya Lúta," Caleb repeated in Lakota.

Red Cloud's eyes teared as he uncovered the sleeping infant.

Complete adoration filled his face. With one hard, callused finger, he traced the baby's pudgy cheek.

"He hasn't had much to eat," Caleb explained. "We gave him what milk my mare had, but that didn't last long."

Red Cloud barked a command to a short, fat woman who stood behind him. She ducked inside the massive tipi, then returned with a willowy young woman at her heels. The Indian maid stepped obediently to Red Cloud's side and looked up expectantly. He softly spoke a few words to her, then handed her the baby from the cradle board. Immodestly, she opened the neck of her buckskin dress, pulled out an engorged breast, and offered it to the child. The baby suckled hungrily, making little gasping sounds as the milk came faster than he could drink. Tiny hands kneaded her soft flesh. The chief looked down on the two and murmured words that made the girl's cheeks redden.

"She is my new wife," he explained, turning back toward Caleb. "She was with child when her husband was killed. We married a few weeks ago. The baby died at birth."

Josie marveled at how well the chief spoke English.

"New wife, eh?" Then Caleb spoke rapidly in Lakota, sending all the women around them into spasms of laughter. They covered their mouths shyly and glanced at Red Cloud. He scowled, then grinned sheepishly, sending the women off into another fit of laughter.

"What did you say to him?" Josie whispered at Caleb's elbow.

Caleb leaned closer. "I told him I thought he was too old to . . . perform."

Josie gasped, and Caleb chuckled, his eyes dancing with mischief.

"Ain't you afraid you'll make him mad?" she asked as Red Cloud frowned sternly and chased away some of the onlookers.

Caleb shook his head. "He and I are old friends. He knows I'm kidding."

"I didn't think Injuns joshed and teased." She edged behind Caleb as Red Cloud glowered dramatically at a laughing squaw.

"You've got a lot to learn about the Lakota, muleskinner." Caleb looked down at her and winked.

"I don't want to learn about 'em." Something about his easy way with the Indians riled her. "I just want to git to a fort and go home."

"Who is the woman?" Red Cloud pointed at her.

Caleb put an arm around her shoulders and drew her close. "She is my woman."

A scathing retort sprang to her lips, but fear, and Caleb's booted foot on hers, silenced her—for then.

"Ah," the chief said with a mischievous grin. "And the other?" He pointed at Petey.

"My woman's brother."

Red Cloud stepped closer and carefully studied Petey. He smiled when Petey grinned broadly. "He is touched?" he asked Caleb.

"Yes," Caleb nodded in agreement. "He is touched."

Suddenly, Petey spilled forth an explanation in Lakota. Josie couldn't believe her ears. Indians scared Petey at least as bad as her. "Where'd you learn that babble, Petey?"

"I dunno, sis." His expression was one of astounded wonderment as he shrugged his shoulders and grinned. "It just come out. I listened to Caleb and Rotten Stomach last night. Reckon I picked it up."

Josie started to explain that wasn't possible, but Caleb silenced her with a whisper. "Leave it be, Josie."

The people quickly surrounded Petey, touching him, murmuring softly. He chatted as easily with them as if they spoke English.

"Those that are touched are treated special, given their own place in the village," Caleb said into her ear.

"But we ain't part of this village," Josie noted.

"Maybe we will be more than you think," he retorted with a raised eyebrow.

Josie watched her twin speak to these people who should have terrified him. His eyes glinted with awareness, with happiness she'd never seen before. He was someone of significance, someone special. Suddenly, everyone wanted to touch him, to ask his opinion, to seek his advice.

Caleb had fallen back into conversation with Red Cloud. Josie's eyes strayed to the young Indian maid suckling the baby. A tinge of jealousy went through her as she watched them. The sound of her name made her jerk her head around to where Caleb stood watching her with a mocking smile on his face.

"You can see the baby whenever you like." He nodded toward the Indian girl and took Josie's arm.

"No." Josie shook her head. "I reckon he's where he oughta be." She jerked her arm out of his grasp. "Good riddance, I say." She wanted Caleb and his self-satisfied look to know she'd be happily rid of both him and his friends as soon as she could.

Caleb caught her arm and pulled her forward. They were moving at the center of a crowd that was guiding them through the camp. Ahead, Red Cloud forged the way through villagers. She would have marched head-on into a group of men if Caleb hadn't jerked her back. Directly in front of them stood a new, half-erected tipi, one whose skins were not yet aged by the sun, the newly cut poles stripped bare.

"What's that?" Josie asked with a growing sense of dread as she watched the lodge go up.

"It's our new home." Caleb smiled and nodded, speaking rapidly to Red Cloud.

"You mean we're gonna live here? Right in the middle of 'em?" She crossed her arms defiantly. "I ain't living in no Injun village."

"You'll live here for now and like it," Caleb spat out in her ear. "This is no time to be stubborn. Is that understood? We need them in order to survive the winter. And soon they may need us."

Josie glanced up at him, wondering at the last comment, but he gazed toward their new home wistfully.

Red Cloud rejoined them, reached out, and took Josie's ragged shirt between his fingers. She flinched at his nearness and backed closer to Caleb.

"Her clothes are thin," he said, rubbing the tattered cotton fabric between his fingers. "The winter will be cold. She must have others." A sharp word brought the heavy Indian woman who had done his bidding before. She listened as he pointed at Josie and made motions with his hands. Then she scurried away.

"Where's she going?" Josie asked Caleb's back as he moved in front of her.

"He ordered you new clothes," he said over his shoulder.

Josie didn't have time to protest before the woman reappeared, her arms full of soft skins. She stepped inside the tipi and motioned for Josie to follow.

"I ain't goin' in there with no savage woman." Josie pulled against Caleb's gentle push.

"I didn't know you were afraid of anything, Jocelyn Hardwick," Caleb taunted, gently nudging her toward the tipi.

"I ain't stupid, if that's what you mean." Josie wrenched away.

Red Cloud frowned and spoke sharply to the woman who poked her head out and frowned in confusion. Caleb interrupted and spoke for several minutes to the chief, his voice barely above a whisper. Red Cloud intently listened to Caleb, glancing Josie's way occasionally. While the men talked, she looked around for the best way out of the camp. The passage that had led them into the meadow seemed a long way off.

Caleb stepped past her and went inside the skin lodge. Reaching out, he grabbed her hand and yanked her in behind him. He secured the flap with a stick through both layers of leather. They were alone in the dark except for the small circle of light on the packed earth made by the smoke hole over their heads.

"What was all that about out there?" she asked, moving

away, the hopelessness of her situation closing in on her. His green eyes seemed to see right down into her soul, and she was afraid he would see what troubled her of late, see that thoughts of him disturbed her sleep and clouded her judgment. He stepped forward and caught her by the shoulders, forcing her to look up at him.

"This is the way it is, Josie," he said slowly and calmly. "Tomorrow it will snow, a huge, deep snow that will bury this village and the passage we took in here. We can't and won't leave here until spring."

Suddenly, he seemed a natural part of this primitive world. He belonged there; she belonged nowhere. Loneliness overwhelmed her. She'd have to live out her worst nightmare, existing in fear of the people who had taken away all she knew and held dear. Ducking her head, she looked away from his mesmerizing eyes.

"I'd have told you before now, but I knew you'd fight me at every step." He tightened his grip on her forearms. "Things were bad enough without that."

Josie blinked rapidly, fighting tears. His voice dropped to a croon. "We're safe here. These are the same people who raised me. We have a warm house and food to eat. When spring comes, we'll leave, and I'll take you to a fort and see to it you get back home." He paused. "If that's what you still want."

The plea in his voice made her glance up. Again his gaze locked with hers, but she didn't see his face. All she saw was the prospect of spending the entire winter with the people who had murdered her Johnny, her parents, her brothers, and her brothers-in-law; the prospect of spending the entire winter in intimately close quarters with this bear of a man, a man who made her knees weak and made her act like an idiot with one kiss. Both thoughts terrified her.

"I'll take care of you, Josie," he said softly, smoothing his hands down her arms. "I promised I would, didn't I?"

"Stop saying that!" she flung at him, tearing out of his grip and from under his spell. "You keep saying that, and then you go and git me into more trouble. I wish you'da left me there in the mine. At least I woulda only had to face a few of 'em, not a whole damn camp of 'em.'' Tears sprang to her eyes, and she angrily wiped them away and turned her back.

"There's no choice," he said from behind her. "This is the way it has to be, at least for now."

Josie's shoulders sagged with resignation. She knew perfectly well she had no other choice, but it seemed too final to hear him say it. Long-held tears tumbled down her cheeks. Strong arms went around her and pulled her close. She turned in his embrace and rubbed her cheek on his shirt. His breathing quickened. Before she could pull away, his lips captured hers and his tongue began a gentle exploration of her mouth. Worse, she felt herself responding. Caleb bent over her, pressing her tightly to his chest while his lips drove all thoughts of tears from her mind.

A shaft of light streaming in the door of the lodge interrupted them. They turned to find the opening filled with the body of a woman. She was almost as tall as Caleb, and her face was long and slim. She stepped gracefully inside and stopped in front of them. Crossing her arms, she looked each one of them up and down. Josie swore she saw disapproval in her eyes and stepped out of Caleb's embrace.

"Owl! *Hau.*" Caleb greeted her in Lakota.

The woman's eyes darted to where Josie stood embarrassed and humiliated, and she wished she could crawl under the nearest rock.

The Indian woman laid back the flap, allowing light to flood the interior. Josie moved deeper into the dark while the woman chatted cordially with Caleb and went about the business of laying down stones for a fire pit. She grinned broadly and pointed toward Josie. Caleb commented in Lakota, and his neck reddened as the woman smiled slyly. Josie's spirits lifted a bit. Could it be this woman had embarrassed Caleb McCall?

Owl threw back her head, and a delicious, deep laugh spilled forth. She laughed until she had to hold her sides, and Caleb grinned sheepishly. Josie would have given anything to understand what they had said to each other.

But she didn't have time to ask before the lodge filled up with other women, each one popping through the flap bearing a gift. Caleb explained each new addition that was laid on the floor of their home. A new buffalo paunch came with the sticks to hold it in place beside the fire. Round stones to boil water from the river were a present from Red Cloud and his wife. Another woman brought thick buffalo robes, and still another brought sweet grass and herbs.

"What are they bringin' grass for?" Josie asked as one woman laid a carefully tied bunch of grass by the fire pit.

"It's burned during ceremonies and on an altar in each lodge," Caleb explained, smiling and nodding as the woman ducked to leave.

People streamed in for the rest of the day, bringing food, clothes, utensils, and weapons. With Caleb as interpreter, Josie learned she was to wear a beautiful buckskin dress from Owl. Josie shook out the garment and held it up. Carefully cut and sewn together with the sinew from the legs of buffalo, the dress was soft and supple and velvety to the touch. An intricate design covered the bodice of the dress, made from a combination of valued glass beads and porcupine quills. Matching moccasins accompanied the dress, as did a beaded headband.

The generosity of the gift touched Josie despite her fear of the woman making the offer. It must have taken many days and nights to make and bead the outfit. But when she glanced up at Owl, she saw not welcome in her eyes, but suspicion, anger. She glanced over at Caleb and found his face expressionless, giving her no hint as to how to behave. She took a step forward and reached out to smooth the leather.

"Thank you," Josie said, taking the garment into her arms. Owl looked over at Caleb and they exchanged smiles. As quickly as she had appeared, Owl vanished out the door, closing the flap behind her.

"Well, I guess I had better set about teaching you how to

set up a proper home,'' Caleb said from where he'd flopped down on a buffalo robe.

Josie frowned, her brief joy evaporating. ''What do you mean?''

Caleb slid over to the ring of stones and laid a fire. ''If we're going to live here . . .''

''What do you mean we?''

''I mean we. You and me.''

''Like hell I am. I thought this was yours. I mean, I thought . . . I . . . thought I'd live with Petey.''

''You'll be safer here with me.'' Caleb poked at new embers just beginning to glow.

''Safer? I thought these people were yore friends?''

''I don't mean safe from them. I mean safer from your own foolishness.''

''My foolishness? I saved yore ass.''

Caleb looked up with a lopsided grin. ''I only meant that I can help you understand these people, to keep you from offending somebody.''

''What about Petey? You just gonna turn him loose out there. He's bound to be more foolish than me.''

''Petey's got his own tipi in the village.''

''He cain't live on his own. He ain't never had to look after himself.''

She started to push past him, but Caleb stopped her. ''Josie, Petey's a grown man. He knows more than you think. He's already fitting in here. You've protected him all his life. Now let him be.''

''I'm damn sure not gonna let him live like no Injun.'' Josie shoved at his chest. ''And I'm damn sure not gonna live here with you.'' She sidestepped and stormed to the door. Then she paused. If not with Caleb, then were would she live? What would she do alone in an Indian camp?

''We've got to do something about your language,'' Caleb said from behind her in a smug voice.

"I could live by myself," she suggested, faltering at opening the flap.

"Women don't live alone here. They have to have the protection of a man."

"I'll live with Petey, then." She whirled around to face Caleb.

He stood behind her with arms crossed over his chest. "You can't live with Petey. He's already been offered brides." Caleb smiled slowly. "Besides, you're my woman."

"I ain't your woman." Josie stamped her foot in frustration. "And what do you mean, brides? Why, Petey don't know how . . . He thinks . . . in Independence he didn't . . . you know what I mean."

"Petey'll know when the time comes. Maybe this is his place, Josie. Let him be a man for once in his life."

Josie kicked at a pile of furs. "Well, I don't need no man's protection." She sniffed, turned on her heel, and stalked to the other side of the lodge.

"You don't have a choice." The closeness of his steely voice made her jump, warning her not to cross him about this. "It's either live here with me . . . as my wife . . . or take your chances with some Lakota brave. And—" Caleb paused, as though carefully weighing his next words. "He'll demand his husbandry rights."

Josie's eyes grew round in fright, and she unconsciously backed away. "What do you mean?"

Caleb stepped closer. "The Lakota value the virginity of their women highly. I told Red Cloud you were my woman, that we planned to marry. That was pushing it. So he has offered to marry us under Lakota tradition."

Genuine terror coursed through her veins.

"Except for the fact he thinks you belong to me, he would have insisted you live with one of the other families until spring. Do you want that?"

"No, of course not, but . . ."

"Chastity is important to them, and only because he considers me his brother is Red Cloud letting you live here with me, where I can protect you.''

She felt as if a shadow had passed over her. The mention of marriage brought back memories she'd rather forget.

''It's not binding, of course,'' he said, slanting a glance at her face. ''Only if you're Lakota. But at least you won't have to worry about some other man taking a liking to you. I'd have to thrash him.''

She ignored his attempt at humor and seized on an earlier statement. ''What do you mean, husbandly rights?'' she asked in a small voice. She knew perfectly well what he meant, but her mind searched for an answer, for something to forestall the one event she'd learned to hate in her brief marriage.

Caleb stepped closer, caught her chin in his fingers, and tipped her face up to his. ''I mean . . . I won't force you. I'm not that kind of man.''

''You promise?'' She pleaded in such a pitiful voice that he dropped his hands and stepped away. Her face was pale and shaking hands held the buckskin dress tightly against her chest. In the time he'd known her, he'd never seen her this scared, not even in the face of an Indian attack.

He reached out to touch her and she jumped. He frowned. Something didn't add up here. Surely, she was no stranger to sex, not when she'd been married and had a child. ''What is it?'' he asked gently.

Her head came up in a cloud of black hair. ''I don't want you . . . like that. You or any other man.''

Caleb studied her face. ''What's the matter with you?'' he asked, slipping his hand beneath the warm mane of her hair. ''Surely it wouldn't be that bad?''

She moved away, and he noticed a fine line of perspiration breaking out on her upper lip. That night on the porch, she was so willing, so warm and yielding. What had happened? Before he could question her further, the flap opened again. Red Cloud entered, the baby in his arms, and in his wake stood several giggling women.

"It amuses them to see a man carry a child," he said offhandedly, jerking his head in their direction with an embarrassed shrug. "I thought you might like to see the child again." He held out the swaddled baby to Josie.

"You speak . . . so good." Her amazement was plain in her voice.

"White Eagle taught me the white man's language many years ago." He shoved the baby into her arms. "White Eagle and I have much to talk over."

Josie took the baby. Bathed and swaddled in a soft buffalo hide, he smiled in his sleep as she pulled back the fur that covered him. Caleb glanced at Red Cloud, noticing he watched Josie with an amused look.

The two men stepped outside into the crisp, moisture-laden air that waited for the cold, high mountain winds to turn it into snow. "It will snow tomorrow, maybe tonight," Red Cloud said as he took a deep breath of the painfully fresh air.

"I know. A heavy fall too." Caleb closed the flap behind him.

Red Cloud turned and smiled. "You are right. You have not forgotten." They walked on in silence, out of the circle of lodges, out into the meadow filled with grass beginning to show the brown tips of cold damage. Already the valley grew quiet in preparation for the storm, leaving only the crunching of the grass beneath their feet to interrupt the silence.

"You should get her with child. A woman needs a child to hold when the father is away."

The sudden words startled Caleb, and he could think of no answer.

"There has not yet been . . . love between you, has there?"

Caleb smiled down at the ground. "You see too much, brother."

Red Cloud put a hand on Caleb's shoulder. "Come. We smoke the pipe and talk."

Caleb ducked to enter Red Cloud's immense lodge. The tantalizing odor of roasting rabbit filled the house as his bride turned a carcass on a wooden spit. Red Cloud sat down cross-legged beside the fire and accepted the carved pipe his wife passed over his shoulder. Caleb sat down on the opposite side of the fire. Lovingly, Red Cloud filled the red rock bowl with the sacred tobacco, then lit it with an ember from the fire. A thin, aromatic swirl of smoke curled up and around his head.

"Where did you find her?" he asked after he took another deep draw on the pipe and passed it to Caleb.

"I guess she found me." Caleb accepted the carved and feather-adorned stem of the pipe and inhaled. "In a saloon in Independence. She joined the train and took care of me when I was injured in the attack."

Brief pain flitted across Red Cloud's face in the firelight. Caleb paused, then said, "Running Elk is dead."

"I know, I saw." Red Cloud glanced away and took the pipe from Caleb's outstretched hand.

"You were there?" Caleb tensely awaited Red Cloud's answer.

"Yes. We were riding north to join the rest of the band, when we saw the smoke. I returned to the train and found her body where you buried her. I knew you had the child and we tracked you up into the mountains until the woman took you to her home."

Caleb glanced over at Pretty Owl, but she seemed intent on her preparations for supper. "Why did the Crow paint their faces like the Lakota?"

Red Cloud inhaled deeply, then blew out a cloud of thick white smoke. "They wish to make trouble with us, wish to bring the white man's anger down on us, to have the white man defeat us where the Crow cannot. I wondered, White Eagle"—he drew deeply on the pipe again—"if you would come for me, to avenge your people."

Caleb let out an unconsciously held breath. "You taught me better than that, brother. They left an arrow with the owner's mark on it."

"Who was it?" Red Cloud's hand paused in midair.

"I don't know. I've never seen a mark like it." Caleb shook his head. He described the red, blue, and yellow slashes on the arrow's shaft.

Red Cloud frowned. "I have never heard of such markings. It does not belong to any warrior I have faced."

They smoked in silence for a time, then Red Cloud rose and they left the lodge. They walked together, slowly circling the camp, enjoying each other's company and the silence before the storm. Village women knelt by the stream to draw water for last-minute washing and cooking in preparation for the predicted blizzard.

"When did you take a wife?" Caleb asked.

The warrior colored like a young boy at his question. "Her father, a friend of mine, offered her to me when I knew Running Elk would not return. I was reluctant at first, for I wanted no other woman, but as time passed, I knew I needed a mate, needed a wife to bear me children. I grew to love her, and I do not hurt here so much now." Red Cloud placed his hand over his heart. "And when will you take a wife, Caleb McCall?"

Caleb stopped at the sound of his English name. Red Cloud never used it. "I don't know. I hadn't thought about marriage again."

Red Cloud studied his face. "Haven't you?"

Caleb smiled and looked away. "Yes, I've thought of it, but she's not ready. She lost her husband and family to the Crow. Then I come along and drag her across half the country, looking for you. She wants no part of me."

"You love her, then?"

Caleb stopped. "I . . . don't know." He looked up at Red Cloud, amazed at himself for overlooking the possibility. "I don't know."

Red Cloud laughed loud and deep, his voice echoing out across the still meadow. "A long winter alone in the same lodge with such a beautiful woman? You will know by spring, White Eagle, you will know by spring."

Chapter Fifteen

Josie sat alone among the gifts, the sleeping baby propped in her lap. She picked up first one primitive object and then another, turning them over and over carefully in her hands. The generosity heaped on her and Caleb amazed her. There didn't seem to be a lot of anything in the village, so why would the villagers give so freely to strangers? And white strangers at that?

She searched through the pile of robes, beaded pouches, bedding, cooking implements, and other necessities, admiring the workmanship. Suddenly the flap of the lodge opened and Owl stepped lithely inside. Josie's heart began to pound as the Indian woman carefully pulled the tipi closed and turned around. From her seat on the floor, Josie looked up at the woman who towered over her, knowing her legs would never hold if she stood. Owl represented her worst nightmare.

Josie shifted the baby to a more comfortable position, a position from which she could lay him down swiftly if needed, while eyeing the large knife tucked into Owl's belt. But Owl didn't move closer, standing barely inside the lodge's opening.

Her light brown eyes swept Josie from head to foot, and Josie returned the stare. The woman had long brown hair instead of black. She was tall and slim, with extremely gangly hands and feet. But her most unusual feature was the streak of silver hair starting above her ear and blending in as it fell far below her shoulders.

"Wasté yaleka he?" Owl's voice rang out in the stillness of the lodge, and Josie jumped. She frowned and shook her head to indicate she didn't understand a word.

"Koykpe he? Koyke ontun cye kte sni, yeló. Wanblí Ska winyan tawa he niye ksto. Ounyapapi ksto."

Josie shook her head again, and Owl frowned.

"You like?" Owl abruptly switched to broken English. She stepped closer, nodded her head at the assembled gifts, and squatted down.

Josie felt an invisible shiver pass over her as Owl's eyes stared into hers unfalteringly.

"You are afraid?" Owl asked, triumph sneaking into her expression.

Swallowing her fear, Josie shook her head slowly.

"I will not hurt you." Owl held out her hands. "You are White Eagle's woman."

Josie's first impulse was to declare she wasn't anybody's woman, but another glance at Owl's towering size made her ironically glad to be associated with Caleb. "Yeah, I like them gifts a lot. Much obliged." Josie laid the baby aside and stood. "How'd you know we was coming?"

"Rotten Stomach, he brought us word." Owl stepped forward in a swirl of fringe. "Red Cloud is grateful for the return of his son. He ordered women to bring gifts for you."

"He didn't have to do that. I mean, we didn't expect him to . . ." She let her words drift off when she realized the woman wasn't understanding her, but was intently staring into her eyes.

"Are you an Injun?" Josie asked, staring into the light brown eyes.

Owl's brow creased into a frown, and Josie wished she could bite back the words. Maybe she'd offended her.

"Yes, I am Lakota," Owl answered slowly. "My father was great warrior, my mother was like you, *wasíchu.*"

"Your mother was wh-white?"

Owl nodded. "Father took her from farm. Next year, I was born."

Josie shivered, her thoughts recreating what must have happened to that poor woman.

"You White Eagle's woman long?"

Josie dropped her eyes. "Not long."

Owl smiled a secretive smile, stood, and walked to the opening of the lodge. "White Eagle is good man. Make good father." Then, without another word, she was gone, leaving Josie to wonder at the familiarity in her words.

The skies had lowered and the air had turned bitter when Caleb and Red Cloud finished their talk. Darkness fell early and supper preparations lit up the insides of the tipis like lanterns. Caleb had turned Cindy out with the Indian ponies, knowing they would all make for shelter when the storm hit. As he walked back toward the tipi he would share with Josie for the next few months, he realized how much he had missed this life. He missed seeing families together, feeling the blending of the young and old, seeing the children play, the freedom of the nomadic life they lived. A fat snowflake landed on his nose as he pulled open the skin door.

Inside, the tipi was cold and dark. In the faint light he could see Josie sitting in the middle of the pile of gifts, staring dismally down at them.

"It's cold in here," he said, quickly laying a fire in the new ring of stones. Tiny flames licked at the wood, then grew until they threw dancing shadows against the wall. "Aren't you hungry?" he asked her.

She shook her head and he felt a wave of compassion. Squatting down at her side, he lifted her chin with his finger. "It won't be that bad, I promise."

She didn't answer. Leaving her to her misery, Caleb filled a paunch with water from a skin bag hanging outside. Suspending the cooking utensil from four sticks beside the fire, he pushed stones into the fire to heat. Then he cut up strips of buffalo meat, another gift from Red Cloud, and dropped them into the bag. When the stones were hot, he rolled them out of the fire, picked them up with a handful of cut grass, and dropped them into the paunch. As the delicious smell of cooking meat began to bubble out of the bag, Caleb sat back on his heels and watched Josie. Had he made a mistake bringing her here? Was it too cruel to make her face the thing she most feared? But what else could he have done? He couldn't have left her at the cabin. Sitting in the dark, shoulders slumped and head hung, she seemed a shell of the spitfire he had first met.

When the stew was cooked, Caleb dipped some out into wooden bowls. Josie took the one he offered, and he leaned back against the wall and began to eat. She sniffed at the food, dipped in one finger, then began to eat hungrily.

Before they had finished their meal, the wind picked up and flapped the skin sides against the poles. Cold crept in, chilling the air. Caleb rose, set his bowl by the fire, and picked up a long piece of buffalo skin. Tying this piece to the inside of the tipi, he then stuffed the space in between with grass from a pile by the door.

"Whacha doin' that fer?" she asked, raising her eyes from her food.

"To keep the cold out."

She didn't comment. When the job was over, Caleb sat down again.

Josie felt his eyes on her. She tried to ignore him until his stare began to warm her cheeks. She turned to look at him, but his thoughts were far away.

"You're thinking about her, aren't you?"

His eyes blinked him back to the present. "Yes," he said slowly, "I guess I was."

"You loved her a lot?"

He stared at her for a second more, then murmured, "More than my own life."

The intensity of his words sent a shock through Josie. What she wouldn't give to have him feel that way about her.

"It reminds you of her, don't it? Livin' here like this, I mean."

"Yes," he said softly. "It's not your fault. It's not anybody's fault."

"Well, I ain't a-wearin' this thing." She held up the buckskin dress. Something about his devotion to a dead wife was eerie, disquieting.

"Better keep your clothes for when you get to the fort."

The note of sarcasm in his voice confused her. Did he want her to stay? Or was he counting the months to spring, when he could dump her and Petey at a fort and be on his way? There was no answer in the emerald eyes that stared at her. What did he want from her? "Yeah, I guess so," she muttered, and sat back down.

The conversation between them waned. Outside, the wind wailed and keened, telling of the approaching storm. There was nothing to do except sit and stare at each other. It took all of Caleb's concentration to keep from crawling around the fire and taking her into his arms, to use her to assuage this burning in his soul and in his body. Evocative memories of nights with Fawn rose like wisps of smoke, swirled around him, then disappeared out the smoke hole into the night. "We better save the firewood and turn in," he said weakly.

Josie nodded silently, then watched as Caleb spread out two large buffalo robes. One, he placed fur side down and the other lay fur side up. He laid out no others—only the two. Helplessly, she glanced up to find him staring intently at her.

"Don't worry," he said. "I have my bedroll. Go on and crawl in."

Josie didn't dare answer. She had no idea how to take the inflections in his voice. Was he being sarcastic, or was he sincerely sensitive to the way the close quarters made her feel? Was he aware of how she felt, or was he uncomfortable with her so near, reminding him of another home and another time? Her questions would go unanswered at least for that night, because by the time she snuggled deep inside the thick buffalo hides, Caleb was breathing softly and evenly on his blankets on the other side of the fire.

Sometime during the night, the wind awakened her. The inside of the tipi was bitterly cold, and the fire had long since gone out. The buffalo hides flapped against the poles, and the whole structure shook with the strength of the blizzard.

"Don't worry. I haven't seen one fall yet." Caleb's voice came to her across the black velvet of the night. She turned toward him, seeing nothing in the darkness except the faint orange glow of the last coals. Burrowing deeper in her robes, she pulled the hides up over her head.

She heard him rise from his bed and began breaking sticks to nurse the ailing fire. She risked a peep. He squatted beside the fire pit. His breath made a cloud around his face and the orange glow reflected off his handsome features as he peered down, lost in the tiny flames. Bare-chested, he wore only his buckskin pants edged in brilliant blue and yellow beads, and beneath the leather bulged muscular thighs. Firelight played in the curls that were wisps around his face, hanging down to the tops of his shoulders. Josie's gaze followed the smooth muscles that rippled across his chest as he ran a hand through his tangled hair. She remembered the smoothness of his skin from the night she'd sprawled wantonly across him on the porch, hungry for the taste and feel of his lips.

The crease in his brow and the sorrow in his eyes told her his thoughts were on Fawn and the life they had had together. The urge to rise and take him into her arms, to press his cheek to her shoulder and smooth the tangles from his curls, threatened to overcome Josie's promise to herself. The intensity of the feeling made her shiver uncontrollably, and she turned onto her side so she wasn't tempted to watch him any longer.

Josie stretched and stirred. Cozy in the nest of furs, she hesitated, then ventured a peek over the edge. Caleb's bedroll lay neatly folded and stored along the edge, and he was gone. The fire crackled with newly placed wood, and she felt a stab of guilt that he'd stoked the fire while she slept.

She crawled out of her bed and searched through their supplies for something to eat. There was nothing except some pemmican in a leather sack Caleb carried with him. Judging even pemmican better than an empty stomach, she bit into a piece of the tough meat and chewed.

When she had finished, she heard someone crunching through the snow toward the house. She ran her hand through her hair and smiled as the skin flap parted. But it wasn't Caleb who entered, it was Owl. Josie's smile faded.

"Nita wicasa wote sni he? Your man not eat yet?" Owl asked with a frown, then shook her head in a manner that said Josie wasn't doing her job. "I get him."

Before Josie could protest, Owl quietly slipped out. Josie followed her to the flap, unnamed resentment chewing at her. The morning light revealed a good foot of snow piled deep around the tipis. The shouts of the children echoed against steep granite walls as they ran and played, sliding and sledding down inclines on buffalo-rib sleds. Josie smiled, watching them. They were just like any other children—deliriously happy in winter's first snowfall.

Owl trudged away from her, a shaggy buffalo robe piled around her shoulders, weaving a crooked path between tipis, apparently searching for Caleb. Jealousy pricked her. Why did she care what went on between the two of them now or what linked each to the other's past? Why did it matter to her? As soon as it was spring, she'd be on her way back to Independence and then on to the green, rolling hills of Tennessee. But thoughts of home were not nearly so warm this morning. Returning to Tennessee would mean leaving this brutally beautiful country and . . . Caleb. Josie rubbed her temples, feeling the beginning of a headache. Jealousy was a new experience to her, and here she was, jealous of two women—one dead and the other very much alive.

Before Josie could finish her thoughts, Owl reappeared with Caleb in tow. He had abandoned his buckskins and wore skin leggings and held a buffalo robe tightly around him. His hair was tousled and flecks of snow melted in the curls. Owl smiled briefly at him as they stopped in front of Josie, then she swiftly disappeared. Josie felt like she'd been scolded for some childish misbehavior, and she didn't like it a bit.

"Sorry I'm late. I wanted to check on Cindy. She and the others found a little gully and they were huddled in there warm and cozy. On the way back . . . well, I couldn't resist just one ride on a sled." He grinned boyishly. "Did you sleep well?" He shook the snow off the robe, sending flecks of ice over them both.

"Yeah. Yeah, I did. 'Cept for the wind. I woke up once." An uncomfortable silence fell between them. Caleb's grin faded and his eyes met hers. Her heartbeat quickened. Did he know she watched him last night? Did he know how guilty she felt intruding on his thoughts of his wife? "Come inside. It's freezing out here."

"How come yore a-wearin' those things." She pointed to his leggings and the breechcloth at his waist as they entered the lodge.

Caleb glanced down. "I thought I'd better save my other clothes. Besides, these are more comfortable," he said with a shrug.

"Well, be careful. They ain't decent." Josie turned her back, embarrassment searing a trail up her cheeks as his lips curved into a suggestive smile.

"I'll try to remember your innocence," he replied, and she

could just see his face as she reached for another strip of pemmican.

"Josie." He touched her arm, his voice suddenly solemn.

Josie turned.

"I told you Red Cloud asked that we marry." He closed and secured the flap behind them. "Well, he says today is as good a day as any."

"Today?" Josie's eyes flew open wide and a subtle panic built in her. "It's too soon. I mean ... ain't there gotta be some fixin' up or somethin'?"

"Because it's winter and food is low, we can skip some of the ceremony."

"What ceremony?" Josie grabbed at her chance to delay the wedding, if only for a few days. Oh, God, how was she going to stand pretending to be this man's wife and still keep her distance from him?

"Well, most brides have a special dress, you know, decorated and fringed and quilled. There's usually a feast that lasts for several days. Here in the dead of winter, there isn't the food for that."

"Well, you don't want 'em to think this ain't the real thing, would you? You want them to think you and me ..." Josie let her words drift off, suddenly aware she was treading on dangerous ground. "Couldn't we wait?"

Caleb met her eyes in a look so filled with desire, it shook her. Quickly, she looked away, afraid if they were married, even if it was by a Lakota chief instead of a Baptist minister, neither of them would remember that it wasn't for real.

"It has to be this way," he said curtly. "I'll tell Red Cloud."

Loneliness closed in around her as the tipi flap fell shut. Caleb had put away some of the gifts, but others lay in piles at her feet. She picked up a beaded parfleche and placed it along the wall. Then another gift and another until only the packed grass and dirt floor remained. Firewood was getting low, and she knew she should go look for more, but each time she got to the door, her feet refused to move. Where in this great, vast openness would she find wood, and who or what would she encounter in her search?

A cold swirl of air told her the tipi flap was open. Red Cloud's face filled the opening. "Do not be afraid," he said with a smile. "I wish to speak to you."

Just seeing him this close made her heart pound. Involuntarily, she backed away from him, unable to answer. Slowly, he stepped inside. His eyes never left hers, and Josie halted her retreat when her back touched the side of the lodge.

"I will not harm you. I only wish to speak to you before the wedding." He approached her with hands outstretched.

Josie swallowed and gripped one of the poles for support. He stopped, sat down by the fire, and threw another branch or two into the flames. Then he set those black eyes on her, and Josie felt as if his gaze drilled through her.

"Come here and sit." He patted the buffalo robe at his side.

Obediently, Josie moved toward him, obeying the note of authority in his voice as she had unquestioningly obeyed her father. She willed herself to place one foot in front of the other. When she stood beside him, he patted the robe again. She crossed her legs and sat.

Red Cloud held her eyes for a moment, studying her closely before he spoke. The faint odor of wood smoke clung to him. His dark hair lay even and straight across his shoulders and down his back. She almost jumped out of her skin when his hand closed over hers. "White Eagle is brother to me. He and I were children together after he came to us. I carry him here." The warrior patted the bare chest over his heart. "I only wish that he find a woman."

Josie swallowed again, trying to dislodge the lump choking off her air.

"What do you feel for my brother?" Red Cloud peered closely at her.

A thousand thoughts raced through her mind. Uppermost were the comments Caleb had made regarding the Lakota. If she didn't live with him, then some other man could make an offer for her. The Lakota didn't believe in single women living alone.

"He is a good man," she heard her voice answering. "He will take care of me," she said, echoing Caleb's own words.

Red Cloud's face appeared expressionless, and she couldn't tell whether he had believed her or not. She sat under his gaze until she felt perspiration begin to break out between her breasts.

"You feel more." Red Cloud's voice was deep and authoritative, telling her what he knew rather than asking.

"What do you mean?" she asked, dragging her gaze up to meet his.

A slow smile spread across his face as if he'd discovered a great secret. "White Eagle does not know." He stated the fact as if it were a truth. "It is good that you feel this way about my brother."

Josie felt her face flush bloodred at his words. "But . . . but . . . you're wrong. We're only . . ." She struggled to set him straight, ominously remembering Caleb's warnings. Red Cloud's stern eyes suddenly softened and he put out a sinewy but gentle hand, and touched her arm.

"White Eagle has known much pain. He came to us as a child, cold and afraid. We took him in and healed his body. But we could never heal his heart. When he and Fawn married, everyone was happy." He held his hands up in a sign of joy. "The broken little boy was healed. Then a child was born. More happiness and celebrating." Dropping his hands, Red Cloud shook his head sadly. "Then his family was killed by the Crow. It will take much time for his heart to heal, for he carries deep scars." Again he touched her arm, giving her a gentle squeeze. "A wife who loves him can do that for him."

Josie didn't answer, and blinked at the tears that burned the backs of her eyes.

"It was once that way for me," he continued with a wistful look. "Her name was Running Elk. She was a white woman."

"The baby's mother."

He nodded. "An evil man took her from me. I thought my heart would die."

Josie nodded her head. Funny, she thought. She hadn't felt that way when Johnny died.

Red Cloud stared at the fire and didn't speak for several seconds. Then he looked at her and said as though it were a command, "You will be happy with White Eagle."

Josie nodded again, wishing with all her soul that Red Cloud could be right. "Thank you," she said in a choked voice as he rose abruptly to leave. She looked up into his face again, only now she didn't see the fierce warrior. Now she saw a father; an ordinary man gifted with great sight and the burden of leadership; a man struggling to overcome a great loss. Her fear fell away as some inner voice told her he didn't speak so freely with most people, that she should consider herself greatly honored.

"I will take care of him," she promised. Her hand shook as she tentatively touched his shoulder.

He turned and smiled at her. "See, you have counted coup on the great Red Cloud again and still you live," he said with a chuckle and a twinkle of recognition.

Josie's eyes widened. How could he have recognized her as the woman he touched that dark night on the plains? Even more surprising was the sarcasm and humor in his voice, and the fact he could make light of his reputation.

Swiftly, he was gone, leaving Josie with a warm feeling. Perhaps the Lakota were not so bad. Perhaps she had judged them too quickly. Even Caleb had told her all tribes were not alike. She fastened the skin flap against the cold, her heart suddenly lighter. Maybe she would go out and gather some wood—all on her own.

Chapter Sixteen

Caleb returned to the tipi in the glow of a pale winter sunset. Muted oaths in Josie's Tennessee twang greeted him as he opened the skin flap. Bending over the steaming buffalo paunch, Josie shook one hand vigorously and put her fingertips into her mouth. Damp ringlets clung to her forehead, and she wiped at drops of perspiration with the back of her hand.

"Confounded Injun ways," she muttered, attempting to pick up a heated rock from the fire pit with a piece of skin.

He smiled as she cursed again and dropped the rock on the dirt floor. She whirled around when he slipped the wooden pin through the tipi flap. She smiled brightly at first. Then the smile faded and Caleb knew his face gave away his thoughts. For a moment she'd looked hauntingly like Fawn bending over their supper.

"The wedding is set for tomorrow," he said flatly, and sat on the buffalo robe by the fire to warm his hands. She resumed her battle with the rocks, and Caleb watched her from the corner of his eye. He had had a long talk with Red Cloud, and once again his brother had insisted the two wed, as much for Josie's

protection as for the morals of the tribe. But Caleb knew she
was afraid, afraid of him, afraid of loving again. He brushed
off the troubling thoughts. The marriage would be temporary
and only for appearance's sake. In the white man's world, the
bond would be worthless.

Josie had made no comment to his announcement, and he
slanted a glance toward her. With her back to him, she carefully
tended the evening meal, fishing the rocks out of the boiling
water and dropping in chunks of buffalo meat. After tomorrow,
they would be considered a family. Mixed feelings rushed
through him, thoughts that pulled at the memories haunting
him. Josie brushed by, and he realized how easily he could
forget this marriage was to be for appearances only.

On the other side of the fire, Josie broke off pieces of pemmican and laid the pieces in two wooden bowls.

"Did you hear what I said?" he asked, standing and moving
so close behind her that his breath ruffled wisps of her hair
and sent her fragrance curling up around him.

"I heard you." She continued her cooking tasks, seeming
unmindful of how near he was.

"Josie . . ." Caleb gently took her shoulders and turned her
around to face him.

In the tiny tipi, he loomed above her more than she remembered. He stared down at her with a hunger that made her knees
weak. But beneath the want was the old, familiar hurt, and she
didn't want to be a substitute for a dead woman. Summoning
all her courage, she met his eyes steadily.

"Josie, I want you to know . . ." His words drifted off, and
he paused as though gathering his thoughts. "I want you to
know that you're safe here with me. I'll take care of you."

"You keep a-sayin' that," she snapped. Chagrined at the
flicker of pain that crossed his face, she said slowly, "I know
you will," hoping her voice didn't tremble like her legs. "But
. . . when will you stop a-pinin' after her?"

Abruptly, he dropped his hands and turned away.

"I won't substitute for nobody, Caleb," she whispered.

"I don't want to talk about her," he growled. "Not to you, not to anybody." Her brief comment had aroused the very thoughts he had just fought to push away. From somewhere deep in his mind, Fawn's lilting laughter bubbled up and he heard it again as though she were beside him. Caleb whirled and stormed out of the lodge, leaving Josie behind in the swirl of cold air.

Sometime during the night, he returned. Through slitted eyes Josie watched him shuck off his shirt and lay down on the blankets she'd unrolled for him. He put his arms behind his head and lay on his back. When his breathing became slow and even, she knew he was asleep. Wiping away a stray tear, she turned on her side and stared at the shimmering shadows on the lodge wall.

The morning dawned clear and cold, the result of another blast of cold air from the north. Outside, the crunching of snow beneath feet awakened Josie. She stretched and turned onto her back to stare up through the smoke hole at the brilliant blue sky. The sounds of daily village life worked their way into her consciousness. Children shouted, dogs barked, people greeted one another in friendly tones. Today was her wedding day. She smiled, then memories of her first wedding day crept into her mind.

It had been hot, so hot, in fact, that her sparse bouquet of flowers had wilted even before the ceremony. An unsuccessfully altered dress, given by a lady on the wagon train, had served as her wedding gown. Beads of sweat had run down between her breasts as she stood, arm in arm with Johnny, before the preacher and pledged their vows. Afterward, eating and dancing continued far into the night. But she hadn't seen her own bridal party, for Johnny had insisted on taking her directly to his parents' wagon after the ceremony. She frowned, remembering her mother's shame as the others asked why the bride and groom didn't attend.

Johnny was frantic in his conquest of her. With girlish anticipation, she'd looked forward to the mystery of her wedding
night, but in reality it was a sorry truth. He hadn't been gentle
and kind as she'd envisioned, but harsh and insistent, barely
getting his own pants down around his ankles before he lifted
her skirts and took her on the floor of the wagon. He sweated
and grunted and pushed at her, making her bare backside slide
across the rough boards. Every splinter bit into her flesh as the
suffocating heat inside the closed canvas of the Conestoga
wagon threatened to engulf her. Sweat soaked her clothes before
Johnny finally finished in a shuddering climax and collapsed
on top of her. She hadn't felt a thing, not a pleasant thing
anyway. She'd felt only revulsion, not just for her husband,
but for the act that had made him such; revulsion for the sweaty,
sticky union men put so much stock into. No, she didn't look
forward to that again. She turned her head and looked over
across the fire at Caleb's neatly rolled and stored blankets.

Outside, Caleb walked in nearly knee-deep snow, striding
across the flat floor of the valley to where the horses had pawed
out a place to eat the dried greenish-brown grass. He moved
easily among the Indian ponies until he reached Cindy's side.
She nickered and pushed her nose into his palm, searching for
the tidbit he often brought her. Quickly, she devoured the dried
apple he'd begged from Pretty Owl. He stroked her tan coat
and laid his head on her back. She was his steadfast friend,
always ready with a gentle nicker and a quick nudge no matter
what the situation. She was his companion for months at the
time on the lonely prairie without a complaint. Caleb sighed,
gave her a good-bye pat, and began the walk back toward the
village.

Red Cloud waited for him at the edge of the tipis. He wore
only a single eagle feather in his hair, and a buffalo robe cloaked
him head to foot.

"Come with me, brother. We have much to discuss." The
chief turned on his heel and headed toward the outskirts of the
village. "You must rid yourself of your past," he threw back

over his shoulder as he trudged through the snow. "Let go of the memories that haunt you. I, too, had to learn this."

"I can't." Caleb shook his head and stumbled in a snowbank. "It's not that easy to forget Fawn and what they did to her."

"You must not forget her, but she will not come back from death. You must go on and give your love to a new wife."

Caleb didn't answer. Red Cloud was saying the same things he'd told himself all night.

"She will be a good wife and bear you many children." Red Cloud stopped so suddenly, Caleb almost plowed into the back of him. "You are lucky your wife is beautiful and in love with you."

Caleb jerked up his head. Red Cloud had turned around and was grinning at him. "Did she tell you this?"

"No, I saw it in her eyes."

Caleb shook his head, the fleeting hope dashed. "She doesn't love me. She grieves for a dead husband as I do for Fawn."

"Ah, that may be, but she loves you. Am I not the best at reading the enemies' eyes?"

Caleb nodded.

"Then, is it not easier to read the eyes of a woman in love than the eyes of a warrior?"

He's got me there, Caleb thought while he struggled not to believe Red Cloud's words. She said she wanted to go home, away from the prairies and back to Tennessee. Far away from the land of Caleb McCall.

As they passed the last row of lodges, Caleb sighted a rounded hut of willow branches covered with buffalo hides. A sweat lodge. Red Cloud meant to conduct the rite of purification, *onikare,* for him before the wedding. Caleb knew his brother hoped the words and chantings would come back to him, would remind him of their shared youth.

Red Cloud held open the skin flap. "You must purify yourself for your bride."

Caleb glanced at the careful preparations already made for the ceremony. The mounded path of soil, scooped from the fire pit inside the lodge, led from the rings of stones, through the door facing the east, and ending in a sacred altar of dirt. A brave bent over the altar, patting the soil into a small hill with dirty hands and chanting, "Upon you, Unci, Grandmother Earth, I shall build the sacred path of life. By purifying ourselves for the people, we shall walk this path with firm steps. . . ."

The other end of the path stopped at *Peta-owihankeshni*, the fire of no end, where a helper would heat the limestone rocks and tend the fire. Red Cloud dropped the buffalo robe, revealing his naked body, lean and slim despite his forty winters. The muscles across his stomach molded to his ribs. His chest was completely devoid of hair, as was the rest of his body, except for his head and his groin. Caleb quickly shed his buckskins, his pale body a complement to the brown one next to him.

Red Cloud entered the lodge first, after accepting the pipe. Other men wandered up, each one dropping his robe as well. As Red Cloud disappeared inside alone, memories of other sweats came back to Caleb, sweats serving both a religious function and offering familiar camaraderie between braves. The words and motions of the ancient ritual came back to him. First, Red Cloud would pass the pipe around in the direction the sun moved across the sky. Then he would sit in the corner designated for the compass direction of west, facing the dugout fire pit. With a pinch of tobacco to the four corners, he would declare the hole an altar.

In rhythm with Caleb's thoughts, a brave leaned inside and passed Red Cloud a burning ember, then a handful of sweet grass. The pungent odor drifted outside as it burned on the ember placed in the bottom of the fire pit. Caleb could hear Red Cloud offering a pinch of tobacco to the winged Power of the place where the sun goes down, from which the purifying power comes, asking this Power to help in the rite. Next, he would place a pinch of tobacco in the pipe and offer pinches to the other three powers—to the east, the place where the sun comes up and the source of wisdom; to the north, the source of the purifying winds; to the south, the source and end of all life. Then he would offer a pinch to Mother Earth.

"How!" A general cry went up from all those gathered outside the lodge as the last offering was intoned.

Red Cloud flung open the door and stepped carefully along the path. He placed the pipe, made *wakan* in the sweet grass smoke, on the earthen mound, the bowl facing the west and the stem the east.

"Hi-ho! Hi-ho! *Pila miya!*" each man said as he bowed low and entered the lodge after Red Cloud.

Caleb ducked to enter, remembering the prayer to Wakan-Tanka he'd learned as a child, the prayer asking the Great Spirit's aid in all they were about to undertake.

The naked men moved clockwise around the lodge and sat down cross-legged on fragrant sage strewn across the floor. Its coarse stems crackled against Caleb's bare skin, each broken twig sending forth a new surge of scent. A few moments of silence gave each man the chance to remember the good things Wakan-Tanka had done for him. Caleb felt a surge of reverence, a returning of his childhood teachings about the gods of the air, water, and earth.

The door to the lodge opened, and a young man handed Red Cloud the pipe. He set the pipe on the floor in front of him, the stem pointing to the west. The lodge flap opened again and the same young man handed in a forked deer antler containing a hot white rock etched with spidery moss. The large rock, placed at the center of the fire pit, represented Wakan-Tanka. Red Cloud tapped the pipe against the rock.

"Hi ye! *Pila miya!*" all responded.

Each rock was handled likewise until they filled the pit. Green cedar, sprinkled over the heated rocks, filled the air with sharp pungence. Red Cloud held up the pipe, offering it to heaven, earth, and the four directions. Then he lit it, puffed a few times, and rubbed the white smoke over his body.

"*Ho Ate,*" he said, handing the pipe to Caleb.

Caleb placed the end in his mouth and drew on the special

tobacco for the first time in more than ten years. The strong, mellow flavor filled his mouth. *"How Ate,"* he murmured, and handed the pipe to the man next to him. Red Cloud smiled, and Caleb knew his memory of the words pleased the chief.

The pipe returned to Red Cloud, and he inverted the bowl and knocked out the ashes at the edge of the altar, ending the phase of the ceremony honoring White Buffalo Woman, the holy woman who brought the pipe to the Lakota.

The empty pipe passed to the man sitting in the east position. He held it high above the altar with both hands, then passed it to the young man outside the lodge, who would refill it and lean it against the mound until needed again.

Then the young man closed the lodge's entrance flap, casting them into complete darkness except for the red glow of the rocks. Red Cloud explained the darkness was the darkness of their souls, their ignorance. They must purify themselves of it so that they may have the light. He began to chant the prayers, his voice filling the tiny lodge made limitless by the darkness. For a few moments the red glow illuminated his face, then he poured a handful of water over the rocks. They popped and sizzled and lost their glow. Steam carrying the fragrance of sage filled the lodge. The temperature spiraled, and Caleb felt rivulets of sweat run down his chest and back. The singsong chant of Red Cloud's voice touched something in him, something he'd suppressed for years. He heard his own voice joining that of the others as they prayed words learned in childhood. Caleb clenched his hands and shut his eyes against the heat. He poured his soul into the prayers, asking the gods who had once governed his life to again take control of it, to guide him in his indecision.

Suddenly, the door to the lodge opened. Caleb squinted against the light as the pipe was once more smoked and passed. Again the flap of skin closed, again Red Cloud prayed and chanted. Four times the procedure was repeated, four times Red Cloud appealed to Wakan-Tanka, but he included a special prayer for *Wanblí Ska,* asking that he remember his teachings and the way of the Lakota. The chanting stopped and only Red Cloud's voice filled the lodge.

"The helper will soon open the door for the last time, and when it is opened, we shall see the Light. For it is the wish of Wakan-Tanka that the Light enter into the darkness, that we may see not only with our two eyes, but with the one that is of the heart, and with which we see and know all that is true and good. We give thanks to the helper, may his generations be blessed! It is good! It is finished! *Hetchetu alo!*''

"Hi ho! Hi ho!" all the men cried as the door opened for the last time. Caleb opened his eyes, realizing that most of the water on his face was tears and not sweat. He glanced over at Red Cloud, who smiled knowingly. He'd achieved his purpose. He'd given new life to the beliefs long dormant in Caleb.

Owl crept into the lodge in her quiet way. Josie heard her and didn't flinch. The Indian woman seated herself by the fire without a word. Josie moved around the tipi, rolling up her sleeping robes and piling belongings around the edge of the tipi, taking care not to look in the woman's direction.

"White woman is afraid?" Owl finally asked.

"No, I ain't afraid of you today," Josie answered, not meeting the woman's eyes.

"Today you will marry White Eagle. The women prepare for the wedding." It was more of a statement than a question, and Josie waited to see where the conversation would go.

"White Woman marry White Eagle, but he belongs to me."

Josie's head came up at that one, and she stared straight at the woman whose expression had never changed. "What do you mean, he belongs to you?"

Owl threw a stick on the fire and poked at the embers. "When his wife died, he should have taken me as his new wife."

She stated it simply, as if any idiot could see the logic in it.

"Fawn was my sister. I had no husband, and we have many

more women than men. He should have taken me. Now Owl has no husband and she is too old.''

"Do you live alone?" Josie questioned her, hoping for an error in Caleb's reasoning to keep her by his side.

"No, I live with friends." Owl shook her head, dashing Josie's hopes for a last effort to get out of this marriage.

"I'm sorry," was all Josie could think of to say. What could she say when she didn't know herself how she felt about the whole thing?

"I will not stop the wedding. He loves you."

"Loves me?" Josie shook her head. "Where'd you git that fool idea? He don't love me."

Owl turned her head to the side, as if perplexed by what Josie said. "He is your man?"

"He takes care of me," Josie corrected Owl.

"No." Owl shook her head. "He loves you. Owl would know if he didn't."

"How?" A prick of irritation made Josie narrow her eyes. "How would you know?"

"Because"—Owl raised her chin triumphantly—"he would have come to my bed."

Where was all that talk about purity now? Josie thought, feeling a sharp pang at the thought. "Well, you can have him. 'Cause I'm goin' back to Tennessee as soon as we git out of here in the spring."

"You not want White Eagle?" Owl looked at her as if she were crazy.

"Once I git out of here, you can have him," Josie said with finality. Owl's satisfied smile pierced her.

The women came for her a little past midmorning. They filled up the lodge, muttering to each other in Lakota. Without breaking the stream of their conversation, they reached for Josie's clothes. She pulled away when she realized they intended to dress her as if she were a child. Pretty Owl patiently explained it was the custom, and Josie decided the longer she fought them, the longer it would take until this whole shooting match was over. Reluctantly, she submitted and allowed them to tug and pull at her until she was attired in the elaborately beaded dress, moccasins, and headband.

Pretty Owl stood at her elbow and explained to her that usually the bride was taken on a blanket to the tipi of her future husband and there dressed and adorned. Then she would be carried back to her mother's lodge, where there would be a marriage feast and much celebrating. After that she was a wife. But today they would carry her on the blanket to the tipi of Red Cloud, where Caleb waited.

The women carefully combed and braided her hair into two long, fat braids and secured each one with a buffalo skin tie decorated with the fluff from an immature eagle. When she was ready, several young men and women arrived at her lodge with a large blanket. They placed the blanket on the ground and motioned her to sit. Then they lifted and carried her through the village, where everyone had turned out to see their favorite son marry.

They wove their way through the forest of tipis until they reached the middle of the camp and the large tipi. There they set down the blanket and helped her to her feet. Owl whispered to Josie to enter the tipi alone and then gave her an unreadable look. Josie stopped before the adorned flap and inhaled before she pulled back the skin and stepped inside.

A tall man stood with his back to the door. He turned at her entry, and she drew a sharp, quick breath. Caleb was stunning. That was the only way she could describe how he looked. He wore a magnificent set of buckskins, the hides tanned until they appeared as soft as velvet and bleached a snowy white. An intricate pattern of quills spread across his chest, and the sleeves hung with fringe almost a foot and a half long. The pants were edged with the same long fringe. Even the moccasins were bleached and beaded and quilled to match the shirt. All around him swirled the aroma of sage and cedar.

Josie let her gaze roam over him until she reached his face. He smiled at her, his eyes the color of spring moss against the soft white background of his shirt. His curly hair was tamed by a rawhide band and adorned with two eagle feathers, one with a horsehair tuft at the end and the other worked with quills. His eyes sparkled as he looked her over, then he held out his hand. She stepped up alongside him, laced her cold fingers with his warm ones, and turned to face Red Cloud.

The chief's headdress of eagle feathers cascaded to the floor. He wore a brown set of buckskins beaded as carefully as Caleb's. As Josie's eyes grew accustomed to the dark interior of the tipi, she became aware of others around them. Just behind Red Cloud stood Pretty Owl, holding the baby. At Caleb's side stood perhaps the oldest woman Josie had ever seen. She was tiny and bent with time, the skin on her face toughened and lined by age and exposure to the sun, but her eyes sparkled.

Josie glanced at the people standing to her left and caught her breath. Close by her side stood a tall, tanned man. He, too, wore elaborate buckskins, his hair tied back with a leather thong. Except for the crooked grin he gave her, Josie would have never recognized her twin brother. She couldn't believe Petey could have changed so much in a few short days.

Red Cloud spoke softly, barely raising his voice so others could hear. Josie shifted her eyes back to his face. Caleb's breath ruffled her hair as he leaned down to tell her what Red Cloud had said. She kept her eyes on Red Cloud's moving lips, but she was aware only of Caleb. How was she supposed to feel? she wondered, chancing a glance at his face. Did she love him? Yes, her heart whispered, and a delicious weakness washed over her.

"Normally, no ceremony is held," Caleb was whispering, his lips close to her ear. "The two young people simply begin to live together once the bride arrives at the groom's door after a night of feasting and dancing."

"Why are we listening to all this, then?" Josie hissed.

"Red Cloud insisted that we needed to know how to act like husband and wife."

She shot him a venomous glance, hoping to hide the heat that crept into her face, but he saw and winked at her. Red Cloud droned on, explaining in detail what was expected of both of them in their marriage.

Caleb listened to the words and interpreted for Josie. When she was to answer, she nodded. Sometime during the ceremony, she became aware that Owl had stepped between her and Petey. Once, when Caleb leaned down to whisper, his eyes met the Indian woman's, and he looked away quickly.

When Red Cloud finished, he motioned to two men waiting by the door, and they threw open the flap. Caleb caught her hand, squeezed, and flashed a brief smile before ducking outside to raised voices and throngs of well-wishers. As they walked through the village, Caleb's warm hand clutching hers, she noticed the adoring faces flanking them, each one jostling to see Caleb. These were his people; these were the ones who had loved him, dried his tears, fed his hunger. He should have married Owl, she thought sadly, and stayed here, where he was apparently very happy.

Somehow, in the short time since they'd left, the women had produced a magnificent meal. Buffalo rump and fowl of all kinds roasted over open fires. Roots and berries, dried and stored in the summer for the winter, were boiled and eaten. The villagers thronged around them, eating and visiting with one another and reminding Josie for all the world of church socials back home in Tennessee.

A hand nudged her elbow, and she turned. "Petey!"

He smiled smoothly and Josie caught her breath. His bare chest was broad and smooth, his arms muscular and sinewy. When had her brother become a man? Slowly, Josie smiled back. "What are you doin' in that gitup?" She nodded at his buckskins.

"Red Cloud had some women bring 'em to me." Petey grinned broader. "He brought me somethin' else too."

Josie swore if her brother had been wearing belt loops, he would have hooked both thumbs in them and rocked back on his heels. "You mean . . ."

Petey looked shocked. "Oh, no, sis. I mean a wife. She's real pretty. I seed her the day we come here and we fell in love just like that." He reached behind him and drew out a giggling, blushing girl.

Not even fourteen, Josie judged. "You're married?"

"Will be tomorrow." Petey turned toward the girl and chattered to her in Lakota. He turned back and leaned close to Josie. "They say I'm touched," he whispered.

Sudden, intense tears stung Josie's eyes and fogged the image of Petey, his arm around the young woman. He was slipping away. Her companion, friend, other half, was a man and veering off onto his own path, and the thought left a terrible yawning void deep inside her.

Josie took his elbow and steered him away from She Laughs, returning the bride-to-be's frown. "What in Sam Hill do you think you're doin'?"

Petey looked astonished. "Whadda ya mean, sis?"

"You lost yore mind marryin' one a-them?" Josie accused.

Petey glanced over his shoulder. "I don't see hits no different than you marryin' Mr. McCall."

"She's an Injun. You ain't gonna be able to take her with us when we leave come spring."

Petey's wounded look tore at Josie's heart. "I ain't leavin', Josie. I like it here and I'm gonna stay. These here folks have been good to me. She loves me, sis. Ain't nobody ever loved me before 'ceptin' you."

Josie bit back the sob that rose at the painful words. "You don't even know what love is," she snorted.

Petey stared at her a moment, giving her one of his looks that bypassed his surface inadequacies and uncovered the simple wisdom that guided his life. "I do too know, sis. It's somebody that wants you no matter how stupid you act or how confused you git sometimes. It's somethin' I hope you find someday,

'cause it's wonderful and you deserve somethin' wonderful.''
His eyes flitted away from her face and back to the girl behind
them. Love softened his eyes and jealousy stabbed Josie, then
immediate guilt for her selfish thoughts.

"See you tomorrow at my wedding." Petey winked, threw
his arm across the girl's shoulders, and they ducked into the
crowd.

Suddenly feeling very alone and deserted, Josie searched the
throng in front of her for Caleb. He stood at the center of a
group to her side, and the other warriors jostled and teased
him. Although she couldn't understand what they said, she
knew she was the topic of the conversation, for occasionally
they cast bashful glances toward her. Caleb seemed in his
element, and he was indeed splendid in his marriage clothes.
The young girls attending the festivities at their parents' sides
giggled and whispered and watched him with envious eyes. He
moved easily among the people, smiling broadly and a full head
taller than all present save Red Cloud, who was his constant
companion.

The feasting continued well into the night, and then the
dancing began. A large area had been swept clean of snow by
the women, and inside this circle the dancers assembled. Drums
pounded out a soul-reaching rhythm, and the warriors filled the
arena first. Caleb stood at Josie's side with an arm casually
thrown across her shoulders, but his eyes followed the dancers.
Red Cloud had abandoned his headdress and joined his warriors
in their dance. Their feet pounded the snow-covered ground,
raising a cloud of dust. Bending and weaving, Red Cloud circled
the ring.

On the next pass, he motioned for Caleb. He looked down
briefly at Josie, then stepped out into the arena. Except for his
pale skin among so much brown, he could have easily been a
Lakota. He maneuvered the steps of the intricate dance with
little trouble, twirling and spinning at Red Cloud's side. The
drumbeats intensified. The dancers whirled faster, Caleb's
fringe becoming a blur around him. Whoops filled the air as

the drums speeded up again, and the dancers followed suit.
Suddenly the beat ceased, and the night was loud with the
silence for a moment before chattering voices filled the void.
Red Cloud pounded Caleb on the back, and they both laughed.
Caleb looked at Josie, said something to Red Cloud, then walked
toward her.

"It's time for us to leave," he whispered when he reached
her side.

A thin layer of perspiration made his skin glisten, and his
brown curls lay tangled against his forehead.

"Leave? What do you mean?"

"We're expected to go to our tipi now and leave the guests
alone."

Josie swallowed, old memories suddenly vivid in her mind's
eye. He'd said he wouldn't force her, that he'd take care of
her. But would he remember in the darkness of the tipi with
the sensuous beat of the drums in the background?

Gently, he took her trembling hand, and they slipped through
the crowd to their home. He opened the flap, and light spilled
out. Someone had laid a warm fire in the fire pit. Sweet grass
smoldered on the earthen altar. Josie's sleeping robes lay by
the fire with another new set at their side, opened to their furry
insides. Color crept up Josie's cheeks as she surveyed what
was obviously a bridal chamber. She didn't have the courage
to look at Caleb for fear of what she would see in his eyes.
They stood side by side for several moments before either of
them moved.

Caleb released her hand and turned back to fasten the flap.
Then he moved away from her and sat down by the fire.

"Come here." He patted the soft buffalo fur.

His voice was soft but firm, and he didn't meet her eyes as
he spoke. It crossed her mind to refuse, to remind him of his
promise, but something in the bend of his head made her go
toward him. When she reached his side, she knelt down on the
furs. He stared into the flames, poking the embers with a short
stick.

"I'm sorry I got you into this. It must be . . . uncomfortable for you." A shower of orange sparks crackled viciously, then escaped the flames and drifted up and out the smoke hole. "The people put a lot of stock into marriage and family. Red Cloud only wanted you to be safe and happy here with us."

Josie didn't answer, but stared at the soft, curly hair that tickled the edges of his ear. Caleb's eyes captured hers before she could look away. A deep, burning desire haunted his gaze.

"Was your wedding to Fawn a lot like this?"

The want in his eyes dimmed. Caleb dropped his gaze. "Yes, yes, it was. Except there were more people then; the band was larger. We married in the summer, when the fields and woods were full of game and berries. The feasting went on for two days. She and I left for a time, a honeymoon of sorts. We took a small tipi and went far up into the mountains along the banks of a small, swift stream." He paused, lost in his thoughts.

Josie didn't interrupt him and stared into the orange glow of the fire, seeing her own marriage to Johnny fade in comparison to the love Caleb must have had for his wife.

"Why didn't you marry Owl?" Josie asked the question with as much innocence as she could muster, but Caleb saw through her ruse.

"Did she tell you that?"

Josie nodded.

Caleb shook his head. "Sometimes there's a surplus of women in the tribes because of wars and raids. The Lakota don't believe in spinsters or widows. They encourage a man to take more than one wife. That way everybody's happy." A mischievous glint crept into his eye.

"Everybody but the first wife."

"Oh, no. She's glad for the help. It's a big responsibility being the wife of a great warrior. Many chores to do. A second wife is a companion and a helper."

"Is that what Owl oughta been?" Josie guided the conversation back to her original question.

"No," Caleb answered slowly. "There wouldn't have been

a second wife with Fawn. But when she died, Owl naturally expected I'd take her. Her height has made it hard for her to find a husband. Indian men don't like their wives to tower over them.''

An uncomfortable silence again filled the tipi as the drums resumed their pounding and stomping feet shook the ground. Josie threw her head back and looked up at the smoke hole. Far above the thin stream of smoke twinkled a thousand stars, glimmers against the fabric of the Wyoming night.

"Would you like to go for a ride?'' Caleb was asking when Josie realized she was daydreaming.

"A ride? On Cindy?''

Caleb shook his head and held out his hand. "Come on.'' He crawled over to the back side of the tipi and lifted up the edge. "Here, crawl under. They're watching the front, and they might think this odd behavior for a couple of newlyweds.''

Josie wriggled under the buffalo skins, and Caleb followed her. He took her hand and they ran out into the cold of the night. Skirting the edge of the camp, they sprinted across the meadow to where the horses pawed the snow for dried grass. I should be freezing, Josie thought, feeling the warmth of Caleb's hand around hers.

With a low whistle Caleb called Cindy to his side. He patted her nose as she trotted up, then nuzzled his shirt for an apple. He whistled again, but this time with a different sound. A movement in the herd caught Josie's eye, and a beautiful pinto trotted forward. She was white and dark brown, her spots forming elegant patterns across her back and withers. Caleb smiled while watching Josie's face.

"She's yours,'' he said.

"She's beautiful. Who . . .''

Caleb smiled warmly and squeezed her hand. "A wedding present from me.''

Josie didn't have time to thank him before he caught her around the waist and lifted her. She threw one leg over the horse's back, and her skirt rode up along her thigh. She glanced over at Caleb as she tugged at the hem, and he smiled.

"Don't worry. Nobody'll see but me, and I'm your husband. Remember?" He grinned, then hopped lightly up on Cindy's bare back.

Slight pressure from his knees urged Cindy forward. Caleb looked back over his shoulder and whistled again for the pinto. Cindy eased into a gentle canter, and the pinto followed suit. Josie grabbed for the horse's mane, but found that the gentle gait of the mare barely rocked her.

Across the moonlit, snowy prairie they rode, the bitterly cold wind biting at their faces. Cindy's hooves threw up little sprays of ice as she cantered along. Caleb reached up, pulled the buckskin thong from his hair, and let the curls spread out along the base of his neck. He turned back once, the expression on his face that of a pleased little boy. Josie took a deep breath of the cold, fresh air. The wind tore at her hair and the crisp moisture nipped at her skin. She thought her heart would burst with happiness.

They rode for miles, making a broad circle of the camp. The constant thumping of the drums drifted out to them, and the whistle of the wind washed all thoughts of sadness from her mind. Just for tonight, she could pretend she was wild and free, a newlywed wife on a moonlit ride with her husband. As they circled the camp, they could see the merrymakers still celebrating by the light of the fires. Caleb led them around the camp back to the rear of their tipi. He slid off Cindy's back and then held up his arms to help Josie down from her pinto. A quick slap to Cindy's rump sent the two horses galloping back to the rest of the herd.

They stood alone behind their lodge, just the two of them, the cadence of the drums, and the silvery light of the moon. Josie could deny no longer that she was in love with Caleb. The thought of it filled her mind and her soul. His very presence made her weak. But the logical side of her knew that his love was not free to give. It belonged to a woman long dead.

Caleb slid his hands up her arms. "You're cold."

"I'm . . . all right." I'm anything but all right, Josie thought as she tried not to think about the warmth of his skin touching hers.

"Let's get inside before someone sees us." Caleb reached down and pulled up the skins again.

They both wriggled inside, smothering giggles over their secret. The beat of the drums had grown more intense.

"How can anyone sleep with that racket?" Josie asked, putting her hands over her ears.

"It's not intended for sleep." Caleb looked at her oddly as she stoked the dying fire. "It's intended for love. The drums are supposed to be . . . exciting to the new couple."

Josie felt her cheeks redden as the rhythm became clear. She started to turn away when Caleb caught her by the shoulders. She looked up at him, and his eyes were once again filled with hunger and want. Slowly, he lowered his face and captured her lips. A gentle fire spread through her, and she was pleasantly surprised that she felt no fear, no panic. His arms tightened around her, pulling her against his chest. Josie lifted her arms and caressed his, feeling the warmth through the velvety buckskin shirt.

"Josie," he whispered into her hair as he laid his cheek alongside hers, and she felt a rush of love for the man she held. She found herself wishing—to her own surprise and embarrassment—that this was indeed her wedding night, that this man would take her into his arms and into his bed and brand her as his.

Abruptly but gently, Caleb set her away from him. He smiled sadly and said, "We'd better get some sleep. Business as usual tomorrow."

A chill surrounded her as he moved away toward his own bedroll. She stood there stupidly, trying to summon the courage to ask him to stay, to tell him she didn't care if it was another woman he loved, that she wanted him to take her tonight, and the devil with tomorrow.

"Something wrong?" Caleb asked as he pulled his shirt over his head.

Josie swallowed. "No. Good night." She slipped into the buffalo robes, dress and all, and turned over away from the fire. Silent tears slipped from her eyes, tears of anguish for what could not be.

Caleb lay awake for a long time, staring up through the smoke hole at the stars winking beyond. He knew Josie was crying, even though she tried to hide it. Perhaps the ceremony had been too much for her, too nostalgic of her marriage to Johnny. Perhaps her memories went too deep, as did his. He closed his eyes and tried to summon pictures of Fawn and their wedding night. But, strangely, those memories were not as clear as before. Tonight they were mixed up with images of a raven-haired woman in a splendidly beaded dress riding bareback across the prairie, an expression of complete abandonment on her face. As sleep finally claimed him, dreams robbed him of his consciousness, and Fawn's brown eyes gave way to eyes as blue as sparkling river water in the warm spring sun.

Chapter Seventeen

Josie dragged the heavy buffalo hide across her lap, wiped at her nose to remove a stray hair, then continued to scrape the flesh side of the skin. Yellow fat rolled off the bone awl in her hand while the stifling scent of buffalo flesh filled the tipi, made thicker by heat from the fire.

To Josie's left, Pretty Owl gossiped with the other women circled around her. Josie raised her head when a woman across from her laughed, breaking her smooth face into rows of wrinkles. They spoke in Lakota and, although Josie didn't understand, their laughter was infectious. In the weeks since the wedding, the village women had taken it upon themselves to educate her in the duties of a proper Lakota wife. Pretty Owl had taught her how to cook using herbs and game from the forest. Moon-Is-Round, the old woman who had stood at Caleb's side during the marriage, had taught her how to sew garments together with sinew from the buffalo's leg. Owl had taught her how to scrape hides and tan them for future use. They were patient and understanding, oftentimes guiding her hands with their own to show her a task.

Josie sighed as the women fell into another conversation. Petey had wed his giggling bride, She Laughs, the day after she married Caleb. Red Cloud explained during the ceremony that wise spirits possessed her brother. The slow-witted boy who had never found a place for himself in the world had found his home with Red Cloud's Lakota.

"Moon-Is-Round asks if you are with child yet?" Pretty Owl's gentle nudge brought Josie back to the present. She raised her head, suddenly aware that everyone was looking at her.

"What? Oh, no," she answered with a shake of her head.

The old woman studied her closely for a moment, shook her head, and muttered something beneath her breath. Josie felt her cheeks flush.

"She is concerned for White Eagle. She is afraid that since he lost his first child, he will want no other." Pretty Owl whispered.

Josie didn't answer, keeping her head down and vigorously scraping the hide.

Moon-Is-Round said something else, and the women in the group agreed with nodding heads.

"She says," Pretty Owl interpreted, "that a man who is gone from home so much cannot make baby."

Josie felt her cheeks flush deeper and the tipi shrink in size. Ever since a warm wind had melted the blanket of snow, Caleb had gone hunting nearly every day with Red Cloud, bringing in rabbits and squirrels from the fringe of woods surrounding the valley. All the while, her heart ached with love she couldn't express, that she dared not admit.

She could feel Owl's gaze burning into her. The conversation lagged and the silence stretched long between them. Owl had visited every day, barging in without notice, increasing Josie's unnamed resentment toward her. Still, they spent many hours by the fire sewing while Owl rattled on in Lakota. Josie had involuntarily learned a few words of the language, enough to get the gist of Owl's conversation that wandered frequently to

Caleb. Each time Caleb came home, Owl's eyes followed him, and Josie felt a ripple of jealousy that painfully reminded her Caleb was not hers to claim.

"Owl, tell me 'bout Caleb and Fawn." Josie let out a deep breath as she asked the question, keeping her eyes on her work. It was good to at least have it out in the open.

Owl continued to scrape and didn't seem to have heard. Josie wondered if she'd trespassed on a forbidden subject, then Owl put down her awl and folded her arms.

"He came to us in the spring. I was a child, but I remember seeing Spotted Bear bring him into our village. He was so small and his skin was pale. He fought the rawhide that held him. It took many days until he liked us. I used to hear his screams at night."

Josie shivered, imagining Caleb's distress, a child alone in a village of savage-looking beings. "What happened to him? Where were his parents?" she asked, her eyes on her work, yet she felt the cold gaze Owl leveled at her.

"White Eagle not tell you?"

More an accusation than a question, Owl's words hinted that perhaps Josie's husband had not taken her into his confidence for some reason.

"No, he didn't," Josie answered honestly. "I'd like to know."

Owl shrugged. "He never say. It was many moons before he run and play with the children, but then he have eyes for Fawn. She was small and thin, but White Eagle think she is beautiful. When their age come, every night he play music on his flute and stand with her in the blanket. Fawn never run away from him. Then they marry." Owl picked up the awl and went back to work.

"Did she love him?"

Owl stopped and looked at her again. "She love him much. When she killed, he scream and rub ashes on his face. We think that he die of his grief. Then he leave, say he go back to the whites."

Josie didn't dare look up at Owl for fear the jealousy would show in her eyes. How wonderful it must have been to have Caleb McCall to come courting. To have a man like that want her. To have him pursue her and play love songs on a flute and come to court her, unmindful of her parents or family. No wonder he can't give her up, she thought with a sinking heart.

"White Eagle get Fawn with baby soon, very soon." Owl smiled and nodded. "White Eagle, he very proud. Daughter born in the winter. Most men want son to be great warrior, but not White Eagle. He proud of little girl, carry her around with him, make the other men laugh."

Josie couldn't imagine anybody having the nerve to laugh at Caleb like that. She remembered his tenderness to Red Cloud's baby, realizing its source. Someday he would marry another Lakota woman and have more babies. The joy went out of her day as she reminded herself for the thousandth time that their marriage was only an arrangement and would disappear like the winter's snow the moment they left this secluded valley.

"You and White Eagle have child?" Owl asked point-blank.

"I don't know. Maybe someday," Josie lied, and scraped harder, not liking the direction the conversation had taken.

Owl appeared to consider the comment as she silently shifted the pelt around. "White Eagle, he have strong medicine. Make baby soon."

Josie knew that she flushed to the very roots of her hair. She could feel Owl's black eyes on her, but she didn't look up. A chilling premonition filled her that Owl had guessed their secret. Yesterday, the Indian woman had arrived early and noticed the two separate sleeping robes lying by the fire. She hadn't said anything, but Josie knew she'd noticed.

Abruptly, Owl dropped the awl and shook off the robe. "Must go. Much work to do," she said as she stood. Without another word, the tall woman disappeared out the flap of the lodge, leaving Josie alone with the women's stares and the cumbersome, stinking buffalo hide.

That evening, Caleb arrived home to a warm lodge with a

rabbit roasting over the fire. Josie glanced toward him as he dropped the buffalo robe from around his shoulders. Once again he wore only leggings and a breechcloth, baring his chest except for a battle plate of reeds. More and more he'd begun to adopt the Indian style of dress, his other clothes rolled and tucked inside a beaded parfleche along the inner wall of the lodge as though he'd also tucked away his other life.

The aroma of the roasting rabbit filled the lodge, and Josie removed it from the fire, tore off a piece, and offered it to him. Their hands touched briefly as their eyes met, and she jerked hers away abruptly.

They ate in silence, and when they finished, Caleb rose from his seat and held out his hand. "Come and walk with me."

Josie stared up at him, afraid to touch the outstretched hand for fear of the torrent of emotions it would set off inside her. But she relented, and her fingers closed around his. They stepped outside. The evening was unseasonably warm, a soft breeze melting away the last remnants of snow still clinging to the shady sides of the tipis. Caleb held her hand tightly and they strolled through the camp where the insides of the tipis glowed and shadowy figures moved about. As usual, a crowd of warriors surrounded Red Cloud's lodge, and he sat in their midst, drawing marks in the sand. He looked up and smiled as they passed. On other evenings Caleb had attended these meetings.

Josie turned her head to look back at the charismatic man who held the loyalty of so many simply by his words and actions.

"He's quite a man," Caleb said in silent response to her thoughts.

"Is he as fierce as everybody says?"

"Yes, depending on what's at stake. Right now it's their home."

"What do you mean?" Josie asked as they reached a log at the edge of camp. The surface of the wood was worn smooth, and she guessed many courting couples held clandestine meetings here beneath the full moon.

Caleb sat down and patted the place next to him. As she sat, a premonition of trouble filled her. He'd acted strangely all day.

"The Bozeman Trail is not far from here. It cuts off the Oregon and travels northwest toward Virginia City and the gold fields." He stared up at the pale moon.

Josie watched his face, and the premonition grew stronger. "Pa always wanted to try his luck there."

"Well, the trail runs right through the only hunting territory we have left."

Josie noted that he'd said *we,* and not *they.*

"Red Cloud has harassed wagon trains for years in hope the whites will have enough and turn back, but they only send more, take more land, push the Lakota deeper into the mountains and away from the buffalo that sustains us. Last summer he went to a council in Fort Laramie along with some impressive chiefs—Red Leaf, Old Man Afraid of His Horses, Spotted Tail—in hope of coming to an agreement."

"Did they?" she asked.

Caleb shook his head. "Red Cloud took a lot of criticism from his people about that. They thought he was a traitor for even talking to the whites. Well, it looked like he'd get his way and the troubles would be settled when Carrington and his troops marched into Fort Laramie, bragging about his plans to establish forts to protect the travelers."

Wondering why Caleb wanted her to know all this, Josie nodded and waited for him to continue.

"Red Cloud was furious. He said he and the chiefs were treated like children, that the white chief had planned to steal the road from the Indians all along. He walked out and took half the chiefs with him. But Spotted Tail and some of the others stayed and signed a treaty giving the army permission to build the forts. Red Cloud waited until they were built and then started harassing them and running off their horses."

Josie looked back to where the fire in front of Red Cloud's

tipi lit the village. "Do you think the army'll come this far to git him?"

"No, not in the winter. But in the summer, I don't know." He turned toward her, the feathers plaited into his hair bobbing in the breeze. "We'll be gone by then."

Josie stared out into the blackness, wishing she hadn't heard the unasked question in his voice. He wanted to know if she wanted to go back. She couldn't answer him. Over the past months, she'd begun to sympathize with the Lakota. It wasn't right to take their home. In Tennessee, folks had been pretty riled when the Yankees ran all over their land.

"What are they talkin' about now?" She nodded to where the men hunched over a drawing Red Cloud made in the dirt.

Caleb didn't turn his head, but stared straight ahead out into the dark. "They're planning the attack of Fort Phil Kearney."

Josie had never heard the name, but she could envision the bloodletting that would result and the heartache for those who lost loved ones. "You can't just sit here and let it happen. You gotta warn the fort." She lowered her voice to a whisper.

Caleb didn't answer, and the skin over his jaw tightened. "I won't interfere."

His answer shocked her. Surely, he realized the massacre that would occur. How could he sit and let that happen to his own kind?

"Caleb, we have to. Think of the women and children."

When he turned toward her, he wore a closely controlled mask of anger. Josie recoiled a bit at the intense hatred on his face.

"The soldiers will get what they deserve." The words seemed to reverberate on the evening stillness.

"How can you say that? What about the wagon trains you've guided right through Indian territory? Why'd you do that if you feel this way?"

Caleb's jaw worked beneath his skin. He rose to his feet and stepped away from her out into the moonlight. She saw the sag of his shoulders and knew he wrestled with himself.

"I can't explain. Not now, at least." He turned back, staring straight through her as if he hoped she'd read his mind.

"It's all right. You don't have to tell me," Josie said softly.

He smiled. "Maybe someday," he murmured, and Josie felt the distance between them grow and a ghost step into the void.

Right after sunrise the next morning, Josie trudged up the hill from washing dishes in a deep pool of the stream. She looked at the high peaks to the west and saw a coating of new snow glistening in the morning sun. By night, snow would fall on the village, and she made a mental note that she must go and gather more wood.

As she started to open the lodge flap, she spotted a tall, slim warrior walking toward her. Behind him, Owl matched his strides. They halted when they reached Josie. The man simply stared at her without speaking, waiting for her to open the flap. Obviously, he wasn't going to tell her his business, so she stepped inside.

Caleb looked up from the arrow he was smoothing. Surprise registered on his face, but then his eyes narrowed.

"Winyan iyaye si yo." The warrior jerked his chin toward Josie.

"Josie," Caleb said slowly. "Leave us for a while."

She looked from one to the other, hoping Caleb would change his mind. "Well, I ain't goin'. This is about me, ain't it?"

"It's all right," he said, but his eyes remained on the warrior.

"I come to offer Owl to you as a wife," the warrior said, switching to English. He sat down by the fire, leaving Owl standing behind him.

Caleb tried not to show his surprise and pretended disinterest.

"She is a good worker and needs a husband."

Caleb glanced up at Owl, who looked very pleased with herself. "I don't know, Crazy Horse. I hadn't thought much about another wife." He glanced at Josie's face, white with shock. Another thin curl of wood fell from Caleb's hands. Even when Crazy Horse was young, he'd enjoyed bargaining with the other boys for their treasures.

"I know your woman does not please you. Owl will." Crazy Horse nodded in Josie's direction.

Caleb saw her rage gathering and hoped it wouldn't erupt until he could explain. Owl had been suspect of his relationship with Josie all along. "You're wrong. She pleases me very much."

Crazy Horse glanced at Owl and continued. "Owl will please you better."

He's stubborn. I'll have to give him that. "I need time to think about it. I'll let you know in two suns." Caleb held up two fingers, then resumed his work, signaling an end to the conversation. He could almost hear Josie's blood boiling.

Crazy Horse rose and left the lodge. Owl turned to follow, but paused by the door. "She is no good. You need Indian woman who will warm your bed as well as your meals."

Steadily, Caleb met her eyes. "I said I'd let you know in two days."

Owl sniffed and stepped out of the lodge with her head held high. Caleb watched her walk away. He knew he'd angered her, and Owl was dangerous when angry.

"Is this what you had planned all along? To take her as your other wife?"

Caleb whirled. Josie stood behind him, her hands clenched into fists. Remembering her fury and her determination to knock his head off that night in the cave, he moved away from her.

"No. This wasn't my idea, although I will admit I suspected Owl was up to something."

"What's 'tween you and her? Don't you lie to me, Caleb McCall."

Caleb backed away as she advanced on him. "Someday I'm gonna have to teach you who you can beat up and who you can't, woman."

Josie flew at him. He caught her wrists, but she kicked him in the shin, then stomped on his toe.

"Dammit, Josie . . ." he began, trying to stay out of the way of her flailing feet and hands.

"Wanblí Ska, wociciyaka wanci yeló." Red Cloud appeared at the door, his brows furrowed. He nodded in the direction of his tipi, then left.

All the fight went out of Josie with one look at Caleb's face.

"They're gonna attack the fort, ain't they?" She dropped her hands, and Caleb let her go and stepped back.

"Yes."

Panic washed over her like cold water. "You ain't goin' with 'em, are you?"

Caleb swung away, turning his back to her as he picked up his knife and tied it to his waist.

"You ain't, are you?"

Caleb straightened, waiting. "I have a responsibility here, a responsibility to these people. They're fighting for their lives, not for the land, as the whites believe."

"Caleb, you're white."

He turned, and she saw the scalp lock braided into his hair. "Only by birth, not by life." He moved toward her and laid a hand on her arm. "These are my people, Josie. They fed and clothed me when I couldn't feed and clothe myself. They doctored me when I was sick, and chased away the nightmares when I was a child. This may be the last stand for Red Cloud's people, for my people. Don't you see?" He shook her gently. "I have to go."

"How can you go around killin' women and children of your own kind?" she burst out, shaking off his hands.

"They aren't my kind." His hands slid away. "The Lakota took me in and cared for me when no one else would. I owe them my life." He turned away, intending to go, but as he walked toward the flap, Josie spoke.

"You owe me your life too."

Her words stopped him cold.

"I took care of you when nobody else would neither. I

cleaned your wounds and changed your diaper and fed you and . . .'' A sob caught in her throat.

When Caleb turned, Josie stood with the back of her hand over her mouth. Tears spilled over the rims of her eyes and streamed down her face. Her chest heaved with panic. ''You're my husband, and you might get kilt,'' she whispered.

He moved toward her and gathered her into his arms. She snuggled against his shirt and sobbed. Her hair was soft and silky as he caressed its length. How long had it been since someone cared whether or not he lived? How long had it been since someone had cried for him. Here, in a bundle of spitfire and bluster, was a woman's heart.

''I didn't plan things this way, Josie. I planned to spend a peaceful winter here and then leave in the spring and take you back to Independence. But . . . things have changed.''

''Things ain't changed. You have.''

Warm tears soaked through his leather shirt. ''I guess I have changed. I've realized I should never have left the Lakota, never should have guided all those wagon trains west. I just brought here some of the same people who are pushing the Lakota out.''

''You're gonna regret this, Caleb. Please, don't.''

She felt his body stiffen. ''I don't have a choice now. I'm one of Red Cloud's war chiefs.''

''War chief?'' Josie pulled away and looked at him incredulously. ''Now it's a war? A war with your own people? Folks that came west for a new beginning same as me?''

''We intend to kill only soldiers, soldiers who were warned to stay away, to keep to their treaty and leave these lands to the Lakota. They are warriors the same as us and know the risks.''

''I never thought you'd do somethin' like this,'' she said, shaking her head. ''You ain't no better'n the Crow that massacred the wagon train.'

The fury and loathing in her eyes stung him more than the

bitter words. He gritted his teeth together, turned, and left the
lodge.

By dawn the second day, Josie was a bundle of nerves. Her
hands shook as she prepared the meals, and barely a word had
passed between herself and Caleb. He spent his time seated by
the fire, sharpening his knife and making arrows decorated with
his own mark of a yellow slash followed by two green ones.
Watching the yellow wood turn beneath his fingers, she thought
of the arrows that had riddled the bodies of her brothers and
her father. Each time the bow string twanged as he tested its
strength, she cringed.

Suddenly, they heard running feet outside. Josie looked up
from her cooking. By the time Caleb leaped to his feet, the
village was in a wholesale panic. He jerked open the lodge
flap and saw people running through the village. Behind them
charged thirty or more painted warriors astride war ponies.
Mothers ran before the charging horses, clutching their children
or dragging them along by an arm, barely out of the way of
flashing hooves. The attackers swung stone axes and welded
knives as they charged through the village of tipis, trampling
household goods in their way.

Caleb pulled Josie back inside the lodge with one arm, and
with the other scooped up his weapons. ''Crawl under the sides
of the lodge and make for the horses. Ride as fast as you can
for the woods. I'll find you later.'' He started out of the lodge
and then paused. His eyes met hers. Suddenly sweeping her
into his arms, he kissed her soundly, then released her so
quickly, she reeled backward. Then he disappeared into the
milling crowd.

Josie was about to crawl beneath the edge of the lodge, when
she heard a shrill scream. She ran to the lodge opening. Standing
alone between two tipis was Red Cloud's young wife, Pretty
Owl, clutching the infant to her breast. Three Crow warriors
surrounded her. Painted in riotous colors, they brandished axes

and knives and grinned at her fear. She cringed away from their touch, protecting her baby with her own body. The attackers lunged at her, nicking her skin with the points of sharp knives. The baby wailed loudly, and its tiny head bobbed limply against his mother's shoulder. Pretty Owl covered his face, but her eyes never left her attackers.

"Thunderation," Josie muttered. The warriors lunged forward again, drawing blood from a long gash on Pretty Owl's arm. Without thought, Josie leaped from the lodge and positioned herself between the girl and the warriors. Caught by surprise, they halted their torment of the girl and turned instead on Josie.

The leader, a tall, slim man, pointed to Josie and muttered something to his friends. Josie peered closely at him as he spoke. Something was odd about him, something not quite right, out of place. But she didn't finish her thought, for at that moment, the two others lunged at her, forcing her backward with the chests of their ponies.

Seeing no way of helping Pretty Owl from where she was, Josie sidled along the lodge wall. "Well, boys, I've had enough of this," she muttered as she fled, their laughter trailing after her. As she ducked into her tipi, she glanced back. Pretty Owl's face was filled with bewilderment. "This oughta even the odds a little," Josie said as she brought her fifty-caliber Hawken out of its leather scabbard, quickly loaded it, and stepped outside.

The Crow had forced the girl and the baby against the side of the tipi again. The leader of the three dismounted and walked over to the girl. He grasped a handful of her hair and forced her head backward. Slowly, he drew his knife from the scabbard by his side. Its metal blade gleamed in the sun, and Josie saw the flash before he placed the cold steel against Pretty Owl's throat.

Josie licked her thumb and put a bead of moisture on her sight. Carefully she took aim for the man's head. "Gotta git him right between the eyes so he don't use that knife," she mumbled as she squeezed the trigger. The gun roared and the

Indian whirled. He faced Josie for a second before pitching facefirst onto the ground. The other two looked bewildered for a moment, giving Josie the chance to leap in, grab Pretty Owl, and drag her to safety. The girl whirled away and ran toward her lodge screaming her husband's name.

The two other warriors quickly recovered and advanced on Josie. She fumbled with the shot bag and powder horn, attempting to reload her gun. Lithe as a cat, one man swung down from his horse and grabbed her. He raised a stone ax over his head and grinned maliciously. A scream died in her throat. A loud swishing filled her ears. The face of the Indian holding her suddenly went blank, and he stiffened. Her braid slipped from his hand and he sank to his knees. For a moment, he extended his hand to her, then pitched face forward onto the ground. Sticking out of his back was the same knife Caleb had so carefully honed only minutes earlier.

"I thought I told you to run," Caleb said as he put a moccasin-clad foot on the man's back and yanked out the knife.

"I couldn't . . . the baby." Josie's heart hammered against her ribs.

Caleb took her hand and pulled her along with him. They wove through the battle and across the open area to where Pretty Owl waited. Caleb put Josie on Cindy and Pretty Owl on Josie's pinto. A slap sent both galloping toward the woods.

The sounds of the battle, the whoops and screams, the clash of body against body, and the dull thud of the stone axes filled the valley. Josie led the horses deep into the forest, where she tied them securely. Then she crept back to the edge to watch the camp. She and Pretty Owl lay close to the ground and saw the horses charge in and out of the battle. Josie tried to recognize some markings, to determine the identity of the attackers, but they were all strange to her. She glanced over at Pretty Owl and found recognition in her eyes.

Suddenly, a rider broke away from the battle and made for

the narrow pass leading into the valley. Then another followed, and several more behind him. The remaining attackers were in full retreat. Several Lakota ran for their horses and gave chase. But the Crow had a head start and far outdistanced them, disappearing into the high walls of the pass.

The Lakota warriors milled about the camp, searching for injured. What should they do? Josie wondered. Should they risk returning to the camp, or should they wait as Caleb had said? Was he even alive, or lying dead with an arrow or knife sticking out of him?

Then, as Josie watched, a man strode out of the camp. He started across the meadow, stopped, then started again. Without waiting to see more, Josie grabbed Pretty Owl's arm and dragged her deeper into the forest.

Caleb trotted into the edge of the woods and looked around him. He'd followed the tracks of the ponies here, but now they disappeared. Smart girl, he thought with a smile. He advanced into the woods, his eyes constantly alert to movement. The attackers had left and he assumed they had not ventured into these woods to hide until later, but he had to make sure. He crept on silent feet deeper into the woods. Suddenly, a form swung down out of a tree, wrapped its legs around his throat, and tightened. They both tumbled to the ground, and he coughed, feeling a cool knife blade slide against his throat.

Caleb twisted in the hold, but couldn't break the attacker's grasp. Then he blinked and recognized Josie lying on the ground beside him, his throat twisted between her calves. He followed a small sound and looked up. Pretty Owl perched on a limb above with the baby.

"Where'd you learn that trick?" he asked, rubbing his throat as Josie scrambled to her feet.

"Pa taught me. That's hill fightin'. Why'd you scare me like that?" Josie's hand shook as she pushed back a curl.

"I had to make sure they were all gone. I couldn't go crashing through the woods, yelling like a demon for you."

"Are they gone?" she asked, looking over her shoulder toward the camp.

"Yeah, they're gone."

"Who were they? Crow?"

Caleb frowned and looked back toward the pass. "No, they weren't Crow, at least not all of them. A band of renegades mostly, painted up like Crow warriors."

"What about Red Cloud?" Josie leaned closer.

"He's fine. He's getting together a force to go after them."

His wife scrambled down the tree and hit the ground lightly. She chattered rapidly to Josie, who caught only a few words, and then set off with a determined gait back toward her husband. Josie quickly retrieved the horses, and they followed her.

The village was in a shambles, but luckily there were few injuries and no casualties. Except that the men were readying themselves for battle, they would have been slaughtered. As it was, almost each man had his weapons laid out, carefully prepared and within easy reach. The renegades were turned with little resistance.

As they entered the perimeter of the camp, families reunited with hugs and mumbled greetings. Dead men lay strewn about, but they were the dead of the enemy. Caleb walked over to the body of the man he'd slain to save Josie. He frowned as a feeling of familiarity overtook him, and he turned the body over with his toe. He wasn't ready for what he saw.

"What is it?" Josie asked at his quick intake of breath.

Caleb reached down and with one finger wiped away a streak of the greasy paint smeared across the man's face. He didn't have the color or the high cheekbones of the Crow or the Lakota. In fact, he was white.

"Who is he?" Josie questioned, looking into the unseeing eyes of the corpse.

"Eric Tolbert."

"Anna Tolbert's husband?"

"That's right." Caleb laughed bitterly. "You don't know

how many times I wanted to kill that man, and today I didn't even know it was him."

Stacked one on top of another, the dead bodies were set afire. The stench permeated the village and filled each tipi. Red Cloud was busy overseeing the aftermath, but he took time to hug his wife and child. Enviously, Josie watched the happy family. What she wouldn't give to have a man love her like that, she thought.

"You have again saved the life of my son," Red Cloud said, advancing toward Josie. He held out a grimy and bloody hand and she took it. His eyes were a warm brown, and his height didn't seem so imposing now.

"Your wife is very brave, White Eagle. She would make a brave Lakota. Tomorrow she will receive her warrior's name."

By night, the camp had returned to normal, although additional guards patrolled outside the village in case the attackers returned. Red Cloud summoned all his warriors to his lodge.

"The soldiers have planned this attack to kill Red Cloud. No more Red Cloud, no more trouble with the trail. The white man can move in and take what he wants." Red Cloud spoke as he paced up and down in front of the roaring fire outside his large tipi.

Although what he said seemed outrageous, Caleb knew it was true. Rumors had floated around Independence that the army had hired cutthroats, thieves, murderers, and renegade Indians to kill Red Cloud. They knew he was a powerful leader whose now-small band of followers would soon swell into an army. They had tried to incite the Crow against the Lakota, but only a few renegades were so foolish. Seeing Eric Tolbert's face solidified what Caleb had long suspected. The government would stop at nothing to get what it wanted, and it wanted the land promised to Red Cloud's Lakota, the heavily forested heights of the Powder River country.

"We must kill all the white soldiers at Fort Phil Kearney.

If we leave one man, he will come back with others, more troops against us. We will march in three suns.'' Red Cloud stalked around the fire, bundled in a buffalo robe against the cold. Caleb distractedly went over the time in his mind. It must be getting near Christmas, he reasoned. December, the Moon of Frost in the Tipi. Soon, too soon, spring would come.

Chapter Eighteen

A huge crowd surged in front of Red Cloud's tipi the next morning when Caleb and Josie answered his summons. The previous night, a silent, hawk-faced warrior had brought them the message that Red Cloud wanted to see them that morning. When they walked up behind the crowd, Pretty Owl pushed her way through, took Josie by the arm, and pulled her to the tipi.

As the group closed in around her, Josie panicked and tried to wrench around to look back at Caleb. Other hands grabbed her arms, propelling her forward and pushing her into the tipi. Inside, the fire's flames crackled and jumped as Red Cloud strode around it, wearing the headdress Josie had seen him wear only at ceremonial occasions. Caleb had told her each feather represented a conquest in battle. As she thought of him, Caleb stepped up beside her, caught her hand, and gave it a squeeze.

Red Cloud stopped his pacing and walked up to face them. Despite the fierceness of his dress, his eyes were soft and a smile lurked in their depths.

"Once again you have saved my son," he said to Josie.

"I reckon I feel like he's part mine too," she murmured, glancing over to where Pretty Owl nursed the infant.

"When you married White Eagle, you became a part of our village. I would like to give you a gift." He walked over to an intricately beaded pouch lying on the floor. Picking it up, he pulled at the rawhide strings, opened the pouch, and took out a necklace. It was an elaborate piece of work, adorned with quills and glass beads. In the center hung a star-shaped piece of leather dyed a beautiful light blue.

"This belonged to my mother," he said wistfully, fingering the piece. "She was a brave woman and much honored by our tribe. Her name was Morning Star." He glanced at Caleb and smiled. "One time before I was born, she accompanied my father on a raid on a Crow village. We had scouted the camp many times, but we did not know more Crow joined the band during the night before battle. When they attacked, our enemies poured out of the tipis. My father's men were outnumbered and many Lakota died. Mother had watched hidden in the brush beyond the village. When she saw the tide of the battle turn against my father, she caught one of the ponies and rode down the hill into the battle."

He glanced upward and blinked rapidly. "Father had fallen from his pony and was fighting on foot. Mother charged down onto the battlefield and picked him up. Other wives joined her, and soon the remainder of the band rode up the hill to safety behind their women. She was honored and held in esteem for the rest of her life. Her name became known throughout the Lakota nation."

Stepping forward, Red Cloud placed the amulet around Josie's neck and tied the string. "She would want you to have her name in return for the life of her grandson."

Josie's fingers examined the beading and tears sprang to her eyes. "It sure is pretty, Red Cloud. I'll wear it proud."

He glanced over at Caleb. "You have chosen well, White Eagle. She will make a good warrior's wife."

Their curiosity satisfied, the crowd thinned out, and Caleb and Josie walked side by side back to their tipi. Suddenly, Crazy Horse and Owl blocked their path.

"What is your decision, White Eagle?" the young Lakota warrior demanded.

Caleb looked over his head at Owl, who smiled confidently. Then he glanced down at Josie's expectant face. His pause in answering jolted her. Of course Caleb would want a second wife. With a second wife he could assuage some of the wants she saw so often in his eyes. With a Lakota woman like his Fawn, he could have children and someone to return to after he delivered her to Independence.

"The answer is no. One wife is all I need," he answered, a protective arm across Josie's shoulders.

"It is your duty to take your wife's sister. She has no husband to provide for her. It is your duty." Crazy Horse pounded his palm with a fist.

"I said no. I do not desire another wife."

"She is no good." Owl stepped forward and thrust a finger into Josie's face. "She does not sleep with her husband. She is *wasíchu*, she is no good," Owl said, and then spit at Josie's feet.

Caleb narrowed his eyes. He'd never especially liked Owl, even as a child, when she was nothing like his gentle Fawn. The product of a union between her father and a white captive, White Owl had grown up defensive and bitter. Chided by the other children because of her light coloring, she soon developed an ill nature and inherent laziness. Very few suitors vied for her attentions. When the girls' father died in battle after Caleb's marriage to Fawn, the family expected him to also take Owl. He had refused then too.

"She is my wife, Owl, and she will remain my only wife. Perhaps you had better look elsewhere for a husband. Crazy Horse grows tired of supporting you." Caleb knew the truth in his words made Crazy Horse bristle. He was the youngest boy of the family of girls. To him fell the responsibility of providing for Owl when she failed to attract a husband. Now he'd reached the age to begin a family of his own, and he wanted to rid himself of the burden his half sister had become.

"This is not the end, White Eagle. I will speak to Red Cloud." Crazy Horse strode away with an angry Owl close on his heels.

The entire conversation was spoken in Lakota, and Josie had no idea what was said, but she liked the familiar way Caleb draped his arms across her shoulders and she rejoiced in the anger in Owl's eyes.

"What did they want?" she asked as they resumed their walk.

"Crazy Horse reminded me of my promise to give him an answer in two days." He looked down. Josie had paled.

"What's the matter? You're turning pale," Caleb asked with genuine concern in his voice.

"It's nothin'. I guess it's the excitement," she lied.

Caleb stopped and caught her by the arm. "Of course I said no. I told him one wife was enough for me."

Josie felt her cold body warm right up to the roots of her hair. "But . . . but I'm not really your wife."

His grip on her forearms tightened. "I'd never take a second wife, no matter our arrangement."

"Why?" she heard herself ask.

"Don't you know?" he asked her, his eyes slowly changing to a dark, sultry emerald, and she felt the electricity pass between them as he moved closer.

All the sounds of the village ceased, and Josie heard only the beating of his heart. Her eyes locked with his and she couldn't tear them away. She'd waited so long for this moment. Caleb dipped his head to capture her lips, but then he stopped and glanced around at more than one set of curious eyes that had stopped to watch. He laughed and the spell was broken. But Josie was happy. It was at least a beginning.

* * *

Even though the coldest part of winter bore down on them, and they were well into December, Red Cloud's warriors still harassed the few travelers who braved the Bozeman Trail. He chafed at the presence of the white man so near his village, and he didn't intend to endure it. Carefully, he and his braves planned their next move to roust the whites forever from the land of the Lakota.

Red Cloud conceived and planned their attack well, going over and over the preparations with his warriors many times before the dawn of December 21, 1866. Many nights Caleb was late with Red Cloud and the other warriors, and on those nights Josie lay alone in the dark of the tipi, trying to accept the fact that the man she loved was going to join a Lakota war party, that he was going to take up arms against the white men who manned Fort Phil Kearney.

The war party formed on the edge of the village in the early dawn hours and the women and children turned out to bid them tearful good-byes. Caleb rode at Red Cloud's side. Bright colors streaked his face, painted in a pattern that made sense only to him, although he'd tried to explain it to Josie last night after the *Inipi*. But she'd found her mind was not on war paint. It was on the fact she might never see him again, that he would ride away and she would never know how it felt to lie in the dark in his arms.

Ever since the day Red Cloud had given her her name, she'd wished she could reach out to Caleb in the night, that she had the courage to make the first move, to crawl over to his blanket in the dark and offer herself to him. But she'd lain on her back, listening to his breathing, on the last night they had together. She was afraid to approach him, afraid she would see that tragic look in his eyes that told her his thoughts were of Fawn. All night she'd struggled to find the courage to tell him she loved him, that she would gladly give up her independence in exchange for his name. But her courage had failed her and they had slept several feet apart, each rolled into their own blanket.

Now, as she stood and watched the crowd before her in the predawn cold, she wished she were free to embrace him, to hold him close one last time as some of the other wives did their husbands. Across the sea of people, Caleb caught her eye and raised his lance in recognition, a poor good-bye for a warrior going out to battle. He reined Cindy around and rode out after the bulk of the warriors as the party moved forward. She felt the world drop out from beneath her feet as he disappeared into the narrow pass. She was left with the plight of the wife of a warrior—to sit and wait.

Red Cloud's warriors covered the distance between the village and the valley of the Peno long before noon. Along the trail they were joined by large numbers of Cheyenne braves. Red Cloud halted his force behind a hill that stood alone on the open ground between them and Fort Phil Kearney. The fortress sat in the distance on a slight rise in the forks of the Little Piney and the Big Piney creeks. A shiver of revulsion swept over Caleb as he remembered what that log stronghold represented.

Crazy Horse rode alongside Caleb and Red Cloud, the feathered skin of a red-backed hawk braided into his hair. Jagged bolts of lightning zigzagged across his face in red paint. Beneath his blanket, red hail marks dotted his body. All around them were more than a thousand mounted Lakota and Cheyenne braves. A cold wind whipped down out of the north and set Caleb's teeth to chattering. Red Cloud appeared impervious to the cold, and Caleb's thoughts wandered to keep his mind off the impending battle.

His surety in this venture had begun to wane as soon as they rode out of the village. He'd found himself surrounded by a throng of painted warriors, each one having prepared himself for death as Caleb had seen warriors do countless times before.

He'd also thought of the many times he'd been on the receiving end of such a war party of Crow or Blackfoot and even strange bands of Lakota.

When he left Red Cloud's village after Fawn was killed, he thought he'd left behind his Lakota upbringing as well. He was wrong. Warring emotion pulled at him. Loyalty to the man riding in front of him, the man who had befriended him as a child, fought with loyalty to the people of his birth, those he had lived among these last few painful years. He closed his eyes against visions of wagon trains stretching out across the windswept plains, their canvas tops swaying back and forth with the rhythm of the wagons. Were these innocents? Did they really not understand they were taking this land from someone? Would they ever understand that the Lakota did not own the land but drew their life from it?

With hand signals, Red Cloud motioned to Crazy Horse. A group of braves on foot moved away toward the wooded edges of the hills to their left. Another small group of mounted warriors broke away and rode ahead. Below them, a wood train sprawled, loaded with firewood for the fort. With an unspoken signal, they charged out of the valley, splashed across the Big Piney, and swept down on the wood train, making its way from the mid-river island to the fort.

Caleb heard shots, then saw the flash of a signal from the top of the hill.

"I want you to see this, brother, to see your revenge," Red Cloud said, raising a clenched fist. They rode around the bare hill, but still out of sight of the fort. Spread below, the battle with the wagon train waned. The Lakotas pulled back and their scouts galloped back toward the Peno valley. As the Lakotas retreated, the wagon train broke its corral and rattled toward the Piney River.

"See?" Red Cloud pointed to their retreat. "Now Fetterman will come."

At the same time, Crazy Horse's small group of warriors had worked its way quite close to the fort. They crept along the edge of the brush, giving the appearance of hiding from the soldiers. A lookout on the fort wall spotted the small group and fired one of the fort's howitzers directly at the party. One of the grass-stuffed decoys plunged from his horse as the shell exploded. Others in the party howled and scrambled north, obviously afraid of the army's superiority.

Crazy Horse spun his pony around and set off after the frightened group, turning and firing arrows awkwardly back at the fort as he rode, appearing to do a clumsy job of covering the back side of the retreat. A new group of soldiers spilled out of the log fort. They dashed after Crazy Horse; who moved his group fast enough to stay out of range of the soldier's rifles. Their shots whined and slammed into the ground behind him as he repeatedly turned and charged the soldiers, taunting them to come after him.

The swift Lakota ponies plunged into the freezing waters of the Big Piney and scrambled up the side of Lodge Trail Ridge with Fetterman and his men in hot pursuit. Suddenly, Crazy Horse pulled his pony to a plunging stop just short of the top of the ridge. While his group poured over the crest and disappeared on the other side, he dismounted and fiddled with the war rope around his pony's neck. Then he frantically picked up the horse's hoof and dug at a stone. The soldiers drew nearer, and their bullets hailed down around him, flinging up gravel where they struck the ground.

Red Cloud reined his horse around, motioned for Caleb to follow him, and galloped around the hill and up the side of Lodge Trail Ridge. Once again Caleb asked himself if he was doing the right thing, seeking revenge through the massacre of his brethren, betraying all his teachings as a white man, turning his back on his own race. Sudden violent memories flashed through his mind—a blur of feathers mixed with blue and yellow, screaming horses and shouting men, his mother's cries, his own wails. The sounds of the battle seemed to echo in his head, and he glanced over his shoulder to dispel the thoughts.

He would need his mind clear of all except the battle before him in a few minutes.

Caleb watched Crazy Horse throw himself onto the back of the little pony and gallop up the rise. Fired with the taste of near victory, Fetterman charged recklessly up the hill behind him. Crazy Horse galloped right past where Caleb and Red Cloud hid in the brush. Caleb ducked his head as the thundering hooves of the cavalry soldiers charged in front of him, down the slope, and toward the forks of the Peno creek. Suddenly, Crazy Horse pulled his horse to a stop and issued a terrifying war cry. From out of the bottoms of the creek, out of the grass behind him, and out of the trees ahead of him charged thousands of Lakotas. Fetterman was caught out of range of his howitzer, out of sight of the fort, and without any hope of rescue. His brave relief force scattered as the Lakotas waded through them.

Taken entirely by surprise, the soldiers jerked their horses to a halt. Some dropped their weapons as the valley filled with thousands of Lakota war cries. Cursing themselves for their own foolishness, the soldiers jerked their horses around to retreat. Swarms of Lakotas fell on them, shooting the horses out from under the men. Once on foot, the soldiers formed a circle, putting all their backs together. But they were far outnumbered and fell in waves as the Lakota reached them.

Caleb felt his feet move and plunge him into the midst of the battle. He saw the look of terror on the face of his first victim, a tall youth with a lock of sandy hair hanging over his eyes. Caleb stared as his knife plunged deep into the boy's belly. The boy's eyes widened in surprise and a trickle of blood seeped from his mouth. Then his weight sagged on the knife. Caleb jerked it loose and the lad fell to the ground.

Turning back toward the fight, Caleb felt himself charge into the melee, swinging the ax and the knife. He felt his weapons make contact with the enemy, felt the sickening thud as his stone knife struck bone, felt the warm blood flow over his hand as his knife jabbed home time after time. His chest heaved with the exertion of the battle, and the thrill of battle ran through his veins, making him feel light-headed and invincible. But he knew better than to trust that feeling and, without a look back at the bloody bodies, he rode after the war party toward Lodge Trail Ridge.

To his left, Red Cloud was still astride his horse, riding through the scattered soldiers and wielding his stone ax with success. A few Lakota fell with the first crack of army-issue rifles, but there wasn't time to see who it was. As wave upon wave of soldier dropped, Fetterman and a few of his men managed to fight their way out of the midst of the battle and up a knoll alongside the Bozeman Trail. The top was bare of trees and a few scant rocks jutted out of the ground. The blue-clad men turned their back to one another and made their last futile stand there.

In less than an hour, Caleb judged by the sun, the entire rescue force, including Fetterman, were dead. Afraid of being taken as captives, Fetterman and his second in command had shot themselves.

Caleb stood at the top of the hill. His hand dangled at his side, tightly clasping his knife, bright red blood dripping off its end. Scores of braves busily stripped the soldiers of their clothes and scalps. Some of the bodies of the soldiers were brutalized and dismembered, to keep them from entering the afterlife. As the rush of battle began to recede, reason returned to Caleb, and the impact of what they had done came crashing home. Unsteadily, he sat down on a rock, still holding his bloody knife.

"You have done well, White Eagle," Red Cloud said, riding his blood-streaked pony up to him. "We have defeated our enemy."

Caleb raised his head as a wave of nausea washed over him. "I have wronged my people, Red Cloud."

Red Cloud frowned. "This is what you have wanted for many years—revenge, justice for your parents."

"Yes, I wanted revenge, but this . . . this is a massacre."

Red Cloud slowly shook his head. "The soldiers had weapons and the protection of the fort.'' He pointed at the log structure, now strangely quiet. ''They knew the Lakota were near, as well as the Cheyenne. No, this was not a massacre. Only a brave battle. The white man will call it a massacre only because he lost.''

Caleb swallowed and shook his head.

''You will feel better when we ride into camp with many fine scalps hanging from our blankets,'' Red Cloud said confidently.

Caleb only nodded, pressed his teeth together, and prayed he wouldn't get sick in front of his brother.

The next morning at dawn, a din awoke Josie out of a troubled sleep. Children cried, women shouted, and songs of victory wound their way through the crowd. The war party was back. Flinging aside her buffalo robes, Josie dashed out of the tipi and stumbled into the thick of the crowd.

Crazy Horse rode in first at Red Cloud's side. His little war pony pranced and plunged, while the young warrior waved a blond scalp in the air. Blood was smeared across his chest and that of his horse. Behind the two leaders rode the rest of the party, scalps dangling from their lances. Several wore jackets from fallen cavalry officers, forming an incongruous picture, their legs and thighs bare and their upper portions clad in the blue and gold serge of the army uniforms. Cavalry caps sat atop some heads, and long, black braids flowed from beneath. Josie stretched up on her toes to look for Caleb, and her pulse pounded when she didn't see him.

The women came forward and took the scalps from their husbands, waving them above their heads and making the tremolo sound of victory while brandishing their braves' weapons. Row after row of warriors poured into camp, and it became a churning sea of nervous horses, shouting women, and crying children. Finally, with a great wave of relief, Josie spotted Caleb. He rode far at the back of the procession. No scalps hung from his saddle and no triumph lit his face. The mass of the crowd followed after Red Cloud and Crazy Horse as they rode through the village to Red Cloud's tipi, leaving Caleb and Josie virtually alone. Wearily, he drew Cindy to a stop. His shoulders sagged and his face was gray even beneath the dust. Blood spattered him from head to toe and was matted in Cindy's coat. He threw his leg over her neck and slid to the ground, his legs catching him uncertainly.

Instinctively, Josie reached out for him. A thousand unasked questions were on the tip of her tongue, but the glowering expression on his face stopped her.

''I'm going to bathe,'' he said shortly.

He pulled the blanket off Cindy and slapped her on the rump, sending her galloping toward the rest of the horse herd. Brushing past Josie, he didn't speak, stumbling out across the meadow toward the ice-encrusted river. Josie watched his broad back as he crossed the now-empty meadow, stripping off his clothes piece by piece while he walked.

The stream fed out of the mountains, and in a bend above the village it was about four feet deep and covered with a thin coating of ice. Caleb waded into the water, crashed through the ice, and squatted down, letting the cold water wash away the guilt and revulsion he felt. He closed his eyes against the cold and saw again the faces of the soldiers he'd killed. Not even the frigid water could remove their images from his mind. His stomach roiled again, although he'd vomited repeatedly on the march back. He had not only disgraced himself in the eyes of the Lakota, he'd gone against everything he'd ever learned about life and decency.

He felt the bile rising in his throat and waded to the shore before his stomach tried in vain to empty itself again. He sprawled out on the cold ground, not caring if he froze to death. Rocks bit into his naked skin. He opened his eyes and watched a single blade of grass quiver in the chilly breeze, thankful the simplicity of the thought shut all else out for a moment.

Suddenly, a shadow stretched over him and he rolled over onto his back. Josie stood over him, holding a buffalo robe.

Wordlessly, he stood, and she wrapped the pelt around him. As he started toward the village, from the corner of his eye he saw her bending to pick up his discarded clothes.

Searching glances met his as he entered the village, now filled with victory celebrations and confusion. He looked over their heads, heading for his tipi, a sanctuary from the explanations he knew they wanted.

Josie followed closely behind him, scowling at those who dared comment, while her own mind whirred with unasked questions. When Caleb entered, she secured the lodge flap, shutting them away from prying eyes. She'd built up the fire before going in search of Caleb, and the interior of the lodge was warm and cozy. Listlessly, he sat down by the fire, hunched his shoulders, and stared blankly into the flames.

She kept to her normal tasks, trying not to give in to the growing fear his behavior aroused in her. Pulling out the dried buffalo paunch, she filled it with water and pushed the rounded stones into the fire. She piled up a little dried buffalo meat, some roots and berries, then waited for the stones to get hot.

She sat down across the fire and watched his face. His eyes never left the flames, but they were widened as if in surprise to some thought of his own. Suddenly, someone outside shouted and she moved across the tipi to open the flap. Owl stood outside. The same uneasiness she always experienced in the woman's presence sent a shiver through her, but Josie shrugged it off.

"The warriors say White Eagle very sick. I come to see." Owl folded her arms and raised her chin.

"My husband is fine," Josie snapped, positioning herself in the doorway.

"Red Cloud say he sickened by the sight of the dead enemy."

"Caleb's reasons are his own business. He'll be all right after he sleeps."

Owl tilted an eyebrow as she looked past Josie at Caleb's back. "Warrior need a woman after battle."

Josie felt the hackles on her neck raise up. "I'm his wife

and I can tend to everything he needs." She didn't bother to disguise the contempt in her voice and never shifted her gaze from Owl's eyes.

Owl lowered her brows and glared. "He need real wife, not *wasíchu.*" She spit out the last word as if it tasted bitter to her tongue.

"He's got all the wife he can damn well handle." Josie didn't give her a chance to answer before she snatched the flap closed.

When she turned around, Caleb was staring up at her, a lopsided grin on his lips.

"Thank you," he said simply.

"What for?"

"For saving me, temporarily, from the questions."

Josie squatted down beside him. She longed to reach out and put her arms around him, give him sanctuary in her embrace for at least a while. But instead she laid her hand on the robe that covered his arm. "You wanna talk about it?"

Caleb shook his head. "No."

She didn't ask again. Rising, she pulled the stones from the fire and dropped them into the water. A cloud of steam hissed from the paunch. When the water began to boil, she took the stones from the water and dropped in little pieces of the dried buffalo meat. She stirred the mixture, dropped in more rocks, and then sat down. Caleb had returned to staring at the fire and ignored her curious glances.

When the meal was ready, she dipped out portions for herself and him, then broke off a piece of the coarse bread she'd made earlier in the day. Sounds of the celebration grew louder and the beat of the drums pounded in her ears. Memories of their wedding night and the seductive marriage drums floated through her mind as she tried to eat and ignore their suggestion.

She took Caleb's bowl when he'd finished pushing the uneaten food around and set it with hers outside the tipi to wash in the stream in the morning. On the other side of the village the sky was bright red with the ceremonial fires, and the ground shook as hundreds of feet danced on the hard-packed earth. The smell of roasting meat wafted through the air, and Josie knew a great feast awaited the returning victors. Sadly, she ducked back inside the lodge.

"Please tell me what happened," she asked his back. There, she thought. She'd said it, and if it angered him, then that was better than his silent stares.

He raised his eyes from the flames to her face. "I killed white men, a lot of white men. I watched their blood run down my knife and onto me." Unconsciously, he rubbed his arm.

"Why did you go and git into that? I know it's more than honorin' a promise to Red Cloud. I know you better than that."

A smile stretched Caleb's mouth but never quite reached his eyes as he stood and walked to the far side of the fire.

"A long time ago, when I was a little boy, my folks had a farm in Nebraska Territory. Pa and Ma carved a home out of the wilderness. Indians were always around, but Pa seemed to have worked out an understanding with them. I remember Ma giving them meal and sugar, and every time they would leave game, or a bit of beading or a carved toy for me."

He turned his back to her and stared over his head up through the smoke hole. "But the army wanted the Indians out of the territory. They wanted to push them farther west, closer to the mountains, away from the fertile farming land. They came around a lot and talked to Pa. They used to sit at the table and argue for hours."

He turned to face her and drew the buffalo robe tighter around him as though he were suddenly cold. "Ma always made me go to bed, so I don't remember all they said, but they didn't like Pa trading with the Indians. The army wanted the cooperation of the settlers to move the Indians out. They needed complaints, not people who befriended the Indian."

"What happened?" Josie asked, feeling a chill herself.

"Well, the visits and arguments went on for months. Then one day we heard that a neighboring farm was attacked and the woman and children killed. Our Indians became cautious and didn't come around as much, but I remember seeing one approach Pa while he plowed. He told him that the Indians had had nothing to do with the murders, that the white men did the killing to make it look like the Indians did it.''

Josie clamped her mouth shut, suddenly aware it hung open. The army, involved in murder? Weren't the soldiers the ones protecting the whites from the Indians?

''Pa believed the Indians and continued to trade with them. Well, the captain came to visit again and he and Pa shouted at each other over the table until Ma made them stop. The army captain never came back to our house, but one day right about dinnertime, our farm was attacked.''

Caleb trembled, and Josie put out a hand, then drew it back quickly. ''They wanted the neighboring farms to think the Lakota did this too, so they used Lakota arrows and axes and rode unshod ponies. They caught Pa in the field and killed him there. Ma was in the house and they shot her as she ran out. I saw her fall and ran and hid under the seat of the wagon. I never knew why they didn't look for me, but they didn't. After they finished, they turned around and trotted off, laughing and joking among themselves.''

Josie put her hand up to her mouth to stifle her own sobs. Caleb turned away from her again, but his voice quavered and his shoulders trembled.

''I was only about ten years old. When night came, I started to get cold and cry. At dawn the next morning, Spotted Bear, the old Lakota Pa traded with, found me and carried me home with him. I was already terrified and I screamed and kicked when I saw the village. Finally, hunger got the best of me and I quieted down. I found out years later that it was Red Cloud's father who had traded with Pa and he who found me and took me home. He even tried to return me once to a white settlement.''

Caleb sat again by the fire and stared into the flames. His jaw worked beneath the skin as he fought for control. ''Do you know what they said? All of them? They said the savages had corrupted me and no decent family would have me.''

Josie found herself crying, crying for the lost, hungry, frightened little boy this man had once been. He needed her more than he had when she'd found him wounded. Now his wounds were on the inside—old, festering wounds. Josie dropped to her knees beside him. She raised her hand and gently brushed back his curls, then entwined her fingers in his hair. She pulled him to her and kissed him, wishing that she could take away his pain. He raised his eyes to hers, and replacing the blank, defeated expression was a deep, burning want. Caleb's arms reached out and encircled her waist, drawing her to him. His lips pressed against hers in a searing kiss, releasing all the anger he felt into his desire for her. Josie vaguely remembered she should be afraid, but she wasn't.

Caleb swiftly pulled her onto his lap, and through the buffalo robe she could feel the stiffening of his body. Her skirts had wriggled up around her thighs, and Caleb removed the leather garment in one swift movement, leaving her as naked as he when the robe fell away.

Josie had unrolled their sleeping robes earlier, and Caleb pulled her over onto the soft fur, then covered them both with another. Beneath the warm covers, his hands roamed over her body but his lips never left hers. The vague memory of Johnny rose, then disappeared like mist beneath the morning sun. Caleb was gentle, his skin like satin beneath her fingers as she traced an old scar on his back. His hands played across her body, and the blood began to throb in her ears. Caleb murmured into her hair, and while she was in a stupor of desire, he moved on top of her. She stiffened in anticipation of the pain, but felt only waves of pleasure as he took her, velvety smooth skin against smooth skin. His rhythms kept time with the drums that vibrated the very air around them. Faster and faster the drums beat and pounding feet danced. Shimmering curtains of pleasure washed over her, and she knew she'd never known such love before. Caleb supported himself with his arms on each side of her and

looked directly into her face as he brought her to pleasure.
Josie closed her eyes against the explosions that went off inside
her, and she clasped Caleb close to her with her arms. Suddenly,
the drums stopped and silence filled the tipi. In the firelight,
his eyes burned into hers, displaying every emotion he felt.
Her heart leaped with joy. He loved her as she loved him. In
this moment of intimacy, there was no covering the truth, no
lies because of old fears.

"Caleb . . ." Josie reached up and caressed his cheek, her
lips curved into a soft smile.

He closed his eyes, dipped his head, and murmured into her
hair, "Faw—" Suddenly, his face blackened, and with a groan
he rolled away from her. The cold air brought a chill to her
damp skin. Without a word, he pulled on the only extra pair
of leggings he owned and covered his groin with a breechcloth.
Then he grabbed the buffalo robe and tore out of the lodge,
sending the wooden peg skittering across the yard and leaving
the flap fluttering in the cold wind.

Chapter Nineteen

Caleb pulled the buffalo robe closely around him and waded out into the knee-deep dead grass at the edge of the village. The full moon drenched the meadow with cold silver light. Hot tears stung his face as he continued to walk with no special destination in mind except to get away from prying eyes.

In a few short hours, he'd turned his life completely upside down. Now his once-certain decision to ride with Red Cloud was fogged by blood and pain. Even as he killed them, he'd felt more kinship with the soldiers than he thought he would. He put both palms to his temples and stopped. Why were his thoughts confused? Where had his strength gone? First, he'd ridden in revenge against the people of his birth, and now he'd made love to Josie merely as a salve for his self-pity and seen in her eyes a love for him he could not hope to return. No, it wouldn't be right to love again. It was somehow . . . disloyal to Fawn.

"You did well today, my brother."

Caleb whirled as Red Cloud walked soundlessly up behind

him. Ashamed and humiliated, he hastily wiped the tears glistening on his cheeks.

"Battle is hard," Red Cloud said, giving him a hard look. "Even for the bravest of men. There is honor in battle, but there is also sadness."

"I'm not afraid," Caleb said with his back turned.

"I know your bravery better than anyone. I should not have asked you to come. It was not your place."

Caleb turned around. "I promised to ride at your side one day long ago. Don't you remember?"

"Yes, I remember." Red Cloud nodded. "But you and I are no longer small boys dreaming of battle. We are men. You have chosen to live among the whites and I must lead my people. Things are not the same."

"The Lakota were good to me. Better than the *wasíchu*. They took me in when the *wasíchu* would not. They fed me, gave me a place to grow up, and a family to love me. I can never repay them for that, only with my loyalty."

Red Cloud put a hand on Caleb's shoulder. "This is not your war. It is mine—Red Cloud's war. Now go back to your woman and your warm tipi."

Red Cloud studied Caleb's face and tilted his head. "There is trouble in your tipi?"

Caleb sighed. He might as well have it all out in the open. "She's not my woman, Red Cloud. I married her only to please you. I'm taking her back to Independence, where she can catch a stage going back east."

A sly smile crept across the chief's rugged face. "Maybe that was true then, but now you love her."

Caleb jerked his head up.

"Do you think your brother does not know you so well?" Red Cloud asked.

Caleb walked off a short distance. "Yes, God help me, I do love her. But I can't. I just can't." He shook his head vigorously. "Life is too uncertain out here. I lost Fawn, I can't lose again." He turned around and dropped his voice to a whisper. "I took her. I took her knowing I could not return her love. I took something precious from her, something she offered only to me.''

"I have seen your eyes when you look at her. Your heart is strong and loyal, as you are loyal to me, but you must carry no promises to Fawn. She is dead, White Eagle, and in a wonderful place. She would not wish you to grieve.''

"Part of me knows you are right, but the other part . . . I don't know.'' Caleb shook his head, now beginning to ache.

"Have I not told you I am a wise leader?''

"Of course you are, but what—''

"Then I tell you as a wise leader, and as a man, that Morning Star loves you. You are a lucky man, just as I was to find Pretty Owl after I lost Running Elk. It is wasteful for a good warrior to grieve himself away. You have been too long without a woman.''

"I haven't told her I love her. She had no reason to . . .'' Caleb searched for excuses not to believe Red Cloud.

The warrior threw back his head and laughed. "Reasons are not necessary. A woman knows her heart, and when she finds the man she wants, she will let him know. As you did not stand in the blanket with Morning Star, perhaps you do not know she favors you, but as a man you know even before she tells you.'' Red Cloud walked over and put his arm across Caleb's shoulder. "You have made yourself unhappy and forced a ghost to live in your soul. Let her go. Let Fawn go to the Spirit World and let Morning Star live in your heart.'' He turned and walked back toward the celebration, leaving Caleb alone with his words.

Caleb returned to the tipi far into the night, just before dawn etched pale pink into the dark night canopy. Josie lay in the buffalo robes the same as he'd left her, except her cheeks were stained with traces of tears. His throat tightened as he looked down on her. He wanted to awaken her, to take her into his arms again. But the damage was done. He'd hurt her, used her to assuage his own feelings of inadequacy, and he didn't know if he could even forgive himself for that.

* * *

The cold of December passed into the chill of January, the Moon of Popping Trees. Caleb and Josie coexisted in the same tipi, but he was gone as much as possible. He tried once to apologize, stumbling over his words and explanations, doing little more than confusing Josie. Finally he gave up and stormed from the tipi. She had cried all morning, oblivious of the compassionate stares that followed her. To live so close with Caleb, to breathe the air he breathed, share the same heat from the same fire yet not be able to hold him, comfort him through these difficult days, hurt. But he'd made it clear this was the way he wanted it.

Repeated snows fell on the high camp, practically burying the village. The women kept busy making paths through the snowbanks. At night, the cracking of the nearby trees from the frigid temperatures gave the season of the year its name.

Caleb and Josie continued to sleep under the same roof but on opposite sides of the fire pit. Each spent a goodly part of the night staring straight up at the roof and wishing for the courage to change things.

January led into February, Moon of the Sore Eyes, and February into March, the Moon When the Grain Comes Up. The piles of snow gradually melted and the ground became visible again, and its rich, moldy scent filled the air. The meadow that held the horses turned a light, airy green as tiny shafts of grass pushed their way up through the mud.

March gave way to April, the Moon of the Birth of Calves, and Josie knew the time to leave was upon them. Small hunting parties consisting mainly of members of the same family went out in search of game. The women went out into the woods to seek the box elder and to tap its trunk for the sap that was rendered into sugar over a hot wood fire.

Most families moved into wigwams and took down the less durable tipis for repair or replacement as steady, drenching rains set in, drowning the entire camp for days. Caleb became restless and spent long hours off by himself, leaving Josie to cope with the changing face of the village. Life seemed to go on all around her. New babies born in the late winter months were brought outside for the first time, and young couples began to court, long lines of suitors lining up in front of an eligible girl's tipi each evening. Flute songs warbled through the village, wafted on the evening's chill, but Josie felt her own life was at a standstill. She loved a man who no longer had a heart. In its place was a vessel filled only with the memories of a dead wife. Watching Petey with his own bride, apparently happy and satisfied, Josie longed for a rich and full life of her own, with babies to love and a man to hold her. She thought her life useless when she was bound to her father. Now she was bound again to an impossible love.

Caleb came home one night after a full day of hunting with Red Cloud. He strode into the tent without a word and sat down by the fire. Josie wordlessly handed him a bowl of stew.

"We will leave for Kansas in a week," he said between bites. The suddenness of his decision stunned her. "Why the hurry?" she asked.

Caleb smiled, but it didn't quite reach his eyes. "I thought you were the one who wanted to go home."

"I do, but . . . this sure is sudden."

"No, I've thought about this for several weeks. Most of the deep snow will have melted by now and we can get down out of the mountains with little trouble. It's time I got you back."

"What will you do?"

Caleb shrugged and looked away. "I don't know. Trapping maybe, high up on the Musselshell. Maybe into Canada."

"You won't come back to Independence?"

Caleb shook his head, his hair now down past his shoulders. "I can't live there anymore. Anywhere," he whispered.

Josie wished for words to soothe his pain, to say she wanted to come with him, to share whatever life he forced himself into. No life, no matter how basic or sparse, could compare with the loneliness already taking root within her. She waited, but he said no more. Not a word about her. Not a word about their marriage. Nothing.

In a week's time, they were packed and ready to leave the village. Standing at Cindy's side, holding her pinto's reins, Josie looked into faces she knew she would never see again, faces she'd come to trust and to like. The hardest one to leave was Petey.

Her brother had made quite a place for himself in the village. His wife was large with child, and he strutted like a bantam rooster. In addition to being quick to learn the Lakota language, he had also quickly mastered the art of herbal medicine. The village holy man believed he might be receiving visions and was encouraging him to delve deeper into his vivid and frequent dreams.

"Do you have to go, sis?" he begged, holding her hands in his. "The baby's comin' anytime and you can help."

She glanced at Petey and smiled. He was as brown as any Lakota brave. His hair had grown long and hung loose, tied back from his face with a leather strap. Around his neck hung his medicine bag, containing items known only to him. His leggings were slick from use and a quilled breastplate covered his chest. The muscles in his upper arms had grown. All in all, her addled brother had become a wise man. "Nope. I gotta go home." She adjusted the blanket on her pinto's back again. "I'll tell 'em in Tennessee all about you. They'll never believe it." She shook her head.

"Josie." Petey touched her arm tenderly. "You could live with us. There'd always be plenty for you to do."

Josie touched his cheek. "There's sad memories here, Petey. Besides, these is Caleb's folk, not mine."

"He loves you." Petey gripped her hand tighter. "You've done figured that out, ain't you?"

Josie shook her head. As much as she wanted to believe, she knew Petey was only trying to ease the pain for her, to keep her with him. No, she'd be a burden to his young family. The time had come to go their separate ways.

"Yore fixin' to do somethin' real stupid, sis." Petey gripped her arm with more strength than she thought he had. "I had a dream the other night about you. I seed you a-ridin' through that pass over there." He pointed to a notch in the surrounding mountains. You was a-wearin' yore weddin' dress and ridin' yore pinto. That's all I seed, but I got the feelin' you was real happy."

"That could mean anything, Petey."

"Standing Bear says I gotta study some more on what my dreams mean, but I got this feelin', sis. I can't explain it, but I know you ain't supposed to leave us and that Caleb loves you, even iffen you don't believe it."

"He don't love me, Petey. He's still mournin' his wife, and I ain't got no use fer half a man."

"What's waitin' back in Tennessee? All our people is gone 'cept for a few old aunts and uncles we never did like nohow. There ain't nobody there. I'm all you got."

"I'll git along." She avoided looking at him, knowing his face held that pleading expression she never could refuse.

"I'll never see you again, will I, Josie?" She looked up quickly. Gone from her brother's face was the idiotic expression he'd worn so often. Instead, his eyes were filled with a gentle wisdom, the wisdom the Lakota had seen buried deep inside him.

"No, Petey. You won't ever see me again," she answered softly.

"Bye, sis." He tilted his head up, but his chin quivered.

"Bye, Petey." She gave his hair a yank. "Look after that fat little wife of yours."

He nodded, and Josie knew he didn't trust his voice.

Before she could start to cry too, Caleb walked up behind them. He again wore his buckskins. Josie had carefully rolled and packed the beaded dress and put on her worn shirt, pants, and floppy hat.

"Keep safe, my brother," Red Cloud said, grasping Caleb's forearm firmly. The two men had said their own good-byes the previous night before Red Cloud's fire and in the presence of the other warriors who had fought at their side.

"I will. You do the same."

"I cannot promise, brother. I will never give up the fight for our lands."

"The whites are here to stay. And if you kill these, more will come, hundreds and hundreds of them will swarm over these hills. You ought to listen and make some kind of deal with them."

Red Cloud shook his head. "My people have always lived in these high meadows. They have hunted the buffalo and roamed these lands, become one with them. I cannot leave them. I belong here."

"Well, I wish you luck, brother." Caleb swung up into the saddle. He turned toward Josie's pinto, waiting for her to mount, but Red Cloud had claimed her first.

"Be good to him," Red Cloud said, lowering his voice so only the two of them could hear.

"I'll try," Josie said, choking back the tears, knowing her time with Caleb was now fast drawing to an end.

Gently, he took her hand. "Our people will long remember you as Morning Star, and each time I look at my son, I will remember here." He touched his chest over his heart.

"I've grown right fond of your people. It makes me sad to leave."

"Then stay. Live here with us, you and White Eagle." He squeezed her hand tighter to emphasize his words.

Josie shook her head. "It hurts him too much. He remembers his wife and the battle. I can't. I'm goin' back home, back home to Tennessee."

"Is this Tennessee near Missouri?" he asked.

"No, it's a long ways away from here."

"Then White Eagle will be very sad."

Josie turned away. She didn't think she could stand someone telling her another time how much Caleb loved her, when he had been barely civil for weeks. Her tears were close to the surface, and she didn't want to ride out of the camp sobbing like a child.

She jumped up and threw her leg across the pinto's back. Caleb took a last look around, then nudged his mare forward. Once they had left the last row of tipis, he kicked Cindy into a trot and they rapidly left the valley behind. As they neared the pass, Josie glanced back over her shoulder at the peaceful scene, and tears flowed down her cheeks as the high stone walls shut out the picture. She faced forward and stared at Caleb's broad back. I gotta keep my mind on goin' home. I just gotta think about them green rollin' hills and the mornin' fogs. There'll be family there, mostly aunts and uncles, but they're family just the same.

They wound slowly down out of the mountains, Caleb pushing the horses hard, and by nightfall they had reached the rolling hills of East Wyoming. They found a small wooded spot in which to spend the night. Caleb hobbled the horses and set them to graze on the plentiful grass all around them.

He'd shot a rabbit along the trail that morning and roasted it over the fire. Josie sat by the fire, her knees drawn under her chin and her arms wrapped around her legs against the chill. The flames leaped and jumped and cracked, and she let the fire mesmerize her.

An uneasiness grew in Caleb as he moved uselessly around the camp. The horses were taken care of and supper sizzled over the fire. Except for watching the shadows for movement, there was little for him to do either. He'd fidgeted with his tack long enough, and with a sigh of resignation he came and sat by the fire.

He glanced over at Josie and found her eyes riveted on the flames. Did she know how disquieting it was to have her riding behind him all day, knowing that they were alone and that she was only feet behind him? "I think I owe you an explanation."

Josie raised her eyes to meet his. "Nope. You don't owe me nothin'." A coldness edged into her voice.

"No, I do. I want to apologize for . . . that night in the tipi."

He spoke haltingly, embarrassed at the length of time that had passed since that night.

"Which night is that?" she asked innocently.

"You know, right after the raid on the fort."

"Oh, you mean the night you made love to me and then just walked yourself off and never said a damn word these four months?" Her hair came loose from its thong in the back and fanned out across her shoulders.

Caleb flushed. "I guess that about covers it."

"Well, I don't accept your apology, Mr. McCall. Not without a good explanation."

"I don't have an explanation, Josie. I . . . I was confused, sad. I'm just not ready for another woman."

"My God, Caleb." She turned to face him and flung back the mane of hair. "It's been years and years since Fawn died. It's only been a few years since I lost Johnny, and I'm not still mopin' around about it."

Caleb's flush turned to anger. How dare she speak that way about his wife. "Now, wait a minute—"

"No, you wait a minute." Josie stood up and glared down at him. "I'm in love with you, only you're too dad-blamed stupid to see it. I fell in love with you the day I knocked you on your butt in the saloon. But all I ever hear from you is how much you still love Fawn and what a wonderful wife she was. Well, that may be true, but she's gone. She's gone, Caleb, dead and gone and I'm right here." Josie punched her own chest with both hands. "Do you think she'd want you wastin' your life a-grievin' over her? Do you think if things was different and it was you kilt, do you think she'd still mourn you after all this time? Well, I can tell you no. No. She'da knowed you wanted what was best for her and wanted her to find another husband and have other children."

She'd worked herself into a fine pitch now. She paced around the fire, striding back and forth in front of him. *I love you.* The words sang in his heart, but did she even realize she'd said them? He studied her face, but she was so caught up in her anger, she didn't seem to know she'd confessed her love. An odd pain twisted in his insides. Could he return her love? Return it with the same intensity he knew instinctively she felt. Josie Hardwick never did anything halfway. No, he decided, and clamped his teeth shut on the answering words. He wouldn't say them until he was sure, sure Fawn had been laid to rest in his heart, and there was only one way to do that.

"But you don't believe that do you?" she continued. "No, I didn't think so. You only want to spend your time hidin' behind her memory and a-tryin' to git around the real business of livin'. Well, go on and hide, Caleb McCall, hide and remember till you're old and gray and got the gout in your joints, then look around and see who's there to tend and feed and love you. Think about that." She ended her tirade with an arrogant toss of her head.

His face flushed a bright, angry red, and he leaned toward her. Josie's triumph fled, replaced by fear as she watched his face. You've gone and done it this time, she told herself. She had no right to say the things she'd said, but they were the things she felt and she was glad they were out in the open. She tilted her chin back and awaited his reaction.

"Of all the . . ." he sputtered. "What I do with my life is none of your damn business, Miss Hardwick. And the feelings I had for my wife aren't any of your damn business either, so you keep your thoughts to yourself. In a few weeks, we'll be in Missouri and rid of each other."

"Fine by me," she snapped, scrambled up from the ground, and stalked off into the night.

"Where are you going?" he called.

"To the bushes, if you don't mind." Her answer was neatly laced with venom.

After banking the fire for the night, they lay on opposite sides, each rolled into a blanket. Caleb lay on his back and gazed up at the stars above. From somewhere in the darkness an owl hooted his loneliness. The sound made a shiver run up his spine. A branch cracked in the fire and Cindy rattled her hobble chains. His eyes drooped and his body grew heavy. He ran through a hardwood forest. The brilliant colors of autumn showered down on him and sparkled like jewels beneath his feet. Someone ran ahead of him, flitting in and out of the trees, just out of his sight. He leaned forward and pumped his legs harder. Leaves flew up from the head runner's feet in a kaleido-scope of color. Then he saw her. She ran lightly, long black hair streaming out behind her. Laughter drifted back to him. High, lilting laughter. Momentary surprise slowed his pace. She looked back over her shoulder and laughed again. It was Fawn.

Caleb lunged forward and caught her arm, bringing her to a sudden stop. Her hair fanned out around her and whirled around them both. "Fawn," he whispered, and clasped her to his breast. Suddenly, she was several feet away. Her eyes danced with merriment as she motioned him closer. He stepped forward and she changed into a young fawn with luminous brown eyes. Effortlessly, she leaped over a log and bolted into the forest. Caleb's arms dropped to his sides and the old pain became new—wrenching grief that made his chest swell until he thought it would burst.

He fell to his knees on the forest floor. A fluttering near his ear brought his head up. A dove hovered near him. Softly, she brushed his cheeks with her wings, a light, caressing touch. The canopy of leaves overhead parted and a brilliant light shone down. The dove moved away, very slowly flapping her wings, moving backward until the light swallowed her up, leaving Caleb in complete and total blackness. Then a pinpoint of light appeared in the heavens, a tiny beam in a world of cold darkness.

Caleb jerked awake and sat straight up. His heart thundered as the wispy tendrils of consciousness drifted around in his mind. Cindy's chains jingled again, and he realized it was a dream. He glanced over at Josie, her back to him, and he couldn't tell whether she was asleep. He sighed, lay back down, and put his hands behind his head. Could Josie be right? Could it be he *was* using Fawn's death to hide from life as Josie accused? Did he use it to avoid facing the decision staring him in the face—life among the whites or life with the Lakota?

Five hundred miles and a month and a half later, they could see the outskirts of Independence, Missouri. Barely after sundown, Caleb stopped along the banks of a sluggish, muddy stream, but it was water and they had seen little enough of that in the past weeks. Caleb stepped down from Cindy and stared across the prairie toward the settlement.

"What are you waitin' for?" Josie asked, wondering why he would choose to camp when another hour of riding would bring them into town.

He ignored her question as he unsaddled Cindy and set her to graze in a lush patch of grass nearby. "There's something I have to do first."

"What have you got to do that's so important we gotta stay in this heat one more day?"

He dropped his bridle onto the horn of the saddle and straightened. "You know things won't be the same once we're there." He pointed toward Independence.

He looked into her eyes, and Josie looked away.

When she looked up, he was rummaging through his saddlebags. He drew out a clay-bowled pipe, the wooden stem decorated with slashes and feathers.

"I'll be gone two days. I'm asking you to wait here for me." He stepped to the side of her pony and looked up, the sun putting golden chips into his green eyes. "But I'll understand if you don't."

"Here? This close to town and you're gonna go wanderin' off and want me to just squat here?"

He reached up and took her hands in his, gently caressing her fingers. "Please, Josie."

"What's so all-fired important I gotta wait here?"

Caleb hesitated. "I'm going to pray, to seek a vision."

Josie wanted to shriek at him that he should've prayed weeks ago, when they had no water. But she held her tongue, realizing how important his religion had become to him.

Caleb dropped his eyes from her steady gaze. "I have to settle some things with myself, get some things straight in my mind before . . ."

"Before what?"

"Before I let you go."

Josie pulled her hands free. "Seems to me we already settled that. You've sure made it plain."

"I'm not asking you to understand and I don't think I can explain it to you now. Just wait for me."

Josie stared into his eyes, straining to see an answer there, wanting to see into his soul, past the sorrow and the walls he put up around himself. Trust me, his eyes implored.

"All right. I'll wait. But only for two days. Then I'm high-tailin' it to town."

He smiled slowly at her, and she thought he would kiss her. But instead, he walked over to his saddle, pulled the long skinning knife from the saddlebag, and started out across the prairie without even taking a gun.

"Thunderation. Damn man," Josie murmured as she made camp. She bridled at his indifference and at the confusion he caused within her and banged the coffeepot down hard on the circle of rocks containing the campfire. The past weeks had taken a toll on both of them. Caleb had spoken little to her, his mouth set in a grim line and his hat pulled low across his face. He rode much of the time out in front of her, and few words passed between them. At night when they made camp they ate in silence and then went promptly to sleep in their respective bedrolls.

Josie tried to keep her mind on Tennessee and closed her eyes, imagining deep hollows and evening fogs, the distant lowing of a cow waiting to be milked and the sounds that echoed back from the forested sides of the hills surrounding her home. But her memories were empty, only fleeting images of her long-ago childhood. The pictures she conjured up contained neither love nor warmth, only deprivation and want, poverty and sickness. She and her family had left and never looked back. They had instead looked forward toward a new life, one filled with opportunity and possibilities. She knew it was futile to go back. Only loneliness and insufficiency waited for her there.

Caleb walked for miles, stopping only for a brief drink from a small spring. Then he found what he wanted—a high knoll overlooking the prairie. He could see no sign of a town, no sign of settlers, only the land, untamed and wild since the dawn of time. The sun had almost disappeared when Caleb reached the apex. Pieces of bones, rounded rocks, and feathers littered the ground, and Caleb smiled. He'd chosen wisely. Others had used this place as a holy spot. He stripped off his clothes and began to dig. The stars were pinpoints of light when he finished. Out of the top of the rise of land, he'd scooped a hole large enough for him to squat down in. An ominous rumble in the west announced an approaching thunderstorm.

Carefully, Caleb filled the pipe with tobacco. Usually, the ceremony he was about to undertake was performed with the help of a holy man, but tonight he prayed he would receive a vision by himself, that somehow the spirits that ruled his life would grant him a solution to his problem and speak to his heart.

The scent of the tobacco drifted up from the bits of orange in the clay bowl. Caleb fanned his hands through the smoke and rubbed it over his naked body. Another rumble in the west, this time with a stab of lightning. Caleb closed his eyes and threw his head back. The first downdraft of the approaching storm brought with it the sharp scent of rain and the hot smell of scorched earth.

His body suddenly had no sensation. He couldn't tell if he was sitting or standing, walking or flying. He was weightless, adrift in the great ocean of stars over his head. Another clap of thunder split the air, and the wind increased. Caleb ran his hands through his hair. The piercing cry of an eagle preceded the storm. His vision would come. The eagle guaranteed it.

Another crack of thunder shook the ground, and the first pellets to fall were hail. Lightning struck the ground below and Caleb could feel the charges running up his damp skin. The winds increased, blowing his hair straight back. Then he heard them. Tiny voices speaking to him, whispering in his ear. He opened his eyes and saw someone walking toward him, someone who cared little for the storm that raged over their heads. Fawn.

Chapter Twenty

Caleb stood and shouted at Fawn, but she gave no indication she heard as she walked confidently across the barren ground. Another shaft of lightning struck in front of her. Without faltering, she continued toward him, dark hair falling across one shoulder in a thick, black braid. The long fringe of her wedding dress swished softly around her ankles. Caleb scrambled to his feet. He had to save her from the storm. Why was she outside in this? Thunder boomed and the ground shook. Icy pellets pounded his body.

"White Eagle," she called, her voice painfully familiar.

"Fawn?" Was she real or a vision? Did visions speak? He had never heard another warrior say a vision spoke to him. Had Wakan-Tanka returned her to earth?

"Your pain is so great, White Eagle, that I felt it in a place where there is no pain." Her words were soft, skittering across his skin as he remembered.

Caleb's feet were rooted where he stood. This couldn't be, but she looked real, sounded real. Part of him longed to join her, to go with her into that unknown that waited, but another part held back, tied to the present by soft thongs.

"Your heart is torn. You must not grieve for me any longer." Her eyes were as soft and kind, yet now they contained some unreadable expression, something . . . unearthly.

She stood so close, he could see the beadwork on her dress, remembered how the rows of work felt beneath urgent fingers. "There is a woman."

"Yes," Caleb heard his voice answer. "A woman named Josie."

"She is of your people."

"She is white."

Fawn smiled, mirth tipping up the corners of her mouth. "You are still confused between your people and mine."

"Your people are my people."

Fawn shook her head. "I feel your doubt. Your soul is not at peace within you. Your answer lies with this woman."

A vision of Josie's face suddenly rose before him. Was she a vision too? Which was real?

"Your path is set, White Eagle, and you will walk it with this woman. Much good will come of this, good for our people."

She'd said "our" people. "What of these feelings I still have for you, Fawn. I cannot put you out of my heart."

"You already have."

Her words were shocking, yet he felt truth in them.

"You cling to my memory for selfish reasons; you hide behind them, use them as a shield against this world you do not want to see. A Lakota warrior does not do this."

"So I am not meant to be Lakota?"

"You must seek to unite the two parts of you, husband. Your soul howls with loneliness, waiting for your heart to join it."

The wind whipped a curtain of rain against him, stinging his legs and arms and dimming Fawn's image.

"I must go soon. Let me touch you." She started up the knoll, leaning into the incline. He fell to his stomach and reached over the edge, stretching his fingers, anticipating the warm touch of her hand. She took one hand away from the bunch of flowers she held and reached out toward him. Their fingertips touched; a jolt rocked Caleb, then her body dissolved and an eagle emerged, a solid white eagle that spread its wings and soared. Spiraling up, the bird rose into the boiling clouds of the storm. Lightning struck a scrubby bush behind Caleb, setting it on fire. Thunder boomed, shaking the air with its anger, and pellets of hail fell harder, bouncing on the hard ground. The thunder gods are speaking loudly, Caleb thought as he watched the eagle disappear.

Suddenly, the ice turned to soft, fat raindrops that soaked the ground beneath him, leaving him lying in a puddle of brown mud. Disappointed, he rolled back into the pit and sat hunched against the storm. He'd achieved a vision, but what did it mean? Muddy water slid up over his hips as the depression filled. The piercing cry of an eagle forced Caleb's eyes to the stormy sky. The white predator dove from the clouds, streaking for the earth with its wings folded back against its body. Grasped in its claws was a brilliant light. The bird reached an incredible speed.

Caleb crawled out of the pit and struggled to his feet. He stumbled to the edge of the knoll. Surely it would spread its wings and stop. But the eagle continued its death plunge. In a ball of fire, it plunged into the ground. The flash was so bright, Caleb threw his arm over his eyes. Thunder rolled so loudly, he covered his ears.

Then, from the fireball marking the eagle's death emerged another figure. This one wore a white buckskin dress and carried a rifle. She was crying, holding out her arms to him. Drawing back her arm, she threw something toward him. The amulet Red Cloud had given Josie sailed through the air, turning in flight. Rising into the stormy sky, it reached the apex of its ascent, then fell back toward the earth. Caleb held up his hand and caught the charm. A shaft of lightning struck the ground a few feet in front of him. The charge ran over his body and set him to quivering. His feet flew out from under him, and he fell back into the pit filled with water.

"Caleb? Caleb. Dear God, please tell me you ain't dead."

Consciousness crept in on Caleb and he became aware of being wet, of smelling burning wood, of Josie bending over him. "I'm not dead."

He blinked open his eyes. A smile split her face as she moved between him and the rising sun. She knelt down and smoothed back his hair. "When you didn't come back, I came a-lookin'."

Caleb rolled onto his side, every bone in his back protesting. He reached out and touched the toe of her boot. At least it felt real.

"Can you git up?"

Caleb hauled himself to his feet and shook a mixture of dirt and debris out of his hair. He stumbled once, then regained his balance.

"What in tarnation happened up here?" Josie asked, pushing her hat back on her head.

Holding an aching head, Caleb looked around him. Behind him smoldered the charred remains of a bush. Slowly, he opened his fingers. Lying in his palm was a perfect star-shaped stone, smooth and polished. He glanced to where the eagle had plunged to its death. There, at the foot of the hill, a hole was gouged in the earth.

"That storm was a nubbin' killer." Josie shook her head. "You all right?"

He didn't answer her immediately, staring down into her eyes with an intensity that sent shivers up her spine. She searched his face, and felt that she wasn't talking to the same man who'd left her last night. Whatever he'd gone looking for, obviously he'd found it.

She turned away from the gaze. "We oughta be gittin' back and git you some dry clothes on."

He followed her down the knoll, barefooted, and spoke not

a single word. Once at camp, Josie threw more branches on the fire she'd banked that morning. Wet from the rain, they sizzled and popped. Caleb sat down with a groan and laid his moccasins by his side. She handed him a cup of day-old coffee, which he took without comment, curling his hands around the cup. Josie spread his dry shirt over his shoulders, but he continued to stare into the flames. Something about the vacancy of his stare frightened her. She'd never put much stock in the Lakota religion, raised on fire and brimstone herself. But now she wasn't so sure. What could have brought about such a change in a body?

He raised his emerald eyes and stared at her. Josie flushed and looked away, uncertain of what to say or how to act. What had he found all alone out there? Had he found peace, the vision he sought, or ghosts?

Darkness crept in on their silence, and the insects of the night began to chirp and sing. The coolness of the evening moved along the surface of the stream, blanketing it with a thin layer of fog. Josie threw another willow limb onto the fire and wrapped her arms around her knees. Across the fire, Caleb was asleep, as he'd been much of the day. She'd busied herself the best she knew how. She went hunting and shot a rabbit for supper, but still Caleb had volunteered no explanation. Was he sick? What could have happened to him? She was reluctant to ask questions, so she waited. Morning had moved into afternoon and afternoon into twilight without comment or explanation. He stirred and turned over. "Did I sleep the day away?"

"Near 'bout." Josie avoided his eyes.

"I'll take you on into Independence tomorrow."

"What are you gonna do?"

Caleb started to say something, then paused. "I'll see that you're settled, then I'm leaving."

Tears gathered in her throat, but she bit them back. If nothing else, she could salvage her self-respect.

"What are you gonna do?"

He sat up and swung his legs around to cross in front. "I'm going up into the mountains for a while. Maybe do some trapping."

Josie paused, the question stuck in her throat. "Are you ever coming back?"

Caleb's gaze darted away. "I don't know," was his muffled answer.

Independence, Missouri, was busy with the usual summer flock of settlers when Caleb and Josie arrived early the next morning. Outside town, a wagon train waited for word from their wagon master. Ironically, the train camped on the very spot Caleb had organized his own trains time and time again. A young man passed them on the road into town, wearing a new set of buckskins and riding a dancing stallion. The scabbard at his knee contained a new fifty-caliber Henry rifle. Tipping his hat to them as he rode past, he headed for the train.

"New wagon master," Caleb said to Josie, and nodded back at the stranger.

Weary and caked with dust, the two rode slowly up the same street they had each traveled before. The town had grown, Caleb noticed, in the year he was away. New buildings had sprung up on the outskirts and there were more businesses on Main Street. Some of the fronts of the old buildings were repaired and patched with new, unweathered boards.

They rode directly to the hitching rail in front of a big white house at the end of the street. Red geraniums bloomed in the planters at the end of the steps. A sign hung over the door by one hook, reading, MRS. OSGOOD'S ROOMING HOUSE. A white-haired old woman sat in a rocker on one end of the porch. Caleb stepped lightly up onto the boards. She didn't look up and leaned closely over the bit of needlework held in her lap. He took a step closer. Still, she didn't notice him. She lifted her needlework and turned it toward the morning sun. Caleb felt a lump rise in his throat. She was far more feeble than the last time he saw her, her skin more transparent and thin. He walked forward carefully, then got down on his knees at her side.

"Emmy?" he said softly.

Slowly the little woman turned her head. At first there was no recognition, and then her face lit up with a smile.

"Caleb, child!" Her voice shook and quick tears filled her eyes. She let the sewing drop to the porch as she struggled to get up from the chair. He put his hands beneath her arms and lifted her out of the rocker.

"Caleb!" She covered her mouth with a frail hand, the skin almost white and etched with fine blue lines. Caleb's eyes burned as he pulled her to his chest.

"I didn't think I'd ever see you again," she sobbed into his shirt.

"I'm not here to stay, Emmy."

She put a soft, withered hand to his cheek. "I've always taken what I could get of you."

Caleb helped her stand, then put an arm around her stooped shoulders and led her down the porch. He noticed she dressed as carefully as ever, her calico housedress perfectly ironed and pinned at the neck with the brooch she'd worn every day as long as he'd known her. She had eyes only for him as she pulled a lace handkerchief from the belt of her dress and dabbed at the tears. "There's somebody I want you to meet." He gently guided her to the edge of the porch.

Josie had stepped down from her horse and fidgeted at the foot of the steps.

"This is Josie. I want you to take care of her for me."

Emmy extended her hand and clasped Josie's fingers tightly. "She's welcome."

Josie glanced up at Caleb, then hesitantly took the hand Emmy offered. Emmy grasped it and squeezed while tossing him a taunting look.

Leading the way, Emmy ushered them into the house and

up the stairs to the top. "I have a lovely room right here. Pretty lace curtains."

"Emmy. I think Josie might like my old room better."

Emmy frowned. "It's just the way you left it, Caleb, and you never were one for decoration."

"She'll like it." Caleb led them down the hall and pushed on the familiar door.

In the window still hung the sheer white curtain that stood out in the morning breeze. The same wedding-ring quilt covered the bed in the center of the room. The washstand against the wall by the door held the same pitcher and bowl painted with a pale pink rose. Clean white towels hung from the bar beneath the towel rack, and a large braided rug covered the floor.

Josie turned and stared up at him. "I like it."

Caleb tossed Josie her saddlebag. "Go ahead and wash up. I want to talk to Emmy for a minute." Josie's eyes were luminous as she stared unabashedly at the surroundings. She suddenly looked very vulnerable and lonely.

"For shame, Caleb McCall," Emmy scolded, her back to him as she stood over the white enamel cookstove.

He sprawled in the chair at the kitchen table, listening to her maternal tirade, remembering this room had always been his favorite. Her speech had started the moment he told her how he and Josie had spent the winter together.

Abruptly, she turned around, a mischievous smile on her face. "Shame, shame," she said, trying to sound serious while shaking a wooden spoon at him.

"Don't you try that fine, upstanding citizen stuff on me, Emmy Osgood. I know better."

She giggled, the laugh of a much younger woman. "Philip Osgood was a mighty hard man to put off too." She giggled again.

Caleb reached over to the fruit bowl and picked out a bright red apple. Rubbing it against the sleeve of his leather shirt until it shone, he bit into it. He'd always felt at ease with her, he thought as he smiled at her lilting laughter. Despite the difference in their ages, he could tell Emmy anything.

"I bet Philip was a pistol when he was younger," Caleb said as he chomped the apple.

"He was indeed. In fact, one time"—she dried her hands on her apron and whispered conspiratorially—"we went buggy riding. He hired a rig and drove out of town the opposite way of where I lived. Then he circled out around and I met him down by Pa's watering hole. I climbed into the buggy and we set out for this little place down by a stream, just outside of town. We were engaged, you know," she added with an earnest frown. "Well, anyway, Philip stopped the buggy and leaned over and—"

A slight sound at the door of the kitchen made them both look up. Josie stood in the doorway. She'd washed and dried her long hair and shaken the dust out of her clothes. Although she felt ill at ease, Emmy put any doubts away when she embraced her in a hug, brought her into the kitchen, and sat her down at the table. Moving to the stove, Emmy ladled out a goodly portion of stew and broke off a piece of fresh bread.

"Go on with your story, Emmy," Caleb said with a twinkle in his eye, in between bites of apple.

She frowned at him, but her lips smiled, and she waved him away with a dish towel.

Caleb threw his head back and laughed, full and deep. "Emmy was telling me about her courtship."

She blushed red and turned her back, fiddling with the pot on the cookstove.

"Did you have a good bath?" Caleb asked Josie, his gaze sweeping her.

"Yeah, I guess, but I ain't got anythin' else to wear."

"Well"—Caleb stood up from the table and tossed the apple core into the pan designated for the chickens that ran in the backyard—"we'll have to remedy that if you're going to be living here in town."

"No." Josie caught his arm. "I can't let you do that." She leaned closer. "Neither of us is got any money," she reminded him in a whisper.

Caleb put a finger under her chin and tilted her head back. "You let me worry about that." Then his expression sobered and he kissed her, deeply at first, then abruptly drew back. His fingers left her face and he was gone. Josie stood stock-still for a second, her legs wobbly from the embrace, and cursed herself for being so smitten.

"You're a lucky girl," Emmy said, motioning for her to eat as she dropped into a chair herself. "But, then, it appears to me Caleb is a mighty lucky man."

Josie flushed under her scrutiny.

"Where'd he find you?" Emmy asked, pulling her sewing from her apron pocket.

Painfully at first, Josie related the circumstances of their meeting, of her knocking him winding in Shorty's saloon, of trailing the wagon train, of the attack on her cabin and their flight into the mountains. She told of the winter with the Lakota and their trip back across the plains. Then she stopped. Should she tell about last night? Would Emmy know anything about his strange behavior?

"Miss Emmy, I don't mean to be forward, but you've known him a long time . . . and . . . well, I'd like to ask you somethin'."

"Ask me anything, dear."

When Josie finished, Emmy studied her needlework for a moment before spreading it across her knee and sighing. "Fawn again."

"His wife?"

Emmy nodded. "He has prayed and prayed to be freed of that memory, or the guilt, but it just won't go away."

"So you think that has something to do with last night?"

"A Lakota man will not speak of his vision. It is a very personal thing and he must tell no one except a holy man what he has seen."

"He said he was going away up into the mountains."

Emmy traced the outline of a red flower on the white linen cloth. "And I suppose he must."

"Do you think he'll ever come back?"

Emmy raised sad eyes. "I do not know, child. He is a strong-willed man, an honorable man. In his own time he must come to terms with this. He's long overdue to find his place in the world." Emmy smiled a small smile. "Maybe you've been sent to guide him."

Tears stung Josie's eyes. She glanced at Emmy, standing on the porch edge, a white handkerchief twisted in her hands, her face like stone.

"You take care now. Don't fall into bad company."

Caleb laughed and yanked a latigo strap tighter. "Now, who am I going to see along the Musselshell to fall into bad company with?"

"People are moving in up there, child. The Rockies are almost trapped out. That's what the papers say."

"Well, I'll be careful." He tied on the last bundle with a snap of leather, then turned. All humor left his face, and a deep grayness replaced it.

"I'm going inside for a drink of water," Josie said, allowing him and Emmy time together alone.

"Take care of Josie. She's so innocent. Unscrupulous people will eat her alive."

"You're making a big mistake, Caleb McCall. That woman loves you. She's just what you need."

Caleb climbed up on the bottom step and carefully took Emmy's hands. "But I'm not what she needs. I'm only half a man, and not much of one at that."

"Oh, horseshit, Caleb." Emmy jerked out of his grasp. "Philip would thrash you good if he ever heard you say anything like that about yourself. You just need some time to think, and I hope that's what all this is about. If you let that little woman get away, you'll regret it all your life." She moved down a step and placed a palm on each side of his cheek. "All your life, child," she whispered. Then she moved away in a soft whisper of fabric.

Caleb stepped up onto the porch. Josie was just coming out, her face contorted with trying not to cry. She moved into his arms and Caleb laid a cheek on the top of her head. Was he making a terrible mistake? Did he belong here or up there in the heights? Was he a solitary man or a family man? White or Indian? Coward or warrior? The only thing he was sure of was that the answer didn't lie in the safe confines of town and Emmy's and Josie's love. He had to push himself, strip himself of all comforts, of all safety. Rob himself of all but instinct, and then he would find the answer. Then, only then, he might be able to return.

"I'm never gonna see you again, am I?" Josie mumbled against his chest.

"I don't know."

"I'm always a-tellin' you good-bye." She raised her head. "Whatever kind of man you find in yourself out there, I'll take him. Remember that." Then she stepped away.

The pain on her face was worse than if she'd been crying.

"Whenever you're ready, Mr. Simmons has a job for you at the store."

"I don't know." She shoved back the ever-present hat. "I'll have to see. I don't know about workin' in no store."

"You can do anything you set your mind to, Josie."

"I can't have you."

"That's not your fault."

"It ain't yours either."

Caleb looked away, knowing there was no way to win this battle. Guilt hugged him like a second skin. He felt like he was abandoning her here in a strange town filled with people she didn't know. Before he'd met her, she'd had Petey, but now life had separated them and she was alone. If he stayed, he'd only do her more harm than good.

"You have to go." She suddenly stepped away from him

and laced her fingers together in front of her. "I've decided. I ain't workin' in no store. I'm gonna help Emmy. She's asked."

"Sounds like a good idea." *Somebody else will see her value and marry her.* The thought suddenly reared up and roared its message to his brain. Regret cut deep. If he didn't go right now . . . He could feel his resolve weakening. He raised his eyes back to hers, memorizing every detail of her face. The small scar above her top lip, the way one eyelid blinked slower than the other, the way her hair curled just above her eyebrows. These images would warm his empty soul on cold nights.

He turned and swung up into the saddle. Emmy smiled a tight-lipped smile and waved at him from the porch. Josie watched, her face contorted but dry. He felt a thousand knives cut into his back as he turned Cindy and started off down the street. When he reached the end, he looked back, but the porch was empty.

Spring had passed in a collage of pastels. Wildflowers rioted through the flat, thick meadows, yet even as Cindy waded through the ocean of color, Caleb thought of Josie. Every passing cloud, every brilliant blossom, brought to mind some small detail about her. He rubbed a rough hand across two weeks' growth of beard. Somehow it seemed pointless to shave when there was no one to see.

The meadow ended and the terrain became immediately rocky again. Granite-flecked walls sheered up from the ground, tenacious plants clinging to each crack and crevice. He swung his gaze around him, turning in the saddle. The wind had shifted and something unseen irked at him. His eyes narrowed and searched the shadows. He hadn't seen another living soul for weeks, but he felt as if someone were watching him, following. A raven rasped from a high pile of rocks, and Caleb jumped, his pistol half out of his holster. With a nervous laugh, he reseated the gun and patted Cindy's neck as she turned to look at him. "I'm just jumpy today, girl."

Suddenly, Cindy stopped and her ears flicked forward. A deep, thick cove of trees loomed ahead. "What's the matter, girl?"

Cindy snorted and sidestepped daintily. Caleb frowned and bent down to peer beneath the low branches. He punched her in the sides and, reluctantly, she stepped forward, her ears perked. Soon he knew the source of her hesitation. Burial platforms raked at the green foliage like gaunt fingers. Tattered bits of hides and cloth waved in the soft breeze. One platform had fallen and bones were scattered across the mat of needles and aspen leaves. Caleb pulled Cindy to a stop, and she quivered as she stood. How long had he been on sacred ground? How didn't he see the warning markers? Had he been so self-absorbed he didn't see?

A raven pitched on a platform, scanned around for a moment, then plucked at a bit of fur. So bleak, yet so . . . alive set amid the green, lush growth. High in these mountains, these people had spent their lives. Had loved and sorrowed, laughed and wept. Now their bones would spend eternity as part of this earth, this place. Sudden tears washed over him, relief pouring from him in their salty brine. He gripped the saddle horn with one hand and covered his eyes with the other. So clear. His path was so clear now. Why hadn't he seen it before?

All things must end. Die. Dry up. Wear down. It was not the number of days, but the richness of those days. Where did he want his bones to spend eternity? Buried in some church cemetery or here, food for the raven, nourishment for the ground, the vines, the trees that had shaded him. He raised bleary eyes and fastened on a tiny feather, red, brilliantly red against the brown and green of nature. Slowly, it turned on the puff of a breeze.

Emmy calmly stitched and listened, hearing more in Josie's words than she knew she told. "You loved him right off, didn't you?"

Josie looked up from her supper. "Yeah, I guess I did."

Josie's face had gone from animated to gaunt, and Emmy felt a pang of regret at having brought up the subject. For weeks, Josie had eaten little and talked less. Recently, though, her eyes had taken on some of their old light, but she seemed more sedate, wiser somehow.

"You know, many a young woman here in town chased after Caleb, but none ever caught him. I expect you're a mighty unusual young lady."

"I been called a lot of things, Miss Emmy, but a lady ain't one of 'em." Josie sopped at the gravy on her plate with a bit of biscuit.

"Nonsense," Emmy said as she bit a thread in two with even, white teeth. "There's many a matron in this town that isn't a lady either. I never put much stock on hanging names on folks like they were dogs or cats." She smoothed the bit of embroidery and flashed Josie a genuine smile.

Josie smiled back. Miss Emmy was the first friend she'd had in a long time. Had it not been for Emmy's gentle concern and welcoming ear, she didn't think she could have made it through the last few weeks. Every morning, Caleb's absence had hung heavy around her, and each night was cold and empty without him beside her.

"I bought you another embroidery pattern today," Emmy was saying as she surveyed her own work. "Let's see if we can't do this one without the permanent soil around the edges."

Emmy grinned at Josie and she smiled back. "Embroidery just ain't one of my interests, Miss Emmy. I just ain't very good at them teeny little stitches."

"Nonsense. You can do anything you set your mind to." Her words rang reminiscent of Caleb's words, and the old pain stabbed at her heart.

"What's the matter?" Emmy leaned across the table and covered Josie's hand with her own.

"Nothing, just ghosts."

"You've got to get on with your life, child." She squeezed

Josie's hand. "I love him too, but I also see both sides of him. He may never find what he's looking for. He may never come back. You have to set your mind to that."

Josie sighed, feeling the closeness of tears again. How on earth could one person hold so many tears? She'd already cried a bucketful, she knew. Mostly into her feather pillow. "I just cain't. Not now. I gotta give it more time. I just cain't think no further ahead than today. I just cain't."

The sun had begun to set before stomping on the porch announced the arrival of the other boarders for supper. "I'll get the dining table set." Josie planted both hands on the table and pushed back.

"When will you come and eat with the rest of us?" Emmy asked, grasping her elbow.

Josie smiled into gentle eyes. "I ain't up to that. I just cain't stand all of 'em a starin' at me and wonderin' 'bout me. Maybe someday."

"Well"—Emmy moved away toward the stove, where large pots rattled their lids and steam poured out—"I hope it's soon. I could use your sense of humor out there with all these sour old maids who have descended on me lately."

Josie laughed. Three spinster sisters had come to town to start a newspaper, each one more sour than the next about their lack of husbands. Each one lamented their situation every night over supper to Emmy's annoyance. Josie silently helped Emmy load the table with food, then disappeared, well aware of the speculative whispers that followed her. As their conversation settled into its well-known rut, Josie crept up to the stair landing and sat down. An evening breeze ruffled the curtains and her hair, bringing with it the acrid scent of the prairie, the mustiness of summer, and a slight hint of faraway rain. She closed her eyes and drifted back, back to the night she and Caleb said their vows. She was again on the back of her gentle little mare, riding bare-legged in the freezing cold, reveling in the wind whipping against her face. Ahead Caleb rode Cindy as though they were one being and not two. His muscles rippled beneath

tanned skin; his hair blew long and free, and for this brief
second in time they were husband and wife. Free, unfettered
by convention or man, responding only to ancient rhythms and
urges, answering only to nature.

A sudden piercing laugh broke the spell, and Josie slipped
back down to the kitchen. The boarders were bringing in their
plates from the dining room and in a short time all the dishes
were washed.

"I'm going up to bed, Miss Emmy," Josie said, wiping her
hands on a towel.

Emmy stopped her at the door. "I'm sorry I made you sad
this afternoon."

Josie frowned. "How'd you do that?"

"By mentioning Caleb."

Josie smiled. "You didn't make me sad. I reckon there'll
always be a part of me that'll be sad because o' him. Just some
days these little memories start peekin' out 'stead of stayin' in
their place."

"Caleb was like a son to me and my Philip, but I have no
illusions about him. He's a confused man. Maybe he always
will be. As much as I love him, I love you too and I don't
want to see you shrivel up like those three out there." She
pointed toward the closed door that separated the kitchen and
the dining room. "You have to get on with things. Starting
tomorrow, I want you to get out of this house and start working
for Mr. Simmons."

"But I got a job here."

"Not anymore you don't. You're fired. But you'll always
have a home here."

Josie wanted to laugh at the stubborn expression on Emmy's
frail face, but the laughter stopped somewhere near her stomach.
Seemed harder and harder lately to get it up.

"All right. I'll go talk to him in the morning."

Emmy grinned. "Good. Now up to bed with you so you can
look fresh tomorrow."

Fresh, Josie thought as she mounted the stairs. Not a word

she'd use to describe herself. The door to her room swung open and reminders poured out. She knew she should have changed rooms long ago. Emmy tried to get her to, but somehow she wanted to cling to this little piece of him. She lay down on the bed and curled on her side.

Outside, far to the west, the sky flashed dimly, promising a storm before the night was over. The breeze picked up, caressing her brow, soothing her skin. When she fell asleep, she couldn't remember, but then she jerked awake, her heart thudding in her chest.

Years on the trail and outdoors had honed some inner sense, and now that sense was telling her someone was near. She lay very still, not moving. There was no sound, no scent, just an invisible force that sent her blood speeding through her. Her heart hammered in her ears and her breath came short and shallow. What could have awakened her? Then she heard it. A soft spatter of water on a wooden floor, rain on the overhang outside, thunder in the east. She listened, separating out the sounds. The drips she heard were inside, not on the roof outside. Slowly, she turned over. A shadowy figure stood in the corner of the room, a floppy hat covering his eyes, a drenched duster hanging on thin shoulders, dripping on the floor.

"I hope you sneak up on other people better than you do on me."

Caleb stepped into the faint light and Josie gasped. His face was thin, his eyes hollow. He towered over her, still, silent. Was he sick? Then she was in his arms, her thin shirt soaked against his wet coat. She breathed as deeply as his tight hug would let her, inhaling him, committing his scent to memory, afraid he would disappear again, an apparition brought in with the storm.

"Are you real?" she asked.

"Very real. Oh, Josie." His voice was weak, tired.

"Did you find what you were looking for?"

"Yes."

"What was it?"

He pulled back from her and a silvery reflection from the streetlights lit his face. "Marry me. Legal and binding."

"Yes." The word leaped from her lips before her mind was fully awake. "Yes."

"Tonight? Right now?"

"Yes."

Then he smiled and looked a little more like the man she remembered.

"I'm afraid if I wait, you'll disappear." His voice broke twice with the simple words. Josie raked her fingers gently through the tough whiskers, pulling the hair beneath her nails. "This very minute if it was possible."

Without another word, without warning, He scooped her into his arms and strode out into the hall. Still dripping water, he rapped on Emmy's door. "Emmy!"

"Caleb? Is that you?" Rustling and padding footsteps came from the other side of the door. The door opened and Emmy stood there, her long white hair tumbling down around her shoulder. "Caleb, child." Tears welled in her eyes.

"Get your clothes on. We're getting married."

"About time, I'd say." Without closing her door, Emmy scurried away, snatched her wrapper off a chair and twisted her hair into a simple knot. "Let's go," she said, her eyes brighter than Josie could ever remember.

"Well, I never," one of the spinsters said, cracking open her door. "The telegraph clerk said this was a *decent* house," she said with a sniff.

"It is *decent*. We just do things quick around here." Emmy finished her retort with an exaggerated sniff and took the steps downstairs at the gait of a young woman.

The judge yawned, then laughed, his nightshirt jumping as his belly jiggled. "Miss Emmy, you've had some strange boarders before, but these two take the cake."

"These two aren't boarders, Clarence. They're my children.'' She smiled, tears misting her eyes. ''They might be odd, but they're mine.''

Josie looked up at Caleb. They were a sight indeed. He had yet to remove the soaked duster. Trail mud dotted his buckskin breeches. She, her hair tousled, still wore the clothes she'd slept in. Emmy wore her bathrobe and slippers and had never looked younger or prettier. Shorty, clutching together his mismatched shirt and pants, stood by his yawning wife, both summoned as witnesses.

''Caleb McCall, do you take this woman as your wife?'' the judge began.

The ceremony only took a few minutes, then Josie was in Caleb's arms again, pressed against him. He was real from the dirt on his clothes to his ragged beard to his dusty, smelly hat. No matter, it was him and he was hers.

''Well, I was going to say kiss your bride, but . . .'' The judge said with a snicker. ''Why don't you take her off home, young man, while these poor folks here and I help ourselves to some of my wife's cake and a stiff drink. Anybody object?''

''I haven't had a drink in years, Clarence,'' Emmy said, taking his arm.

Caleb pushed the door open with his boot and carried Josie over to their bed. Then he removed the trail-weary duster. He was so thin, he looked as if he hadn't eaten for weeks.

''I didn't expect you to say yes,'' he said as he removed his shirt.

''Neither did I,'' Josie answered, helping him slide it off his shoulders.

''Why did you?'' He paused, running a hand through his hair.

Josie walked across the bed on her knees and put her arms around his neck. ''I don't know. Maybe it was just one of them things we ain't supposed to question.''

His lips went down hard on hers, possessing her, branding

her. Josie yielded, no doubts floating to the top of her thoughts, a feeling of supposed-to-be enveloping her. His kiss was different, freer. No holding back, no hesitation like before. As he lowered her to the bed, far-off thunder rumbled and the thunder gods spoke.

Chapter Twenty-One

Caleb held the bridle as the stallion rolled his eyes in fright. Slowly, he tied a red bandanna over the horse's eyes, tucking it securely beneath the bridle straps. The horse stood docilely while Caleb swung up into the saddle, then he leaned down and whisked off the cloth. The stallion began to rear and plunge. For a brief few seconds, Caleb maintained his seat and then he felt himself slipping and hit the ground hard underneath nervous hooves. Crawling swiftly out of the way, he added one more to his list of times thrown. Across the paddock the horse halted abruptly and stood switching his tail in aggravation as he watched Caleb warily.

Rubbing his throbbing backside, Caleb hobbled over to the fence and decided to give the horse time to calm down. With his old hat, Caleb knocked the dust off the legs of his pants, folded his arms on the top rail, and rested his chin on them, studying his equine adversary.

An odd assortment of people passed the livery, people from all over the eastern half of the country. The end of the war back east brought a flood of emigrants west, broken families and individuals fleeing the war-torn east, looking for a place to start over. How his life had changed in three short months, he thought as he watched yet another wagon rumble by, its back end filled with shouting children. He and Josie had settled in at Emmy's boardinghouse, as Emmy would have it no other way. As soon as they had earned enough money, they planned to outfit themselves and return to Red Cloud's people. That was where he belonged, he now knew. The newspapers every day were filled with horrific stories of Indian raids and massacres on white settlers. The days of the Sioux were numbered. They would live with them and accept whatever fate the Sioux were dealt.

Caleb had taken a job at Mr. Woods's livery stable breaking and training to harness horses for sale to the settlers. It was hot, dirty work, but Caleb enjoyed it and didn't miss the responsibility that went along with guiding the wagon trains. Mr. Woods had recently acquired an especially difficult bay stallion. He was a fine horse with obviously good bloodlines, tall and durable, good breeding stock. To Caleb fell the task of breaking the animal. He'd never really considered himself a horse wrangler, but it brought in a little money and kept him home at nights—home with Josie.

He glanced past the corral toward the end of town. Beyond the line of storefronts was the open prairie. An ancient urge pulled at his heart. The confines of town often were too restricting, too limiting. He longed for the freedom of the prairie, the cool green of the mountains, the freedom of life among the Lakota. Vivid, violent memories returned, voices screaming in his ears, the death rattles of dying men. He closed his eyes, willing away the thoughts that often haunted his dreams. They came to him in the night, silent stalkers that robbed him of his sleep and his peace of mind. Cold sweats drenched his bed, and he would awake in Josie's arms to her voice softly crooning to calm him. Shaking his head, he diverted his attention back to the horse. Nothing would make him change his mind, not even these demons who nudged him and whispered in his ear that he did not belong here, that he belonged nowhere.

Caleb smiled and looked toward the two-story house barely visible at the other end of town. He'd learned to love Josie as he'd never thought to love a woman again. He had quickly found her marriage to Johnny was empty and unfulfilled, merely a young girl's dream gone wrong. Clumsy, cruel, and self-centered, her first husband had taught her nothing, and only in Caleb's arms had she learned the art of pleasure.

His body stirred in response to thoughts of his wife, and he quickly slammed his hat back on his head and turned to where the bay horse regarded him with a look nothing short of speculation. Caleb couldn't resist a chuckle at the calculating look on the horse's face as he approached slowly and prepared to mount again.

At the other end of town, Josie swept the last pile of dirt out of the living room and onto the porch. She straightened a moment and put a hand to the small of her back, massaging the spot that insisted on aching. Little ringlets of dark hair clung to her forehead as the heat of the day settled in. Heat waves shimmered in the street, making the buildings appear to dance just above the ground. Josie blinked her eyes and ran a hand over her face. With the way she felt these days, she didn't need dancing buildings. The slight nausea made her stomach churn, and she sat down for a moment in the porch rocker and propped the broom on her knees.

She smoothed her hand across the skirt of the gingham day dress she and Emmy had stitched together. Although plain and with little decoration to enhance its pink checks, Josie was proud of the garment, one of the few dresses she had ever owned.

A cloud of dust rose from down the street toward the livery stable, and she smiled, imagining Caleb sailing through the air from the back of the bay stallion again and the string of curses sure to follow. She'd laughed at him last night until her sides ached as he related his numerous spills from the stallion's back.

Some of that cloud would surely come home on his breeches, she thought with a chuckle.

Her stomach churned again, and she thought of the glass of cool tea she had left in the kitchen, but she felt too lethargic to go and get it. She would tell him tonight, she promised herself as she leaned her head back and shut her eyes. She wasn't sure until yesterday when she went to the doctor and he'd confirmed what she suspected—she was pregnant, about two months along, the doctor had said with a kind smile and a gentle pat to her shoulder. At first she'd wanted to rush right home and tell Caleb. Then, on the way, she'd changed her mind. What would he say, knowing they planned to leave soon for the mountains and the Lakota. Would he insist they stay here? Would he try to give up his destiny in preference to her? She couldn't let him do that. No, maybe she should wait to tell him once they were on the trail. He and she could deliver the child. Lakota women did it themselves sometimes. So could she.

The little man standing on the porch startled her.

"I'm sorry if I frightened you, madam," the man said in a shrill voice, sweeping his hat off in an exaggerated motion of respect. "My name is Jeremiah Farthington. My card." He held out a little piece of white paper.

Josie slowly took the card and at the same time looked the man over. He was small, his head, hands, and feet seemingly too small for his slender body. No taller than she, he reminded her of a little sparrow. The hand he extended was bony and pale, each knuckle raised, each vein outlined in blue. His hair was long, a dull sort of brown, and he wore it tied at the nape of his neck with a thin black ribbon. His spectacles were the thickest she'd ever seen, making his eyes look huge behind the lenses. He had a large nose that seemed ample to support his gold-rimmed glasses, but they nonetheless kept slipping down that great nose, and he unconsciously pushed them up with one finger. A thick coat of dust covered the suit he wore, and the deep blue of the material had faded to a nondescript gray.

As she took the card, Josie was careful not to touch his hand, for she could imagine it was as cold and lifeless as it looked. "You're with a freight company?" she asked.

"Yes, I'm with Masters and Brown, as it says there."

Josie bristled under his patronizing tone. "I can see that. What can I do for you?"

"Well, for starts, I'd like to rent a room, please."

"How long you gonna be here?" she asked, rising from the chair.

"I'm not sure. I'm here looking for someone."

"Oh?" She opened the screen door and preceded him into the cool, darkened living room.

"Yes, I'm looking for a rather colorful gentleman named Caleb McCall."

Her heart skipped a beat, but she didn't turn around. Out here, she'd learned, it was best not to say too much too soon to strangers. "We got a purdy room up at the top of the stairs, Mr. Farthington. Here, let me show you."

She led the little man upstairs and opened the small room down the hall from theirs. As the door swung open, a draft of cool air met them. "It ain't been opened today and the curtains is still pulled. I'll open 'em and let in some light." She started across the room toward the window.

"No. No, that's quite all right," the little man protested. "I prefer the room darkened, if you don't mind."

She turned to study the queer little man again.

"All right. It'll git stuffy in here 'fore dark, though, if you don't let in some air."

"I'm sure I'll be quite all right, Miss . . ."

"Just call me Josie."

"I left my satchel on the porch. I'll go fetch it."

He headed back downstairs and Josie managed to fiddle around until he returned with the luggage, went into his room, and shut the door. Then she hurried back downstairs and out into the kitchen, where Emmy stood at the dishpan, peeling potatoes.

"I'm goin' down to the livery for a spell," Josie announced hurriedly.

"You two just saw each other over breakfast and it's not even noon. For shame." Emmy's voice was scolding, but her eyes danced with mischief. "Go on with you. One day you'll get enough of each other and won't be able to stand to look at one another."

"That ain't gonna happen," Josie threw over her shoulder as she ran out the door.

She stepped carefully over a fresh pile of horse manure in the street and worked her way down the crowded sidewalk. It seemed like businesses and stores had grown up overnight, extending the sidewalk far beyond where it had ended when she came down this very street in the back of her father's wagon nearly five years earlier. Merchants were pouring in from the east, bringing with them goods and merchandise not obtainable before west of the Mississippi River. Independence had grown into a sizable town, and with it came all the problems of large masses of people. Just before she and Caleb had returned, the town had had to build another jail to house all the prisoners that would fill the cells on a Saturday night alone.

She turned sideways to allow a woman with a batch of rowdy children to pass her on the covered sidewalk. The woman was heavy and had a child by each hand. One hung onto her apron, sucking a dirty thumb while he half dragged and half walked down the sidewalk, his eyes huge with wonder at all the sights. Josie smiled and remembered that she, too, had been amazed at the hustle and bustle the first time she saw it.

Crossing the street in front of the livery, carefully avoiding the wagons and buckboards, she stepped inside, out of the sun. Closing the huge double barn doors, she waited for her eyes to adjust to the darkness. The big barn smelled like hay and horse dung, leather and sweat, and she breathed deeply of the aromas. Somewhere in the deep shadows, she heard a familiar nicker, and she squinted to make out the perfectly formed head of her pinto. Brownie, as Josie had named her, hung her head over the top rail of the stall and whinnied again, her ears pitched forward to catch her voice. Josie smiled and rubbed her velvet nose. Caleb had laughed at the horse's name, saying Josie had no imagination, but the name had stuck and she'd grown attached to the mare.

Josie scratched her between the eyes and Brownie lowered her head to receive the ministrations. She was shut up now in a stall because Caleb wanted to breed her to the bay stallion. The bay's bloodlines combined with Brownie's native sturdiness and surefootedness should make a good line.

"It's not so bad, girl," Josie said as she scratched. "You just might enjoy it."

"I'll say she might. Why, if I was half as lusty as that stallion, I'd keep you in foal." Caleb grasped her around the waist and hugged her to him.

Josie turned in his arms and wrinkled her nose at the smell on his clothes.

"Do I smell that bad?" he asked, releasing her and taking a step away.

"You sure do, but I'll settle for a kiss instead of the hug." Pursing her lips, Josie closed her eyes and turned up her face.

Caleb politely obliged her, wanting to do more, but he could feel the wet, sticky spot on the leg of his pants where he had fallen into horse dung. "What brings you down here? Couldn't wait until dinner to see me?"

"Emmy says we're gonna git tired of each other." Josie moved upwind of his pants.

"Don't let Emmy fool you. If Philip Osgood had let her, she'd have followed every wagon train he ever led." Caleb picked up a handful of hay and rubbed at the offending spot.

"She must've loved him a great deal."

"Not as much as I love you." Caleb put his arms around her and pressed her against him again, which set off a bout of wiggling.

"Please, Caleb. I promise I'll make it up to you tonight. I don't want to wash this dress again this week. I'm afraid I'll wear it out.'' Wriggling away, Josie moved out of arm's reach and smoothed the material.

Caleb smiled. ''It becomes you.'' He'd helped Emmy pick out the material as a surprise for Josie soon after they arrived. She'd never owned a dress, not a firsthand dress anyway, and now she had three. ''You know you can't wear them on the trail.'' He pointed at the dress.

''I know, but I don't care. I'd rather have britches anyway.'' She leaned forward and tweaked Caleb's cheek, then stepped away to straighten her skirt. ''Oh, I came down here because you've got a visitor waitin' for you at the house.''

''Who?''

''He said his name was Jeremiah Farthington and he was lookin' for you.''

''For me?''

''Yeah, he called you by name.'' Josie frowned. ''You think somethin's wrong?''

''No, probably wants to hire a wagon master.'' Others had approached him many times to take another train, but he always refused, insisting that was behind him now. He wanted only to save enough money to leave some for Emmy and outfit them for the trip.

''I don't know. He didn't look like the rest. Somethin' spooky about him. Said he was with a freight company.''

Caleb wrinkled his nose. ''If there's anything I'd hate worse right now than a wagon train full of settlers, it's a wagon train full of freight.''

''He took a room at Emmy's.''

''Tell him I'll see him at supper.'' Caleb leaned down and kissed her again. ''You know there's a pile of soft hay in the loft and Woods'll be gone until nearly suppertime.''

Josie giggled and pushed him away. ''Not till you wash.''

''Have the water ready.'' Caleb made a grab for her, but she was too quick.

She paused as she started out the door and watched his silhouetted form saunter away, and her heart surged with love—

and fear. Almost every night he awoke, drenched with sweat, writhing, and screaming. Sometimes he never fully awoke and calmed only when she slid her arms around him and drew him close as though he were a child.

At supper, the regular boarders filled the table, people Josie knew from the three months they had lived there. Most of them made their home with Emmy, single people without ties or family. There was Miss Dodd, the spinster who was always waiting for the right man. Some said she had often considered that man Caleb, and she flirted outrageously with him. Caleb, amused by the whole thing, often flirted back just to annoy Josie.

Mr. Satterwhite was a traveling salesman, selling ladies' underwear and lingerie. He covered the entire area but made Emmy's his permanent residence. Mr. Wills was a widower. Once the best ranch foreman around, he'd retired when his wife died. Now he seemed content at Emmy's, spending his days gossiping on the porch with passersby.

Mr. Farthington rounded out the number at the table to ten, including Emmy. Besides the usual boarders, there were always a few overnight guests and transients who stayed only a few days and left. And the three spinsters, whose paper was now a small success. Caleb had returned as supper was being served. Josie had a bath waiting for him, and they had made love before coming down to eat, making them conspicuously late. Emmy raised her eyebrows when they came down with flushed faces, and Miss Dodd had murmured something about decent behavior as she shoved the mashed potatoes at Mr. Farthington.

During the meal, Josie noticed Caleb quietly studying the little man. Farthington's mannerisms, from the way he daintily tucked his napkin in his shirt to the way he carefully cut his meat, marked him as a dandy and probably an Easterner.

After supper was cleared and the dishes washed, Josie took a seat in the wide porch swing that hung across the south end of the porch. Tonight she would tell Caleb about the baby. She would wait until everybody else went back inside and the moon rose and they were alone on the porch. She smiled as she rehearsed the words she would say.

"You're certainly looking self-satisfied. It wouldn't have anything to do with why you were late for supper, would it?" Emmy asked, flopping down in a caned rocker facing the swing.

Josie blushed. " 'Course not."

"Humph," Emmy snorted, giving her full attention to her needlework and the threads of conversation going on around her.

Caleb left the house right after supper to go down and check on the bay stallion. When he returned, Farthington was waiting for him on the porch.

"Mr. McCall?" Farthington inquired, holding out his hand. "It is indeed fortuitous I found you in the same rooming house. It makes my task all the easier."

"Yes," Caleb said with a glance to where Josie swung herself with one foot.

"I have a matter of business I would like to discuss. Is there someplace private where we might talk?"

"Of course. Emmy? I'm going to use the parlor."

Emmy waved her agreement with one hand while holding her place in her work with the other. "Remember to close the blinds and straighten the rugs," she said without looking up.

Caleb led the man through the living room to the parlor behind the stairs. The door swung open with a gentle creak, and the air that greeted them smelled slightly musty. A single lamp sat on a marble-topped table. Caleb lit it with a match. The wick sputtered and flared up. Quickly replacing the glass chimney, Caleb turned down the flame until a pale yellow glow bathed the room. Then he opened the blinds, letting in some of the dying sunlight.

"Now, Mr. Farthington, what can I do for you?" Caleb asked as he sat down on the horsehair couch.

Farthington strolled around the room before answering, carefully studying the displayed whatnots and running his finger across the fine cherry wood tables Emmy kept dusted and polished. He paced back across the colorful hooked rug on the floor and stopped, facing Caleb. The sun was setting behind him and through the dusty window it cast an orange light onto the things in the room. "Mr. McCall, I understand you used to be a wagon master, and quite a good one."

"Mr. Farthington," Caleb said, leaning forward to get to his feet. "Let me save you some time. I don't lead wagon trains anymore."

"I am aware of that," Farthington said coldly, causing Caleb to look up in surprise. "My company has authorized me to offer you quite a tidy sum for your resuming your career."

Something told Caleb not to ask the amount, to stand and walk out of the room. But he remembered Emmy. How he would love to leave her enough money to take care of her once they were gone. "What's involved in this?" he asked suspiciously.

Farthington smiled. "A group of miners are stranded in Montana territory, a rather large group, and they are in desperate need of medical supplies. A large mining concern back east is responsible for those men and has hired my company to see to it these supplies get through. You came highly recommended as a guide into that part of the country."

A cold sweat broke out on Caleb's body. His palms became clammy, and dread was a stone in the pit of his stomach. "Where in the mountains are they?"

Farthington leveled his gaze on Caleb. "At the end of the Bozeman Trail."

Caleb stood up and paced around the room. "Do you know what you're asking? Red Cloud's Lakota have harassed trains along that trail for more than two years."

"I am well aware of the danger. I also know these supplies must get through or those men will die."

Caleb paced back across the room. What a turn of events, he fumed, asked to switch sides again, to defy Red Cloud after fighting by his side only a few months before, to represent the whites as they again trespassed on Lakota lands. He felt Farthington's beady little black eyes on his back.

"Well, Mr. McCall?"

"No," Caleb said, stopping in front of the man. "I can't do it. I gave up scouting and guiding, and I won't go back on my promise to my wife."

"Don't be hasty, McCall. Think about it, and we'll talk again tomorrow night." Farthington tipped his head to the side. "You haven't even asked the price."

"All right," Caleb said reluctantly. "How much?"

"A thousand dollars."

He gave a low whistle. "That's a lot of money for one trip. You sure all it is is medical supplies?"

"That's all, but the mining company will stop at nothing to assure the safety of its men."

Caleb let the words sink in. Something didn't smell right here. Why so much money? And it was a great deal of money, enough to leave Emmy well cared for, all her bills paid. "I'll think about it and let you know tomorrow," he said, wanting to buy enough time to talk to Josie about it.

"Very well," Farthington said, still smiling that self-contented smile. Then he clasped his hands behind his back and walked out of the room, leaving Caleb standing, staring into the orange sunset beyond the windows.

He blew out the lamp, straightened the rugs, and shut the door behind him. Most of the boarders had filtered into the house and upstairs, but he found Emmy and Josie still on the porch, enjoying the cooling evening breeze. He sat down in the swing alongside his wife.

"Well, what did Mr. Farthington want?" Josie asked as she moved the swing with one foot.

"He had a very interesting offer," Caleb admitted. "He wants me to take a wagon-train load of supplies up into Montana territory." He conveniently left out the destination.

"You said no, didn't you?" Josie asked with a slight frown, stopping the swing.

When Caleb didn't answer right away, Josie leaned forward to get a better look at his face. "You did, didn't you?"

"I didn't give him an answer yet. I wanted to talk to you. He's offering a lot of money."

"You promised. You said you wouldn't do that anymore." A seed of panic gripped her as she thought about the months apart, and the joy of her announcement faded.

Caleb took her gently by the shoulders. "A thousand dollars, Josie. We could have enough to outfit us and leave Emmy well cared for."

"I don't care about the money. I only want you here with me." Tears filled her eyes, and she squeezed Caleb's arms.

He studied her face. She was serious about his not going, and he had his answer. "I won't go if you really don't want me to. I promised you I'd stay here, and I will." Caleb kissed her nose. "We'll earn the money in time." He put his arm protectively across her shoulders and she relaxed against him, her head on his chest. Caleb stared off into the darkness and thought about all the security a thousand dollars could buy.

Chapter Twenty-Two

Farthington was still around the next morning when Caleb came downstairs for breakfast. Seemingly unperturbed that Caleb had flatly refused his offer of the night before, he calmly read the local paper while Emmy served eggs, bacon, biscuits, and coffee. Caleb watched him politely converse with the other boarders, pointedly ignoring him.

After breakfast, Caleb resumed breaking the stallion, who would now let him mount and ride him for a short distance before rebelling in a series of bucks and jumps. Just before noon, Caleb felt someone watching him. He glanced over his shoulder. Farthington leaned against the rear barn door, his arms folded across the chest of his faded gray suit. Caleb dismounted and walked over. "I gave you my answer last night, Farthington. Is there anything else I can do for you?"

"You gave me a conditional answer, Mr. McCall. You said you would think about it."

"Well, I have and my answer's the same—no."

"Perhaps I didn't completely explain the situation last night." Farthington pushed away from the barn door and clasped his hands behind him. He walked a little distance away, staring at the ground, deep in thought. "Don't you wonder how I got your name, how I knew of your experience in that part of the country?" He turned and gazed pointedly at Caleb, a mocking smile on his lips.

"I suppose you asked somebody," Caleb answered, the beginnings of a chill running up his back.

"Indeed I did. I asked Colonel Carrington, commander of Fort Phil Kearney."

Farthington's slow smile told Caleb his shock showed on his face. "I don't believe I know the colonel," he replied evenly.

"Ah, but he knows you." Farthington began to pace again. "And that's what's important, isn't it?"

"What's your point?" Caleb grew angrier and more apprehensive each second.

"My point is"—Farthington turned and walked up to within inches of Caleb—"Carrington can identify you as one of the Lakota who attacked a party of soldiers gathering wood last December and killed eighty men under the command of Captain William Fetterman."

Caleb's heart thudded in his chest. "That's ridiculous."

Farthington was undaunted by Caleb's denial. "In fact, Carrington has a witness who will swear you and Red Cloud grew up together."

Caleb's laugh sounded hollow. "If you'd convict a man because he grew up in an Indian village, Mr. Farthington, I'm afraid you'd lose a lot of scouts."

"Perhaps." Farthington rocked back on his heels. "This witness also says you and your . . . wife spent last winter in his camp, and you knew well in advance of plans to attack the fort. You did nothing to warn those eighty good men who lost their lives."

"If that's true, why hasn't the army brought charges against me?"

Farthington unclasped his hands and walked over to examine

a bridle hanging above an end stall. "It seems Colonel Carrington has reason to doubt the validity of the witness's claim, but I"—he dropped the leather and walked closer—"I have followed your movements quite closely. I believe you were involved."

"What do you mean?"

"I mean you managed to lose your entire wagon train last July in an Indian raid designed to rescue Red Cloud's son. Only it wasn't the Lakota who attacked, it was the Crow. I also know you and Red Cloud were raised as brothers, you were once married to a squaw known as Fawn, and you lost her in a raid also by the Crow."

"That doesn't make me a murderer, Farthington." Caleb clenched his teeth against his rising anger.

"Ah, yes, but you *were* in Red Cloud's camp last winter and you suffered, shall we say, an unfortunate tragedy caused by the army some years ago?"

Caleb felt his face grow red. His hands formed into fists as he faced the arrogant little man immensely enjoying making him squirm. "Are you here to bring charges, Farthington? Because if you are, then you need to bring charges against the officers who stole that land from the Lakota after a treaty gave them possession of it as hunting grounds."

"I know nothing of treaties." Farthington shrugged, dusted his hands off on his pants, and examined his fingernails. "I am simply a freight agent interested solely in the safe delivery of my valuable cargo. I came into possession of this information as a part of my investigation into a suitable guide for the expedition." He stepped forward and placed a hand on Caleb's shoulder. "The offer of a thousand dollars still stands, McCall. I merely offered the other information as . . . encouragement."

Caleb knew he had him. Public knowledge of his part in the massacre would send him to the gallows. Justice wouldn't take into consideration what had been done to him at the hands of the mighty United States Cavalry. Slinging aside the bandanna he held, Caleb walked over to a stall and braced both hands against the top rail. He was being forced to sell out again—that or die—and now he had Josie to consider. "All right, Farthington, I'll take your wagon train, but under my conditions and orders. Is that plain?"

"I wouldn't have it any other way. You are, after all, the expert in this matter." Farthington smirked and adjusted his lapels.

Caleb turned to face him. "I'll give you a list of the things we'll need."

"I assure you I have already seen to the outfitting of the wagon train. It's waiting outside town."

"Sure of yourself, weren't you?" Caleb asked through clenched teeth.

"Let's just say, I had to hedge my bet, but I knew you were a reasonable man."

Caleb turned away and headed back toward the corral. Then he stopped and turned around again. Farthington hadn't moved, standing as before in the doorway. "Just for curiosity, who is the witness Carrington has?"

Farthington frowned and scratched his head. "An Indian woman, a former member of Red Cloud's band. I believe he said her name was Owl."

"A woman scorned," Caleb whispered beneath his breath.

Caleb didn't return home for supper, purposely waiting until he knew the rest had eaten and retired to their rooms before he slipped in the back door. The house was dark and a single lamp burned low in the center of the kitchen table. At its base was a plate filled with food and covered with a red checked napkin. Caleb raised the edge for a look before moving out into the dark living room. He felt his way toward the stairs. As he stepped onto the upstairs landing, he saw light pouring from beneath Farthington's door. He moved down the hall toward the room he shared with Josie. Slowly he turned the doorknob, hoping she was already asleep.

She lay curled on the bedspread, asleep. A lamp burned by the side of the bed, framing her face with its yellow light. A fist cushioned her cheek, and her hair fell around her shoulders and across her face. Caleb bent down and gently kissed her.

Her eyes flew open and she blinked in bewilderment at first before she smiled slowly and put her arms around his neck. "Hi," she murmured.

"Hi, yourself. Saved me some supper, did you?"

"Why are you so dad-blamed late? I thought you mighta been hurt."

"No." Caleb rose from the side of the bed. He couldn't look her in the face when he told her about his decision. Going back to the Lakota meant so much to her, and now their future was in Farthington's hands. He walked to the window and looked out over the sleeping town bathed in silver moonlight.

"You decided to take the job, didn't you?" she asked softly.

He turned and met her eyes, expecting to find anger in them, but instead he found sorrow. Returning to the bed, he eased himself down beside her and took her hand. "Farthington knows about my part in Red Cloud's attack on the fort. He'll use the information against me if I don't go."

Josie's eyes widened in disbelief. "How . . . ?"

"Somehow Owl got word to the commander of the fort that I was involved."

"Owl?"

"A woman scorned, isn't that the saying," he said bitterly.

"What's Farthington goin' to do?"

"Nothing, if I cooperate. He says Carrington has reason to doubt Owl's claims, but apparently Farthington has made it his business to know all about me."

"You can say he's lyin'," she suggested, rising from the bed.

Caleb shook his head. "No, he's got too much on me."

"Then, let him use the information and we'll explain what the army did to your family and that you were raised by the

Injuns when none of them white families'd have you.'' Her eyes flashed with anger.

Caleb shook his head. ''The white courts won't understand that, Josie. All they see is land going to waste, land white settlers could farm. They don't see the plight of the Lakota. They don't understand their lifestyle and don't want to understand. No, they'd never believe us.''

Josie didn't reply. The mysterious, slim little man had shattered all her dreams. Why hadn't she said they had no rooms and sent him down the street? Maybe he and Caleb would never have met. No, she reminded herself, he would have found them anyway, because everybody in town knew Caleb. ''I want to go with you.'' She stepped up to face him.

''No.'' Caleb shook his head vigorously. ''No, it'll be too hard.''

''Too hard? Have you forgotten where you found me, Caleb McCall?'' She planted her hands on her hips.

Caleb smiled, looking down into the deep blue of her eyes, then he gently pulled her to his chest and rested his chin in her soft, fragrant hair. ''No, I haven't forgotten, but I don't want you to ever have to live like that again. I want you to stay here with Emmy. Promise me.'' He grasped her by the shoulders and held her away from him so he could look into her eyes. ''Promise me, Josie.''

She felt tears burning the backs of her eyes. He didn't even know about the baby and he was about to ride away again, possibly never to come back. But now wasn't the time to tell him. She bit her lip and nodded. ''All right, I promise.''

''That's my girl,'' Caleb said with forced lightness. ''I'll be back before you know it, and then we'll leave as soon as we can.''

Josie nodded, not trusting her voice.

''Now, I want to see what I'll miss,'' he said thickly, slowly undoing the navy blue buttons that led down the front of her dress. He gently pulled the garment off her shoulders, letting it float to her waist. Beneath the thin material of her chemise, she felt her nipples spring to arousal at his touch. He cupped one breast in his hand while his lips claimed her mouth. Slowly, he eased her down onto the bed and tugged the dress over her hips, followed by her underclothes. He stood up long enough to remove his shirt and pants, and then he joined her and slowly, languidly, made love to her, forcing out of her mind all thoughts of the lonely months that lay ahead.

The wagon train was quickly brought into town and outfitted. Winter wasn't far away from the high peaks over which they must pass. Caleb's days were filled with preparations for the trip, but at night he loved her tenderly, desperately—almost as if he didn't expect to return.

All too soon, the ten wagons were ready with a driver and shotgun rider for each. Farthington had insisted on accompanying them, and Caleb reluctantly agreed. The train stretched the length of Main Street at barely dawn the morning it was to pull out of Independence. Josie pushed aside the curtains and looked down on the wagons, clutching the sheet against her bare body while tears rolled down her cheeks. She and Caleb had said their good-byes last night, and still she hadn't told him about the baby. It wasn't fair to let him ride away and worry that he wouldn't be back for the birth.

Down below, the drivers and horses milled about. She could see Caleb as he trotted back and forth astride Cindy, wearing the same buckskins as he did when she first saw him, his hat shielding his eyes. He didn't belong here in town. He belonged up in the mountains, up among high passes. She knew his horse-wrangling job dulled in comparison with scouting for wagon trains, and she remembered the anticipation in his eyes even as he talked of his reluctance to leave her.

As the sun became an orange ball on the horizon, Caleb gave the order to the lead wagon to pull out. The wagons groaned forward as the horses leaned against their harnesses and the train moved slowly. Caleb held Cindy back and shouted orders to the drivers. Then he looked up at the window where Josie stood. Slowly, he raised his hat and waved it at her before spurring Cindy and galloping forward toward the front of the train. A sob caught in her throat as she watched him until he was out of sight.

Josie had to remind herself every day of her promise to Caleb, but each day it became more difficult to keep. She had no one in Independence except Emmy. The memory of the far blue mountains and the man she loved beckoned. She spent more and more time on the porch, looking toward the west and going over in her mind the months until Caleb would return. Then one day the pull became too great to resist. She was going home, home to the high Rockies, where she belonged.

She found Emmy in the kitchen, starting preparations for lunch. Emmy had hired a local girl named Beth to come in and help with the chores, and the two of them were busy making biscuits.

Josie got as far as the door of the kitchen before she stopped and stood watching Emmy's bent back. She was as close to a mother as Josie would ever get again, and Emmy didn't have many years left. Worrying her bottom lip, Josie tried to think of a way to tell the old woman she was leaving, some way to cushion the blow. But she could only stare at her hands as they lovingly shaped the biscuits.

Emmy softly dismissed Beth without turning around. When they were alone, she slowly wiped the flour from her hands. "You're going after him, aren't you?"

Josie was taken aback, but she answered, "I cain't just wait here, Emmy, wonderin' if he's ever gonna come back."

Emmy didn't answer at first and stared down at her hands as she turned them over and over in the cloth to remove the last of the dough. "I wish I could tell you you're doing the wrong thing, that you shouldn't even think about going after him. But I won't tell you that, Josie, because I'd be lying. Every time Philip Osgood rode down that street''—Emmy turned, tears welling in her eyes, and pointed west—''I wanted to go with him, but I never had the courage. So I waited here and made a home he rarely saw. Lord, how many years I waited for him to come home to me. And then, when he did, he died in a stupid barroom brawl before we could make up any of the time we had lost.'' She shook her head and sat in a nearby chair. ''No, Josie, I can't give you any good advice you should listen to. I can only tell you life is short, too short, and that men like Philip and Caleb come along only once.''

''I'm goin' after him. I figure I can catch 'em in a few days on horseback. He'll be mad, but he'll git over it.'' Josie dropped to her knees in front of the chair where Emmy sat. ''But I'll miss you.''

Emmy waved her away with a flour-coated towel. ''Don't worry about me, child. All these boarders are like children, and I have them to worry over.'' Emmy leaned closer. ''Promise me one thing.''

''What?''

''Let me know when the baby's born.''

Josie's eyes widened. ''How . . . ?''

''Ah, I knew weeks ago.'' Emmy smiled. ''Just be careful, child.''

''I will Emmy, I will.'' Josie tearfully kissed her wrinkled cheeks, and noticed a sparkle that wasn't there before.

Josie was ready to go by dawn the following day. She retrieved Brownie from Mr. Woods—over his voluminous objections—packed her supplies, and then all that remained was to say good-bye to Emmy. She'd packed only one change of clothes and the buckskin dress and necklace given her by Red Cloud. Looking around the room one last time as the rising sun cast a warm glow, the memories of nights spent with Caleb floated through her mind. Then she quietly closed the door and hurried down the stairs.

Emmy met her at the bottom, wiping tears with the corner of a flour-covered apron. "You and Caleb are like the children Philip and I never had. I'll miss you both."

"We'll miss you too, Emmy." Josie felt a tear slip down her cheek.

"Here, I've got a present for you. Now, don't open it until you find Caleb. It's for both of you. Godspeed child." Emmy gripped her in a hug and then she turned, straightened her back, and walked back into the kitchen, shutting the door firmly behind her.

Josie stepped out into the early morning heat, swung her saddlebags over Brownie's back, and mounted up. As she neared the edge of town, she stopped and looked back over her shoulder once more toward the two-story frame house. She could barely see Emmy standing on the porch, shading her eyes from the sun, framed by two pots of red geraniums. Josie turned around and looked out over the prairie that stretched beyond her. Digging her heels into Brownie's sides, she headed out across the grass-covered prairie at a gallop.

The wagon train's tracks weren't hard to follow. Josie was gaining on them by late in the week. She'd sighted their dust before noon, and Brownie perked up her ears as she caught the scent and the sounds of the other animals. Slowing the mare to a trot, Josie tried to think of a way to approach Caleb. He'd be furious, but he wouldn't send her back—she hoped.

After dark, she skirted their camp, staying outside the fire-light. Then she saw Caleb. Stretched out beside the fire, his hat was pulled down over his eyes and his head rested on the seat of his saddle. Far out in the dark, she heard Cindy nicker as she caught Brownie's scent. Josie dismounted, dropped her reins, and crept toward the fire.

"I was beginning to wonder when you'd get the courage to come in, muleskinner," Caleb said from beneath his hat.

Josie froze in her steps. She peered closely at his shadowed face and saw him smile.

He rose on one elbow and pushed his hat back off his eyes. "I expected you before now."

Josie stood, straightened her clothes, and walked proudly into the light of the fire. Caleb scowled darkly at her, but she didn't miss the twinkle of delight in his eye as they took in the curves of her figure beneath the tight pants and shirt she wore.

"How'd you know I was here?" she said as she sat down tentatively, braced for the fury of his anger.

"I knew you were following us for the last day and a half. I saw you myself yesterday when we topped a rise. That pinto is unmistakable."

"Why didn't you let me know?" Josie asked irritably, remembering the uncomfortable nights alone.

"And have you miss the satisfaction of surprising me? Now, would I do that? I figured you'd get tired of all that sneaking around and come into camp sooner or later." He grinned broadly.

"Ain't you mad?" Josie asked hesitantly when there was no storm of recriminations.

"Well," he said as he stretched back out on the ground, "I was at first, but then I should have known you'd follow me. In fact, if you hadn't thought of it, I was sure Emmy would have suggested it to you before too many days went by."

At Josie's frown, Caleb chuckled. "Emmy's said over and over that she wished a thousand times she'd gone after Philip. I figured she couldn't stand to see you do the same thing she did."

"Then, you're not gonna send me back?"

Caleb smiled, the warmth reaching the deep green of his eyes. He reached up and grabbed her wrist. "There are certain advantages to having one's wife along." He pulled her down on top of him and kissed her soundly. "That's one of them."

"Caleb! The others!" she whispered frantically as he undressed her.

"Let 'em get their own woman," he murmured into her hair.

Reaching out a booted foot, he kicked sand onto the fire, throwing them into darkness while his hands and lips remained busy on her body.

Chapter Twenty-Three

The drivers were surprised when they awoke the next morning to find a woman among them, but Caleb offered no explanation except to tell them she was his wife and would be accompanying them. Looks varying from amazed to lecherous passed between the men, but none dared to comment, not even Farthington, who simply clasped his hands behind his back and pursed his lips.

The first nip of fall was in the air by the time they sighted the distant peaks of the Rocky Mountains. A month on the trail and they had encountered no trouble. Caleb halted the train with a raised hand when they topped one of the prairie's many rolling hills, and purple, snow-capped peaks filled the horizon. Josie pulled her mare to a stop beside him. He stared off at the snowy summits miles in the distance. Yes, this is where he belongs, she thought, noticing the way his lips almost curved into a smile.

They hadn't seen one Indian by the time they reached the fork of the Oregon and Bozeman trails. Leaving the deep, wellworn ruts of the Oregon, the train bumped and jostled into the shallow, less-used Bozeman, which took them higher up into the mountains toward Montana territory. They passed Fort Phil Kearney without stopping and camped a short distance away from the log fortress. Caleb instructed each man to check his weapon and keep a supply of ammunition at hand. Only Josie knew how much pain those instructions caused him. Only she knew how the ghosts of the battle haunted him when his eyes strayed to the little cemetery high on a hill behind the fort—a stark reminder of the men he had helped kill.

Farthington went into the fort alone soon after they made camp and returned with more bloody stories of Red Cloud's conquests along the trail. Farthington didn't mention again the charges he had leveled at Caleb, nor did he mention Owl. The information had achieved its purpose, and he seemed content to let it drop.

The prudish little man turned his nose up at them all, constantly brushing at dust and lint, complaining about everything from the weather to the brightness of the moon. His disdain for Caleb set Josie's blood to boiling. He didn't understand anything about a man like Caleb. There was no understanding what made men like him seek the solitude of these craggy heights as opposed to the comforts found in the many towns springing up along the way to Oregon. As long as Farthington's freight got through, his job was well done. That's how she saw it.

The Bozeman Trail proved little better than a dim path in the thick grass, its use having dropped off because of Red Cloud's campaign. After Fort Phil Kearney, it began an immediate ascent into higher country, and the wagons groaned across spacious meadows and rock-strewn passes. They traveled for several days without mishap, although Caleb reminded them to be constantly on their guard. Sentries were always posted at night and changed every two hours.

The trail took them past the deciduous tree line, into towering pines, and past the first patches of virgin snow lying on the shady sides of rocks. Outcroppings hung over the narrow trail as the wagons careened dangerously close to the edge in some places and the air became brisk and thin and filled with the heavy scent of pine. Surprisingly, Josie's thoughts began to turn to the little cabin she had shared with her father. She remembered cold nights when the cabin was warmed by the crackling of blue spruce logs, and in the morning air was so crisp it often took her breath when she opened the door. In some ways, the mountains reminded her of home—the thin, cool air, the towering summits. But in other ways the Rockies were nothing like the Smokies. There were no lingering morning fogs, no sounds of wood chopping from a distant hollow. Still, there clung to the heights the feeling of being close to one's maker—whoever he might be.

The weather held, cool and crisp in the day and cold at night, but no early snows hindered them. Josie still hadn't told Caleb about the baby, finding no appropriate moment. Either he was too tired or there was some small, nagging problem to handle. Now, she began to dread telling him as her pregnancy advanced and the swell of her stomach became hard to hide. He would be angry when he learned she had come all this way, carrying his child. But, she rationalized, it was their child, the child of a man raised by the Indians, a frontiersman, and a woman who had traversed the Plains three times, lived through an Indian attack, and spent the winter in an Indian village ruled by the most feared of Lakota chiefs. Surely, this child could stand a cross-country journey one last time, she thought with a slight smile to herself.

"You want to let me in on the joke?" Caleb reached over and slapped her behind while pulling Cindy to a plunging walk.

"Just remembering last night," she said coyly.

Caleb's eyes searched the deep pine woods beside them and she knew he hadn't heard her carefully contrived answer.

"Is something wrong?"

"No, nothing's wrong. That's the problem. Red Cloud knows we're here. I'm sure of it. I can't figure why he hasn't shown himself."

"Maybe he knows you're along."

"Maybe," Caleb said distractedly.

He had been aware of another presence for days. Someone or something was following them, out of sight even to him, but he knew for sure they were there.

They were deep in the mountains now, the craggy pinnacles soaring up all around them and casting the trail into a dim twilight. Caleb stirred uncomfortably in his saddle and again searched the forest. He was sure someone was out there somewhere, simply watching and waiting. And he was just as sure that someone was not Red Cloud or any of his people.

They made camp for the night beside a rushing, clear stream pouring out of the mountain between two huge boulders. The water fell with such force that it made a roaring sound, dimming out all other noise save to sharp ears. Caleb nervously paced around the camp, disliking the choice, but it was the only level place they were likely to find for several miles as they steadily traveled higher into the mountains.

As darkness fell and Caleb's eyes adjusted, he thought from time to time that he caught movement in the woods beyond. Leisurely, he rose from the fire where Farthington was laying out the final leg of the journey, and moved over beside Josie at their small campfire. Gripping the stock of his rifle, he flopped down beside her. "A penny for your thoughts." He tipped her chin back with one finger.

"I got something to tell you, and I . . . don't know if you're gonna like it." Her eyes twinkled mischievously.

"Tell me and I'll be the judge."

She turned to face him and drew a deep breath. "My apron's a-ridin' high."

Caleb frowned.

"I'm in the family way. You know, a baby."

Caleb went numb. Another child, and this one in danger too. They had talked some about a family and always the word "someday" was included in the conversation. Someday was here. The old fear washed over him anew.

"Josie . . ." Before the words were out of his mouth, the woods were suddenly filled with painted warriors. They swarmed over the wagons, wielding axes and clubbing the drivers and the guards. Caleb heard Cindy scream as strange hands grabbed her bridle. In the confusion of painted tanned bodies, he tried to read the patterns striping their faces. They were Lakota, but not Red Cloud's. They moved in so quickly, they met no resistance, and soon had Caleb, Josie, and Farthington captive. Everyone else was dead.

One warrior held Caleb immobile, his hands bound together behind him, and another held Josie. Whoops of victory filled the woods around them as a lone brave strode into the circle of light, dragging Farthington behind him.

Caleb spoke quickly in Lakota, but the man gave no indication he understood or even heard.

"Who are they? They don't understand you," Josie whispered.

"Oh, he understands all right," Caleb answered.

"Who are they?"

"I don't know. They're Lakota, but I don't recognize anybody."

The three hostages' hands were bound together, and they were seated on a rotten log with their backs to one another. The Indians milled around and ransacked the wagons. Those responsible for the capture of Josie, Caleb, and Farthington disappeared into the dark trees. Suddenly, the brush parted and a regal brave stepped out. He wore a war bonnet that dragged nearly to the ground, each feather carefully trimmed and beaded to announce his accomplishments.

"Crazy Horse," breathed Caleb.

"Talk to him," Josie whispered urgently.

But Caleb remained quiet, studying the man before him. Crazy Horse was little more than a boy last winter when he had offered Owl to him and had taken his first coup during the attack of the fort. Since that time, he must have been busy to acquire all the feathers he wore.

The warriors chattered urgently to Crazy Horse, who stood with his arms crossed over his chest plate of porcupine quills. He regarded the prisoners with disdain, his eyes flickering over them occasionally as he listened to his advisers. Then he suddenly strode toward them. He jerked Caleb to his feet and brought his face inches away, studying him intently.

Caleb opened his mouth to speak, but was silenced with a slap from one of the other men.

"We meet again, White Eagle." Crazy Horse sneered. "But where is the brave warrior Red Cloud has told us to respect, that he has held up to the young braves as an example?"

"You've taken many lives from the looks of your head-dress," Caleb said, his eyes watering from the pain in his cheek.

Crazy Horse spit at Caleb's feet. "White Eagle has gone back to the whites. He had no stomach for the way of the Lakota."

"No," Josie cried as Crazy Horse raised his ax. He jerked his head around at the sound of her voice.

"Silence, woman," he shouted. Another brave stepped forward and hit her across the mouth. She tasted blood.

"Take them," Crazy Horse ordered, releasing Caleb so suddenly that he stumbled backward.

The three hostages were loaded onto their horses and led out of the clearing.

The party swerved off the Bozeman and plunged deep into the evergreen forest. Josie ducked as branches came her way, and she felt the old familiar nausea sweep over her. Warriors led them through narrow passes and dense forests until she was completely disoriented. They had ridden about two hours, descending back into deciduous trees, when they came to a small camp. About fifty tipis were pitched in a clearing hidden on all sides by dense undergrowth and rocks. Victory cries went up all around as the group broke through the edge of the brush.

They were led to the ceremonial grounds in the center of the village, heralded by wailing women announcing their men's accomplishments. Crazy Horse halted in front of a tipi set apart from the rest, threw one leg over his horse's neck, and slid to the ground. A nervous woman quickly led the mount away. Crazy Horse turned to his hostages. At his signal, the warriors grabbed each of them and jerked them to the ground. Josie stumbled and pitched forward, but a strong brown hand caught her and steadied her on her feet.

"I have taken captives," Crazy Horse proclaimed with upraised hands to his gathered listeners. "I have conquered the white train that dares to cross our territory." A general shout went up, and its volume hurt Josie's ears.

"Tonight, we will have much feasting before we kill them." Another shout echoed his words. He turned in a flurry of feathers and quickly disappeared inside the tipi.

Loyal braves dragged the captives away to a smaller tent and shoved each of them inside, sending them sprawling into the dirt.

"Why ain't they a-listenin' to you?" Josie asked as she spit dirt out of her mouth and scrambled to her feet. Across from her, Caleb sat calmly with feet outstretched, listening to the conversations outside the tent. Farthington lay in an unconscious heap in the center of the lodge, having passed out as soon as he hit the ground.

"They understand me, but Crazy Horse has split from Red Cloud and formed his own little group."

"But why? The army's already after Red Cloud. Why'd Crazy Horse want to go out and borrow trouble?"

"Red Cloud only wants to protect the Lakota hunting grounds. When we left, he was thinking of talking with the army, of ending the war that will only cost more Lakota lives. He knows the days of the Lakota are few, but Crazy Horse tasted glory at Fort Phil Kearney, and he wants more."

"Will they kill us?" Josie asked, thinking about the baby in her womb.

"Probably," he answered honestly. "I hurt Crazy Horse's pride when I refused to marry Owl. As the eldest male of her family, he saw it as his duty to find her a husband. Now he's stuck with her. He wants to get even."

In the stillness of night came the pounding and dancing Josie remembered most from her days among Red Cloud's people. The small band of followers were making the most of their conquest by working themselves into a fevered pitch. She closed her eyes and listened to the drums foretelling their deaths.

Suddenly, the flap of the tipi parted, giving them a glimpse of the huge bonfire built in their honor. Invisible hands grabbed and hauled them to their feet. Outside, the sky glowed orange. Dancers' feet stirred the dust until it formed a thick layer that snaked through the village like a fog.

Caleb, Josie, and a still-unconscious Farthington were dragged to the center of the ceremonial circle and placed in the midst of the dancers. Three poles were lodged into the ground, and to each one, a captive was tied. The pounding and dancing resumed, the dancers whirling around and around with their faces painted into frightening masks. Josie felt her stomach roil and willed herself not to be sick. How different this was from the celebrations last winter in Red Cloud's camp. Then, she had been part of that world. Now she, like Caleb, was part of neither. If she was about to die, she wouldn't humiliate herself first.

The drumbeats suddenly ceased and a deathly quiet descended. Crazy Horse stepped forward out of the darkness. Directly behind him in the crowd stood a tall, gangly Indian woman.

"I have brought you the white men that cross our land. I have brought them to you so that you may see their death and know Crazy Horse will stop the whites. I will do what Red Cloud could not." Crazy Horse stabbed at the ground with a magnificent war lance laden with ermine tails and eagle feathers to accentuate his words. His people responded with deafening shouts.

"There must be a lot of rivalry between Crazy Horse and Red Cloud," Caleb whispered.

"I have brought them to you that you may take their life."
Crazy Horse's announcement was met with more shouts.

"Would the great Crazy Horse kill a woman who is with
child? Would he do what he condemns the *wasíchu* for?"

Caleb's words brought silence to the crowd. Josie recognized
Owl and several other familiar faces as Crazy Horse slowly
turned.

"I think you got his attention," Farthington whispered,
finally regaining consciousness.

Crazy Horse advanced on them, his face contorted in anger.
Caleb stared unflinchingly into the brave's eyes.

"Why did you leave Red Cloud's camp, Crazy Horse? Was
there not enough bloodshed for you there?" Caleb whispered
rapidly in Lakota, and Crazy Horse's neck turned red. "Are
you afraid to tell all these families why you brought them here?
You don't want them to know that beneath all those feathers
and paint you're just a young boy with his nose out of joint
with the man who taught you everything."

Crazy Horse didn't answer and continued to stare into Caleb's
eyes. "Why do you have no fear?"

"I'm not afraid of you," Caleb said with as much noncha-
lance as he could muster. "What happened? Did Red Cloud
tire of your arrogance and send you packing?"

Crazy Horse's face reddened again and his eyes narrowed
in anger. "I am no longer the young warrior I once was, White
Eagle. I have become a war chief. I have taken many scalps
and counted many coups. I am as great as Red Cloud." He
beat on his breastplate with his fist. "Red Cloud has become
an old woman. He talks of meeting with the *wasíchu,* of seeking
peace."

"Red Cloud is a wise leader. He knows he can't fight the
flood of whites forever, that he must reach an agreement for
the sake of his people. I don't like it any better than you do.
I, too, grew up on the lands the *wasíchu* now claim, but I know
that for every *wasíchu* you kill, ten more will come. Red Cloud
knows that too. Are you such a wise leader?"

"I will kill you myself," Crazy Horse growled. "I will kill you and take your scalp to Red Cloud to prove you are not the great warrior he thinks."

"If you are a wise leader, how would killing a woman with child make you look to your people? Is there honor in that?"

Crazy Horse paused and slid his eyes in Josie's direction. "Do you carry the seed of White Eagle?"

Josie nodded. The crowd murmured and several of Crazy Horse's advisers whispered in his ear.

"Release the woman," he said loudly. "Your death will be enough." He pointed at Caleb. "You were once a brave warrior and I will not destroy that seed."

A brave quickly untied Josie's hands.

"Get your horse and ride for the fort," Caleb whispered.

"No, I won't leave you," she argued.

"Go, dammit." He turned his eyes from Crazy Horse and stared down into her soul. "I love you."

"Caleb, I love you too, but . . ."

"No buts, Josie, go. Think about the baby."

Josie looked around her at the angry faces ringing them. She couldn't help him here, she reasoned, so she turned and disappeared into the crowd unhindered. At first, she ran with no particular direction, tears blinding her. Then reason began to take over when she realized she was not followed, and she slowed to a walk. No one was paying her any attention at all. Looking back over her shoulder, she could see the entire population of the village assembled at the ceremonial grounds. They wanted Caleb, wanted his blood.

She stopped and looked back to where the tips of flames illuminated the tops of the tent poles, providing a brilliant orange backdrop. Surely these people could not be so different from Red Cloud's band, she reasoned. They were kind and caring people, people concerned with family and honor and respect. An idea began to form in her mind.

She darted among the lodges. Disoriented, she couldn't remember from which direction they had come as she ran from tent to tent. Finally, she found the large tent covered with paintings of horses. She crept around to the back, and seeing no one around, she raised the edge of the cover and crawled inside. A low fire smoldered in the fire pit, casting a yellow glow over the contents of the tent. Crazy Horse had obviously been successful attacking supply trains. Fabrics, dress goods, beads and guns, furniture, and other booty stuffed the tipi. Quickly, she searched for her saddlebag, remembering one of the warriors taking it off her horse.

Caleb held Crazy Horse's attention with attempts at dissuasion until he was sure Josie had escaped the camp. "So, you will take my life and so capture my spirit. Are you sure you can manage the spirit of a real warrior?" He thought for a moment he had gone too far when Crazy Horse did not respond, then he threw back his head and issued a piercing war cry. The pounding drums ceased, the dancers stilled, and all eyes turned toward the two men. Slowly, Crazy Horse drew a knife from a scabbard by his side. The smooth handle, carved from an elk horn, ended in a bright steel blade. It flashed as the chief brought it high over his head, ready to plunge it into Caleb's breast. A stir at the edge of the crowd caught his attention. Crazy Horse turned his head toward the commotion.

Josie stepped into the circle, the beaded fringe of the buckskin dress swishing around her ankles. Her thick, black hair was gathered into two fat plaits that hung over her breasts. She moved into the light, and a general gasp from the crowd stilled Crazy Horse's hand in midair. Around her neck hung the leather necklace that had belonged to Red Cloud's mother.

Josie showed no sign of fear, although her insides were trembling. She walked calmly toward Crazy Horse, concentrating on putting one foot in front of the other and trying to keep her eyes off the knife in his hand. She stepped between Caleb and Crazy Horse. "When Red Cloud gave me his mother's name, he told the story of how she had once saved his father's life. Do you remember?'' she asked Crazy Horse in a soft voice that only they could hear.

Slowly, Crazy Horse lowered the knife. "I remember."

"She was a brave woman, a warrior, someone the Lakota tell stories about around evening fires and in sweat lodges."

He nodded, his eyes on the necklace at the base of her throat.

"White Eagle, too, is brave. He came back to the Lakota and fought by their side. He killed the *wasíchus* and he *is wasíchu*. Would you kill somebody so brave? Would you kill the man of Morning Star?"

Murmurs filled her ears. Crazy Horse stared at the amulet, a frown creasing his brow.

"You are now Morning Star, bearer of a great name, but he is still *wasíchu*."

Josie's mind whirled. She'd relied on their respect for her position to spill over on Caleb. "He received a vision and a gift. Here." She dug in the pouch at her side and retrieved the star-shaped rock Caleb had found in his hand after that night on the prairie. "This gift was from his dead wife, Fawn. She was killed by the white men and she gave him this to show she forgave them. Are you gonna argue with that?" She held out the stone, and several men stepped back. There. She'd played her trump. She could only hope the Lakota's reverence for the sacredness of visions would prevent them from going against it.

Slowly, he reached out his arm and callused fingers picked up the star-shaped stone. "It is true. You are Morning Star, the white woman who saved Red Cloud's son. She was a brave woman, the mother of Red Cloud. And you have been given to White Eagle to replace the wife he lost." He fingered the piece of leather around her neck, then let it fall back onto her chest and looked at her for the first time without the gleam of defiance in his eye. "You have risked your life for the life of your man as Morning Star did," he said softly and thoughtfully.

"White Eagle stood beside his Lakota brothers. Now he only wants to return to the Lakota, to live out his life as one of them. Please"—she laid her hand on his arm—"let them go. The little *wasíchu* man is no threat to you. He is a coward."

Crazy Horse seemed to consider her words for a moment, and then he slowly lowered the knife. "I think Red Cloud chose well a keeper for her name," he said softly.

He raised the knife again and Josie's heart leaped into her throat. The flashing blade cut through the leather thongs that bound Caleb's hands. "Come, we will talk," Crazy Horse said as he also released Farthington.

The crowd opened a path, but suddenly, Owl stepped into their way.

"You let them go after they took your honor?" Owl asked her younger brother. For a moment the fierce warrior seemed to shrink beneath the scowl of his sister.

"They have dishonored you. Did White Eagle not refuse your offer?" she reminded him.

Crazy Horse suddenly seemed to recover. "You convinced me to take the train when you saw White Eagle leading it days ago. Your poison tongue convinced me to kill the wagon drivers and bring the others here. Perhaps I am not the leader I thought. I let a bitter woman whisper in my ear. He did not dishonor me. He dishonored you by refusing to take you as a wife because of your sharp tongue. Many others have done the same. Would you have me kill them all?" Without a look back, he swept regally past her, and Josie glanced back to see a brave whose dark hair was streaked with white put his arm around Owl's sagging shoulders. A toddler grabbed at the hem of her dress.

The sun had climbed well into the sky by the time Caleb, Josie, and Farthington emerged from Crazy Horse's tent. Her eyes burned from the wood smoke and the effort to hold them open. Caleb and Crazy Horse had talked far into the night about the Bozeman Trail. Red Cloud was indeed coming around to thinking of negotiating with the whites for peace in their land, but all the tribes were not in agreement. They wanted all the land back, as it was before the *wasíchu* came, but Red Cloud was wise enough to realize that wasn't possible, that the white man was here to stay, and to continue to fight him would mean only more killing and wasting of young lives. He wanted peace for his people.

Honored for his performance in the attack on Fort Phil Kearney, Crazy Horse had received his first taste of glory. In his imagination he saw a magnificent battle, the entire Lakota nation fighting and expelling the white man from their lands. To the desperate Lakota, it was an attractive prospect. Many had followed the young war chief, leaving the safety of Red Cloud's camp to join this band. Caleb had pointed out it was only a matter of time before the army crushed Crazy Horse as it had attempted to do to Red Cloud, and might well have done had the chief not known when to quit.

By the time Caleb left the tipi, Crazy Horse had agreed to return to Red Cloud and reunite the bands. Many sad days were in store for the Lakota, and their greatest strength was in their numbers, Caleb reminded him.

Crazy Horse led them to the edge of camp and ordered their horses brought around. After brief good-byes in Lakota, the three mounted up and rode back toward the Bozeman Trail. Farthington pressed a wad of bills into Caleb's hand, then wasted no time in kicking the little horse into a trot down the trail toward the fort. Their Indian escort vanished back into the dense forest, leaving Caleb and Josie alone in the still afternoon.

"Well, Mrs. McCall. Shall we head back to Independence?" He smiled, threw a leg across the saddle horn, and jumped to the ground.

"I've been thinking," she said, leaning down into the arms he offered.

"Thinking? About what? The idiocy of what you did last night?" He pulled her tightly against him.

"No, about the village."

"What about it?" he asked, nuzzling her hair.

"I want to go back there."

Caleb's exploration of her neck stopped, and he pushed her away from him. "Now?"

"Now. I want our child raised with the Lakota."

Caleb let his arms drop and walked away from her. He turned his back and looked out across the valley toward the mountains. "This world won't be here a few years from now. Here, where we stand, will be houses and towns. The Lakota won't be able to run and hide much longer. It's only a matter of time before they're all herded up like cattle and forced onto reservations. I don't even know where he is or if he's still alive."

"I know." She stepped up behind him and put her arms around his waist. "We found him once, we can find him again, cain't we?"

"I suppose, but what about the baby?"

"You've told me a hundred times the whole trouble with the Injuns is the whites don't understand 'em. Ain't that right?"

"Yeah, that's part of it."

"Well, suppose our son grows up with 'em and then he knows all about 'em. Right? Then maybe he can teach some of them others about visions and White Buffalo Woman."

He turned in her arms. "You'd go back for me?"

"Well, not just for you. I guess I got pretty attached to 'em myself. Besides, Petey's there and the baby's gonna want to know its uncle, and—"

"Hush, woman," Caleb muttered as his lips and tongue began their magnificent torture.

AUTHOR'S NOTE

Little is known of chief Red Cloud's early life. He told his friend Charles W. Allen that he was born in May 1821 on the banks of Blue Water Creek near where it empties into the Platte River. This assertion was one of many by Red Cloud that he lived along the Platte. We assume that he spent his youth learning to hunt, fight, and ride, as did other young Sioux men.

Red Cloud's private life is even less documented. Several stories circulate as to his marital status. One story is that he married a young Indian maid named Pretty Owl and remained monogamous, as did many Sioux chiefs. Another tale relates that he had six wives, taking the last when he was twenty-four.

Thanks are in order to the late Enos Poorbear, Sr., who, along with several other senior citizens on the Pine Ridge Reservation, translated the dialogue into Lakota Sioux. A special thanks to Delane Boyer, who assisted in the translation and read the manuscript for authenticity.

ROMANCE FROM ROSANNE BITTNER

CARESS   (0-8217-3791-0, $5.99)

FULL CIRCLE   (0-8217-4711-8, $5.99)

SHAMELESS   (0-8217-4056-3, $5.99)

SIOUX SPLENDOR   (0-8217-5157-3, $4.99)

UNFORGETTABLE   (0-8217-4423-2, $5.50)

TEXAS EMBRACE   (0-8217-5625-7, $5.99)

UNTIL TOMORROW   (0-8217-5064-X, $5.99)

Available wherever paperbacks are sold, or order direct from the Publisher. Send cover price plus 50¢ per copy for mailing and handling to Kensington Publishing Corp., Consumer Orders, or call (toll free) 888-345-BOOK, to place your order using Mastercard or Visa. Residents of New York and Tennessee must include sales tax. DO NOT SEND CASH.

PASSIONATE ROMANCE
FROM BETINA KRAHN!